the **Eloquent Scribe**

Books and stories by T. Lee Harris

Twenty-Seven Cents of Luck (Short)
Cat in the Middle (Short)
Sweet Water From the Rock (Short)
Muddy Waters (Short)
Winter Wonderland (Novella)

In the Miller and Peale Series

Chicago Blues
New York Nights

In the Josh Katzen Series

Hanukkah Gelt (Short)
The Pecan Pie Affair (Short)
The Case of the Moche Rolex*

In the Sitehuti and Nefer-Djenou Bastet series

To Be a Scribe (Short)
The Scribe Vanishes (Short)
Wanting the Fish (Short)
3 Tales of the Cat (Collection)

* Coming Soon

the **E l o q u e n t** **S c r i b e**

T. Lee Harris

Per Bastet

The Eloquent Scribe

Published by Per Bastet Publications LLC, P.O. Box 3023 Corydon, IN 47112

Cover art by T. Lee Harris

ISBN 978-1-942166-22-1

Dedicated to all those companions
who have gone to join the Great God.

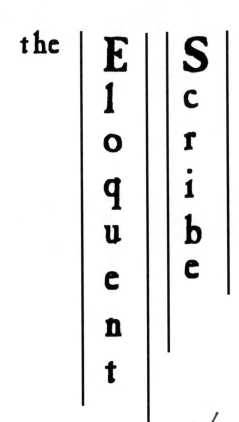

the **E l o q u e n t** **S c r i b e**

ENJOY!

T. Lee Harris

Cast of Characters

Sitehuti — A scribal student and the unsuspecting object of A temple cat's loyalty.

Nefer-Djenou-Bastet — An opinionated temple cat who has adopted the young scribe Sitehuti as his own.

Khenemetamun-pa-sheri — Sitehuti's scribal master.

Ahmose — A beginning scribal student.

Pedibastet — High Priest of the temple of Bastet in Pi-Ramesses, son-in-law of Ramesses II and brother-in-law of Crown Prince Merenptah.

Ramesses II (Userma'atre Setepenre Ramesses Meriamon) — elderly pharaoh of the Two Lands.

Merenptah — Crown Prince of the Two lands. Son of Ramesses II and the Royal Wife, Isetnofret.

Tepemkau — Stolist priest at the temple of Bastet in Pi-Ramesses. Shameless gossip.

Paseti — Lector priest at the temple of Bastet in Pi-Ramesses and closet cat-hater.

Huya — Elderly servant to Pedibastet.

Senbi — A city policeman who ran afoul of Nefer-Djenou-Bastet.

Khu — A city policeman who recognized trouble when it padded his way.

Tiaa — Sitehuti's widowed aunt and weaver of fine linen.

Maya — A basket weaver.

Isisnofret — The neighborhood brewer and possibly a part-time lady of the evening.

Butehamun — A porter and ardent admirer of Tiaa.

Ptahetepmose — Sitehuti's youngest cousin. Familiarly called Mose.

Aha — A weaver's apprentice.

Maatre — Another weaver's apprentice.

Merysobek — Sitehuti's older cousin, apprentice to a fisherman.

Hapuseneb — Junior priest of Bastet. Cousin of Tepemkau. Shameless gossip is a family trait.

Pamiu — Amulet maker and devotee of Bastet.

Kyky — A son of Pamiu.

S'kem — Neighborhood friend of Sitehuti's. Barber extraordinaire.

Wosret the Nubian — Mercenary Nubian bowman now very dead.

Captain Djedmose — Nubian head of Merenptah's personal Medjay guards.

Lieutenant Si-Montu — Nubian soldier, second in command of Merenptah's personal Medjay guards.

Sasobek — Brother of Paseti and captain in the Seth Division of the Egyptian army.

Captain Jebahou-Nefer — Captain of a riverboat and all around smart lady.

Jiji — Foreigner deckhand on Jebahou-Nefer's boat.

Userhet — Senior scribe from the House of Life at the temple of Bastet in Pi-Ramesses.

Ta — Head Scribe of the House of Life in the temple of Bastet in Memphis.

Intef — Officious servant of the high priest of the temple of Ptah in Memphis.

Ptahneb — High Priest of Ptah in Memphis

Khety — Missing scribe from the temple of Ptah in Memphis.

Heru — Trusted servant of the high priest of Ptah.

Bakare — Overseer of the House of Life for the temple of Ptah in Memphis.

Shepenwepet — Wife of Khety. Singer in the temple of Amun in Memphis.

Henut-Wedjebu — Elder singer to the god in the temple of Amun in Memphis.

Addaya — toddler who likes cats. Youngest son of Shepenwepet and Khety.

Den — Eldest son of Shepenwepet and Khety.

Renen — temple boy sent to assist Sitehuti

Anan — Vineyard owning priest with grumbling employees.

Peser — Grumbly employee of Anan.

Ma'aheru — Owner of a large estate near Memphis. Paseti's and Sasobek's father.

Neferhedjet — Second wife of Ma'aheru. Mother to Banufre.

Banufre — Youngest son of Ma'aheru. Half-brother to Paseti and Sasobek.

Amenhotep — Wastrel son of Ramesses II and a concubine. Failure as landowner, but great at throwing parties.

Meriramesses — Amonhotep's younger brother. Overseer of his brother's estate.

Wurusemu — Hittite wife of Meriramesses, mother of Iaret.

Iaret — Youngest daughter of Meriramesses and Wurusemu. In love with Banufre.

Yuni — Prince Meriramesses' Chief Butler.

Ipuy — Chief Scribe of Amunhotep's estate and disgruntled employee.

Kerer — Overseer of the vineyards on Ma'aheru's estate.

Nedjem — Noble friend of Prince Amunhotep. Lover of chariots and racing.

Seti-Merenptah — Son of Merenptah and commander of the Army in Memphis.

Iker — Former soldier. Aide to General Seti-Merenptah.

Meritamon — Late concubine of Ramesses II. Mother of Princes Meriramesses and Amunhotep.

Dedi — Personal servant to Prince Amunhotep.

Rebu — Riverman attached to the Princes' estate.

Hentaneb — Senior member of the Princes' kitchen staff.

Nekure — A nobleman in Memphis and a lousy farmer.

Tali — Former lady's maid to Lady Wurusemu. Deceased.

Maia — Another deceased former lady's maid to Lady Wurusemu.

Merit-Ptah — Amunhotep's personal physician.

Kha'Emteri — The Chief Royal Butler of Ramesses II.

Weni — Member of the Seth Division under Sasobek.

Isetnofret — Wife of Merenptah.

Hori — Captain of the Sherden personal bodyguard of Rameses II.

Hesi-ra — Sitehuti's youngest brother.

Mahu — Medjay soldier of exceptional skill.

ONE

The day hadn't started any differently than most other days in the ten years I'd lived in the capital. Up before sunrise and at Master Khenemetamun-pa-sheri's scribal school bright and early. It was already hot and the unrelentingly clear sky gave little respite from Amun-Re's glory. The school's porch retained the morning cool longer than anywhere else, so I usually hid out there before lessons, copying the assigned text so as to be line perfect for my master's inspection. That particular day the text was the dreaded "Tale of the Eloquent Peasant" — for the millionth time. At the point where Khun-anup had almost convinced the judge to hear his case, a crash and swearing erupted from inside. I'd have recognized that cursing anywhere. It was usually directed at me.

A cautious peek around the doorway revealed my teacher, lying prone on the tiled floor, writhing and bellowing that he had wrenched his back. Several students scurried about, collecting his scattered writing tools while others attempted to help him up. Considering the way he was flailing, that was no job to rush into. Sure enough, a few moments into the performance, the Master's beefy forearm took one of the smaller students up beside the head and knocked him sprawling against the wall near my refuge. The Master stopped flailing as soon as he noticed me.

"You! Sitehuti! Come here!"

Once he'd seen me, there was no help for it. I crept forward, bowing low. "Yes, my master, shall I run and fetch a physician?"

"No! No, Ahmose can do that." He gestured toward the student still sprawled against the wall. Miraculously, the boy recovered,

1

bowed respectfully, and fairly flew past me out into the street. Master Khenemetamun-pa-sheri turned his attention back to me. "I have a different task for you, Sitehuti. I was on my way to the Temple of Bastet to take correspondence for the High Priest, Pedibastet. My injuries will prevent me from sitting and holding the papyrus properly. As my most senior student, you must take my place. Convey my apologies to Pedibastet for the inconvenience."

I was stunned. Instead of abuse, my master had given me a job — an important job at that. I was also suspicious. Writing private correspondence for a High Priest who was also a son-in-law of the Pharaoh was a very big honor. True, my graduation loomed, and I *was* the most senior student currently at the school, but I was still only a student. Not a favored student, either. There had to be something wrong. It beat revisiting the Eloquent Peasant, though. Khun-anup and his endless speeches had not only been seared into my memory, but had taken a prime spot in my nightmares. Before my teacher could change his mind, I bowed even lower, snagged my writing kit and followed close on the heels of the recently-fled Ahmose.

~*~

My timing was good. Services were finished and the High Priest received me in the formal salon of his private quarters inside the temple complex. He sat in a folding wooden chair flanked by a Stolist-Priest on his right and a Lector-Priest on his left. It was working up to be a stifling day and I didn't envy them the leopard skins they wore draped around their shoulders. The Lector had the additional burden of his badge of office, a folded linen sash worn diagonally across his chest. At least as priests, they were able to go without wigs. Mine was already itching up a storm and it was only just past midday.

High Priests are usually elderly and, while Pedibastet was no exception, the eyes regarding me from under shaggy white brows showed no dimming of age. He tapped his ornate staff fitfully on the stone floor as he mulled over the tale of Master Khenemetamun-pa-sheri's mishap. Fear that he would send me away as unacceptable was growing when he stood and said, "You hardly look old enough to have even learned your letters . . . but . . . you'll do."

He turned and strode deeper into the cool, shadowed private quarters followed closely by the two priests. A servant, hovering in the background, shot forward, folded the chair and glided after them. There was nothing else to do but fall in behind the procession and try to keep up.

For a man who supposedly relied on a walking stick for support, Pedibastet moved at a pretty good clip. Soon we entered a small courtyard with a pool in the center. The servant, who looked to be almost as old as his master, unfolded the chair in the shade of an acacia tree, then retreated to a position by the door. Pedibastet seated himself and waved me to sit on the limestone paving next to him. Before I could, there was a disturbance back the way we'd come. I turned and was amazed to see the attendant trying to put as much space as possible between himself and something on the floor. As he strove to become one with the painted column, a temple cat emerged from within and stood blinking golden eyes in the sunlight. It was a very large male, whose coloration marked him as one of the cats most sacred to the goddess as well as linking him with the great god Amun, himself. Considering that this was the temple of Bastet, and cats had free run of the place, the reaction of the servant was curious.

Behind me, Pedibastet sighed. "It appears that Nefer-Djenou-Bastet has decided to honor us with his presence."

The young Stolist, who'd had his back to the doorway, wheeled, saw the cat and gave an involuntary yelp. Clutching his robes protectively to his backside, he bounced a good distance away from the creature, then realizing the impropriety of his actions, blushed all the way up his shaven head. He didn't move, though. The Lector looked momentarily alarmed and quietly stepped back so that Pedibastet was between himself and the cat. I was beginning to see a pattern.

Tail swishing slowly, Nefer-Djenou-Bastet watched the human activity with what appeared to be a faint air of amusement. Then he fixed his golden gaze on me and after a moment of consideration, sauntered over. I greeted him with respect — well, he *was* a temple cat dedicated to the goddess. Nonetheless, I braced myself as he sniffed my bare toes. My flinch was undoubtedly visible when he grimaced and closed his eyes, savoring my scent. Whatever his criteria were, I must have met them because he then sat down beside my feet with a deeply satisfied purr.

The purr was drowned out by an odd coughing sound. Pedibastet was laughing. "You are a lucky man, Sitehuti! Our opinionated Nefer-Djenou-Bastet has taken a liking to you."

The jumpy Stolist snorted and the High Priest riveted him with those piercing eyes. "You spoke, Tepemkau?"

Tepemkau flushed again and ducked his head. "No, Your Eminence."

"Good. Leave me now. You and Paseti have duties that are going wanting and the scribe and I have private business to attend to."

They skirted the purring animal at my side and fled, leaving me alone with the cat and the Sem-Priest. I sat cross-legged on the pavement taking dictation until the sun dipped low enough in the sky to make it difficult to continue. All that time, Nefer-Djenou-Bastet stayed beside me, stretched out on the stone, napping in the sunshine.

~*~

Shadows stretched long across the courtyard by the time the elderly servant emerged again to ask when his master wanted his evening meal.

"Is it that late?" Pedibastet glanced at the sky with mild surprise. "So it is! And there are many more letters to write. Sitehuti, you will return tomorrow morning, and we shall finish then."

He stood. I did too. An involuntary moan escaped me at the stiffness of my legs from sitting in the same position all day. The Sem-Priest coughed his laugh again. "Such groans from such a young man. You have a few more decades before you are allowed such noises."

I tried to hide my grin with a respectful bow, but it didn't work. The old man was far too sharp. Leaving instructions for the servant, Huya, to pay me for my time, he disappeared into the house, having a good chuckle. That was fine by me. My own stomach had been reminding me for quite some time that all I'd given it was a stale bread roll at breakfast. My stomach could quiet down; if the High Priest paid me tonight, there'd be more bread on the way home. Even better, I had a legitimate job tomorrow. I could duck out of morning classes with Master Khenemetamun-pa-sheri and no one could say a word about it. As far as I was concerned, life couldn't get much better than that.

I was wrong.

As a rule, a student will receive a fraction of the pay a master scribe is given. Usually, this is for good reason as a student is prone to more errors than an experienced scribe. As much as I would like to claim otherwise, I am forced to admit I was no different. In light of this, I waited in the courtyard expecting the servant to return with, at best, a small bag of grain or a loaf from the temple's bakeries. When he finally did return, my jaw dropped at what he was carrying. It wasn't the biggest payment I'd seen to that point, but it was certainly the largest ever presented to *me*.

Honor demanded I protest. "There must be a misunderstanding. I'm only a student. Surely this is too much."

Huya suppressed a grin. "Yes, Scribe, but my master had already measured out the payment. He saw no reason to change his original plans. If it is not needed. . . ."

"Oh, no! It is both needed and appreciated. Please express my thanks to his Holiness."

He bowed again and left me to find my own way out. I was elated. There was enough for not only bread, but beer and little honeyed fowl, with some left over. My heart was in the clouds, and my eyes were certainly not on where I was walking. I ran right into two men in the street outside the temple gates.

"Here, boy! Where do you think you're headed in such a hurry?"

Just my luck. The men were city policemen. Two of the larger specimens, to boot. My heart came back to earth quickly. It might have even dropped a few cubits below street level before it stopped. "My apologies, officers, I wasn't watching where I was going."

The other policeman chuckled. "We kind of noticed that. You didn't answer my partner's question. Where are you off to in such a hurry?"

Okay, time to drop a name or two. "My work for the High Priest, Pedibastet, is finished for the day. I was going home."

The first officer jabbed toward the pavement with his club. "Not with temple property, you don't."

I followed his point and to my horror, saw that the temple cat had followed me out of the complex. "Oh, no, no, no! Officers, there's been a mistake. This cat is Nefer-Djenou-Bastet, he must have followed me. . . ."

"Followed you, huh?"

We were attracting a crowd. It was the tag end of the day and the vendors were grateful for a little excitement before closing up shop. A row between a scribe and the police was just the ticket to end a boring day.

"Look, I'm not stealing the cat!"

The second officer eyed the cat with a faintly worried

expression. "Um . . . what'd you say that cat's name was?"

"Nefer-Djenou-Bastet," I repeated as I tried to shoo the animal back into the temple compound. He didn't shoo. He sat down and yawned.

The first policeman was having none of it. "Not stealing the cat, huh? Let's take a look at that pouch and see what else you aren't stealing."

His partner looked uncertain. "Hey, Senbi, maybe we ought to forget. . . ."

"Forget nothin', Khu, stealing temple property is a capital offense," Senbi said, jabbing me in the chest with his club. "We're not finished here. What say we go ask the priests abo-ow-owow-oooooOOOOOO!"

The policeman suddenly dropped his club and collapsed onto the pavement rolling and clutching his shin. Blood oozed from under his fingers. Nefer-Djenou-Bastet gazed up at me, then fell to washing his face.

Just as I was expecting the sky to fall on my head in the form of the other officer's club, the temple gates disgorged a flood of priests. The Stolist, Tepemkau, was at the head of the wave. He took in the scene and raced back inside, returning almost immediately with the High Priest, himself.

The sight of the High Priest had a miraculous effect on the crowd. The merchants suddenly got busy packing up their wares. The injured policeman stopped howling and scrambled up to join his partner in bowing respectfully before the august personage. His shin was a nasty sight.

Pedibastet suffered the babble of explanation only briefly before he brought his staff down on the pavement with a crack like to split the stone. The resulting silence was almost deafening. "Sitehuti, it appears our Nefer-Djenou-Bastet has decided to leave with you."

"Yes, Your Eminence, but. . . ."

"If the Sacred One has decided to stay with the scribe, who are we to say otherwise?" Having made his pronouncement, the Sem-Priest turned and the crowd of gawkers melted before him as he strode back to the temple. At the gate, he stopped and gestured toward the policeman's torn shin. "You should get that looked after."

I was suddenly alone with the cat. The priests had filed back inside the temple, the policemen were headed away in search of a physician as fast as Senbi could limp, and the merchants had almost all vanished. The cat trotted out into the street and stopped to look over his shoulder as if to say, "What's keeping you?"

Glaring, I slogged off after him. "Y'know, you're lucky it's a crime to kill a cat, or I wouldn't give two figs for your chances after that stunt."

Nefer-Djenou-Bastet looked up at me, crinkled his eyes and trotted ahead with his tail in the air.

As a student, there was no way I could afford a house of my own, so I lived in the home of my widowed aunt, Tiaa, behind and above her weaver's shop. Tiaa is my mother's sister and that part of the family has never been noted for shy and retiring womenfolk. My aunt was a prime example of that. Mind you, I'm not saying my aunt was a termagant, she was just rather forceful in her beliefs. One of those beliefs was that I would probably never amount to much. It didn't help that most of what my parents sent from home (that was the Village of the Workmen in Western Thebes) went for supplies and to Master Khenemetamun-pa-sheri. I tried to contribute, but it was infrequent, and never very much. Lately I'd been cadging a little on the side by playing public letter writer for the folks in the neighborhood. It still hadn't added much to the household coffers or to my aunt's opinion of me.

Tiaa also hated animals of any kind — including humans, apparently. Here I was bringing home a cat. Maybe the fact this animal was sacred might make a difference. Yeah. Sure it would.

All that was why I was lumbering home lugging a huge rush basket laden with a honey-sesame roasted duck and several pots of vegetables. It had taken a big chunk of my pay, and I still owed Maya, the basket weaver, a letter. But if springing for family dinner mollified Aunt Tiaa a bit, it was worth it. As if the load wasn't heavy enough, Neffi had discovered it was better to ride than walk. He lounged across the top of the basket, enjoying the scenery, flicking me in the face with his tail from time to time. It was cumbersome and his added weight made the basket harder to hold, but, on the whole, it was better than having him weaving around my feet.

Approaching the lane my house was on, Neffi's ears twitched and he jumped to the ground. It took me a few more steps before I heard what had alerted him. A woman's angry voice rose above the normal hubbub of the neighborhood. Given that it was a working neighborhood and most of the residences along there doubled as storefronts, that was going some. The worst of it was that I knew that voice. It was my aunt's. Apparently, the show had been going on for a while. Other residents were leaning against door-posts and some had pulled stools close to the edge of their roofs in order not to miss a moment. The notion of spending a bit of my new wealth on a room at an inn trickled across my mind only to be dismissed summarily. One, it would be worse when I showed my face again. Two, I didn't have enough left for a room after buying dinner for the family.

A woman cooed from off to my right, "You can camp out with me on the roof tonight, Sitehuti, and I might not even ask for any of that delicious-smelling whatever in return."

Glancing in the direction of the voice, I found Isisnofret, our neighborhood brewer, leaning against the wall of her tavern lazily waving a fan of woven red and yellow palm fronds. Even though the evening was cooling, she probably needed the fan for more than effect; her heavy, elaborate wig with its many beaded braids made me hot just to look at it. At least her pleated linen gown would be cooler — anything that filmy and transparent couldn't possibly hold in the heat. It was rumored that from time to time she sold something more than beer in her back rooms. At that moment, though, patrons in various states of inebriation struggled to decide which show was more entertaining, the one down the street or the new one closer to hand. A fresh stream of invective followed by several whumps made up their minds and they moved closer to the mayhem.

Isisnofret may once have had the beauty of Isis that her name implied, but that must have been before I knew her. Under all the jewelry and makeup, she was a skinny woman who was at least the same age as my mother. I grinned. "Tempting, but not this evening. I'm afraid I have to brave the den of the lioness. What happened this time?"

She rolled her heavily kohled eyes. "It's Bu again. He fell into a rack of linens while delivering a jar of my best red beer."

I winced. Butehamun was a porter who seemed to spend equal time moving cargo on his donkey, in Isisnofret's tavern and trailing my aunt around like a sick puppy. He seemed to think the sun's barque sailed the skies just for a glimpse of her. The donkey had more sense.

"Poor Bu. Why doesn't he just go down to the river and pelt crocodiles with stones. He'd get the same result — but quicker."

Isisnofret laughed, and shooting a glance at her patrons to be sure their attention was still down the street, moved away from the wall. She swiveled toward me. Her voice was pitched low as she said, "I wasn't joking, you know. It gets lonely up there at night and I have a jug of wine of Inet. . . ."

A low rumble sounded from the ground. Isisnofret froze mid-swivel and waggled her fan toward the source. "What's *that?"*

I looked down to find Neffi crouched sphinx-like in front of me, ears pinned back and tail lashing. "Ah. Isisnofret, allow me to present his sacred felinity, Nefer-Djenou-Bastet. He's part of the reason I have to go home tonight."

"A sacred cat? What in the Two Lands are *you* doing with a sacred cat?"

Good question, but we were attracting attention again. It looked like that was going to happen a lot with Neffi around. "He's following me home."

The brewer snorted. Not a pretty sound, but it managed to convey her opinion admirably. The tavern patrons pressed in for a closer look and Neffi, whose eyes had never left the tavern keeper, growled again.

Isisnofret backed up a pace. "That cat doesn't like me."

"No, he must like you. He didn't give the policeman he mauled anywhere near as much warning."

Immediately, the crowd gave way to a respectful distance. Isisnofret glared at us for a moment, then threw back her head and roared with laughter. "Sitehuti, with you the gods don't smile, they laugh themselves sick! Get on with you, I think Bu is running out of stones for the crocodiles."

The way parted and we continued into the fray. The nearer we got, the clearer my aunt's words became. She shouted, "Butehamun, you big oaf! Put that down. I'm perfectly capable of picking up the wreckage myself. NO! Leave it where—"

There was the sound of splintering wood.

I quickened my pace and arrived on a scene of utter chaos. My aunt's palm stick cloth racks, that had been so neatly arrayed when I left this morning, were now tossed every which way as if a whirlwind had struck. The whirlwind, in the form of Butehamun the porter, lay sprawled in the splintered remains of two other racks. He attempted to stand but was impeded by lengths of dirty, torn linen. He looked like the rubbish pile outside a mortician's tent. He said, "I'm sorry, I'm sorry. Here, let me set it right. I'm sure I can fix. . . ."

"I'll show you what'll be fixed!" Tiaa grabbed a broken palm stick.

I plunked the basket down and lunged forward. She managed to land several good blows before I snatched her up. That was probably a mistake, but it was the first idea that came to me.

She twisted around in my grip and started in on me. "Curse you, Sitehuti! Put me down!"

Not bloody likely. Her leverage was horrible from where she was and most of her swipes missed me by a finger's breadth. There was no way I was going to let her down to get better aim. Turning my head to avoid the latest flurry, I caught sight of my youngest cousin Ptahetepmose and the two apprentices, Aha and Maatre, peering around the shop door in wide-eyed fright. I shouted, "Mose! You and Aha get Bu out of here NOW!"

Mose isn't real great at thinking, but he's wonderful at taking orders. He instantly lost his glazed look and ran forward dragging Aha with him. In a few moments they had the linen unwound and two of Bu's erstwhile drinking buddies bore him out of the jaws of danger and hurried him along in the direction of Isisnofret's tavern. Why they hadn't done that before I'll never know. I didn't let Aunt Tiaa loose until the crowd had closed in their wake, then I let go and ducked. I needn't have worried, she was far too interested in hurling abuse at the retreating Bu.

I was just congratulating myself on an easy escape when she wheeled on me. "You idiot! Why did you pull me off of him?"

"Just trying to keep you out from in front of the magistrates, Aunt. Er — not that it wouldn't have been purely justifiable homicide. Let me guess. He was trying to help?"

"Wouldn't you know it?" She brushed gray-shot hair out of her flushed face and sighed. "What a mess. That was some of my finest linen and now. . . ? Maatre! Pick these scraps up and take them to the washing tub. Maybe they'll clean up enough to be used. With luck we may be able to sell it to the morticians and make a little back on the flax."

Aha and Mose were already gathering fragments of the racks; I confess to a certain relief when Tiaa relinquished her weapon to them. Then she asked, "You're later than usual. What kept you?"

"Oh! I had the most wonderful stroke of luck today, Master Khenemetamun-pa-sheri fell and hurt his back — NO, I'm not glad he had an accident, just listen!" With my aunt's incipient tirade abated, I continued, "He was going to take dictation from the High Priest of Bastet, but since he couldn't make it, he sent me. I was there all day and he wants me back tomorrow, too. The High Priest, not Khenemetamun-pa-sheri although I imagine I'll have to see him tomorrow, too, but I got paid and. . . ."

I stopped breathing as I suddenly remembered the basket.

When Tiaa grabbed the stick, I had simply let go the handles and left it in the street where anyone could — the air split with a bloodcurdling shriek. One of the erstwhile tavern patrons ran past clutching a bleeding hand. Back on the basket, Nefer-Djenou-Bastet yawned, stretched and sharpened his claws on the edge of the lid. I turned back to my aunt and with a wide grin and a sweeping gesture, announced, "Dinner!"

"Looks like a cat to me."

~*~

Aunt Tiaa's house was decent sized for a working-class neighborhood, but not so big that everyone had their own room. I shared a small bedchamber with Mose on the uppermost floor. Until a few months before we'd also shared the space with Mose's older brother, Merysobek. Mery moved out and into his own place when he took a wife, the daughter of the man he'd learned his trade from. Considering that trade was fishing, additional elbow room in our small, windowless digs wasn't the only reason we weren't sorry to have Mery out of there. As a rule Mose was a pretty good roommate, except for those times he got a bit wound up about something.

"Wow! A sacred cat and he's *yours*. That is *great*." Mose was on his knees pulling things from his clothing chest so he could put away his neatly folded kilt. I never grasped the concept that all things had to come out and be rearranged in order for one item to be stowed neatly. It seemed to work for Mose, though. I sat on the edge of my cot, watched the performance and kept an eye on Neffi. At that moment, he was perched on top of my clothes chest also watching Mose excavate.

"Your mother didn't seem to think it was so great."

"She'll come around, she never takes to anything new. You know that."

"I hope you're right. She doesn't like animals, sacred or no." No sense in sitting like a lump, I tossed Neffi on the floor and busied myself with stowing my own jewelry, clothes and writing kit.

"Sure she will, you remember when Mery brought that — Hey! Give that back!"

I'd been vaguely aware of an odd snuffling noise, but now, roused by Mose's shout, I realized Neffi had moved. He was in the middle of the floor, rolling on one of the sandals Mose had pulled from the box, with an expression of ridiculous rapture. Before long, he rolled onto his face and, head firmly in the straps, began to claw and bite the toe thong. Then to the accompaniment of Mose's frantic cries, he flung the sandal into the air, sprang after it, landed squarely on it and raked the sole vigorously with his hind claws. At length, enemy subdued, he dropped his guard and Mose was able to scoop the footwear up.

"What was that all about? These are my new sandals — well mostly new — new to me, anyway. They're real leather."

I continued to stare at the cat, who was now rolling all over the floor, purring with deep satisfaction. "I have no idea, he's only been with me today. Maybe it's the leather?"

As if to prove me wrong, Neffi pounced on my ratty woven rush sandals. I had an awful time getting them back. Finally, I tossed them into my clothes chest and slammed the lid. It was heavy wood; no way a cat could lift that. Mose followed my lead and we put out the lamp, secure in our victory.

In the end, Mose and I wound up sleeping with our sandals tucked under our bed linens. Neffi contented himself with stretching out along my leg with his head against the footboard.

TWO

The sun was just topping the horizon when Neffi and I arrived at
the scribal school. More precisely, at Master Khenemetamun-pa-
sheri's house. Classes were held in the master's own home and, as
usual, I took a moment in the street outside to appreciate the
gleaming white walls and brightly-painted gate posts. Master
Khenemetamun-pa-sheri was a well-known scribe — not famous,
but well-known. My family were craftsmen and couldn't afford a
truly famous scribe. The place was still magnificent, reflecting its
owner's importance, stopping just short of a villa. Someday, I
wanted a house like that. A villa or two and some land outside the
city wouldn't be bad, either, but I wasn't greedy.

Sufficiently motivated and reminded of why I was in the
clutches — I mean under the tutelage — of Master Khenemetamun-
pa-sheri, I continued inside in search of him. Having a job lined up
was one thing, skipping lessons without permission was another
thing entirely. It wasn't hard to locate him. Simply follow the
shouting. Neffi padded along beside me, sniffing the doorposts
and furniture with great interest. We found the master in the central
courtyard, dressing down a student at the top of his lungs. He
seemed remarkably fit for a man who had taken a serious fall the
day before.

The student was one of the newer boys, roughly the same age
as me when I first entered the school. I had no idea what his
infraction was, and quite frankly, it didn't have to be much. The
Master was a firm believer in the adage that the ear of a student is
on his back. The small boy, now cowering in front of him, was

about to receive this form of instruction if the stout stick clenched in my teacher's fist was any clue.

My heart went out to the kid. The master scribe was a large man who looked even larger and more terrifying from the boy's angle on the pavement. I know. I'd been there.

The Master's stick rose, but it never struck. As it reached its apex, Nefer-Djenou-Bastet hopped lightly onto a bench, stretched out a paw and placed it on the master's backside. Khenemetamun-pa-sheri, wheeled, saw the cat and recoiled so violently, he nearly fell over backward. Trailing a high-pitched scream of panic, my teacher was across the yard with a wooden column between himself and the cat in an instant.

The reprieved student crab-crawled to one side, eyes wide.

My teacher's voice shook even more than his hands. "By Thoth! The demon. It's here!"

Neffi regarded me with half-closed eyes, then dismissed the lot of us, extended a hind leg, and concentrated on cleaning his splayed toes.

I stared at the scene — until I remembered where I was and why I was there. Stepping into the courtyard, I bowed and said, "My apologies for interrupting, Master."

"Sitehuti! Be careful! The demon!"

"Ummmmm . . . that's not a demon, Master, that's Nefer-Djenou-Bastet, he's a cat from—"

"I *know* where it's from. What's it doing here?"

Now, I might not be the swiftest boat in the race, but if you give me enough clues, I eventually get there. As I looked from my scribal master, cowering behind a pillar, and the cat, putting the fur on his leg into place, it all became clear. I understood the melodramatic fall. I understood why a prime job had landed in *my* lap. I understood all of it. I'd seen the same behavior in the priests at the temple. My Master was terrified of a cat.

Given what Neffi had done to the city policeman who'd

stopped me the day before, they probably had a valid point. I plunged ahead. "He's with me, sir. Sort of. He kind of adopted me at the temple yesterday."

"Adopted you? Nonsense. Take him back! Immediately!"

Strange. That was very similar to what Aunt Tiaa had said. I said, "I can try, but he probably won't stay. That does bring up why I have to speak with you, sir. I need to be excused from lessons today. The High Priest wants me back at the temple today after morning services."

Master Khenemetamun-pa-sheri looked hopeful. "To take the demon back?"

"Uh, no, sir. To write more letters."

There was silence for a few heartbeats, then the Master straightened and made an effort to reclaim some dignity. "Very well. You may have the day. Be off. Don't keep the High Priest waiting, boy." He took a step toward the open doorway to his study. "And take that . . . *creature* . . . with you!"

The master bolted into the room, slamming the door behind him. After a moment, the student, forgotten in the chaos, rose slowly to his feet. He looked from the closed door to the bathing cat to me and asked in a hushed voice, "Where can I get one of those?"

~*~

Everything was in turmoil when we arrived at the temple. The place was normally an anthill, but this morning someone had poked it with a stick and stirred hard. I swung Neffi onto my shoulder to keep him from getting stepped on in the crush and instantly changed my opinion about the priests' hot leopard skins. I'd have given anything for even a secondhand moth-eaten one just then.

Heading into the public courtyard, I spotted Khu and Senbi, the two policemen that Neffi had tangled with the previous evening. To be more accurate, they spotted us and veered to intercept. No way to duck it.

Senbi sported a large swath of bandage around his shin and several new amulets including a blue faience Bastet. I wondered if it was there to make him more acceptable to felines or because the wound was caused by one of the goddess' sacred cats. Whichever, he was limping badly. To give him credit, he didn't flinch like most of Neffi's victims, but his hard glare was formidable. He called out, "Well, well, if it isn't the illustrious Sitehuti of Western Thebes and his pet cat-demon."

Great. They knew my name, but that was inevitable given the circumstances. I tried to be casual. "Looks like something big happened here."

Khu nodded, "Someone attacked the High Priest's personal servant last night. One of the priests — that Lector — what's his name?"

Senbi offered, "Huya."

"No, that's the servant. The other guy. The priest."

"Oh. Paseti."

"Yeah. Anyway, this Paseti was taking a walk before service and found Huya lying on his face in the street with his head bashed in."

I gasped, "Dead?"

"Almost. If a group of amulet hucksters hadn't showed up to give Paseti a hand, it might have been different. One of them ran for the Sem-Priest, one of them ran for a doctor and the rest helped lug the guy into the temple."

"But Huya? Who would want to hurt that old man?"

Senbi said, "We asked that one ourselves. If you get the answer, we'd love to know, too. Oh, yeah, his Holiness wants to see you. He's sent a flotilla of servants and lesser priests out looking for you. You're a fellow in demand, Scribe."

For the life of me, I couldn't figure why. "Then, I better get to him and find out what he wants."

The quickest path to the high priest's quarters was straight across the courtyard. I'd reached the deep shade of the hypostyle colonnade that divided the public areas from the private ones when I was intercepted by Paseti who didn't look real happy. I said, "Hey, I heard about your exciting morning. Lucky for Huya that you and the merchants happened by."

The Lector glared off toward the pylon gates where the pair of city policemen were talking to a small group of priests and scribes before he responded. "Yes. Things would surely have gone differently had that not happened." His gaze shifted to my passenger and his lip curled in distaste. "I see your companion is still with you."

I scratched Neffi's rump; he smacked me in the face with his tail. "So far he's shown no signs of leaving."

"Ah, then we have *two* things to thank the goddess for. Have you heard the Sem-Priest is looking for you?"

"Yeah, those two policemen already told me."

He looked startled. "The police? Why were you talking to them, what did they say?"

"It was more like they were talking to me." I nodded toward the group still in conversation by the gate. "Kind of looks like they're talking to everybody."

If Paseti was going to reply, he never got the chance. The Stolist, Tepemkau, came running through the colonnade making directly for us. If he'd been a horse, he would have been in a lather. It was a rather undignified entrance for a priest of his level and from yesterday's performance, seemed to be characteristic. No doubt he was frequently reprimanded for it, but I found it refreshing. Most priests of my acquaintance were stiff, formal and a bit off-putting.

As if to prove my point, Paseti turned on the new arrival with a frown. "Tepemkau, you shouldn't be running in the temple precincts."

Between puffs, the Stolist gasped, "These are the public areas,

Paseti, besides the Sem-Priest heard the scribe was here and told me to make haste to bring him."

From Paseti's expression, he apparently found running in a public area more distasteful than running in the sacred precincts. Before he could voice this, I turned to the Stolist and said, "The two policemen at the gate told me the Sem-Priest as asking for me. I was already headed that way."

Tepemkau nodded, and motioning me to follow, hurried back the way he came. Uninvited, Paseti joined us, and along the way we collected an honor guard of minor priests who tossed around theories and questions all the way to Pedibastet's study. Even the servant who let us into the house joined the entourage. This might have been out of fear that such a large crowd as we'd accumulated might cause breakage. He had a good point.

We went deeper into the house than we had the day before. Neffi seemed to know where he was going — or rather where he was once we got there. He'd ridden quietly, draped across my shoulders, until we stopped in front of a set of beautifully carved cedar doors, when he dropped to the floor. This action caused a wild flurry among the accumulated priests who had apparently not noticed him until that moment. This, in turn, caused a rapid reduction in numbers. Paseti quirked a smile and rapped the carved wood with the back of his knuckles. The door was opened by yet another servant who ushered only Neffi and me into the august presence.

The High Priest was agitated, pacing his airy study, but when Neffi and I entered, he stopped abruptly, seeming to relax. Completely at home, Neffi strolled over to the Sem-Priest's chair and got comfortable on the beautiful and expensive silken cushion. I came to the center of the room and bowed. "I was told you wanted to see me, sir. Do you need a letter written?"

"It is a letter I wish to speak to you about, although not one for you to write. You heard about the assault on my servant,

Huya?" He didn't wait for me to respond, but turned, dislodged Neffi, then sat, eyes closed, holding the cat close and stroking him. Surprisingly, Neffi submitted to this and flowed onto the Sem-Priest's lap staring up into Pedibastet's face, purring. After a moment, Pedibastet opened those piercing eyes and riveted me with them. "This will be complicated. Please sit down."

I started to seat myself on the floor as per custom, but he stopped me and motioned me toward a low chair. This was definitely not how a scribe is usually treated by a high priest, but I did as he directed — even though it made me a little uncomfortable. "You are aware that the Crown Prince, Merenptah, is my full brother-in-law?"

"Yes, sir." I wasn't lying. I really did know that Pedibastet's wife was the Crown Prince's younger sister, both born of the Pharaoh's Great Wife, Isetnofret.

"Good, then you may know that my brother-in-law and I have always been close. We enjoy many of the same pastimes."

Well, I didn't know that, but he didn't wait for an answer, so I didn't have to confess my ignorance.

"Don't think I'm trying to increase my importance in your eyes, I'm merely giving you background so you'll understand why I was entrusted with a particular task that has now gone very, very wrong."

I looked at him with utter amazement, both for the self-effacing commentary and for the extraordinary way a high priest was speaking to a student scribe almost as an equal. "Sir, I would never accuse you of inflating your importance. I well know the difference between being important and merely making it seem you are."

He surprised me by coughing his laugh. Offended, Neffi hopped out of his lap, stalked a distance away and fell to reordering his coat. "Yes. Yes, you would. I have known your teacher for many years and Khenemetamun-pa-sheri is a good scribe and a good teacher but . . . ah! That isn't what we're here for. It appears I'm reluctant to give voice to the problem, but avoiding it won't make it go away." He sobered and seemed to fall into himself as he continued, "To put it simply, a plot to assassinate the Pharaoh and the Crown Prince has been discovered. It apparently originated in Memphis where my brother-in-law has many connections. One of his people got wind of the plot and procured a list of the conspirators. He wrote it into a letter that was sent to me in care of an overseer of one of my estates. We believed it would attract less attention if Huya went to pick it up under the pretense of delivering a message of my own to that overseer. You know the text, Sitehuti. You wrote it for me yesterday."

I did remember it and could see no way to have deduced all this from a list of instructions on how much which workmen were to be paid for what work. I asked, "Then your servant was returning with this list when he was attacked?"

"It seems so. It also seems that the original writer of the list has gone missing. His name was Khety. He was a scribe of the temple of Ptah and has not been seen or heard from for several weeks. This is why you must find who attacked Huya. That's now our best chance to learn the identities of those involved. We don't expect to find the list intact; you know yourself how easy it is to destroy a written document. What we hope is to find the culprit and force the names of his associates from him."

If I hadn't been so stunned, I would've blanched at the mention of that kind of force. As it was, I hardly heard it above the roaring in my ears and, for an eternity, the thick silence of the study was only broken by the faint click of Nefer-Djenou-Bastet's teeth as he groomed the fur on his tail. At length, I managed, "Me, sir?" I probably squeaked a little when I said it, too.

The high priest merely sat back in his chair and regarded me with the air of a job well done. Or a job well passed off, if you look at it in an uncharitable light. I cleared my throat and tried again, "Your confidence honors me, Eminence, but I'm just a scribe. Just a *student*. Shouldn't this task fall to someone a little more qualified?"

"No, the task is yours, Sitehuti. We've looked into your background — we had to know who our Nefer-Djenou-Bastet had gone with. It's a good history. Your family has served the Great House well for many years and. . . ." I opened my mouth to protest, but Pedibastet raised a hand for silence and continued more firmly, ". . .and the Sacred One has chosen you."

I stared at the Sacred One who was now busily washing his privates and heard myself saying, "Oh. That settles it, then."

It felt like I was walking to my own execution as Neffi and I left the Sem-Priest's study. Coming from a family of craftsmen, I knew nothing about running anything resembling an investigation. My father was a painter, he the son of a sculptor. The closest my family ever came to investigation was the cousin who used to be a Necropolis Guard in the kings' burial ground, but nobody ever talked about him anymore. I glared down at Neffi who was sticking to me like sand to wet skin. "Okay, you got me into this, how about you tell me where to start."

He yawned and trotted off down a corridor. Lacking other ideas, I followed him. He led me out of the private quarters, across the public courtyard, through the huge pylon gates and deep into the temple proper. Several times I thought we would be stopped and told to leave, but each time the priest in question looked down at my guide and decided he was needed elsewhere. Quickly.

Just as it was beginning to look like he was going to barge into the holy of holies, Neffi veered off and trotted into a side office full of scrolls and bound sheets of papyrus. In the middle of all this was the Lector, Paseti. He didn't look happy to see us — but then again, I'd never seen him look happy about anything.

"What are you doing here? The public isn't allowed this far

into the temple."

Okay, start with the guy who discovered the crime. What a great idea — wish it had been my own. "At the moment, I'm not the public. The Sem-priest has charged me with investigating this morning's attack on his servant."

"You? You're not with the temple police or even the city police."

"No, but I've apparently been deputized by a higher authority." I pointed at Neffi who'd leapt on a small bench and was nosing through a stack of papyri with great interest.

The Lector curled his lip and pulled the texts out of the cat's reach. The man didn't seem to like cats much; I wondered how he'd landed in the temple of Bastet. Neffi turned his attention to the stone ink palette and water jar.

Paseti snapped, "All right. Go ahead and ask your questions, but I don't see why you're wasting time here. The people who did this are probably back in the city by now."

"You seemed to be the logical place to start since you were the first one on the scene. What were you doing outside the temple at that time of morning? I'd have thought that was when you'd need to be preparing for the morning offerings."

"That's exactly what I was doing. I find that a brisk walk on the temple grounds before entering the Sanctuary clears my mind and lets me better concentrate on reading the prayers. I do it almost every morning."

"I see. Did you see anyone else in the area?"

"Look, I've already been over this with those blockheaded city policemen until I'm sick of it."

"I understand that and I apologize, but the high priest has asked me to. . . ."

"*All right!* Go ahead, what was it you asked?"

"Did you see anyone else while you were walking?"

"Only the amulet sellers — get away from that!" He snatched

his ink palette away from Neffi, but it was too late. He'd managed to get his front paws into the wet ink and danced just out of reach, leaving black and red paw prints across the bench top and on the edges of the documents scattered there. Paseti took a gingerly swat at him, but wise man that he was, didn't get his fingers too close. It was seemingly close enough for Neffi, though. He dived off in a flurry of papyrus, pens, scrapers and burnishers, then darted behind me and peeked at the irate Lector from behind my legs. I swear he was snickering.

Paseti's fingers briefly closed on the alabaster water pot, then he got control of himself and fell to gathering up the scattered papyri. The polite thing to do was help, so I bent to collect those sheets that landed near me. It was a mishmash of documents. Everything from supply lists to bad love poetry all written in different hands intermingled with blank, freshly scraped papyri. I recognized the signs. These were secondhand sheets and Paseti had apparently been busy scraping them for reuse when Neffi and I interrupted him. I groaned inwardly at the thought. Being the favorite brunt of Master Khenemetamun-pa-sheri's wrath, I had spent many hours resurfacing papyrus for use at the school. It was odd though, why would a temple with the rich coffers of that of Bastet need to recycle papyrus? Sure, it was expensive stuff, but. . . .

Just then another voice sounded behind me. "Good heavens! What happened here?"

I turned to find the Stolist Tepemkau, and another young priest in the shadowy hall just outside Paseti's office. They were gathering sheets that had skimmed out and come to rest against the far wall. It was Tepemkau's companion who had spoken. He lifted a sheet to the lamplight, saw the large inky pawprints and stopped abruptly. Two pairs of eyes swiveled and rolled in long-ingrained panic as they saw Nefer-Djenou-Bastet crouched comfortably on several papyri. It seemed that they would bolt, then they caught sight of me.

Tepemkau gave an audible sigh of relief, then straightened and jabbed his companion with his elbow. "Hapuseneb, this is Sitehuti, the scribe I was telling you about."

Hapuseneb, who looked to be even younger than Tepemkau, regarded me with awe, bowed slightly and said, "Good day, Scribe. We understand you have been appointed to look into the matter of this morning's unpleasantness. We have all been instructed by the high priest to cooperate with you fully."

News traveled fast in the temple. Having grown up in the relatively closed society of the workers' village on the west bank of Thebes, I shouldn't have been surprised.

Tepemkau brightened even more. "Yes, we have. What can we help you with?"

Paseti spoke for the first time since Neffi had scattered the contents of the table. "At the moment, he's helping me pick up everything that . . . animal . . . scattered. *You* can help by handing those papyri over before you soil them."

The younger priests' eyes gave a different kind of roll, then Tepemkau stepped forward with the sheets extended toward me. As he did so, the lamplight picked out the roughened surface. He put them into my hands and smirked, "Being 'frugal' again, Paseti?"

Paseti came around and snatched the papyri away and spat through gritted teeth, "Some of us were not raised in the lap of luxury and see no reason to forget the value of things because there is now plenty. You may leave us, Stolist."

Unsuccessfully suppressing a laugh (Not trying too hard, truth be told.), the young priests bowed again. Tepemkau spoke for both of them. "As you wish — Lector." He again bowed to me. "We will be in the hypostyle hall should you have need of us, Sitehuti."

I was going to have a hard time getting used to being on the receiving end of that bowing stuff.

Neffi stood, stretched and sauntered out after the departed priests, leaving a huge smear of ink on the sheet he'd been lying on. It seemed wise to follow him if for no other reason than to make sure he didn't catch up to them and frighten them straight into the embrace of the Great God. I handed my stack to Paseti and hurriedly took my leave.

I overtook Neffi not far down the hall. He was strolling along, sampling the scents left by other temple cats and adding a few of his own. I scooped him up and draped him around my shoulders again, then winced. If he was determined to stay with me, I was definitely going to have to take to wearing a stole of some kind.

This time I knew where I was going and it didn't take me long to reach the hypostyle hall. After the windowless gloom of the inner temple, the hall seemed bright and the pure white linens of the two young priests glowed in comparison to everything else. I paused just inside. There were a number of things that bothered me about what had just taken place, but I was at a loss to say whether it was because Paseti was an unpleasant person or if there was really something amiss. On the one hand, it was a pretty good bet that whoever attacked Huya was connected to the temple — or at least had free run of the place. Ruling out the temple cats, that left a limited number of people with the opportunity to learn that Pedibastet was using his personal servant as a messenger for the throne. There was also the problem of the recently scraped papyri. On the other hand, there were a lot of people associated with the temple who could have been in a position to learn of the high priest's plans and intercept the slave. From the young Stolist's comments, it was clear that Paseti made a practice of recycling papyri. In short, it was a muddy mess. My instinctive shrug won me some claw-pricks from Neffi and I sucked air sharply before heading out into the hall to talk to Tepemkau and Hapuseneb. I was praying I'd know what I was going to ask them about by the time I reached them.

I needn't have worried. They already knew what they were going to talk to *me* about before I got there.

They both started at once. What they had to tell me wasn't much use; I already knew that Paseti was an officious bastard. It didn't take a real detective to figure that out. They ranted on for a while, but other than proving that people were people regardless of their titles and outward trappings, it got me nowhere. And that's exactly where I was going standing there listening to juicy but unhelpful stories about the goings-on inside the temple establishment. I was just working out how to detach myself from the pair when Neffi, with his remarkable timing, decided to stretch and yawn. Doubtless, both had prior experience with those teeth and claws displayed so briefly, but prominently. They suddenly remembered they had other duties to attend to. It was remarkable how that seemed to keep happening.

And it kept happening all day. I had no idea there were so many people in so many different capacities associated with a temple. There were hundreds and I think I talked to them all. During this I discovered several unchanging facts, No one liked Paseti; everyone liked Huya and everyone was real glad Nefer-Djenou-Bastet was happy living with me.

Finally, I found myself being led to yet a different part of the high priest's sprawling quarters. This time it was at the back of the house in the not so light and airy rooms of the servants and slaves. Pedibastet sat in a tiny room watching over his servant who was sleeping fitfully under the attending physician's drugs and spells. The injured man's head was swathed in an intricate bandage woven around protective amulets and the air smelled of honey, wine and herbs. The high priest sat in his folding wooden chair, looking tired and almost in as much need of a physician as Huya. Once again Neffi hopped down from my shoulders and jumped into the Sem-Priest's lap. Pedibastet scratched the cat's ears and motioned me toward a low stool. He treated me to a wan smile as he said softly, "You are a very respectful man, Sitehuti. You are the only person entering this room today who has not expressed the opinion that I ought not to concern myself over a mere servant — a slave in fact."

Truthfully, I was more alarmed at seeing the vigorous priest looking so tired and drained. What I *said* was, "I would never presume to do so, Your Eminence."

"No, you wouldn't." He chucked Neffi under the chin. If anyone else had done that, they would have ended up with bleeding fingers. With the high priest, he arched his neck so that his chin pointed at the ceiling and purred like rolling thunder. "Huya was taken from Syria as a captive of war and was given to me when I still wore the side-lock of youth. We're very close in age, although I suspect Huya is a little younger than I. We grew up together and I would trust him with my life. As it was, I trusted him with the crown and this is how he's repaid for it." Pedibastet regarded me over Neffi's head. "Have you found the perpetrator of this crime?"

I hesitated, wanting to voice my uneasiness about the Lector-Priest, but still torn about how much of that feeling was based on reality and how much on plain dislike. The high priest took my hesitation for a negative answer and continued almost to himself, "Of course you haven't. It is far too early for anything definite and it is merely my impatience showing through. Go on home, Sitehuti." His voice faded more as he added, "Sitehuti. Son of Thoth, the writer of Truth. The great magician. . . ."

Okay, now I was really worried, I stood and bowed low. "With respect, sir, you aren't doing Huya much good wearing yourself out here."

He roused himself with difficulty and lowered Neffi to the floor. "Perceptive as usual, young scribe. I doubt any more harm will befall him now that what he was carrying is vanished. Huya can neither read nor would he be inclined to read a message addressed to me. Another servant can watch over him as well as I until after morning services — and I must consult with my brother-in-law." He stopped and frowned. "Your back is all over scratches. If you're going to let the Sacred One ride on your shoulders, you had better get something to protect your skin."

I grinned. "Yes, sir, that thought had occurred to me, too."

He chuckled and preceded me into the corridor. I stood mute guard at the door as another servant was summoned to sit with Huya, and recalled the High Priest's words. Perceptive? Yeah.

~*~

Exchanging the relative quiet of the temple for the noisy city, I went looking for more information. Neffi followed close at my heels. A marketplace had grown up around the temple walls and it was in full swing by that time of day. I knew who I needed to talk to, but had no idea where to find them. I stopped at the first booth I came to. They sold pottery and were disappointed that I wasn't a customer. Still, they were aware of what had happened that morning and were able to point me to the merchants who had come upon Huya and Paseti that morning.

Approaching the booth, the reason the men had been on site so early became clear. The brightly colored sunshade occupied a prime spot; right at the junction where the temple's avenue of sphinxes met the public street. If I were selling *anything*, I'd get up early for a spot like that, too.

The pair behind the tables had to be related. Probably father and son. The older one was burly and looked more suited to moving stones than doing fine faience work. The other seller was a younger, slightly smaller version of the first, but he was young enough, there was probably ample time for him to catch up to or surpass the elder. They were both busy with paying customers, so I occupied myself examining their wares until they were free. I knew as soon as I got close enough to see the items on display that I was following in the footsteps of Khu and Senbi. If the Bastet amulet Senbi wore that morning hadn't originated there, I'd eat my writing kit.

Their work was wonderful. I'd spent the first seven years of my life living among the finest craftsmen in the two lands and the pieces spread before me in that market stall were well up to that standard. I was examining one of the beautifully detailed little figures when the father finished with his customer and came over. "The goddess is very popular today. She is also reasonably priced, Scribe, and today only, we are throwing in an exquisitely woven cord to wear her on."

Draping several lengths of linen cord across his beefy forearm, he held them out for inspection. They were indeed fine work. Unfortunately, the dangling ends attracted Neffi's attention. The cat sauntered over, stood on his hind legs and deftly snagged the knotted end of a pretty blue one. The man clearly recognized the thief. That in itself wasn't a surprise. I was rapidly coming to realize that it was doubtful anyone could work so close to the temple without becoming aware of the infamous Nefer-Djenou-Bastet. Still, his response was amazing in light of the other reactions I'd witnessed over the last two days. True, his eyes bulged momentarily, but then his face broke into a brilliant smile.

He bowed low, saying, "Forgive me, honored scribe! It is unthinkable that I did not recognize you and the Sacred One. How may poor, stupid Pamiu be of service?"

His reaction had me nonplussed until I heard his name. At that point, everything including the booth's location and preponderance of items devoted to Bastet became clear. Pamiu. Old Tomcat. Certainly, it was not the name he'd been born with, but he was doubtless a devotee of the goddess.

His grin and good humor were infectious. I found myself smiling as I returned his bow. "Honored to make your acquaintance, Pamiu. I am Sitehuti of Western Thebes. The High Priest of Bastet,

Pedibastet, has asked me to speak with you about what you saw this morning."

The man's beaming face fell. He shook his head. "Oh, yes. A terrible business. Good thing my sons and I happened along when we did. I don't think that skinny Lector would have been strong enough to carry the old man out of the street, although he was trying very hard to lift him."

"Paseti — the Lector-Priest was trying to carry the servant? What exactly was he doing?"

"He was . . . PFAH! Far easier to show you." Turning to his son who was now watching from a distance, he called, "Kyky! The Sacred One and his scribe need to know what happened this morning. Come over here and help me."

Kyky came as did four others of varying ages and sizes who had apparently been wandering through the market hawking their family's wares. Together, they demonstrated how they had come upon the scene to find Paseti trying to lift the old man by himself. They ran forward, saw the situation and took charge. Mind you, the story as they told it was far more elaborate and entertaining. It was punctuated with much arm-waving and dashing about.

The performance collected quite an audience. This resulted in several more sales for the amulet sellers, but left me virtually empty handed. I hadn't learned a single new detail. Maybe it was fated to be that way. Further proof I wasn't cut out to be an investigator. The hope that if I continued to come up with nothing, they'd let me go back to being a plain old scribe lurked in the back of my mind. I know. The rest of my mind didn't believe it, either.

At the finale, that consisted of Kyky and another boy roughly his size hefting a younger boy between them and hurrying toward the temple, Pamiu stood, arms flung wide. "So you see how it happened now?"

"I do, indeed, Pamiu. Thank you — and your sons."

Flushed with pride and exertion, they insisted on presenting me with the amulet I'd been admiring and a fresh, unchewed cord to go with it. It didn't take a lot of perception to see that if I refused the gift or insisted on paying, the whole family would be offended. They were good people and deserved better than that. So, I let Pamiu fasten the pendant around my neck, and with Neffi in tow headed farther into the market.

There was one more stop to make, but I was clueless where this would be. The person I sought had only recently relocated to the temple area. It was a big place and no one was familiar with the man I was asking after. So we wandered. We cruised countless stalls for what seemed to be most of the day. I was buying a meat roll when the familiar, nasal voice I'd been listening for cut through the hubbub of the market. It was calling my name.

"Sitehuti! Hey, Sitehuti!"

Scanning the throngs, I finally caught sight of a wildly waving arm. It was covered with a countless number of the gaudiest bracelets known to mankind and terminated in a be-ringed hand gripping a razor. I pushed my way through the crush and found that, as I suspected, the arm was attached to my friend S'kem, the barber.

We punched shoulders and greeted each other with unfeigned enthusiasm. I exclaimed, "Hey! Where have you been? I haven't seen you around the neighborhood in ages. Not since you finished your apprenticeship."

"I moved closer to the temples when I got out on my own. Business is great here! I'm earning a lot, but it makes it hard to get back to the old neighborhood." He gestured at the crowd of waiting customers. The queue consisted of mainly priests. Being the new shop was practically on the temple grounds, that was no surprise.

He gestured at Neffi, who was now draped around my neck, and continued happily, "Oh, and there he is. The Sacred One! You know, Sitehuti if you're going to carry him around on your shoulders, you better start wearing a stole or something. You're all scratched up."

"Uh, yeah. That's been mentioned — hey, how did you know about Neffi — I mean the Sacred One?"

"Oh, everyone knows how Nefer-Djenou-Bastet chose you. It's a great honor, you know. You're destined for great things. Oh, yes. No doubt about it."

There was also no doubt that S'kem knew all about everything before everyone else did. That's why I sought him out. He seemed to have the ability to collect information like a bee collected nectar; almost as if he absorbed it through contact with his customers' skins. One moment you were sitting getting a nice shave, then the next, you're leaving and S'kem is telling the next guy all about your love life and the incident with the donkey and you didn't remember telling him any of it.

Warm reunions notwithstanding, I had come with a purpose and I needed to get to it. Enough time had already been lost.

"Hey," I said. "I need to talk to you."

I pulled S'kem a little away from his waiting customers. This didn't make them too happy, but most of the waiting priests were from the temple of Bastet. They eyed Neffi and didn't grumble too loudly.

"Look, I need your help," I said. "The High Priest asked me to look into his servant's assault."

He waved airily, making the bracelets rattle. "Oh, I already knew that."

All right. See the previous mention of the incident with the donkey. More fool me. I'd been writing and rewriting what I'd say when I finally found S'Kem. He'd just rubbed out half of my prepared speech. I regrouped and got to the crux. "Well, what you might not have heard is that I *may* have stepped into a pile of political doo-doo."

He looked grave, but didn't reply. For S'Kem, that was a

worrisome development.

I hurried on, "Before I *really* slip and wind up on my face in it, is there anyone who'd know who was doing what to who . . . and that sort of thing?"

"Oh." S'kem started twisting his rings. "Oh, Sitehuti, you better stay away from that stuff. Oh, yes. Politics are bad. Very bad."

Tell me something I *didn't* know. "Believe me, I'd like to avoid it, but I have no choice. High Priest Pedibastet expects me to be able to tell him something by tomorrow."

"Mmmmmm. The high priest? Not a good idea to disappoint a high priest at all." His brow furrowed and he stood pinging his thumbnail against the edge of his copper razor. Before long, he announced, "Wosret the Nubian. Definitely. If anyone can tell you what's going on politically, it's Wosret."

"Great, so where do I find Wosret the Nubian?"

"But then again, maybe not. He's a mercenary and you know how they are. Haven't seen him around much lately. Been talking about packing up and going home to the Land of the Bow, but I doubt he'll do it. There's not as much wealth in Nubia as here in the capital."

"Fine. If he's still in the city, how do I find him?"

"Nubia. Now *there's* politics for you. Half of 'em want to overthrow the Pharaoh and the other half get paid to defend him. No accounting for folks like that." He looked up as if struck by a new thought. "Hey! You look like you could use a fresh shave. Have a seat."

I eyed the waiting priests. They looked even less happy than before. "I don't think your other customers would appreciate me breaking line."

"Oh, don't worry about them. They'll be happy to let you and the Sacred One go first."

I'm not sure I'd have used the word "happy", but the waiting priests did cede their place to me. A half-hour and a good shave later, I knew more about the political goings-on in the Two Lands than I'd ever wanted to — and all from a guy who said he didn't know a thing about politics.

I also knew where to find Wosret the Nubian, although after my crash course in international politics, I wasn't so sure I wanted to tackle him. Still, I couldn't fulfill my obligation to the Sem-Priest unless I tried.

This Wosret lived in the back of a spice warehouse near the waterfront. It wasn't a good section of town, but then again, I've never seen any location near a waterfront or dock that I'd call a good section of any town. It got even better when I learned he preferred to do business after sunset. That made me feel real comfortable.

~*~

It was so late when we finally got back to my aunt's house, there wasn't much left in the way of the evening meal. Neffi and I made do with some bread, beer and a few limp leeks left over from yesterday's dinner. The news that I had spent all day at the temple and been talking with the police had beaten me home and my aunt was livid. As far as she was concerned, any contact with the police was bad news and she was just waiting to see what kind of dishonor I'd brought on the family.

Mose, Aha and Maatre, on the other hand, thought it was the greatest thing to happen since the dry land separated from the chaos of the water. I thought Mose would never calm down enough to drop off to sleep and there was no way I'd attempt to leave the house as long as Mose was still awake.

THREE

The house S'kem told me about was a warehouse owned by a Nubian spice merchant. The mercenary, Wosret, lived in back of the building ostensibly performing the function of night watchman. That section of town comes alive when the sun goes down and I spent more time dodging people on the narrow streets than moving toward my destination. I wore my oldest clothes and cheapest jewelry and had also raided the family storage chests for an old wig some long-departed relative decided not to take with him. It wasn't so much a disguise as a precaution. If anything was stolen or damaged, I didn't care. The only thing was new was the length of heavy linen that I'd weaseled out of Aunt Tiaa earlier that evening. It was draped around my shoulders for Neffi to ride on. He still managed to knead through the cloth periodically, but it was less painful than him riding on my bare skin.

Neffi spoiled any hope of navigating the area unnoticed. I knew he would, and had vainly tried to leave him at home. Apparently, doors and shutters pose no impediment to a sufficiently determined cat. At least not to Nefer-Djenou-Bastet.

We'd managed to keep a low profile until we passed a group of young ladies wearing more paint than clothing. They were lounging on mudbrick benches built onto the outside of a dilapidated two-story building, and were calling out lewd invitations to passersby. One of them caught sight of Neffi and, suddenly, he and I were surrounded by giggling women all making over him. He ate it up. I didn't exactly complain, either.

Pleasant though the interlude was, we had to cut it short. I didn't want Wosret to leave his rooms before I got a chance to talk to him. S'kem had given me an idea of where to look if that happened, but I wasn't anxious to tour the places he outlined. Most of them made the run-down brothel we'd just seen look like palaces by comparison.

The spice warehouse wasn't far from the brothel and before long, I was standing outside the place looking it over. The building was on a corner and the street it fronted was as busy and narrow as the one I'd just left, but that didn't matter. According to S'kem, I wanted the side door. He said to go down almost to the end of the wall and there would be an alcove flanked by windows; the door was in that alcove. If I tapped three, then two, then three times, Wosret would know I was legitimate and open to me.

How S'Kem came by this knowledge, I didn't know. I didn't ask and he didn't say.

I confess that my heart pounded in my ears as I moved down that side street. It was dark and deserted and I couldn't make up my mind if the lack of people was a good thing or a bad thing. It didn't bother Neffi. He jumped from my shoulders and led me right to the door. That was pretty dark, too. I think I'd hoped to find lamplight spilling out from under it or from around the shutters. Instead, the place seemed deserted. Neffi rubbed and twined around my legs encouragingly. I called myself several uncomplimentary names and tapped at the wood planks as instructed.

Then I waited.

And waited some more. I was standing there looking silly and working out what to do when Neffi simply pushed the door open and strolled through. I grabbed for him, but he slid out of my hands and disappeared into the blackness beyond.

I hissed, "Come back here right now!"

That worked as well as expected. I stuck my head in to call again, and was assailed by the mingled scents of exotic spices. If nothing else, it proved I had the right place. Obviously, Neffi wasn't going to come back. He'd left me no choice but to go in after him. I slid in and shut the door behind me. Last thing in the world I wanted was to have visitors from outside at that point. I stood with my back pressed against the door and eyes closed until they could adjust to the extreme darkness inside the building.

When I opened them again, dark shapes of piled sacks loomed around me like a wall extending into the gloom. My questing fingers contacted the nearest stack of bags, releasing an increased scent of cinnamon. Not bad at all. I groped along the stacks inhaling appreciatively of the aromas of cumin, coriander and anise seed released by my touch until I came to a turning point in the way. To my left, a flicker of lamplight shone from under a closed door. I could see Neffi — or at least the shadow of his feet — pacing in front of it.

Rushing forward to snatch him up, I was hit with a smell that was definitely not spice. It was so startling, it stopped me cold. It came from beyond the door ahead of me.

I reached for the latch, but never touched it. The door burst open, slamming me back into a stack of spice bags that toppled and broke, raining cloves everywhere. The lamplight from the room beyond was bright by comparison and a slightly-built man wearing the long hair and robes of a Semite was briefly outlined against it. I glimpsed a cloth headband and heavy braided beard before the first blow landed. After that I was too busy defending myself to notice anything.

I was groping for something — *anything* — to act as a weapon when the man started screaming and clawing at his head. Confused sounds resolved into furious cat screams intermingled with human ones. Nefer-Djenou-Bastet had wrapped himself around my attacker's head like a living wig.

The man lurched from side to side trying to dislodge the whirling ball of fur and claws, bringing the fight into the wedge of light streaming through the now-open door. I still only saw the coarse robes and curled hair of a Semite before he dove for the far exit. This frenzied run dislodged Neffi who slid to the floor still clutching something in his teeth. I heard the plank door bang against the outer wall and the man's scuffling footsteps as he continued to put distance between himself and the angry cat.

I collapsed with my face against the bags; the odor of cloves choked me and made my eyes water. I rolled onto my back and gulped air, fully expecting someone else to burst through from either the door beside me or from outside. Amazingly, no one did. I took advantage of the respite to do a little thinking.

The man who attacked me couldn't have been Wosret, he was far too small to have been the mercenary described to me. Someone the size of the person I'd just tangled with would only take a name meaning "strong" as a joke. I massaged my jaw. Then again. . . .

Still, Wosret was described to me as a big man. Emphasis on big. The one I fought was bigger than me, but that wasn't saying much. Okay, then where *was* Wosret the Nubian? Before long, a sound resolved itself over the muted hubbub of the streets that filtered through the thick mud brick walls. It was Neffi. Purring.

Roughly at that same time I decided that lying across bags of cloves wasn't accomplishing anything other than making my fusty old wig smell better. Besides it was lumpy and damned uncomfortable. I hauled myself up shedding loose cloves all the way and peeked into the lit room.

I pulled back real fast.

A huge black man lay on the floor of the other room in a pool of blood. He had to be the missing Wosret. He also had to be very, very dead. I gulped hard and crept in closer to be sure. The unpleasant smell that warred with the spices was stronger the closer I came to the body and it *was* a body. No doubt of that. The man's bowels and bladder had released at the point of death and I didn't need to be a physician to pinpoint the cause of that demise. His throat was cut. The guttering lamplight revealed several more stab wounds. The hilt of a copper dagger still protruded from his chest. An empty scabbard at the man's belt made it a good bet the dagger was his own. Morbid curiosity sent my hand out to the hilt; the blade was stuck fast. My father was always banging his chisels back straight and complaining how easily copper bent. Now, I was grateful for it. If the dagger hadn't bent, it would doubtless have been used on me, as well.

Neffi meowed and roused me from shocked immobility. He hadn't come into the death room with me; as a matter of fact, he hadn't moved from where he landed when he fell from my assailant's head.

As usual, he was showing more sense than I was. We needed to get out of there fast. I stood and bent to scoop him up — then stopped. He seemed to be sitting on a dead animal of some kind. He stretched and stalked over to me, proud of his kill. I prodded it gingerly, then lifted it. It was a wig. No, not a wig. A false beard cut and curled in the fashion of the Assyrians.

I folded the beard into my linen shawl and reinstalled it and Neffi onto my shoulders. We left the warehouse quickly and took the long way back to my aunt's house. I needed time to think. I was also sick a couple times along the way. When I finally reached home, I didn't go right in, but spent quite a while leaning against the side of the house, rubbing Neffi's fur, wondering what to do next. When the man's body was discovered — and it surely would be — everyone in the area would remember the man with the cat.

Would they also remember the Semite who left without his beard? I doubted it.

That night seemed to never end.

FOUR

I couldn't face breakfast the next morning. Aunt Tiaa forgot all about my dealings with the police in her concern, fluttering and fussing until she'd seen me drink a cup of beer. She also forced a chunk of bread into my hands as I left. I gave the bread to a one-legged beggar at the corner and managed to make it half-way to school before I lost the beer. I needed to talk to Pedibastet, but he wouldn't be available until closer to noon when his priestly duties were finished.

The plan was to behave as normally as possible, then excuse myself from school, high-tail it to the temple and beg an audience with the Sem-Priest. As I said, that was the plan. That wasn't how it worked out.

I must've looked like a candidate for the morticians' tents when I first dragged in, because even Master Khenemetamun-pa-sheri left me alone. We stayed to the back of the class. Neffi stretched out beside me and, from time to time, patted me with a paw or groomed my arm. I tried to concentrate, but it was no use. No matter what the lesson, the staring eyes and gaping mouth of Wosret the Nubian kept floating in front of the papyrus. I made more mistakes than the first year students that day. The way Khenemetamun-pa-sheri was glaring, there was certain to be scraping duty later no matter how sick I looked. It never happened.

We were in the courtyard taking dictation of a set of admonitions praising the occupation of the scribe and comparing it with other careers. Do I need to say the other careers show up badly? Anyway, Master Khenemetamun-pa-sheri had just intoned the phrases,

The soldier drinks water every three days and it is foul with the taste of salt.

His body is broken with dysentery.

The enemy comes, and surrounds him with arrows, and life is far away from him.

when a contingent of the royal Medjay guards pushed past a flustered servant and invaded the garden. The class grew silent and drew back a little. They had good reason, too. These Nubians were the Pharaoh's crack troops, personal bodyguard and royal police force all rolled into one. They didn't pay courtesy calls on citizens, either — even those of the standing of my schoolmaster.

The captain of the contingent stepped up in front of my pasty-faced teacher and demanded, "You are the scribe Khenemetamun-pa-sheri?"

My master couldn't answer. His lips worked, but no sound came out. At length, he managed a nod.

The captain thrust a letter into Khenemetamun-pa-sheri's hands, then stepped back waiting, straight-backed and severe. The master scribe looked at the seal, and paled further. His hands shook as he broke it and opened the message. He read for a few moments, then gasped, "Sitehuti of Western Thebes, you are to go with these men."

My classmates melted away like wax in a flame leaving me alone with only Nefer-Djenou-Bastet standing guard. The captain gestured and four of the soldiers came toward me. Neffi growled and bristled, but this wasn't the time for a showdown. Besides, I didn't know if the Medjay had any kind of prohibition against killing a sacred cat and didn't want to find out. I grabbed him, plopped him on my shoulders and allowed myself to be led away.

We walked in silence. From the glowers of my escorts, it wouldn't have done any good to ask questions, anyway. I'd hoped we were maybe going to the courthouse where I could ask to talk to the high priest, but my heart sank as we took a direct route for the palace. To my mind, that could only mean one thing: Wosret the Nubian had been found and I had been accused of his murder. If I was being taken to the palace under guard, it could only be for judgment of a capital offense because only the Pharaoh can pass such a sentence.

Strictly speaking, it wasn't a long journey from the school to the palace, but it felt like an eternity. The stares of the people we passed and pushed out of the way were unbearable. My worst moment was when we passed the policemen Khu and Senbi. They started toward our little parade, but were thrust back and told in no uncertain terms that it didn't concern them.

Each step brought another "what if." What if I hadn't gone to Wosret's rooms? What if I hadn't talked to S'kem? What if I had simply told the high priest I couldn't do this. . . ?

That was the real sticking point. I *should* have told the Sem-Priest right away that I couldn't handle the job, that it was beyond my ability to do as he asked. Instead, I'd played at being an investigator. I confess, I'd been having fun with it and was sort of enjoying the notoriety my association with Neffi lent me. But it wasn't fun anymore. Real people were real dead — and I might have been the next in line.

All through this Neffi curled protectively around my neck. I'd been afraid he'd cause a ruckus, but he was quiet and only growled if one of the Medjay came too close. That became more infrequent the farther we walked.

Inside the palace grounds, our troop veered away from the official wings, entered into a spacious garden and on into the depths of the private apartments of the Royal Family. I was still trying to work out the significance of this when we entered a beautifully appointed study where two older men were going over a stack of scrolls and papyrus sheets. One of the men was Pedibastet and I was so relieved to see him that for a moment I didn't register the taller man next to him.

That was only for a moment, though.

If his fine jewelry hadn't marked him as a member of the Royal Family, his distinctive profile would have. He looked toward us as we entered and for a brief instant, I locked eyes with Merenptah, Crown Prince of the Two Lands.

It is the dream of every scribe to be called into the Royal Presence and I was no different. However, in my dreams the circumstances were a bit more felicitous. Abruptly, I realized I was the only one in the group still standing. Not only that, I was staring with my mouth hanging open. I fell straight to the intricately woven matting to kiss the earth. Neffi mewed a complaint, bounded from my shoulders and stalked away, tail swishing.

Without rising, the captain of the contingent announced, "We have brought the scribe, Your Highness."

From the corner of my eye, I saw His Royal Highness smile slightly. "Excellent, Captain Djedmose, you may leave us now, but remain in the hall outside. I want no extra ears in on this discussion."

Captain Djedmose glanced at me doubtfully, but knocked his forehead against the floor in a sign of obedience. "As you command, Highness." He and the rest filed out past me, leaving me with the Crown Prince and his brother-in-law, but they didn't like it. If looks were swords, I'd have been dumpling filling.

As soon as I heard the doors shut, I launched into the proper litany that Master Khenemetamun-pa-sheri had drilled into me, "Thou art like Re in all that thou doest, everything happens according to the wish of thy heart. . . ."

"Right, right, right. At the moment, Scribe, the wish of my heart is that you stand up so that I may see the face of the man my brother-in-law speaks so highly of without craning my neck."

I glanced up in confusion. The great man made an impatient motion with his hand indicating that I rise, then dropped into a chair addressing no one in particular. "We really don't have a lot of time. A pack of Nubian representatives are already waiting in the formal salon clamoring for an audience concerning the violent death of one of their own. Never mind that the man was a criminal. Never mind the man had likely done the same or worse to others, he was one of their own and by all the gods they'll have justice!" The crown prince stopped and glared at his right foot. He'd been jiggling it as he spoke and his beautifully tooled leather and gold sandal had dislodged. He jerked the footwear off with a very unregal curse and flung it against the far wall. "These damned things don't even bend! They fall off my feet when I'm sitting down, how in the name of the Eater-of-Souls am I supposed to walk in them? I've half a mind to send for my military shoes. They're at least broken in."

Pedibastet coughed his laugh. "Better not throw those too far, Brother, you'll need them for court. And if you try to wear those smelly old army sandals, Djedmose himself would kill you outright as a threat to the general well-being of Egypt."

Merenptah glared at the high priest with familiar scorn. I'd seen the same pass between members of my own family. With a sniff of disdain, he returned his attention to me. "Now, about this Nubian?"

Heart in my throat, I bowed low again and managed to squeeze words through my fear-paralyzed lips. "Majesty, I am innocent. I swear by the Feather of Ma'at that the man was already dead when I got to his lodgings—"

"Ha!" the crown prince barked. "You were right Padi!"

"Of course," the High Priest said. "A young man with a big spotted cat on his shoulder? Who else would it have been?"

The room reeled and I was glad I'd dropped to my knees again because they surely wouldn't have held me up. "I didn't—"

"No one thinks you did, boy." Crown Prince Merenptah seemed determined not to let me finish a sentence. That was fine. I wasn't sure I could anyway. For someone whose life's work was words, all command of them had fled.

It took a bit for the import of the Crown Prince's last statement to sink in. By that time, the Sem-Priest was speaking, so the ball wasn't on my side of the line, anyway. He said, "I don't like this a bit, Merny. Our informant in Memphis has gone missing and whoever their operative is here in Pi-Ramesses has thwarted us in finding the letter. The conspirators remain several steps ahead of us."

"Mmmm. That letter. I would give a lot to see what was in it."

"I doubt there's much chance of that, Your Highness. I think it's been scraped clean."

Both men turned to look at me and I realized it was me who'd said that. Well, I was in for it anyway, so I continued. "The Lector-Priest, Paseti, might be your Pi-Ramesses operative, Highness. Not only was he supposedly the first to come upon the injured servant and so had opportunity to be the attacker, but in the midst of all the turmoil yesterday, he was making himself busy scraping papyri."

Pedibastet blinked. "Why didn't you say this yesterday?"

"I wasn't sure then — I'm still not, but it seems to fit. I didn't want to make an accusation without having something more solid than...."

"Than what?"

"I don't like him, sir — sirs."

Pedibastet snorted. "If I had a silver deben for everyone who didn't like Paseti, we'd have enough to build a whole new temple."

Merenptah grinned. "I think that's the young man's point, Padi.

Anyone so disliked would be too easy to point suspicion at."

"Point well taken. As it happens, over the time Paseti has been at the temple of Bastet, he's been accused of everything from pocketing offerings to making the Inundation fail."

"Isn't his family from Memphis? I seem to remember his father from summers at my half-brother, Amunhotep's estate. Solid family if I recall." Without waiting for his brother-in-law to answer, the Crown Prince turned back to me. "Since it appears that our reports of a young man and a large cat being in the area when the Nubian mercenary was killed did indeed point to you, young man, what did you learn there?"

"Not much, Your Highness. He was already dead when we got to his rooms. Whoever killed him was still there and attacked me, but Neffi — Nefer-Djenou-Bastet — fought him off."

"Did you see him at all?"

I became aware of an odd snuffling noise. I'd heard it before and cast my mind about for where. Then I remembered and surreptitiously searched the room for Neffi. To my absolute horror, he was rolling around with a ridiculously ecstatic expression on his face in the Crown Prince's discarded sandal. I edged closer in an attempt to intercept him before . . . too late. With a throaty growl, he launched himself and the gold-decorated leather into the air, then landed square on it and rolled across the floor biting and scratching it under the amazed eyes of the Crown Prince and the High Priest of Bastet.

Just as I was about to grovel and apologize profusely, Merenptah threw back his head and roared with laughter. "By Amon! I'd forgotten he was here!" He pulled off the other sandal and tossed it to the enraptured cat. "Here! Break them in for me!' Still laughing, he repeated, "Back to where we were. Did you get a look at the man?"

I stole an uncertain peek at Neffi who was shifting his attack to the newer opponent, then answered, "Well, yes and no, Your

Highness. He was dressed like a Semite, but I don't think he really was — oh wait!" I pulled my linen stole from around my shoulders and unwrapped the false beard. In all the other excitement, I'd completely forgotten it until then. I held it out for inspection. "He was wearing this, but Nefer-Djenou-Bastet pulled it off. He also had long, curled hair and Asiatic-style robes."

"But you're guessing it was all a disguise?" The crown prince took the false beard and looked it over carefully. "Nice work. Whoever our opponent is, he has deep coffers — maybe a high-level priest?"

Pedibastet came forward and ran the curled locks through his fingers. "He's probably used this disguise before. Not much sense in paying for anything like this if it's to be used only once."

"True, Brother." Merenptah smiled at me. "No longer, though. You and Nefer-Djenou-Bastet. . . ." He broke off and his smile widened as he continued, ". . .Neffi — have spoiled that for him. He's been seen and will be recognized again even if he replaces his beard. The rest of the disguise probably ended up on a rubbish tip shortly after your encounter."

Pedibastet nodded, "And will have been found and turned into who knows what other saleable items by the local residents. Too much to hope that the Sacred One marked him."

I shrugged. "It's possible."

Unexpectedly, the high priest slapped the surface of the small table. "Curse me for a blind man, I spent several hours with the wretch at the services for the goddess this morning and didn't look at him once."

The Crown Prince smiled. "Padi, no one knows better than I how complicated the ceremonies to the gods are. When you're serving the goddess, your attention is on her, not on the reciter of the liturgy."

"It will have to be checked."

"Indeed it will be. As much as I would like your presence and support at today's audience, you and Sitehuti will have to see if our errant Lector-Priest bears scratches. But that doesn't alter the fact we still need to know what happened to our man from the temple of Ptah and who is ultimately behind this plot. *You* must find this out for us, Sitehuti."

The only thing I can say in my defense is that I was dazed. The last few days had been too big a change for me; the previous night and that morning a total shock to my system. Words poured out of me unbidden. Thank the gods tears didn't come, too. I heard myself saying, "But I can't find *anything* out. I'm not a policeman and I don't know how to investigate anything! I don't know why Nefer-Djenou-Bastet chose me.

"It was an accident that I saw Paseti was scraping papyri. If anyone can be thanked for catching him at all, it's Neffi! He *led* me to him.

"It was pure desperation that I searched out, S'kem the barber, and asked him who would know about political dealings in the city.

"It was pure stupidity that took me to Wosret's place, and brought me to fight with his murderer. I've never seen a murdered man before! I don't want to see another! I was sick all night and . . . I think I'm going to be sick again." I fell to my knees and knocked my head against the floor. "Please let me go home. I'm not an investigator, I'm not even a real scribe, I'm just a student."

The only sound I heard for a long time was Neffi purring in my ear. During my tirade, he'd abandoned the Prince's sandals and come over to me in concern. He now nuzzled, head-butted me and licked my ear.

Finally, the Prince spoke, "You're right again, Padi. The boy has anything but an inflated opinion of himself. The Sacred One has indeed chosen well."

I banged my head against the floor a little harder. It didn't accomplish anything other than bruising my forehead and knocking my wig off, but I couldn't stop myself.

Pedibastet agreed, "Oh, absolutely. There isn't much to be done about the other things, but we can do something about him being only a student, can't we?"

"Of course we can. It will be necessary if we're to send him to Memphis."

My head snapped up. "Memphis?"

The prince glanced briefly in my direction. "That's the obvious next step. My son, Seti-Merenptah, is General of the Armies there. You'll need to report to him as soon as you arrive in the city. I'll send a letter of introduction with you."

I shooed Neffi off my crumpled wig. Plunking it back on my head, I wailed, "But sirs, you must not have understood what I just said. . . ."

Merenptah fixed me with a stare even more piercing than his brother-in-law's. "Boy, who am I?"

I did a brief suffocating fish imitation before I fell to my knees and knocked my head against the matting again. This time I managed to keep my wig on. "Oh. Yes, Your Highness! Thank you. I've never been to Memphis before."

FIVE

We returned to the temple in force. Captain Djedmose sent four of his men back with us. The initial plan was to seize Paseti and take him off for questioning, but that died the death that most plans do. When we got to the Lector-Priest's workroom, he wasn't there.

He'd been there — and not all that long before by the look of it; the lamp on the work table still had more than half its oil left. An elegant writing kit sat beside a prayer scroll that had been weighted open for copying and a sheet of papyrus lay nearby with the first characters of the prayer inked onto it. A new-looking reed pen with ink on the tip rested across the top of the alabaster water bowl. I examined the pen and ink palette.

"They're both dry, Your Eminence. It appears he left in a hurry. Could someone have warned him off?"

Neffi leapt up onto the bench and nosed through a stack of scrolls.

The high priest took the pen from me and rolled the hardened tip between his fingers, nodding slightly. "We can count on it. It would take something that drastic to make Paseti abandon anything as expensive as this kit."

"But who?" I said. "And how? We didn't even know we were coming ourselves until a little while ago."

The high priest laid the ruined brush back on the water pot. "I wonder. . . ."

We never got to find out what High Priest Pedibastet was wondering because, at that moment, the Stolist-Priest, Tepemkau, poked his head around the door. He looked annoyed. Sounded it, too.

"About time you got back—" he broke off when he came fully through the doorway and fell into a low bow with a horrified expression on his face. "Oh! Forgive me, Your Eminence, I heard voices and I thought the Reciter had returned."

His act was good, but I had doubts. We hadn't been particularly quiet as we'd come down the hall. The Medjay were even less so. Add in that our procession had stomped right past the Stolist's office door, it was more likely he was angling to find out what was going on. Tepemkau was a horrible gossip and never wasted the opportunity to catch some good dirt.

I doubted Pedibastet was fooled, either. In spite of this, he waved the apology away. "It is of no import, Stolist. How long has the Reciter been away from his workroom?"

"I'm not sure, Sir. He was here when the porter brought the letter from his brother. Maybe an hour ago?"

The high priest made a non-committal noise deep in his throat.

The Stolist appeared to rethink his interruption. He drummed fingers against a clay pot he clutched and appeared to be considering a retreat.

The pot caught my eye. It looked out of place. "Tepemkau, what's the pot for?"

The Stolist looked down at the jar as if he'd forgotten it was there. "Ah, yes. This is healing salve. Lector Paseti asked me to fetch some for him from the stores."

Pedibastet looked interested, but said nothing.

"That's a little strange," I said. "Why he would need healing salve? Do you know?"

Tepemkau's demeanor underwent a subtle change. There was something about the answer he enjoyed. He must have realized this, because the look was quickly replaced by one of pious concern. "Oh, the poor Lector had a bad night. He awakened with a terrible queasiness and spent most of the night in the privy. Then, to make matters worse, he tripped over one of the temple cats on his way back to bed." Again the Stolist had to work to choke back a look of glee. "I'm afraid the cat expressed her displeasure with him in a rather physical way."

"He was scratched?" High Priest Pedibastet demanded. His eyes gleamed under his projecting brows.

The Stolist flinched a little at his superior's intensity. "Yes, Eminence. All down his back and shoulders. It looked quite painful."

Pedibastet abruptly turned to the Medjay. "Have any of you ever seen the Reciter-Priest?"

One stood straighter. "I have, Your Eminence."

"Good. You and one other. Go to the docks and see if our missing priest is there."

The soldier saluted and bowed. "Right away, Your Eminence." He gestured to the man next to him and they hurried out.

Mouth agape and eyes wide, Tepemkau stared after the departed soldiers until High Priest Pedibastet commanded his attention. "Stolist? Stolist Tepemkau! How do you know the message was from Paseti's brother?"

The Stolist pulled his attention back to the Sem-Priest with difficulty. "Ummm . . . I heard the Porter tell him so. He said it was from Captain Sasobek of the Seth Division and there was a messenger at the gates waiting for his reply."

"I see."

The younger priest fidgeted in silence for a moment. "Your Eminence, is Paseti in real trouble?"

Pedibastet considered before answering. At last he said, "Yes, Stolist Tepemkau, he is. It appears that Lector Paseti was responsible for the harm done to my servant yesterday morning."

Tepemkau stood wide-eyed and silent. That didn't last long,

though. After a moment he blurted out, "I knew it! There was always something. . . . You know, none of the temple cats ever liked Paseti. Maybe we ought to pay more attention to them. Animals know, I always say. I had an uncle on my mother's side who had this dog—" abruptly, Tepemkau yelped and bounced a distance to his left. I recognized the signs and looked toward the floor where the priest had been standing. Sure enough, there was Neffi. He sat cleaning his face with innocent nonchalance.

The Stolist stammered something about getting the salve back to the stores since it wasn't needed, then edged around the bathing cat and fled up the passageway. Tepemkau was a resilient fellow; I had no doubt that by the time he got to the Scribe of the Temple Storerooms, he'd be recovered enough to give a rousing account of the raid on Paseti's workroom. Most likely, by the time it was finished circulating, it would have been a near fight to the death involving an entire regiment and the Pharaoh's own personal squadron of Sherden guards.

Pedibastet's coughing laugh pulled me back to the abandoned workroom. He spoke softly, "Animals know, all right. If Nefer-Djenou-Bastet hadn't intervened, we might have been gossiped to death."

The two remaining Medjay didn't try to suppress their snickers.

The high priest gestured toward the table. "Bring the lamp, Sitehuti. We'll return to my rooms and wait to hear any news from the docks."

~*~

We heard nothing at all from the docks. Surprised? I wasn't. Chaos ensued, anyway.

As in any other situation where people find themselves at a loss for a normal way to proceed, they fell back on shouting and useless running around. Routines were disrupted, rooms were searched and people were questioned. In the end we learned, Paseti was scratched up the night before, he got a letter from his brother,

57

and was no longer to be found in the temple precincts. In short, exactly what we knew before the chaos.

What I got out of it was time to sit in the cool of the high priest's quarters, sip pomegranate juice and think things over. I'd like to say I formulated a brilliant plan on how to proceed once I reached Memphis, but all I can say with honesty is that I was just as confused at the end of the day as I was at the beginning.

Several days passed with no word of Paseti, but I was too busy to give it much thought. I had my hands full preparing for the journey to Memphis. I'd gone on journeys before, but this one was different. Not only was this a trip to the old capital, but I was going as part of a temple envoy. The up side of this was that it even impressed Aunt Tiaa. Sure, she grumbled and called me a half-wit, after all, it *was* Aunt Tiaa. We'd have all run for the doctors if she hadn't pronounced doom for the whole family due to my incompetence. Still, she supplied me with new linens. This was all under the pretext of protecting the family from ineffable shame if I were found dead in the old capital wearing rags, you understand.

Three days later, Neffi and I stood on the deck of a boat watching the city of Pi-Ramesses recede in the distance. I was bedecked in crisp new linen and armed with a private letter from Crown Prince Merenptah to his son, General Seti-Merenptah.

It was Inundation and the river was running fast. Fortunately, the wind was with us, so we made good time in spite of the fact we were traveling against the current. The priests and scribes traveling with me soon pulled out game boards. As far as I was concerned, there was too much going on for me to join in. This was only my second long boat journey. The first was the voyage to Pi-Ramesses from my home in Western Thebes when I was seven. That was a while back and I confess to being too frightened at the prospect of leaving home for the unknown to notice much. This time, I found a shady place under the cargo awning and sat back to watch the purposeful scurrying of the crew and the amazing variety of crafts plying the Nile.

There was amazing variety in the crew, too. We were on a large boat and, as such, it had a large crew. In addition to the Egyptians, there were a couple Syrians, with their squared off beards; one man wearing large gold earrings that I swear was a Phoenician and a small, wiry man who wore gold double loops in each ear who was as dark as a Nubian and tattooed all over. Their different dialects and clothing styles made watching them at work endlessly interesting.

When we first boarded, I'd been worried how Neffi would behave on a boat. On the whole, cats and boats mixed well, but those other cats weren't Nefer-Djenou-Bastet. I had visions of the terrorized crew putting us off by force half-way to Memphis. I figured if we were lucky, they'd pull ashore before doing it. Neffi surprised me, though. After an initial inspection of his new domain, he wandered back to where I sat, found a sunny perch and went to sleep. It was exactly what the high priest told me he'd do. One of these days, I'd learn to trust what Pedibastet said.

I was drowsing a bit myself when someone sat down beside me. It was Hapuseneb, the young priest I'd met my second day at the temple of Bastet. At the time, he'd been in the company of the Stolist-Priest, Tepemkau. I later learned they were cousins, so I figured he liked his gossip. True to expectations, he glanced around to see if anyone was within earshot, then leaned closer like a conspirator. "Excuse me, Sitehuti, we were wondering what your mission was."

I stared at him. If I'd been fully awake, I might have managed more than, "Huh?"

"You know, the rest of the scribes and me. What's the *real* reason you're going to Memphis?"

My wits were slow to come back, but I managed to say, "I'm going to make copies of scrolls from the old temple. I'm part of the temple envoy, just like you."

He snorted. "Oh, yeah. Sure." He scooted closer. "I'm betting you've been sent to hunt down Paseti and bring him back for judgment."

My mouth must have dropped open because a bug flew in and I choked. Between wheezes, I managed, "Do I look like a policeman or a Medjay? I'm a scribe! A junior scribe at that. I'm being sent along to the old temple for the same reasons you are: to learn from my seniors."

"Right." Hapuseneb grinned. "Sure, I understand."

I was alarmed and hoped it didn't show. Here I was entrusted with a job for the Great House of Ramesses and everyone knew all about it — thought they did, anyway. My reasons for going to the old capital weren't as simple as a runaway Lector-Priest. I was supposed to find someone, yes, but someone entirely different. Someone who was probably dead. I didn't want to think about that.

"That's a ludicrous notion, Hapuseneb. Who in their right mind would send the youngest scribe in the temple after Paseti? Why not send the police instead?" I said, and meant every word.

Hapuseneb's grin never dimmed and his eyes slid toward Neffi. He'd picked up a ton of nuance from his tutelage under Tepemkau, or maybe it was a family trait. "I get you. The youngest scribe in the temple — who just *happens* to have been chosen by the Sacred One of Bastet."

I joined him in regarding the Sacred One who was sprawled on his back with his legs splayed wide to catch the most sunshine. He looked like he'd been squashed by a sledge. It was my turn to snort. "It seems more likely they chose me so as to get Nefer-Djenou-Bastet away from the temple for a while."

The knowing leer faded a bit. Hapuseneb had been at the temple long enough to learn Neffi's reputation. As if on cue, Neffi rolled over, stretched and yawned, displaying the claws and teeth of infamy. The junior priest's expression became even more doubtful and he sat quiet for a moment longer, then stood and straightened his kilt. "Maybe, but in case you change your mind about Paseti, his family has an estate just outside Memphis. If I were going to look him up, I'd start there."

~*~

Everyone in my party had been looking forward to stopping at Bubastis. The city was the most sacred one to the goddess Bastet and her oldest temple was there. There was also the fact that, as a party from the goddess' temple in the capital, we would have been assured of real beds there. That didn't happen. We were still short of the city when dusk fell, so we anchored at a small village for the night and had to pitch our beds on deck again. It was a large boat, but it wasn't a yacht. It was a working boat, so cabin space was at a premium. That meant the most junior members of the party slept on the deck. That was fine by me. I liked sleeping under the stars. The roof was my favorite place to pitch my bed during the summer. Our party was a good sized one, though, so between the junior priests, junior scribes and the crew, the deck was pretty crowded.

As darkness fell, Neffi roused and left my side to prowl, no doubt looking for mice and other vermin. My papyrus box, wrapped in a linen stole, served as my headrest. I stretched out on my back, smiling to myself at the complaints of the other priests and scribes and watching the stars wheel though the silent sky. That was how I fell asleep.

How I woke up was an entirely different matter.

"Help! Murder!"

A series of crashes and more piercing screams brought me bolt upright. The deck filled with lamps and shouting people. Someone hurtled over me, knocked me sprawling as they vaulted over the side of the boat. Several more somebodies followed. I felt the wind of their passing on the back of my neck as I tried to become one with the deck planking.

The captain stormed from her cabin, fastening a brightly embroidered caftan around her large frame and shouting commands into the chaos. Remarkably, she soon brought order to the situation. All fell silent — except for whoever was still being murdered under the fallen awning. Screaming and thrashing continued there.

When members of the crew lifted the heavy fabric, Hapuseneb emerged from one side and a furry streak that looked suspiciously like Nefer-Djenou-Bastet shot from the other.

The captain planted herself in front of the moaning priest and roared, "What in the name of Ma-ha-ef is going on here?"

Hapuseneb sat up, clutching his chest. "He-he had a knife!"

The captain looked startled. "A knife? Someone attacked you with a knife?"

The junior priest's breath was coming more easily now. "No, not exactly."

"Well, what exactly?"

"I was sleeping under the awning. Someone . . . a man . . . stepped on me. I grabbed his leg and then I saw the knife . . . then the cat jumped on top of the luggage . . . then the awning fell—"

The captain shushed the priest and said. "Well, if he wasn't killing you, what was he using the knife for?"

The Mate stood up from the far side of the baggage pile with a linen pouch in his hands. He waggled his fingers through a long cut in its side. "To slit bags and open chests, Captain."

The captain grunted. "Of course."

Behind the mate, several wet and muddied men hove up over the side, breathing heavily. One bowed to the captain and said, "We lost him among the village houses. Sorry, Ma'am."

The captain and the mate exchanged a long inscrutable look. Finally, she shook her head. "Must have been a villager looking for something to steal. Fat lot of good this did them. I have all the valuables locked in my cabin," she said carefully.

My heart stopped. Almost everything stopped. If you counted the small roll of papyrus bearing the official seal of the High Priest of Bastet and the two bearing the royal seal of Userma'atre Setepenre Ramesses Meriamon, not *all* valuables were secured in the captain's cabin. Those particular items nestled among the other rolls of papyrus in the case I'd been using for a headrest.

I gathered my things and muttered to no one in particular, "I'd better go see if Neffi's all right."

SIX

The next day when we were well underway again, I sat, staring at the passing shore and scratching Neffi.

"That cat all right?"

Startled, I looked up into the face of Captain Jebahou-Nefer. She was a big, square woman, burned dark by sun and wind. She towered over me even after I scrambled to my feet. "Yes, Ma'am. He's fine, he was just mad."

Her gravelly chuckle boomed. "Mad, huh? Most cats would have been scared witless. I'm hearing rumors that there's more to you and this cat than meet the eye."

Hapuseneb again. "You know how rumors are, Ma'am. Just because a temple cat decided he liked me, all of a sudden I'm chosen of the gods."

She eyed the two of us critically. "Y'look like a scrawny kid with a big tomcat to me."

The big tomcat in question had been busy sniffing and savoring the captain's scent. Abruptly, he looked past her and growled, hackles raised. To give the lady credit, she didn't startle, she simply swiveled to follow his gaze. So did I. The only thing back that way was a group of crewmen readying the ropes for our next stop.

After a moment's consideration, she turned back to me and lowered her voice. "He been doing that a lot?"

Embarrassed, I pulled him back, but he oozed out of my grasp and continued to glare at the crewmen, ears pinned back and tail lashing. "Ummmm . . . yes, Ma'am."

"Smart cat," she said approvingly, then grinned at my confusion. "Unless I miss my guess, he's growling at Jiji. See the wiry guy with the tattoos and double earrings?"

"Yes, Ma'am."

"If he wasn't our troublemaker last night, I'll kiss a crocodile."

"But I thought. . . ."

"That it was someone from the village?" she finished for me. "That's what we were supposed to think and I didn't see any reason not to play along. What good would it do to mention that Jiji wasn't on deck when I came out, but still returned with the search party? That man's been a pain in my backside since the day he signed on."

"Oh."

"Which brings me to why I wanted to talk to you, boy. It might be a good idea if you pitched your bed closer to the crew until we reach Memphis."

I must have looked alarmed because she raised a calming hand. "Don't worry. I don't know what the deal is and don't *want* to know. The temple of Bastet at Pi-Ramesses has been a good customer and I don't want old Pedibastet coming down on me for letting one of his scribes come to harm on my boat." Suddenly she pointed over my shoulder. Her voice rose to its normal level as she said, "Ah! Here's Bubastis, kid. Told you we were close. Too bad we won't be stopping long. You and that cat of yours would be a big hit there."

She left, then, shouting orders to the crew as they maneuvered the boat into the already crowded port of the sacred city of Bastet. No sooner had we docked than several priests (Hapuseneb included) hotfooted it down the gangway toward the goddess' magnificent temple complex.

Jebahou-Nefer leaned over the side and bellowed after them, "You lot better be snappy! I'm not about to fall behind schedule for a bunch of shaven-headed laggers."

I grinned as they quickened their pace. Given what she'd said earlier about her relationship with the temple and the high priest, himself, I doubted she'd leave without them — but they didn't have to know that.

It would have been nice to see the great temple. It *was* the main center of worship for Bastet, after all. The previous night's excitement had left me shaken, though. My writing box was too bulky to comfortably carry through town and handing it over to the captain at this late date would only draw unwanted attention. Like it or not, Neffi and I were stuck aboard. It wasn't all bad, though. We had the best view of both the sprawling city and the organized chaos of the port right where we were. I'd seen that frenetic activity many times before and have many times since, but I've never lost my fascination with it. The marvel is that with all the shouting and running around, things actually got done.

Neffi, however, never took his eyes off of Jiji. After a while, I got so I could even tell how close the man was by the volume and pitch of the growls.

~*~

We made good time after leaving the city and weren't far from where the delta joined the main river, when we put to shore in the reddening light of sunset. It was overcast and the night promised to be particularly black. We were far away from any town and the darker it got, the more attractive the captain's advice to sleep nearer the crew became. Gathering my belongings as unobtrusively as possible, I moved everything closer to the cabin. My bedding was barely unrolled before the Mate plunked his mat down beside me and grinned. "Gonna be a cold night tonight, kid. Best stick close."

A burly crewman I'd seen talking to the captain earlier claimed the spot on the other side, grinned wordlessly, then lay down with his back to me. Looked like I was being guarded. Neffi apparently thought that was a good idea, too, because my head had hardly gone down, when a furry weight pressed against my shoulder.

I awoke once in the night sure I'd heard growling, but nothing and no one seemed to be moving, only Neffi, grooming his front paws.

~*~

After the excitement of the attempted robbery, Captain Jebahou-Nefer circulated among us, confiscated anything that looked to be worth anything, and locked it up in her cabin with the other valuables. A precautionary measure, she told us. One of the items she secured was my scroll box. I had to make do with a rolled-up cloak for a headrest after that, but I still slept easier.

The voyage settled into a lazy routine. The days aboard passed in gaming, talking and, when we stopped over in a city long enough, playing tourist with a few of the other priests and scribes. At the stopover at Giza, our group went out to admire the magnificent pyramid complex, marvel at the sphinx and buy offerings to leave at the funerary temples. It was close to sundown before we came dragging back to the boat, tired and dusty, only to find it in turmoil.

As we neared, the captain's bellow cut though the clamor of the busy docks, "What d'you mean y'lost 'im?

The three crewman cringing in front of her were unmistakably worse for drink. One spoke up. "A thousand pardons, Ma'am. One minute he was with us in the beer house, then the next, POOF! No Jiji."

The other two nodded unsteady agreement.

One added, "It was like magic."

"By the magic of his own two feet, more like. He wasn't holding your pay was he?" Captain Jebahou-Nefer surveyed the sorry trio, then heaved a sigh that shook the sails. "Oh Sacred Wadjet! Three shit-faced, one runner and us scheduled to sail at daybreak!"

The Mate shifted uncomfortably. "Ma'am, I have a couple of

cousins here in town. . . ."

She swung around. "They available to work?"

"I can ask."

"Then what are you standing here for? GO!" The Mate nearly took flight as the captain roared at the milling crew, "What are the rest of you doing standing around? There's plenty to be done. You can start by getting these drunken sprats dried out."

With that, she stomped toward her cabin, catching sight of Neffi and me in the midst of the returning party — and winked. That took me aback for a moment until I realized that, in spite of her angry appearance, she wasn't any more sorry to have Jiji gone than I was. It was getting tiresome hearing Neffi growling whenever the man was in sight. It wasn't that big a boat and the man was in sight a lot.

The other scribes noticed neither my relief nor the wink. They were too busy buzzing about the scandalous occurrence. One of the older scribes huffed, "Oh, that's nothing! I was on a trip once where the *whole* crew went missing. The captain spent the next three days searching for replacements."

Grinning to myself, I hoisted Neffi onto my shoulder and retired to our favorite spot by the railing to watch the crew bustle around in the fading light. They were moving double-time after the captain's outburst. If they kept up that rate, they wouldn't need a replacement for Jiji or the three drunks.

The next morning, the three drunks were gone, too. In their place were three new men, the Mate's two cousins and a friend. Although technically, the boat was still short-handed by one, the three new men were good and more than made up for the lack — at least to my eye. The captain didn't seem displeased, either.

SEVEN

The rest of the voyage was smooth and uneventful — which wasn't actually that good a thing because it let me forget that: 1) I actually was going to Memphis to do more than copy scrolls and 2) that I had absolutely no clue how to go about what I was really there for.

My first task was to deliver a letter. That seemed simple enough on the surface, but it was a letter no one was supposed to know about. A junior scribe didn't have a whole lot of freedom, either. For instance, when everyone else was packing up to head for the temple, I couldn't simply raise my hand and ask to be excused because I had something else to do. That would have been bad on so many levels, they couldn't be counted.

Next, I was supposed to figure out what happened to Khety, the scribe from the temple of Ptah who originally uncovered the plot and promptly went missing. I was leaning toward went dead, but I didn't want to think about that too hard, either. Khety was a relatively senior scribe, so it didn't require a big leap of logic to say if a senior scribe could vanish so completely, how hard would it be to make a junior one go poof as well? The answer, of course, was "not very".

I was also supposed to find out what the plot against the great house of Ramesses *was* since the details had vanished with the vanished scribe's missing letter.

The problem was that I didn't have a clue how to do any of that. Before leaving Pi-Ramesses, I'd asked for instructions. His Royal Highness, Crown Prince Merenptah told me, "Use your head, boy!"

I have always found that to be particularly unhelpful advice.

Anyway, I'd joined the throng of passengers on the deck, watching the famed white city walls of the old capital coming ever closer. As excitement grew for my fellow priests and scribes, my own sense of impending doom deepened. I was so wrapped up my fears, that I didn't notice the rest of my scribal party melting away until I realized with a start I was standing at the rail by myself. I was baffled until I heard Master Scribe Userhet call my name.

"Ah! Sitehuti of Western Thebes!"

I turned toward the voice and found my new master standing in front of the cabin holding a box in his hands. He held it up. "There is a special task for you. You are to deliver these messages to the temple's estate overseer here in Memphis."

It was a *big* box. I understood my disappearing colleagues now. There would always be estate business and either the lowest ranked scribe — or the slowest one — would play delivery boy. And I'd thought it couldn't get any worse. I went forward, bowed and took the box.

"Yes, Master," I said. "How may I find the overseer's house?"

"It's to the south. If you get lost, the locals can surely point you in the right direction. Don't confuse the overseer's house with that of General Seti-Merenptah. They're close together, but the general's home is much larger. You'll come to it first."

Words left me. I looked into Master Userhet's eyes and understood. He knew. He likely didn't know why I had to visit the general, only that I did. I also understood he was angry beyond words that a junior scribe was entrusted with the task.

He was saying, "Don't worry about your luggage. It will be taken to the temple with my own. Come to the House of Life when you've finished." He turned away, then turned back as if struck by an afterthought. "Take your writing kit. There may be replies."

~*~

It was a long walk to the general's house. I was a junior scribe and poor, so I couldn't afford to hire a porter. Considering I was paying an unscheduled call on the Crown Prince's son rather than going straight to the temple's estates, though, a porter could have been more of a problem than the long walk, anyway. The only positive thing I can say for the box of estate correspondence was that it made an excellent seat. Neffi and I made use of it several times along the way.

When I finally reached General Seti-Merenptah's house, I saw that Master Userhet hadn't been exaggerating how close the overseer's home was. I could see the estate's gateposts and the trees in the gardens from the general's own gate. At least it wouldn't be too hard a slog later.

The servant who answered my knock was an older man; tall, with the bearing of a soldier. Looking down on me from his superior height, he curled his lip at me. With good reason. The long hike had left me dusty, wind-blown and sweaty. I probably smelled like a goat. A dead one. He seemed to be considering slamming the door on me until Nefer-Djenou-Bastet meowed loudly, then stretched and kneaded the beautifully painted door post. At the sight of the cat, the man's expression changed. It wasn't the usual terror on recognizing the cat demon of Pi-Ramesses, it was more recognition of something expected. Pausing for another moment of consideration, he opened the gate wider and stood back allowing us to enter. Well . . . allowing me to enter. It was too late to allow or deny Neffi. After pawing the door post, the cat had simply wound around the man's legs once, then sauntered past and disappeared into the shadowy cool of the area beyond.

I was led to a large room off a formal garden and pointed toward a wooden couch with woven reed seats. Considering how much dust I had on me, that was a good choice. It would be easier to clean off later.

"Please wait here. The general will see you shortly," the servant said. With a slight bow, he disappeared deeper into the house.

Left on my own, I took the opportunity to step into the garden and shake as much dust out of my clothes and wig as I could. It created quite a cloud, but I felt a lot lighter, if not cleaner, afterward. I was re-seating my wig when Neffi trotted out of the plantings, face and front paws wet. Most formal gardens, like the one we were in, had decorative pools and ponds. He'd probably located one of the water features and taken a long drink. I hoped there weren't fish in it. Or if there were, that they weren't rare or valuable. On the other hand, I also felt like I'd swallowed as much road as I'd walked. Part of me wished I could go looking for the pool, too.

It turned out I didn't need to hunt for the pool. The general's was a well-run household. Shortly after Neffi reappeared, a pair of servants brought a basin of water so I could wash the dust off my feet and a tray containing bread, roasted meat, a beaker of beer for me and a bowl of fresh water for Neffi. By the time the general summoned us, I felt almost human again.

The study we were ushered into was immaculate and ordered, very like the man who stood on the portico looking out over a small courtyard as we entered. General Seti-Merenptah was a tall man like his father, but of a more slender, yet athletic build. Sunlight outlined the familiar strong Ramesside profile as he turned to greet me.

"Ah! Welcome, young scribe. I hope you've rested and refreshed a bit. My aide, Iker, tells me you appeared to have walked some distance — with a chest?"

I bowed. "Yes, sir. Thank you. We came directly from the docks. The chest is correspondence for the temple of Bastet's estate overseer just up the road."

"Ah. I sense the hand of Userhet," the general said with a slight chuckle. "Userhet is a good man, even if given to occasional fits of petty vengeance. Still, it was a good cover for you. No one expect that a junior scribe given such a dusty, thankless task would have any other purpose."

A sigh escaped before I could stifle it. "No, sir. No one at all."

He gave in to an open laugh and swept a hand toward a chair carved from a dark wood. "Sit down, boy, and rest your feet while we talk. If you have business next door, I'm certain your day is far from over."

I sat, he didn't. It didn't feel right for me to sit in the presence of a prince, but he'd told me to sit, so I stayed sat. The general paced, head down, and started speaking in a way that sounded like he was continuing a conversation already running in his head. "You look even younger than I expected from my father's message earlier this week, but that might work for us. It could put you above suspicion like Userhet's messenger job did — at least for a while."

Neffi, who had followed me into the study, now leapt onto a chest and trilled. The general broke into a smile and ran his fingers over the sleek, spotted fur. "And we mustn't overlook the fact that the Sacred One has selected you." He looked up from the the purring cat and directly at me. "Still, we have to bear in mind that you are young and have had no training for a job like this."

"Please, sir! I'm not a soldier or policeman. I haven't got the first idea how to find Paseti—"

General Seti-Merenptah straightened abruptly. "Absolutely not! Don't even think about trying to capture Paseti on your own. That priest is a desperate man; that makes him doubly dangerous. There are others tasked with hunting him down. As a matter of fact, if you so much as *see* him, steer clear and send me word. I'll see to it the traitor is taken care of." He paused, then said almost to himself, "He's probably nowhere near Memphis, anyway. He'd be a fool to come back here. Family wouldn't be a draw. He wasn't all that close to his father."

"What about his brother, sir?" I asked.

For a moment, the general looked puzzled, then he said, "Ah! You mean Sasobek. Yes. That one. We've got eyes on him, but he's being a perfect little soldier at the moment. Doubtless, he knows he's being watched. He has been since Paseti did a runner."

"I wonder if that's what Sasobek's letter said, 'You messed up, Brother. Get out of Pi-Ramesses'."

The general raised a heavy eyebrow and nodded slightly. "That would seem likely."

"My apologies, sir, but what exactly *is* my job? I mean, I know I'm supposed to find out what happened to Khety — the scribe from the temple of Ptah — but I have no idea how to do that."

He looked a little surprised. "Didn't you receive any sort of instruction from my uncle and my fath—" He broke off as realization dawned. "Oh no. Not 'use your head'."

I nodded.

I barely heard him mutter, "As if that was ever helpful." In a normal tone, he said, "It's relatively straightforward, really. Simply talk to people. You'll find that as you learn more, a path will become apparent. Well, that's the theory, anyway. I've rarely found it to work differently. You have the letters for the High Priest of Ptah, correct?"

I nodded again.

"Good. That's the best starting point. Once you begin — and if I know Userhet, there will be a delay — I'd like for you to write out a report at the end of each day. I have a man at the temple who will collect it, so you won't have to traipse all the way out here each time. Clear?"

"Yes, sir! Thank you!"

He slapped his hands together. "Excellent! Now, I'll have Iker fetch a servant to help you with that chest and you can be about your temple duties."

~*~

74

It was a very good thing I visited General Seti-Merenptah's home before I approached the Overseer's. As Master Userhet had predicted, there were replies. Many, many replies.

It was very late by the time Neffi and I made our way back to the House of Life of the Temple of Bastet with the help of one of the estate's farmhands and a very surly donkey.

~*~

As I was the most junior scribe, the other members of the party kept me running. Master Userhet especially seemed to have it in for me. I'd be hard pressed to say how much of this was because I'd had orders to deliver a message directly to General Seti-Merenptah and how much had to do with the wild stories Hapuseneb had been circulating about Neffi and me. It didn't really matter, because, regardless of why it happened, for the first full week I was in Memphis, I never once got to set pen to papyrus.

Those initial days were spent fetching scrolls, taking them back, breaking up fights between Neffi and the Memphis temple cats, grinding pigments, mixing inks, fetching clean water, breaking up fights between Neffi and the temple cats, fetching new reed pens, breaking up cat fights, smoothing papyrus and breaking up cat fights. All the while, my letter of introduction and the Crown Prince's message to the High Priest at the temple of Ptah languished in my papyrus case.

Eventually, though, even the most junior scribe gets a day off. I had Master Ta, the Head Scribe for the Memphis temple of Bastet, to thank for it.

Master Ta was one of those people whose age was near impossible to guess. He was a short, squat man with a square face that seemed to be frozen in a perpetual frown. His eyes were wide-set and protruded slightly, making him look like a frog magically transformed into a human by a prankish sorcerer. From what I understood from the resident scribes, the man's apparent frown wasn't usually indicative of his mood. As a rule, he was a jovial man and a maker of bad puns. Usually. As a rule. Not then, however.

Master Ta wasn't the least bit happy to have his House of Life invaded by our group, and Master Userhet's officious manner really seemed to get on his nerves. He stood it for a week. On the last day of that week, he proclaimed the following day to be a holiday for the whole House. Since he was the master of that particular House of Life, and we were his guests, his word went for us, too. The announcement was met with heartfelt cheers. I tried not to make mine too loud.

The following morning, I put on my crispest linen, tucked Merenptah's letter into my shawl, plopped Neffi on my shoulder and set out for the temple of Ptah with Pedibastet's letter of introduction clutched in my hand.

Well, I set out in the direction of the Temple of Ptah. There were a lot of distractions along the way. I was used to the grandeur of Pi-Ramesses, but Memphis was the *old* capital. Where the new capital impressed, the old one awed. Something was happening on every street corner and the fact that the river was rising and festivals were coming almost back to back didn't hurt. The temple precincts sported a bazaar-like feel. I browsed from merchant to merchant and booth to booth coming slowly ever closer to the grand temple of Ptah.

It was at one such booth that I heard a sudden roar of laughter behind me. Call me paranoid, but in my short association with Nefer-Djenou-Bastet, I'd learned that such outbursts rarely boded well. Holding my breath, I glanced down at the ground and found it suspiciously catless. Oh, no.

Dread drew me toward the laughing group. Sure enough, the crowd parted, and a big well-dressed Nubian pushed through. The sun was behind him and he wore a heavy wig of beaded braids that further shaded his face, but even so, it looked as if his eyes widened when he saw me. Whether it was my imagination or not, the big man veered off and all but ran down the street to be swallowed up by the milling crowds. The people ahead of me were still roaring with laughter, though, so I shouldered my way through. In a clearing at the center, just in front of a food booth, I found Neffi hunched over the remains of a couple of meat rolls.

I plunged forward, snatched the growling cat up and launched into an unfortunately well-rehearsed apology. "I'm very sorry, he's a temple cat and. . . ."

The stall owner waved me down, still laughing uproariously. "That your cat?" he managed at last.

"Well, yes . . . sort of. . . ."

"Nothing to apologize for. That was the best laugh me and my boys have had in a long time."

I blinked. "I . . . I don't understand."

"Did you see that big Nubian who just tore out of here as if the Eater of Souls was after him?"

"Ummmm, yeah." Neffi squirmed from my grip, dropped to the ground to resume his demolition of the pastry.

"Of course! Who could miss him? Big fella. Didn't look like he would be afraid of nothin'."

One of his assistants snickered. "Except cats."

This observation was met with gales of fresh laughter from the surrounding bystanders. Neffi, having finished his snack, sat up, blinked and washed his face.

"I've missed something," I said.

"That you did, Scribe, and it was a good show. Right after the big guy came up to the booth, your cat jumped on my counter. I was getting ready to send him packing when I noticed he was staring at the guy, not the food. The Nubian noticed it, too. You'd have thought a demon was eying him instead of a cat. Looked pretty sick, didn't he, boys?"

His assistants sniggered again and the merchant continued gleefully, "He tried backing away first. You know, all casual-like, but that cat wasn't having any of it. Dropped right down and started winding around the fella's legs." He paused again, seized by another laughing fit that left him wheezing. "I swear, the way he looked at that cat, I thought he was gonna have some kind of fit or something. Suddenly, he plunked payment down and tossed a couple rolls on the ground. When the cat pounced on them, the big guy ran for it."

The crowd burst out laughing again, but I didn't see anything too funny. The whole thing made no sense — or rather, it made a different kind of sense to me than it did to them. I'd *seen* that sort of reaction before. It sounded like the Nubian had *recognized* Neffi.

"Ummmm. I didn't get a real good look at him," I said when the laughter subsided. "Could you describe him?"

"You know. . . ," the pastry vendor waved his hands in the air, sketching a person both tall and wide. ". . . *big*! Rough-looking for all his finery. Decked out in those tiered braids and beads the people from the Land of the Bow wear."

One of the assistants observed, "Looked like a mercenary swanning around to me."

The other one nodded. "Yeah, he was dressed up like a merchant but he wasn't no merchant."

Numbly, I thanked the vendors, bought a meat roll and slunk to a shadowed corner away from the crush to chew on it and what I'd just heard. I didn't have to coax Neffi to follow. He probably would have followed that pastry into the middle of the river.

A rough-looking Nubian who recognized Neffi, but didn't want me to see him? That made no sense in Memphis. No one in Memphis knew me. Very few would know Neffi to that extent, either. Most people in this city who knew Neffi's reputation were associated in some way with a temple. The person I saw didn't seem to fit that bill. As the vendors said, he carried himself more like a soldier. He had to be someone from Pi-Ramesses. Maybe someone connected to Wosret? That seemed likely. But why? I hadn't killed Wosret. With a dull, sick feeling I realized that didn't make one whit of difference. Only the actual killer and I knew that. Also, Neffi and I had been seen in the neighborhood. . . .

It suddenly seemed like a good idea to get to the temple of Ptah. Considering that was where the first scribe had disappeared from, it might not be all that safe a destination, but at least I wouldn't be sitting out in the open as I was in the market.

~*~

When High Priest Pedibastet put his sealed letter into my care, he had stressed that his message should be delivered in private and directly into the hands of his counterpart at the Memphis temple of Ptah. He'd stressed *private*. In fact, he'd been so insistent, I'd been tempted to question him about it, but in spite of his openness, a junior scribe just did *not* question an order from a man of his importance. Instead, I'd bowed and figured I'd find out why when the time came.

"His Eminence, Ptahneb, cannot be disturbed. I'll take the letter and give it to him later at his convenience."

The servant's name was Intef and he looked like a cross between something remotely human and an ibis; the ibis being dominant. He stood looking down his beak — er nose — at me, hand extended for the roll of papyrus.

Fat chance. Even if I hadn't been specifically told to deliver it myself, attitudes like Intef's rubbed me the wrong way. Add in that the encounter with the Nubian had already put me on edge, his was a cause lost before it began. I tucked the fist holding the scroll closer to my chest. "Sorry. My instructions are to see this into his Eminence's hands. Personally."

I squared my shoulders, making Neffi complain and jump down. I barely noticed. Intef tried to loom, but compared to my former scribal master, he was a rank amateur. We glared at each other for quite a while before a sharp cry pierced the doors the Ibis guarded. From Intef's instant attention, it had to be his master, High Priest Ptahneb.

The cry was followed by a bellow, "Who let this cat in here?"

Without a backward look, Intef turned on his heel and dashed into the chamber. Since I had a pretty good idea as to the identity of the offending cat, I followed on his heels. When I reached the inner rooms, my suspicions were borne out. A very fat man in opulent robes stood in the center of a richly decorated room, waving his arms and shouting profanities at Neffi, who perched on a tripod table delicately helping himself to roasted goose from a golden platter.

Intef let loose with an inarticulate cry and dived for the cat. This was a mistake.

The gangly servant had no sooner launched himself, than Neffi sank his teeth into the remnants of the bird and sprang from the table scattering utensils, wine cups and plates in his wake. I cringed as the platter hit the floor with a tremendous KLOOOONG! Neffi, prize still clenched in his teeth, headed for a doorway in the far wall, but before he reached it, it disgorged a bevy of alarmed kitchen servants. The cat pivoted and reversed course, his path taking him between the spindly legs of Intef, sending the man off balance and toppling him to the floor where he skidded into the wreckage of the table. My heart sank. Sure, I wanted to get in to see the high priest, but this was more likely to get me flogged than listened to.

Clutching his prize tighter, Neffi made for the shaded walkway that led to a lush garden just visible beyond the doorway at the end. One of the kitchen servants jumped in front of him with a triumphant shout. I couldn't bear to watch, but even with eyes tightly closed, I could trace Neffi's path up and over by the hapless man's shrieks. I opened my eyes as the cat dashed down the cool walkway, out into the sun-dappled garden and disappeared into the plantings. He was followed by a shouting crowd, Intef at the lead. I returned my attention to the room.

Calm reigned once more. One elderly servant had righted the

table, coaxed his flustered master back to his chair and was providing him with a fresh cup of wine.

"Cats! Horrible creatures!" the fat man muttered.

Distant shouts sounded from the garden.

"It is of no consequence, Your Eminence," the elderly servant soothed. "I have already instructed the kitchen to ready another bird for you."

I held my breath, unsure what to do or say. The old servant glanced up at me and I could swear he winked. "Master," he whispered. "There is a messenger here to see you."

The servant bowed again and moved to a respectful distance as the High Priest of Ptah looked up from his wine and glared at me. "Messenger? From who?"

I bowed, moved forward and presented the roll of papyrus. "I am Sitehuti of Western Thebes, sir. I bring greetings from his Eminence, Pedibastet of the temple of Bastet in Pi-Ramesses."

High Priest Ptahneb snatched the message and grumbled, "Pedibastet, is it?" A fresh spate of shouting made him glance speculatively toward the gardens. "Wouldn't put it past that old bastard to have set that cat on me himself."

I stayed silent and forced my face into the expression of respect I used when confronting my schoolmaster when he was irate. I sensed that hard-won lesson was going to prove more useful outside of class than I'd ever dreamed.

Ptahneb opened the message and I watched his progression of expression as he made his way through it. At length, he looked up warily and said, "He says you have a second message."

"Yes, Your Eminence," I said as I pulled the other papyrus from under my shawl and handed it to him with the seal facing up. He paused for a beat, eyes riveted on the Royal seal, before he stood, took the message and said, "Heru, the scribe and I will retire to my study. Please see to it that we are not disturbed." The ancient servant bowed, then Ptahneb turned and stalked through another ornate cedar doorway, motioning that I should follow.

The study was a smaller, more intimate room than the one we'd just left. It was lit by a row of windows set high in the wall and bore the unmistakable clutter of a habitual scholar. Once inside, he indicated I should shut the doors, then sat in a massive chair as intricately carved as the doors themselves and broke the seal on the Crown Prince's message. When he finished, he was silent for a while, pudgy fingers worrying a turquoise scarab that hung on a heavy gold chain around his neck. It was very old and the craftsmanship was fine enough for it to have emerged from the Royal workshops. I wondered if it was a gift from the Great House for some long ago favor.

At length, the man spoke, his voice quiet, "I'm afraid I can't help you much, boy. I didn't know this Khety and my Overseer of the House of Life had not informed me that he had disappeared. A pity. Had I known what the man had knowledge of, I would have taken him to the palace myself. My family has served the great Ramesses faithfully for many, many years. I may not look it now, but I was a soldier myself once." His hand strayed to the scarab again, then he roused himself. "You'll need to talk to Bakare, the Overseer of the House of Life. I'll send a servant along with you to assure that Bakare knows you have my blessing."

My face must have betrayed dismay because the fat man laughed. "No, not Intef. The man is an officious idiot. Heru will accompany you." The Sem-Priest heaved himself out of his chair with difficulty, saying, "He's as old as dirt, but loyal as they come. I swear, he's smarter than most of my priests."

At that moment, Neffi appeared at one of the high windows and dropped lightly to the floor in front of Ptahneb who momentarily startled. The Sem Priest looked from the cat to me and I could almost hear the click of his brain putting the pieces together. I decided to come clean.

"I'm afraid he's sort of with me, Your Eminence," I said. "This is Nefer-Djenou-Bastet of the temple of Bastet in Pi-Ramesses."

The Sem Priest looked at the cat with new respect. "So, *this* is Pedibastet's infamous demon cat? I should have guessed." He looked shrewdly back at me. "Yes. I should have realized. . . ." He marched briskly to the ornate door and I could almost see the soldier he had once been. "Heru!" he called. "Take Sitehuti of Western Thebes to the House of Life. Everyone there is to answer his questions and give him the same respect they would give me."

Heru bowed. the High Priest turned back to me. "I'll expect you to keep me informed, too, boy. This was one of *my* scribes and I don't take kindly to this sort of skullduggery. I take an even dimmer view if it's happening in my own temple."

I bowed, too, snatched Neffi up and followed Heru out.

~*~

After introducing me to the Overseer of the House of Life, Heru retired to a discrete distance as he had done in the Sem Priest's chambers. Most likely, he could still hear every word we were saying if he tried, but if he was trying, he was being discrete about that, too.

Head Scribe Bakare, was relieved that someone was finally interested in his missing colleague and was more than willing to talk to me. While we were talking, Neffi hopped off my shoulders and started nosing around Bakare's legs. I watched him nervously. The last thing I wanted was for him to chomp the Master Scribe of Ptah in the calf. To my relief, Bakare smiled, leaned down and scratched the cat between the ears; Neffi purred and leaned into it. I breathed a little easier.

Bakare continued, "I've been telling the temple police for weeks now that something bad must have happened, but they wouldn't listen to me. Okay, I know that, from time to time, some of the workers here might go off on a drunk or something like that, but not Khety. You could have compiled a handbook on responsible behavior by following that guy around." Bakare stopped suddenly and frowned. "Oh, my. I'm talking about Khety in past tense. I don't want to do that. It's just wrong. He deserves better."

"Were you close to him?" I asked.

Neffi sauntered away and rubbed against one of the other scribes — more to the point, on the small reed basket the man's lunch was probably in. After two and a half meat rolls and the roasted goose, I couldn't believe the cat was still trying to cadge treats.

"I wouldn't exactly say close, but I liked him. Almost everyone here in the House of Life did. He was a good scribe; good husband and father, too."

"He was a family man, then?"

Neffi moved on to a large stack of papyrus. He suddenly attacked a spot directly in front of the stack and pawed madly at something on the floor — well, he pawed at the floor, anyway. From where I was standing, I couldn't see anything there to paw at. Suddenly, he yawned and turned his attention to a small chest. After sniffing it, he scratched his chin against its corner and wandered toward a stack of papyri being pressed under a large stone.

"Definitely. His whole world was wrapped up in his wife, Shepenwepet, and those two sons of his. She's a singer to Amun over at the big temple, but it's her off time right now, so she's at home with the boys." The head scribe had been following Neffi's progress, too. Humming nervously, he said, "Ummmm . . . is that cat going to . . . um. . . ."

I caught his drift. "Oh! Oh no. He's pretty good about that. I'm a scribe in the House of Life at the temple of Bastet in Pi-Ramesses and he's never . . . ummm . . . watered anything there."

"Good. Good." Bakare nodded, then returned his attention to me. "Yeah. Definitely a family man. They were all he talked about until a couple months ago."

"What happened then? Did something go wrong with his marriage?"

Neffi had finished a circuit of the room by then and returned to stretch out on the floor by my feet. He gazed up at the Head Scribe with half-closed eyes.

"I don't think so, but. . . ." He shrugged. "No clue, really. He just sort of turned in on himself. Seemed like one day he was chattering away like normal, the next he was as jumpy as a hare in a hawk's shadow. I was very concerned for him, but he wouldn't talk to me or anyone else. Just said it was nothing. When he didn't show up one morning, we thought maybe he'd been taken ill. A sickness would have explained the change in him. But, when he had a bad tooth last year, his wife sent one of the boys or one of her brothers around with a note from him each day he was out. We knew something bad was happening when Shepenwepet, herself, came here looking for him. She said he'd left for the temple the day before just like he always did, but never came home. . . ." The Head Scribe's voice had become very soft as if his thoughts trailed after his missing colleague.

"Was that the same day he didn't show up here?" I asked.

Bakare suddenly snapped back to the here and now and nodded. "Yes. It was the same day. It was as if he'd stepped out the front door of his house and fallen out of this world. We searched, but could find no sign of him and no one remembered seeing him that morning."

He became thoughtful, frowning at the floor, then asked, "Have you talked to Shepenwepet, yet? I can give you directions to their house, if you haven't."

EIGHT

Bakare might have been a wonderful scholar and a crack scribe, but I hope he never decided to set pen to a guide book. Memphis is an old city and maybe the Head Scribe's directions would have made sense to someone who grew up in it, but not to a man more familiar with either the new capital or one who grew up in the dark warrens of the tomb builder's village for the Place of Truth. Then again, maybe not. It did take a while for the local I finally hired to guide me to stop laughing when I read off what I'd been given.

Anyway, the multi-story house shared by Khety and Shepenwepet was not all that new but very well cared for. Improvements had been added to the original structure and the paint that adorned it was relatively fresh. The wooden door I tapped on was solid and I wondered if the decoration of painted reeds was from Khety's own hand. I was admiring the brushwork when the door opened, revealing a very elegant older lady. She was definitely not a servant and was not as young as I'd been given to understand Shepenwepet was. Regardless, I asked, "Is this the house of Khety and Shepenwepet?"

The lady nodded regally and gave me a fishy look that reminded me of my aunt Tiaa. *Uncomfortably* of my aunt Tiaa. I bowed slightly. "I am Sitehuti, Scribe of the House of Life at the temple of Bastet at Pi-Ramesses. I would like to speak with the lady Shepenwepet about her missing husband."

The lady didn't budge until Neffi, who was sitting by my feet, chirped and rubbed against the doorway. The lady regarded the purring cat, shifted her icy gaze to me, then opened the door and stood back. "I am Henut-Wedjebu. Enter Sitehuti. I will tell my sister you are here."

Sister. I was probably speaking to another Singer to Amun, then. It made sense that the other singers would gather to support one of their own in a time of need — and this would be a very rough time for the lady. I followed the older woman into the house until she stopped, indicating I should wait in a spacious sitting room. The reed mats over the windows were down, filtering the light and shielding the interior from the scorching midday heat outside. The room was clean but bore unmistakable marks of having been used by children. A couple wooden toys and a faience top rested beneath a chair and tell-tale hand prints marred the otherwise pristine walls at a far lower height than any adult could comfortably make.

Neffi took an instant interest in the top, or maybe it was the string partly wrapped around it. I entertained myself watching him feint and strike at the cord as if it were a snake until a gasp from the hall startled me. Turning, I found a small boy about five or six peeking into the room with an enraptured expression on his face.

"Cat!" he whispered.

The boy headed toward the cat like a fly to spilled honey. Neffi could be prickly with adults. I had no idea how he'd be with a child.

The boy knew how to pet — even if he was a little rough with it. Neffi shot me a long-suffering look and I released the breath I'd been holding. I crouched down beside the two of them and said, "Hey, my name's Sitehuti, what's yours?"

The boy looked up from patting Neffi. "I'm Addaya. Is this your cat?"

"Well, sort of. His name's Nefer-Djenou-Bastet. He's a temple cat and one day he decided he liked me. He's gone everywhere with me ever since."

"Wow!" said Addaya. Then he looked at the writing kit slung over my shoulder. "You're a scribe. My papa's a scribe, too."

I didn't know what to say to that. Yes, his papa was a scribe and I was here because of that. I was saved the need as a woman said behind us, "Adi! What are you doing down here pestering guests? You're supposed to be upstairs practicing your letters with Den."

We both looked up at a statuesque lady in layered linen robes wearing a carefully styled wig that brushed the broad beaded collar draped over her shoulders. Her face was freshly made up, but her eyes were reddened as if she'd been crying. Henut-Wedjebu and another younger lady stood just behind her. The younger woman's eyes held concern, but the older lady's held something I couldn't read, and they were fastened hard on me.

The boy said, "But Mama, he has a pretty cat and it's letting me pet it!"

I rose and bowed. "Lady Shepenwepet, thank you for receiving me."

The younger woman came around and held out her hand to the boy. "Come with me, Addaya. We'll go upstairs and I'll show you how to write a poem about a cat."

The boy shot a backward glance at me, then at Neffi, but allowed himself to be led away. Neffi shook himself, jumped on a stool and set about reordering his fur.

The two ladies glided into the room and seated themselves. The elder woman took the younger one's hand in hers and patted it comfortingly. Lady Shepenwepet motioned me to sit, also. I perched on the edge of a low, cushioned, wooden chair feeling very much like I was sitting for my own judgment.

I hardly knew where to begin, so I decided to just jump into the middle and hope I didn't sink. "Lady," I began, "my master, Pedibastet, Sem Priest of the temple of Bastet has sent me to look into the disappearance of your husband, Khety."

Lady Shepenwepet's fingers clenched reflexively against those of her companion. Lady Henut-Wedjebu didn't seem to notice, but sat back and regarded me with those shrewd eyes. She said, "I wonder. Why is the high priest of the temple of Bastet in Pi-Ramesses sending an agent all the way to Memphis to ask about a mid-level scribe to Ptah?"

"Oh, ma'am, I'm not an *agent*, I'm just a scribe."

"Hmmmm," she said dubiously. "Isn't Pedibastet the son-in-law of the Pharaoh, the great Ramesses, himself?"

"Yes, ma'am, he is."

She leaned forward sharply and pointed to Neffi, who had gotten his fur back in order and was lounging on the stool regarding the older singer coolly. "You also admitted to the child that this animal was a temple cat."

"Admitted? Lady forgive me, but I've never tried to hide the fact Nefer-Djenou-Bastet is or was a temple cat."

I was seriously confused at the direction of the questioning, but before I could say more, the lady smacked her open palm against the inlaid arm of her own seat. "Yes. I knew you had to be the one." Turning to the younger woman, she gripped her hand reassuringly. "This is the scribe my sister in the great temple at Pi-Ramesses wrote me about. Talk to this boy, dear. He represents the Great House, itself."

The younger singer seemed to fall into herself as relief unclenched the fear that had previously held her frame in rigor.

The older singer flashed a triumphant smile. "Finally, we'll see something done! Now, I'll head out to the kitchen and get some refreshments. It's a nasty, hot day and the scribe must be drier than the dust itself."

Open-mouthed, I watched the older Singer bustle out of the sitting room in a cloud of efficiency, until I realized that the lady opposite me was crying quietly.

Neffi left the stool and jumped lightly into the weeping

woman's lap, pushing his head under her hand.

"Lady?" I said.

She blotted her eyes with a linen square and said, "It's all right, Sitehuti. It's just that I've been holding my grief back for weeks now." She waved the linen square vaguely in the direction the younger woman had taken the child. "I had to be brave for the boys. I don't know how to tell them they are now fatherless. If it hadn't been for my sisters from the temple, I don't think I could have stood it."

Again, I didn't know what to say, but I didn't need to. The lady squared her shoulders and lifted her head, saying, "Yes, I do recognize that my husband is dead, Sitehuti."

I was taken aback. Oh, she was undoubtedly right, but I was amazed at her certainty. I knew in my heart that the lady had nothing to do with his disappearance. Neffi trusted her, too. As far as I was concerned, that sealed her innocence. Still, I had to ask: "How can you be so sure?"

She started to speak, then stopped and shook her head. "You'll think I'm silly."

"Try me."

After a moment of consideration, she looked at me almost defiantly and said, "He came to me in a dream the second night after he went missing."

I leaned forward. "Did he speak? What did he say?"

She stared at me with wide eyes. "You believe me?"

"Why wouldn't I? I work in the temple's House of Life and one thing I've learned is that dreams are very important. What did he say?"

"He begged me to find his body so he could be properly buried and pass over to the next world."

~*~

The light filtering through the clerestory windows had faded and the servants brought in lamps on tall wood and bronze stands.

Shepenwepet and I had pretty much wrecked any semblance of order Khety had in his study. I sat cross-legged on the floor surrounded by scroll cases and stacks of papyrus. There had been nothing of value in any of them. As I repacked the loose papyri into the case they'd come from, Shepenwepet led two servants into the room with two more boxes.

"These are the last ones," she said. Shrugging, she added, "At least the last I know of."

The lady instructed the servants to set the cases on the floor beside me and remove the one I'd just repacked. I didn't hold much hope for the new ones. They were covered in a layer of dust that bore only the marks of the servant's fingers.

"I keep wracking my mind for anything he might have said that could help," she said.

"I know I keep asking, but he didn't tell you anything at all about what he knew? Not even some off-hand comment that seemed odd?"

She sat on a low stool and brushed a piece of her wig back from her face and sighed. "Not a word. I can pinpoint when he learned whatever it was, though. It was one night just after the last harvest celebration. When we came home from one of the big banquets, Khety was deeply distressed, but he refused to tell me why. He kept saying that his knowledge was dangerous and that the less I knew of it, the better off I was." She paused and looked like she might burst into tears again. "It seems he was right. Whatever knowledge he had was very dangerous."

I concentrated on replacing scrolls in the boxes I'd emptied. Just like all the others, they held nothing in them of importance. We'd spent the better part of the day examining old letters, household accounts and bad, but sincere, poetry Khety had written for his wife. There'd been no lists of names or even anything that could have been a cipher. Neffi had lost interest in the procedure early on and had draped himself across the top of a painted chest.

He was so deeply asleep, he was twitching in his dreams.

I closed the lid of the last scroll box. "It looks like he was pretty careful not to even bring anything regarding it into the house. Do you know of any other place he might have stored something?"

She looked at me and got quiet. "Sitehuti, I'm not asking you to tell me what this is all about. It killed my husband and has brought a scribe from the Great House all the way to Memphis. There is one thing I need to ask, though: if we can't find out what Khety discovered, it will be very bad, won't it?"

"I think you already know the answer."

She nodded. "Yes. I think maybe I do."

NINE

I was never so happy to have a message leave my hands as I was when I handed the written transcript of my interviews to general Seti-Merenptah's man. It wasn't that I hadn't realized there would be danger. I had. I'd understood clearly that this was serious business before I was even dragged into it. Who could doubt it after the violent attack on poor old Huya? That was still at the upper levels, though. The high part of society that was, until now, far above me. However, seeing Khety's family pulled apart and watching the ripples of this still-unknown plot disrupt the lives of ordinary people upset me at my core. I felt drained. All I wanted to do was sit in the House of Life with the other scribes and copy texts. Mindless activity. Safe.

The gods had something entirely different in mind for me. Well . . . someone did, anyway. I'm just blaming the gods because they're the usual suspects.

A full week had passed since I'd sent off my report and I was settling comfortably into routine. My group's visit to the House of Life of our sister temple was almost finished. We'd soon return home. I was sleeping soundly in the guest quarters with the other scribes when I was shaken awake by the door porter.

"Sitehuti!" he hissed. "Wake up, Scribe, someone wants you."

"Hunh?" I managed. I'm never at my best when coming from a sound sleep.

The porter picked up his oil lamp and stood. "There was a boy at the door, said his name was Den. Said it was urgent and that his mother wants you to come right away."

It took a moment longer to register the name. Den. It was the name of Shepenwepet's oldest son.

When I got to the house, I was alarmed to find the place as busy as an anthill. Torches and lamps burned in the small courtyard. Servants crammed household goods into chests and baskets, then loaded them onto waiting donkeys under the watchful eyes of three very large men. As I approached, one of the men straightened and stepped into my way. I tensed and braced myself for something unpleasant. At my feet, Neffi bristled and growled. The man's eyes slid from me to the cat and he visibly relaxed. "Oh! You're the scribe from the Great House," he said. "Go on in, I'll fetch my sister-in-law."

When Shepenwepet came in, she was pale and trembling. There were dark smudges under her eyes that hadn't been there before. She hurried over to me and grabbed my hands. "Oh, Sitehuti! I'm so glad to see you. I was afraid we'd be gone before you got our message."

"The door porter told me Den had come." I looked around in amazement. "But, where are you going — and why so suddenly?"

"We're going to stay with my sister and brother-in-law. I . . . I just don't feel safe in this house any more."

She was still gripping my hands, and I felt her sway. I steered her over to a chest by the door and asked, "Lady, what happened?"

"It started this afternoon," she said. "A big man — he looked like a dressed-up Nubian mercenary with the heavy braided wig and all the armbands. He came around, asking questions."

My heart stilled. There was no proof that it was the same Nubian I'd seen in the marketplace, but it would be a hell of a coincidence if it wasn't. I gulped. "What kind of questions?"

Neffi jumped up onto the chest beside the lady and rubbed his face along her arm. She retrieved a hand to stroke him. "The same kind of questions you were asking, Sitehuti," she said at last.

"Did you tell him anything?"

She shook her head, eyes wide. "No, he frightened me too much to even talk to him. Henut-Wedjebu sent him packing. I was so shaken, I could hardly sit still."

I wasn't surprised the man had fled before Henut-Wedjebu. I'd been ready to do the same at a couple points. "But, you're all right?"

The brother-in-law who challenged me outside came to stand beside her. Resting a protective hand on her shoulder, he said, "Henut-Wedjebu sent me a message, so my wife and I brought Penwi and the boys over to our place for dinner. When we got back, we discovered someone had broken in and ransacked Khety's study."

I went cold inside. "Was anything taken?"

"It was hard to tell," the shaken woman answered. "The room was such a wreck. I think a scroll box was missing, though. At least we haven't been able to find it. It was the one that contained the current household accounts."

Through the buzzing in my ears, I heard the man say, "My brothers and I decided to take her and the boys to our sister's place farther up river. It's a busy estate with many eyes to watch for trouble."

"Good idea," I said, snapping back to reality. "Please let me know when you've gotten settled, I know my master, High Priest Pedibastet, will want to know."

The burly man nodded and returned to the packing. Shepenwepet started to follow, then stopped and said, "I told him about you. You and Nefer-Djenou-Bastet."

I froze. "The Nubian?"

A smile broke over her face and she laughed. It was a silvery sound that made you want to hear it again. "Of course not the Nubian. Khety. My husband. He came to my dreams again last night and I told him the Pharaoh had sent you to help. He was very pleased."

Good thing someone was.

~*~

Day was breaking by the time I re-entered the temple compound. I was so tired by then that being afraid of the mysterious Nubian was too much work. To add insult to injury, my way to the guest house was blocked by the senior scribe and a soldier. As I got closer, I recognized the soldier as one of the Royal Medjay — worse, he was one of the contingent that had been sent to collect me and march me off to see Crown Prince Merenptah without warning. Suddenly my life seemed overrun by Nubians.

This particular Nubian was arguing with my senior scribe. I had to laugh. Royal Medjay or not, he was doomed before he'd said the first word. Master Userhet was the stubbornest man I'd ever met. I bowed respectfully, stifled a yawn and edged around them, intent on the side entrance and my bedroll.

The Medjay was saying, "Look, I *told* you. I can't take them out there because I have to get back to the boat. This will take at least a day and I have messages to deliver at several more places upriver after this."

Userhet groaned, "But why us, Lieutenant Si-Montu? We're finishing up our copying here today. We're all ready to head home in the morning."

"That can't be helped. The Crown Prince asked your High Priest to provide a messenger to deliver the official Opet festival requests, and he sent us to you. He trusts your people. You should consider it an honor."

Master Userhet closed his eyes as if in pain, and sighed. "Honor, indeed. If it's such a blasted honor, why don't you go in there yourself and tell a bunch of tired scribes they don't get to go home tomorrow after all."

I had almost edged past the two when Neffi suddenly chirped and trotted straight over to the soldier. I stifled a yell. I'd had enough brushes with the Royal Medjay guards and wasn't anxious to repeat the experience. I dived to grab him, but he dodged me and proceeded to rub all over the soldier's legs. Lieutenant Si-Montu looked down at the cat, then glanced my way.

He brightened and I knew I was doomed. "Well, no one said *all* of you have to play messenger. Why not that one? The one with the cat? He doesn't look like he's good for much else."

Master Userhet regarded me with speculation. I was beginning to despise the entire nation of Nubia. The cat was getting on my nerves, too.

~*~

Next morning was cold enough to form a thin sheet of ice on the washing water. It was still dark because, when the head scribe saw the list of stops, he declared it was at minimum a *two* day job and I needed to get an early start. At least the Great House had provided funding for the journey, and Master Ta had provided Renen, a local boy from the temple estates, to act as a guide. The master had even conscripted a donkey to carry the chest of scrolls that I had to deliver.

Both boy and donkey were waiting for me as I left the temple's guest house. Neither looked any happier than I felt. The donkey was especially twitchy. Can't say I blamed him much, since Nefer-Djenou-Bastet had decided that riding beat walking, and had curled up on the beast's shoulders, wedged between the scroll box and the animal's neck. We were a pretty sorry crew when we hit the road.

My task was deceptively simple. I was to visit all the estates on the list I'd been given, read from my copy of the Pharaoh's official Opet offering request, hand over the landowner's copy, then wait for a response. Simple, right? Sure. If I'd had any doubts I'd been handed a crap job, the first stop removed it. It was a vineyard owned by a priest named Anan.

When we reached the vineyard, the sun had risen enough for me to read the official request. I was glad of that. At the house, I was told that it was Anan's time to be at the temple. He'd be gone three more weeks and I needed to talk to the foreman. By the time I'd located said foreman, the sun was even higher. I greeted the man respectfully and read out the request of the Great House: "Foodstuffs and jars of wine are to be sent to the storehouses at Thebes" in the clear voice I had been trained to use. Before I reached the end, quite a good-sized group had gathered. My final words and the presentation of the official copy of the request was met with silence.

From somewhere in the back of the knot of workmen came, "Why does he want us to send that much wine?"

Another said, "Yeah, it's not like he doesn't have his own vineyards. There's one just the other side of town."

This elicited a number of snorts. Someone called, "You got your answer, Peser. That estate's owned by Prince Amunhotep."

This elicited even more laughter. Someone else yelled, "Yeah, by the time Amunhotep and his noble pals get finished there ain't enough wine to fill a new skin, let alone his daddy's warehouse."

The foreman joined in the laugh, then said, "Come back later, Scribe. We'll have a list of vintages for you then."

The voice from the rear called out, "Just don't let Amuny see it! It'll never make it to Thebes!"

Turned out I would hear that a lot.

We covered a lot of estates and even more ground, so all four of us were dragging by the time we reached an outlying village large enough to have a marketplace. I left Renen to water the donkey and headed off in search of food. I'd hoped Neffi would stay asleep on the donkey's back as he had been for most of the journey, but that wasn't to be. He jumped down, stretched and trotted along behind me as I entered the market. Turned out this was a good thing, though. The woman I bartered with for lunch was a cat lover and Neffi really turned up the charm for her. She gave us two extra boiled eggs and the biggest loaf she had in her stall. I swear the cat was dancing as we went back to where the boy and the donkey waited in the shade.

I broke the bread in half, pulled a little off for Neffi, then handed bread and a couple hard boiled eggs to Renen. The boy looked at me as if he were afraid I'd bite him.

"You got bread for me, too?" he asked, wide-eyed.

"And eggs." I shoved the bread into his hands and balanced the eggs on top. "You've been walking as long as I have and the road has been as dusty for you as for me." I broke the seal on the jug of beer and poured it into two rough earthenware cups. "The vendor had this cooling in water, so it ought to go down pretty well, too."

The boy bowed and said, "Thank you!" Then he fell on the food as if he hadn't eaten in a week. From the look of him, maybe he hadn't.

The food seemed to make a big difference in Renen. He was much less surly and more talkative on our last few stops before the sun dropped toward the horizon. The route laid out by Master Ta took us south along the river, then looped us up and back toward the city to catch the estates that lay to the west. The Medjay, Si-Montu, had declared it a day's worth of travel; the Head Scribe figured on two. It looked to me that the head scribe was closer to right. According to my list, the really large estates still lay ahead of us. That meant fewer houses, but more territory to cover. Truth to tell, I didn't feel like pushing it. The Great House was paying for food and lodging — and I wasn't having to deal with junior priests and my fellow scribes. It wasn't a bad trade-off.

The next estate on our list was a fair distance away, so we located an inn well before sunset. Lodging for us and board for the donkey. Once again, I shared dinner with Renen who happily tucked into the warm stew and bread.

The boy made it through the stew before he nodded and

announced, "You know, you're not like the other scribes that have come through the temple." Putting his empty bowl beside him for Neffi, he said, "None of the other ones ever shared meals with the servants."

"Really?" I said. It wasn't all that long ago that I'd been treated like a servant, myself — but I didn't say that out loud.

Renen said, "I mean, I can understand sharing with the cat. After all, he *is* the Sacred One and I've heard what some of the others have been saying about *that*."

I had to laugh. "I'm not sure if Nefer-Djenou-Bastet is as magical as some make him out to be."

The boy shrugged, took another big bite of flatbread and chewed thoughtfully. At length, he nodded. "Whether or not he is, I figure I'm your servant now."

I was surprised. "How so?"

"Well, Master Ta and the estate overseer told me to go with you and attend to your needs. That sounds like I've been given to you. I wasn't real sure about it at first, but you haven't hit me all day — even when things didn't go right." He didn't try to stifle a snicker. "And things didn't go right a *lot*."

I was about to object when he sat a little straighter and said, "Hey! There's that big guy again. I keep seeing him — almost like he's following us."

I looked where he indicated and almost choked. The man from the market in Memphis was standing by the gate talking to the innkeeper. The big, rough-looking guy with the aversion to cats, who dropped meat rolls to delay Neffi while he disappeared in the crowd. I looked down. Neffi's huge copper eyes were riveted on the scene, too. Oddly, he wasn't making a sound, just watching the man in the heavy braids. Suddenly, the mercenary/merchant glanced toward the stables and saw us. His stance changed, and he hurried away losing himself in the street traffic. I stared after him with an odd, nagging feeling of familiarity. Maybe it was the fleeting glimpse of him in the market at Memphis — but I wasn't so sure.

Renen was looking from the street to me. "Do you know him?"

I settled back against the mud brick of the stable wall and pulled another piece off my bread. "Um . . . No. I think I've seen him around, though."

"Don't think I'd want to know him, myself," Renen announced after a moment. "He looks kind of mean to me."

I kept watch for the Nubian after that, but he was either not following us any more or was keeping out of sight. Either way, that prickly feeling between my shoulder blades was there to stay.

TEN

Ever since Renen decided he was going to be my personal servant, he'd treated me to a running monologue of local gossip and background on the landowners we visited. From time to time the information had proved useful, but most of the time, it was just amusing. What he told me as our next to last destination hove into sight, was a little bit different.

"Oh!" the boy said, pointing at the buildings ahead. "This is the estate of Ma'aheru!"

I must have looked blank because he added, "You know. The Lector Priest Paseti's father."

I squinted at the sprawling structures ahead. "I didn't think Paseti was from a wealthy family."

"Ma'aheru married into the land and acted as overseer for his father-in-law for years," Renen said. "He inherited it when his father-in-law died. Then his wife died and he . . . Hey! How do you hope to arrest Paseti if you don't know anything about him?"

I stared. "Arrest him? Do I look like a policeman?"

"No . . . not really." The boy shrugged. "All I know is what the scribes in your group were saying."

Habuseneb. Again. "Look, Renen, I don't care what Hapuseneb or any of the others said. I am not a policeman. I am not a royal spy. I am simply a junior scribe who has recently been drafted into messenger duty."

Renen looked at me dubiously.

"Just because *that cat*," I pointed at Neffi for emphasis. He was sound asleep, sprawled across the donkey's back like a dusty, spotted blanket. "Decided he likes me, everyone is acting like I'm suddenly some kind of magician!"

The boy regarded the cat silently. He still looked dubious.

"Seriously! If I was some sort of favorite of the gods, would I have been given a crap job like the one we've been doing for the past two days?"

I thought my logic had him for a moment, but then he broke into a brilliant smile. "Ah!" he said. "But it's a great way to throw off suspicion."

I groaned. but Renen ignored me and launched into another spate of information about the estate and the family that owned it. I confess, I was amazed at the store of knowledge the boy held. I could foresee a career in record-keeping for him some day.

When we reached the gates of the estate, we found an elderly house servant waiting for us. The man was so thin and fragile-looking, that when he bowed and greeted me, I half-way expected to hear him crack and rustle like an escapee from an ancient cemetery. His voice was surprisingly strong and he invited me up to the house with the promise of cool water and fresh fruit. Another younger servant offered to show Renen where to water the donkey.

The welcome took me by surprise. In all the other estates we'd visited, we'd been greeted with a wide range of manners — mostly bad, but never with such old-style courtesy. Yes, I was technically representing the Great house of Ramesses, but at the same time, I was just a scribe playing messenger — and a young one at that. Add in that the request for festival goods came in addition to the tribute most landowners already paid to the state, I was delivering an *unwelcome* message to boot. I couldn't really blame them for not exactly welcoming me with open arms.

As I started toward the inviting shade of the porch, Nefer-Djenou-Bastet roused himself and hopped to the ground to follow me. Neffi was a hit with the servants. A woman had fetched a blue faience bowl that looked to be part of the household feast ware, filled it with water and put it down in front of him. He sniffed it and ignored it in favor of the basin meant to wash the road dust off my own feet. The water felt wonderful against my hot, gritty skin, but having a servant use a fine linen towel to dry them afterward was something I was definitely not used to.

Ma'aheru and his wife greeted us formally in the large hall of their house. The lady was much younger than her husband and, while her artfully made up face wasn't what anyone would call beautiful, it was pleasant and looked accustomed to good humors. At that moment, however, her expression was worried and her eyes had the shine of unshed tears

According to the gossip Renen had been pelting me with, the lady Neferhedjet was the old man's second wife, his first having died of the fevers when Paseti and Sasobek were boys. A young man, who looked to be my own age, stood just behind the couple. This had to be Banufre, the only child this second marriage had produced. As Ma'aheru rose to greet me, the lady laid a gentle hand on his arm. The smile that passed between them said there was a genuine affection there in spite of the difference in years.

Ma'aheru met me half-way, bowing and reciting a respectful, but archaic greeting that I remembered all too unfondly from some of my student copy exercises. Those lessons did come in useful, though, because I also remembered the proper response. I delivered it to the old man as I returned the bow and gave him his copy of the sealed royal message. To my amazement, Ma'aheru froze at the sight of it. At length, he took it from my hand as reluctantly as he would have a hot coal. Slowly, he clenched it in his fist and held it tight to his chest, motioning for me to read the copy I held.

I opened my scroll and started reading. For once, I made it all the way through without a sound from the people assembled in the airy hall. When I finished, I looked up. The old man stood stone still, crushing the rolled papyrus against his chest.

After a moment, he drew a shaky breath and asked tightly, "Is that all? His Majesty Ramesses— Life, Prosperity and Health to him for a million years —only requires wine and foodstuffs from our lands?"

Confused, I tucked the scroll back into my belt. "Yes, sir. Your house is asked to supply the same as the other estates in this area. I understand it's unexpected and—"

To my horror, the old man paled further and sagged toward the floor. Alarmed, I leaped forward to catch him, then helped a couple servants ease him into a chair.

I glanced over at the lady and found her softly crying, clutching her son's hand. The lady slowly opened red-rimmed eyes and whispered, "Thank you. You have brought wonderful news to us. When we heard you were being sent to our house from Pi-Ramesses, we were sure it was to seize all our land and possessions because of my step-son, Paseti's, crimes."

Words escaped me. This interpretation of my mission had never crossed my mind. Truthfully, though, their assumption was understandable.

The old man rebounded quickly, and before I knew it, I was being steered into the dining area and sat down beside tables where servants were laying out dishes for a meal. I started to object, but I was hungry and the scents wafting from the outside kitchen were very good.

A servant poured date wine into a blue faience cup decorated with lotus blossoms that was a match to the water bowl that Neffi had been given earlier. The man handed it to me bowing and smiling broadly. As I looked around, I realized everyone in the room had a happy, almost festive air about them. Sort of like they'd all been spared the executioner's blade. I raised my cup to my host and took a sip. The wine was rich and sweet. A few jugs of this sent to the royal table would go a long way to pleasing the Crown Prince and maybe even his father. I made a mental note to pass that along to the steward when he gave me his lists for the Opet. Another servant brought a bowl of yogurt and set it on the floor for Neffi, who tucked into it with relish.

I took another sip and bowed slightly toward my host. "Sir, I think this is the finest wine I've ever tasted."

The old man beamed. "Thank you, Sitehuti. We can't tell you how much of a relief it is that the message you brought was not what we feared."

"It must have been a terrible weight to bear, sir. I can't imagine how awful it must have been."

The old man shook his head and some of the strain around his eyes returned. "It was, indeed, a weight. Then when we heard you and the Sacred One had arrived in Memphis to track down my son, Paseti . . . ."

That won Hapuseneb a few more silent curses. That blasted priest's big mouth had caused me more trouble than Nefer-Djenou-Bastet, himself. It was probably a good thing that he was well on his way back to the capital with the rest of the visiting group or I'd have been tempted to head straight to the city to give him a good kicking.

"I assure you, sir, I wasn't sent to Memphis to track down your son. I'll admit, they told me to keep an eye out, but as I keep telling people I'm a junior scribe, not a policeman." That was all truth, too. The only way Paseti had figured in my instructions was to keep clear if I saw him. The main reason for coming to Memphis had been to discover what happened to the scribe Khety. I hadn't exactly failed miserably with that, but neither had I added much to what we already knew. I pulled my attention back to the table where Ma'aheru was continuing to speak.

"Paseti was such a wild youth. Angry all the time." The old man eased back against the cushions and spoke sadly. "When we landed the position at the temple of Bastet for him, we'd hoped the responsibility would settle him down; give him a channel for his anger like the military did for his brother, Sasobek."

The servants brought out serving tables bearing yet more of the blue faience ware, each laden with fragrant delicacies. They set the tables in front of us and busied themselves preparing cups of fresh grape juice. The juice was just as rich as the date wine. The wines made from these grapes would probably be magnificent. After a moment, I said, "According to the doorkeeper of the temple complex in Pi-Ramesses, Paseti received a letter from his brother in the Seth Division just before he disappeared. Would you have any idea what that could have been about?"

"Sasobek?" the old man said with a frown. "He got a letter from Sasobek?"

Lady Neferhedjet set her cup down on her table and offered, "We haven't seen Sasobek for quite a while. Not since he won his post with the Seth Division — even before that, he kept in touch more with letters than visits."

"He's quite a letter writer, too. Some of the stories he's told . . . ," Ma'aheru chuckled. "It was probably an unfortunate coincidence that the letter came just as Paseti was preparing to flee." The old man became serious again. "I was always afraid Paseti's temper would get him in trouble, but to commit such a violent attack upon the servant of a man who has been so generous to him? Insanity."

Unless Ma'aheru was the best actor I'd ever witnessed, the family had no idea as to why Paseti launched his attack on

Pedibastet's servant. Then again, if I were involved in a plot to usurp the throne of the Two Lands, I sure wouldn't want to let on about it to a messenger from the Great House.

"I assure you, Sitehuti," the old man continued with some heat, "Paseti certainly wasn't raised that way. I've gone out of my way to instill the old-fashioned values in all my boys."

Banufre snorted into his cup. His father didn't seem to notice, but his mother shot him a warning glance. The boy wasn't cowed.

About this time, I saw a large, spotted paw snake up at the edge of Ma'aheru's table. I considered flicking an olive pit at it, but my aim isn't that good and I was afraid I might zing my host instead.

"So you haven't seen him at all?" I asked. "Ummm. Paseti, I mean."

"*No!*" Ma'aheru sat forward so violently, I was afraid he'd topple out onto the floor. His dinner table wobbled dangerously and Neffi took that as an opportunity to hook one of the savory meat pastries and dart away. "Paseti knows better than to come here. He'll get no warm welcome from us, I promise you that!"

"I'm afraid Paseti's relationship with the family has been strained for a while, Sitehuti," came Lady Neferhedjet's quiet comment. Sadness tinged her words, but the remnants of laughter in her eyes made me wonder if she'd seen Neffi's thievery. "You see, Paseti has never approved of me. He sees me as trying to replace his mother."

Ma'aheru started to protest, but she held up a hand to silence him. "No, that's just the way of it, Ma'a, and denying it won't change anything. In Paseti's eyes, I was trying to supplant his beloved mother. Nothing could be farther from the truth, but sometimes truth doesn't speak as loudly as the heart. He was unhappy and made sure we all knew it. When my husband got him his first position at the temple of Bastet in the capital, he left and never returned."

"Never returned *here*, anyway," said Banufre.

"My son has a point," the old man growled. He jabbed a finger toward another house barely visible beyond the garden wall. "He'd definitely be welcome over there, no matter what he's done."

I followed the point. "That would be the estate of Amunhotep, the son of the Pharaoh, wouldn't it?"

"That it is. It was originally the estate of their mother, Lady Meritamon. The princes, Amunhotep and Meriramesses, grew up there." The old man sighed heavily and leaned back in his chair. "You might as well say my oldest sons did, too. They certainly seemed to spend more time over there than at home."

At the edge of my vision, the paw groped for the plate again. I was casting about for what to do, when my suspicions that the lady had seen the earlier theft were confirmed. Lady Neferhedjet casually shifted in her seat, her hand grazing a ball of herbed labna. The cheese curd rolled off her plate and bounced once on the matting before a spotted streak was on it. I saw the lady shake with silent laughter as the cat disappeared behind a group of vases with the morsel in his mouth.

She schooled her face into placidity. "To be fair, Ma'a," she said, "they were also permitted to study with the scribes sent from the Great House to give the Royal sons their lessons. We could never have afforded tutors of such quality."

"Filled their heads with all sorts of crazy notions, you mean," the old man grumbled. He gestured dismissively. "And there was nothing wrong with the tutors I provided. Nothing!"

Neffi emerged from behind the vases licking his whiskers, then trotted over to the lady's side. I cringed thinking what those claws could do to her delicate linen skirts, but I didn't need to worry. He rubbed against her legs and she reached down to scratch him between the ears. She said, "Still, it didn't hurt in later years that they were the childhood friends of two of the princes."

Ma'aheru looked like he'd bitten down on something sour. "Yes, that did help. I doubt we could have managed to get their positions without it. I just don't like how that Amunhotep grew up. If you can call it growing up."

Neffi turned his attention to Banufre, standing up against his leg and trilling. This earned him a tidbit of chopped meat and won the young man a purring, furry headrest along the back of his chair. This was fine until Neffi shoved his face into Banufre's wig and all but knocked it off.

"Hey!" Banufre grabbed the hairpiece and held it in place. I admired his restraint. I usually yelled a lot louder.

Lady Neferhedjet frowned. "This is also true, Sitehuti — although I'm loathe to mention it. I don't approve of his habits, either, especially when he should be a good example to the young people of this community."

I gathered from the sullen look that crossed her son's face just then, that he was one of the young people Prince Amunhotep was providing a bad example for. The concerned glances his mother sent his way confirmed it.

Banufre said nothing, but suddenly became absorbed in spreading a chunk of the labna over his bread. I wondered if I could swing a private talk with the youngest member of the clan. I wasn't sure what I could find out, but it seemed like it would be worth a try.

Neferhedjet sighed softly. "It really is sad about those boys. Their father might have been the ruler of the Two Lands, but their mother, Meritamon, was a concubine, not a royal wife. The Divine Ramesses gifted her the estate and vineyards. It made a perfect place for the two boys to grow up."

I said, "I thought the princes were raised and educated at Pi-Ramesses?"

"That is usually the case, especially if the prince is in line for the throne. Unfortunately, Lady Meritamon wasn't a particular favorite," Ma'aheru said.

"She may not have been a particular favorite," Lady Neferhedjet added, "but His Divine Majesty spent plenty of time there at the estate — even after the boys were grown and in the capital being trained for administrative positions. That just didn't seem to work out, though."

"For Amunhotep," groused Ma'aheru.

The lady shot him an exasperated look, then told me, "Their mother was taken ill with the fever. The same fever that took Paseti's and Sasobek's mother. Meritamon survived it, but she never fully recovered. That's when Prince Amunhotep left his position at the granaries to return and help his mother run the estate."

Ma'aheru barked a laugh. "So he *said*. I'm of the opinion the Pharaoh sent him back here because he was tired of the embarrassment the sot's drunken parties were causing back in the capital."

He turned to me, "Not that he was any better at overseeing an estate than he was the granary they parked him at. The granary burnt down and everything on the estate went to wrack and to ruin until his older brother Meriramesses was sent to sort things out."

Neferhedjet looked thoughtful, then said, "Life is funny, isn't it?"

I was puzzled by the seemingly unconnected statement. "How so?"

"If not for an accident of birth, Amunhotep would be Crown Prince instead of Prince Merenptah," she said. "He's two years older than the Crown Prince. Meriramesses is a few months older than Merenptah, too, but since their mother was a concubine and not the Royal Wife, Merenptah is in line for the throne, Amunhotep is a gentleman farmer and Meriramesses oversees his elder brother's estate."

"Don't make farming sound like the end of the world," the old man said. "It's been good enough to give this family a living and our sons a leg up in the world."

"Oh, Ma'a, you know that isn't what I was saying. Even you will have to admit that being poised to take the throne of the Two Lands beats tending livestock and vineyards."

Ma'aheru apparently didn't think he had to admit anything of the sort and turned to me. "Now, Meriramesses isn't a thing like his brother. He's a damned fine overseer! Since Prince Meriramesses took over, their production *and* quality have increased. The vineyards produce a fine wine and such a quantity that even his drunken sot of a brother can't drink it up."

This was too much for Banufre. He set his dinner knife down on his table with a thump. "Father! That is a horrible thing to say about Amuny!"

"Hear that? Amuny, not Prince Amunhotep. My son has a serious case of hero worship."

"Father, I don't idolize Amunhotep. I'll readily admit that he drinks too much and isn't the most responsible person around, but he's not as bad as you paint him."

"And I think you maybe ought to follow the other prince around. You might learn something more valuable than how to wreck a chariot."

Banufre went very still, then he stood, turned to me and bowed. "My apologies, Sitehuti, I didn't intend to air a family squabble in front of you. Now if you will excuse me, I need to meet with our own overseer. He's teaching me how to check for signs of disease on the grapevines."

He solemnly bowed to his mother and father, then went out the kitchen door.

Ma'aheru watched his son leave, then said, "Ban is a smart boy. He'll be the equal or better of Prince Meriramesses as a farmer some day."

Neferhedjet leaned forward and squeezed her husband's hand. She said gently,"You should tell *him* that, dear."

I set my juice cup down and weighed what I was about to say. "Forgive me for intruding, sir, my lady, but what you've said is making me wonder what I'll be encountering next door. I've been on the road delivering these requests for two days now. Ever since my first stop, I've been hearing jokes about Prince Amunhotep and his friends and how there wouldn't be any wine left to send to his father's storehouses."

The old man's disgust showed. "Yes, that would be about right. Likes his wine a bit too much does Amunhotep. Hosts wild parties all the time over there, too. They last all night and you can hear the commotion all the way over here."

The old man shook his head. "I truly pity Prince Meriramesses. Now there's a responsible man. He does more than just look after the estate, he's practically his brother's minder. That might be why the Pharaoh — Life, Prosperity and Heath for a million years — actually sent him out here. The gods know Amunhotep was a failure at making the estate work. Once their mother died, the property fell to Prince Amunhotep. That was a sad day in more ways than one."

"Ma'a...," his wife warned.

He waved surrender to her and said, "Mind you, Banufre has it right: Amunhotep isn't a bad sort, but the boy doesn't recognize that the man is just plain lazy. Likes his pleasure more than hard work. Most intelligent thing Amunhotep ever did was to turn the reins over to his brother."

The Lady looked troubled. "I probably shouldn't say anything, but. . . . Yes. I should. Be cautious around Prince Meriramesses wife, Sitehuti. Lady Wurusemu is known for her temper and I'm at a loss to tell you what sets her off. I know full well that the Hittites have different customs than we do, but I fail to see how we offend her so easily — especially after so many years here in Kemet." She considered again. "I truly feel for their youngest daughter, Iaret. She's the last one in the nest and her mother picks at her terribly."

"She probably won't be in the nest for long," Ma'aheru said. "As a granddaughter of the Pharaoh, she has great prospects. Her sisters and brothers married well and hold down excellent positions in the Two Lands. Yes, I think the Prince will do quite well by his little girl."

The Lady laughed. "You can't call her little anymore, Ma'a. She's almost as old as Banufre."

"It's hard to think of either of them all grown up. It really seems like yesterday they were playing with toy boats down by the pond."

This got a stream of reminiscence flowing. Once again, I saw the genuine affection between the couple. Neffi hopped up in Banufre's recently vacated chair and made himself comfortable. I confess I did much the same. The familiar banter reminded me of my childhood in the Place of Truth more strongly than anything had in a long time. It was comfortable and warm listening to them talk, so I nursed my cup and eavesdropped until a servant came to tell me the overseer had finished the list of their Opet gifts.

With the overseer's scroll tucked safely away, I took a reluctant leave from the family and made my way down to the barns to collect Renen and the donkey. I was just out of sight of the house when Banufre stepped out onto the path and hailed me. I got the distinct impression he'd been watching for me.

"Forgive me for lying in wait, Sitehuti, but I wanted to give you my version of the princes before you left with the wrong impression. Sometimes my father lets his disapproval of prince Amunhotep get away from him," Banufre said. "I'll admit, I'm friends with Prince Amunhotep, even though he's old enough to be my father. He treats me well when he could treat me like what I am: the youngest son of a not-quite noble farmer."

There was something in the way he said the last part that struck me. I said, "That sounds like a direct quote and I'm guessing it didn't come from Prince Amunhotep."

"Too right," he said leaning against the mud brick wall that bounded the road. Neffi, who had been trotting along beside me hopped up, and rubbed his cheek along Banufre's shoulder. "Not to put too fine a point on it, I think it's my father who has a case of hero worship and he's favoring the wrong brother."

Interested, I leaned against the wall, too. "I'm assuming it was Prince Meriramesses who made the insulting comment, then."

He nodded. "And the Lady Wurusemu. They both make unpleasant comments about my parents when they know I can hear. Why my elder brothers are so thick with those two is beyond me."

The way Neffi reacts to people tells me a lot. The same goes for how people react to him. Right then, he was purring and leaning into Banufre's hand that was stroking down the cat's back.

I said, "I gathered they grew up together. That makes bonds stronger a lot of times."

"Also true — and I think my father's marriage to my mother didn't sit well with the Prince and his Lady, either. My mother was once an attendant to the late Lady Meritamon."

"The princes' mother?"

"Yes. It was a court position back when they both lived in the palace at Pi-Ramesses. She's the daughter of a wealthy merchant — *ow!*" Neffi had climbed onto his shoulder and given him one of his stone-breaker headbutts. Banufre lifted the cat off his shoulder and plopped him back onto the wall. "Does he always do that?"

"If he likes you, I'm afraid so."

He edged slightly farther away, keeping an eye on the still-purring animal. "Anyway, my mother was no slave in spite of all their insinuations. Mother remained friends with Lady Meritamon even after she and the boys moved out here. That's how she met father."

A lot was becoming clearer. "Of course, they say none of this to your father's face."

Banufre laughed bitterly. "Sounds like you've seen this before."

I had. When you grow up in an isolated village composed of the best craftsmen in the Two Lands, you see many different types of snobbery.

"Mother already knows how they are. We haven't even tried to tell my father, because we know he won't hear us. It hurts to hear him praise a man who speaks so scathingly of him and how he got his land and position." Neffi flipped over on his back and wriggled around for a belly rub. Smiling, Banufre obliged him. "My father worked hard for what he has and I'm proud of him for it. The trouble is, it's narrowed his view of things. I love my father, and the fact that he has such respect for a man who has so little in return for him is just . . . wrong."

Neffi had enough pets and tried to wrap himself around Banufre's hand. The boy was ready for him and pulled away before the claws locked on. The momentum carried the cat off the wall. He landed on his feet in the dusty path, shook himself and went to stalk a particularly threatening leaf.

Banufre continued as if nothing had happened. "Father can look down on Prince Amunhotep all he wants, but he has completely the wrong idea of him. Yes, he drinks too much and is a total loss at anything resembling responsibility, but Amuny has been very generous with my family and with me. I think the gifts he's given me are really what sticks in my father's craw."

"Expensive things?" I asked.

"Most haven't been that expensive, but a lot were things my father couldn't really provide. When I was younger, Amuny arranged for me to sit in with his nieces and nephews when the royal tutors visited. Recently he gave me some hunting gear, a couple dogs — that sort of thing." A grin stole across his face. "When he gave me one of his old chariots and a horse to pull it for my birthday last year, I thought my father was going to choke to death."

I whistled. "Wow! That *is* a generous gift."

"He did it so I could come with him and his friends when they go racing over at the old necropolis. He says that every man of substance needs to know how to handle himself in a chariot. I don't race, but Amuny and his friends like me to come along. I think they look on me as a sort of mascot," he said with a smile.

"Did your father want you to give it back?"

Banufre gave a genuine laugh. "That's the truly funny part, Sitehuti. He didn't like the horse and chariot on any level, but the old-fashioned ways he's so proud of have him stuck. You don't return a gift to a member of the Royal family. Ever. No matter what."

I grinned along with him. I didn't know any boy or young man anywhere who wouldn't have given his eye teeth to be gifted with a chariot and horse. Even a second-hand one.

He got serious. "It's hard to think of Amuny as a prince, sometimes. Meriramesses, yes, no doubt about it, he's as officious as they come, but Amunhotep? He's more like one of his dogs. Big, friendly and never met anyone he didn't like."

I was starting to like Prince Amunhotep, myself, and I hadn't even met him. "What about the parties?" I asked. "Are they really all that wild?"

Neffi, having won a pitched battle with a dead palm frond,

came back and stretched out on the sun-dappled surface of the footpath.

Banufre rolled his eyes, an expression of amazement rather than disgust. "You have no idea!"

"You've been to some?"

"I've been invited and I've slipped out to a few, but they're usually too much for me. Most of the time I don't even tell Father about the invitations. The strain of not being able to say no to a royal would tear him in two. I did slip out to see the one he had for the last Festival of Drunkenness, though."

I laughed. "Why do I think the prince likes that one in particular?"

"His favorite," Banufre agreed. "He went all out last year. He even brought in this troupe of acrobats from Syria and these dancing girls . . ." He rolled his eyes again. "They could even touch the top of their heads with the soles of their feet!"

"So what does Prince Meriramesses think of his brother's lifestyle?"

"Do you really have to ask?"

I grinned. "Not really, but I thought I would anyway."

"The mansion is divided in half. It was built that way for when His Royal Majesty came to visit. Now, Meriramesses and his family live on one side and Amunhotep on the other."

"Prince Amunhotep isn't married?"

"Not now, anyway. I gather he's had three wives. I know one died very young and I know of two others who just couldn't take his way of life. Truthfully, I think the thing that makes him saddest is the fact he has no children. He always doted on his brother's children."

And maybe his neighbor's son, too, I thought.

Banufre's face brightened as an idea occurred to him. "Tell you what, there's usually a sort of picnic going on down by the big pond this time of day. Why don't I go over with you and introduce you to Amuny? Maybe we can hang around long enough for them to gear up for a full-fledged party this evening."

I didn't even have to think hard. "You're on," I said.

~*~

Since the princes' estate was in walking distance, we left Renen and the donkey enjoying the hospitality of Banufre's parents' stables with instructions to catch us up later. We veered off the main road and onto a foot path that took us through a vineyard and up a hill dotted with carefully tended trees, then along a shady path flanked by lush plantings. As we walked, I became aware of a mass of sound: people laughing and shouting; musicians and the sound of many types of animals. It sounded like a festival in the distance.

Banufre laughed, "Amuny must have some friends in from town. We might not have to wait for evening for you to see a big do."

As he spoke, we rounded a bend in the pathway that brought a large, beautiful pond, framed by more of the carefully manicured plantings into view. The princes employed fine gardeners. The pond had been planted with papyrus, reeds and all sorts of water plants until it looked like a chunk of the river bank had been torn up and plopped down in the middle of the lawn. It was designed to surprise the walker. It succeeded.

I said, "Your father said you and Prince Meriramesses' youngest daughter, Iaret, used to play by a pond. Is that the one?"

Banufre started a little, caught himself and said, "Yeah, that's the one." He smiled, apparently remembering happy times. "There's a little pavilion built out over the water. It's hidden by the trees and papyrus from here. We used to launch fleets of miniature boats from it."

After another moment Banufre said, "The woodcrafters on the estate doted on Iaret — me, too, by association, I guess. We were the only kids around here by then. All our brothers and sisters were grown and had moved away. They used to make all sorts of little wooden toys for us. My favorite was a bird that flew if you tossed it up into the wind."

He resumed walking. With some reluctance, I tore myself away from the pretty view and joined him. I said, "Oh, I know the kind you mean! Those are fun. The wood workers in my village made those for us kids, too."

"Village? You're not from Pi-Ramesses?"

"Not originally. I grew up in the village of the workmen, the Place of Truth."

"Oh! Then you've seen the Great Place, the Place of Beauty and all the temples across the river in Thebes itself. I'd love to see Thebes — especially at Opet. The processions sound magnificent." He shrugged and gave a rueful grin. "Well, I can dream, anyway. We've never gone any father than Memphis."

I laughed. "Memphis is pretty magnificent on its own and Saqqara? Saqqara, the *ancient* necropolis. Not to mention the Serapeum and a whole bunch of pyramids. I've never seen those, so we're even."

"Oh yeah? How about I arrange for you to see Saqqara? Then you'll be obligated to show me the Place of Truth, the Great and Majestic Necropolis *and* the Place of Beauty."

I clapped him on the back. "Deal!"

The path made another sharp turn at a heavy screen of vegetation and abruptly ended at a broad flight of stone steps. Before us spread a scene of chaotic merrymaking. There was something happening everywhere I looked. It reminded me of festival time in Pi-Ramesses, but distilled to its essence.

We both paused and let it all soak in, then Banufre told me to wait while he found Prince Amunhotep. He trotted down the steps toward a knot of men playing draughts. I stood on the top landing and let the noise and sights wash over me. Even Neffi seemed uncertain and stayed by my side.

The revelers were men and women, some about the age of the princes, others closer to Banufre and me, with everything in between represented. To the side, a group of nobles threw dice. Suddenly a woman yipped "*YEAH*" and raked a pile of gaming chips toward herself amidst the groans of the other gamers. She threw back her head, and laughed uproariously, then challenged them to see if they could win it back.

Down by the pond, about a dozen men and boys lobbed brightly painted throwing sticks at wooden target ducks floating on the water. The pond itself looked like it might once have been a well that had silted up, then widened and turned into a centerpiece for the yard and gardens leading up to the gleaming white mansion I saw in the distance. Baying dogs danced around the throwers and dived into the water to fetch the sticks. One excited hound retrieved a wooden duck to the extreme merriment of the crowd.

Under the shade of a colorful awning and a stand of date palms, a throng people ate from folding tables laden with food. Nearby, dogs fought over scraps the people tossed to them. I looked down, concerned about Neffi. To my knowledge, he'd never been around that many dogs, but he didn't seem bothered by it. The true test was when one of the hounds bounded up the steps and careened toward us. Neffi never flinched, he just reached out a splayed paw and sent the animal yelping back into the crowd. Still, that was only one dog and not a large one at that. Taking a cue from the nobles with pet monkeys or ferrets on their shoulders, I hoisted Neffi up onto my now-dusty stole. He seemed happier and stretched across my shoulders protectively.

I'd also been watching Banufre's progress through the crowd. It had been slow going because every few steps, someone would hail him and exchange a wave or a few pleasantries. He'd made it about half-way to the water's edge when there came a shout: "BAN! Ban! Over here!"

I scanned the crowd just as Banufre was doing and saw a large, beefy man beckoning him over with wide sweeps of a broad hand more like a paw than anything else. One time in Thebes, I'd seen a Syrian bear. The big man shouting to Banufre brought that animal strongly to mind.

Banufre turned and motioned me to follow. I caught him up and, together, we pushed through the wall of revelers toward the prince. When we made it through, Prince Amunhotep pounded the young man on the back. It nearly knocked the slightly-built Banufre off his feet, but the prince didn't seem to realize it.

Prince Amunhotep said, "Ban! Glad you could make it. I didn't think we'd see you for a long time after that stupid business when the boar we were chasing ran through your father's sheep pen."

"Yeah," Banufre said. "He's still a little hot about that one, but that's not why I'm here. There's a scribe from Pi-Ramesses with a request from the palace for Opet goods. I thought I'd bring him over and introduce him to you."

The prince said, "Scribe from the capital? Oh yeah, I heard the requests were making the rounds. Where is he?" He looked around and spotted Neffi and me for the first time. Immediately, his face broke into a smile that would light a darkened room. "Ah! The scribe with the magic cat!" He hauled off to give me a shoulder wallop like the one that had rocked Banufre, but Neffi pinned his ears back and objected. Loudly.

At first, the prince was taken aback, but after a heartbeat, he roared with laughter. His companions followed suit. "Oh yes!" he said. "I've heard about how protective the Sacred One is. I heard that cat even chased a Nubian mercenary right out of the market."

I'd almost managed to forget that. The reminder made my breath catch in my throat. I said, "It wasn't quite —"

Prince Amunhotep wasn't listening. He threw back his head and roared a laugh to the skies. "I wish I could have been there. I don't particularly like Nubians."

A lovely dark-skinned woman elbowed him and cleared her throat pointedly. Prince Amunhotep grinned, planted a kiss on her cheek and hugged her to his side. "Well . . . Nubian *military* types, anyway," he amended.

Like Crown Prince Merenptah, this prince had inherited their father's famous height. Amunhotep was heavier, though, both through muscle and high living. The arched Ramesside nose was unmistakable as he leaned down to tell me confidentially, "My half-brother's Royal Medjay were a Royal Pain-in-the-Ass when I was in the capital. Especially that big guy — Djed . . . " he snapped his fingers searching for the name, then gave up. "Djed something, anyway. Real sour customer."

My thoughts flashed back to the terrifying march from the scribal school. I murmured, "Captain Djedmose. Yeah. I know the one."

The prince turned to Banufre. "Speaking of sour customers, Ban, what's the word from Paseti? He's dropped himself into a steaming pile of it now, hasn't he?" He shook his head in genuine sadness.

Ban looked troubled, then shrugged. "Your guess is as good as mine, Amuny. You know he won't come around our place. He won't speak to Father and he certainly won't talk to me."

Prince Amunhotep surprised me by going solemn. He said, "Very, very true. It's a hard thing when a father and son don't get along. Hard when brothers grate on each other, too."

The prince's tone and choice of words made me wonder who he was talking about: Paseti? Or himself?

Suddenly the bonhomie was back, erasing the sadness like

a palm broom across sand. "Well, since you came all the way out here, Sitehuti, I guess we better take care of business so we can get back to the fun."

I started. The day had been so enjoyable, I'd forgotten I was supposedly there on business. Pulling out the scroll, I bowed, presented it to Prince Amunhotep and launched into my spiel, "Prince Amunhotep, I bring you greetings in the name of the Divi —"

To my amazement, the prince stepped back from the scroll like it was a snake and waved it away. "Hell no! Save that official stuff for my brother. A little court folderol will make his day. Bores me to tears, but it's the stuff of life for Meriramesses." He grinned and motioned Banufre and me to follow. "Come on, I'll take you up to the house and turn you over to my brother's guard dog — I mean his chief butler, Yuni."

All the way up to the house, Prince Amunhotep chattered away, talking about hunting, what fish were biting at the moment and how Banufre's horse was getting along. The only time he touched on the Beautiful Feast of Opet was to mention some entertainment he'd heard was going to be there and to ask Banufre if his family was finally going to go up to Thebes for it. It was cheerful banter, but there was an edge to it. It was as if the closer we got to the magnificent house, the more uncomfortable Prince Amunhotep became.

When we reached the entry hall of the big house, the sounds of the lawn party were distant and muted. I was just marveling at that when Prince Amunhotep said, "Quiet, isn't it?"

He laughed and swept a hand at the trees and shrubs ringing the house. "That's the way my brother likes it. Lucky for him this old pile of mud was built the way it was. His family apartments are on this side of the great hall and mine are on the far side. He had the gardeners plant this forest around the place to muffle outside noise." He grinned hugely and added, "Outside noise. That means me and my friends."

A staid elderly man in stiff linens emerged from the shade of the entry hall and treated our little group to thinly disguised disapproval.

Amunhotep greeted the man heartily. "Ah! Yuni! Just the man I wanted to see."

I could tell that each booming word was like a cane blow to the chief butler. So could Amunhotep. I was sure of it.

The butler bowed and said, "I am at your service, Your Highness."

The prince swept a massive paw toward us, "Our neighbor, Banufre, has been good enough to escort the royal scribe, Sitehuti, over to deliver an official request from my father. Please inform my brother there's official business to attend to. Officially."

"Yes, Your Highness. I will do so at once."

True to his word, the prim man disappeared back into the shadows of the house.

Prince Amunhotep watched him go, then turned to us. "I'll get back to the party, then. No sense in me going in with you and ticking off His Royal Hemorrhoid and the Hittite Harridan with my uncouth presence. Come find me again when you've finished here. Nedjem heard of a way to maybe get more speed out of that old set of wheels of yours, Ban. We're itching to try it out."

You could almost see relief roll off him like steam as he hurried back toward the picnic, leaving Banufre, Neffi and me standing, dwarfed by the columns of the elegant entry hall. Shortly, a group of servants came out to fetch us. They led us into the loggia where they had set out water, food and drink. One of them even removed my stole and brought it back well dusted and expertly folded it across my shoulders again. Prince Meriramesses and Lady Wurusemu didn't keep us waiting long, but I confess, I didn't mind. The stools set out for us were cushioned and comfortable, and even after the relaxing time at Ma'aheru's, I was *still* glad I wasn't walking the dusty road.

The attendants were divided on how to react to Neffi. Some were leery of a cat his size — and reputation — and others were pleased to have a sacred animal under their roof. As for Neffi, he didn't pay much attention to the controversy. The pro cat side had brought him out a bowl of cheese crumbles with bits of meat on top of it. Once again, he ignored the bowl of fresh water they put in front of him in favor of the water I had my feet in. If I live to be a million years old, I'll never understand that cat.

ELEVEN

The reception in the mansion couldn't have been more different than the one we got at the lawn party. Meriramesses and his wife, Wurusemu, received us in the main hall. They sat on twin, ornately inlaid and gilded chairs on a raised dais, similar to the ones found for the master's chair in middle-class houses, but larger. This one more resembled the throne platforms I'd seen at royal functions: higher, paved with polished stone and sided with faience tiles decorated with a blue and green peacock feather pattern. Prince Meriramesses looked like a distilled version of his brother, obviously of the Rameside line, but, where Amenhotep was large and broad, Meriramesses was thin and drawn out like a wire. A taut wire that hummed with impatient energy. A tall, gilded staff leaned against the chair arm and the Prince's nervous fingers worried an elegant inset in the shape of a papyrus blossom.

The woman sitting next to him looked like a work of art, as beautiful and exotic as her perfume that tinted the air of the pillared hall. Her gown was an unusual blue with a border of embroidered peacock feathers that mirrored the sides of the dais. It might be because I was looking for it, but her eyes held a hooded, aloof look with a hint of temper shrouded behind the veil.

A lovely young woman stood behind them, quiet enough to be unobtrusive, but too beautiful not to be noticed. She was a perfect blend of the tall, willowy side of the Ramesses clan and the exotic glamour of the older woman. She could only have been Iaret, the couple's late in life daughter.

Out of the corner of my eye, I caught a brief, moony expression flash cross Banufre's face. I recognized the symptoms immediately. I'd seen that goofy look on S'Kem's face often enough and it was fixed permanently on Butehamun's. It usually spelled trouble. Simply put: Banufre was in love with his childhood playmate. I quickly returned eyes front, wondering if the lady returned the affection. I stepped forward as the chief butler announced me and stole a glance at her, but the face beneath the heavy, curled wig maintained a serene and court-perfect expression. It was impossible to tell.

Once again, I had cause to thank my old master, Khenemetamun-pa-sheri. The lengthy and archaic greeting he'd forced me to memorize came smoothly and seemed to impress the prince. I wondered if he had more in common with his neighbor, Ma'aheru, than he dreamed. I stomped on a smile as I bowed and presented the scroll. Meriramesses accepted it graciously and listened with head politely tilted as I read from my copy. That copy was becoming a bit tired and dog-eared. I was glad this was my last stop, or I'd probably have had to recopy it before the one I was using fell to bits.

All during the reading of the Pharaoh's request, the family stood as still as ka statues. I don't think I've ever seen anything as perfect — but I'd never been at the royal court before then, either. When I finished, Prince Meriramesses inclined his head and said, "It shall be done as my father asks."

He handed the scroll to Yuni, who was hovering like a cloud of gnats, and murmured that it should be passed on to the head scribe of the stores. The butler scurried off and the prince sat back, regarding me with a furrowed brow.

"Sitehuti. I have heard this name," he said at last.

I braced myself. This was rarely good — especially since I'd acquired Neffi.

He thought for a while longer, then smiled. "Ah, yes! The

boy from the Place of Truth. You studied under Khenemetamun-pa-sheri, didn't you? Excellent teacher."

"You do both me and my teacher honor, Your Highness," I said, bowing deeply. I was beginning to think that Master Khenemetamun-pa-sheri was a pretty good teacher, myself. I'd already had cause to use many of the formal manners he'd drilled into us students. I'd honestly never thought I would.

Lady Wurusemu leaned forward in her seat and fixed Neffi and me with a gaze that hit like a physical blow. Her intensity took me by surprise and set something deep inside me squirming. It took every scrap of discipline I had to keep myself from turning on my heel and running out of the house.

"This would be the Magic Cat, then?"

The lady's voice was deep and still held the strange accents of her Hittite origins. I realized with a shock that she, herself, reminded me of a cat. One of the cruel ones who play with and torment their prey for hours before killing it. Up until that moment, I'd taken Lady Neferhedjet's warning lightly. Not any more.

I bowed again. "Yes, Your Highness, this is Nefer-Djenou-Bastet." The cat in question sat beside me as regally still as the royals on the dais.

"How wonderful," she said, although that same deep-inside-something told me she meant the exact opposite. "We have heard so many amazing stories about you and the Sacred One."

I forced a smile to my face. "I'm afraid there are many fantastic tales circulating, Your Highness. I assure you, I am just a scribe doing the bidding of my Pharaoh."

The lady leaned back and regarded Neffi with speculation. Nefer-Djenou-Bastet was, for once, every inch the temple cat, returning her gaze with half-closed eyes. Aloof and undisturbed.

Movement from the side broke the spell as Yuni scurried back into the great hall with a harried-looking older man in tow.

The writing kit over the newcomer's shoulder identified him as a scribe and he was that nervous kind of thin that puts you in mind of a bird. The chief butler left him fidgeting by the door, and stepped up onto the dais, whispering into the prince's ear.

Prince Meriramesses tapped his golden walking stick on the stone tiles and said, "Excellent! Ipuy, the head scribe of the stores is here." He motioned the scribe forward. "Are the lists being prepared?"

"Even as we speak, Your Highness," Ipuy said.

"Very good. You must give our guest a tour of the property in the meantime." To me he said, "We are very proud of what we've done with this estate, Sitehuti. I trust you can make a good report of us to my father when you return to the capital."

I was dismissed and damned glad of it.

~*~

Once we were well away from the house and on the path to the granary, Ipuy literally shook himself and said, "Silly, isn't it? Every time I leave that audience chamber, I feel like I've escaped with my life."

No, I didn't think it was silly. I felt the same way. What I *said* was, "I've felt like that before. Usually when called into my scribal master's study."

We shared a laugh, then he said, "Where would you like to start?"

I shrugged. "I don't know. I'm not real familiar with working estate farms."

"How about the vineyards, then the wine press? The storage houses are on the way, too."

I suppose I didn't have much of a reference point, but the storage houses weren't very thrilling. Ipuy got excited in the vineyards, though, and fluttered like a nervous bird about the vines.

"We check the leaves frequently to make certain there isn't

any mold getting to them. It's an awful, white powdery stuff. If we keep them pruned so plenty of sun and air get through, we're good," he said.

"Oh!" I said in sudden realization. "That must be what the foreman over at Ma'aheru's place has been teaching Banufre to do. He — I mean Banufre — said he was learning how to check the vines, but I had no idea what he meant at the time."

Ipuy's head bobbed in agreement. "Yes! That would be it and the boy couldn't learn from anyone better than old Kerer, except maybe his own father."

"His father seems a little strict, though," I observed.

"Well, it's true. Ma'aheru might be a little straight-laced, but he's fair. He's worked for what he has. Didn't just fall into his lap in spite of what some people say."

His statement piqued my interest. "That sounds like someone who saw what really happened."

He nodded. "My father was the foreman of this place before the Divine Ramesses purchased it. I was born and raised on this land."

"You must have grown up with the two princes and Ma'aheru's older sons, then."

"Well . . . more or less," He fussed with a vine. Finally he leaned close and said in a low voice, "Between us scribes, there's a world of difference between family and the hired help. I'm sure you've seen it before."

I had to agree. I had certainly seen my share of it.

"Now, even as a boy, Prince Amunhotep wasn't like that and has become even less so as he's grown older, but his brother?" Ipuy glanced around. "It's been worse since Prince Meriramesses brought that snooty foreign wife home. I tell you, that woman has a real mean streak."

His words fit in well with lady Neferhedjet's warning. I said, "You're not the first to make that observation to me."

"Too right," he said, busy with another vine. "A bit too fond of the rod and the whip if you ask me. There have been more than a few maids who ran away because of it."

"Ran away?"

He nodded gravely. "Just up and scarpered in the night. Packed up and left not a hair behind." Suddenly, he straightened, dusted his hands and announced, "Well, that's vineyards. Let's look in on the wine press next, shall we?"

~*~

It turned out Ipuy was excited about the vineyards and the wine press because he was the overseer of the press. Up until then, all I knew about wine presses was that I usually liked what came out of them. Ipuy was determined to change that and launched into a lecture full of terms and details. I looked around the mudbrick building that housed the press and catch basin making "uh huh" noises until I lost track. I shook myself out of it in time to hear him say:

". . . and the estate is noted for several excellent vintages. The fine red is especially prized."

Neffi was about to drop down into the basin where the juice from the crushed grapes collected. I snagged him and tried to settle him on my shoulders. He wasn't having it.

"Your production is impressive, Ipuy. I confess, I'd been given a completely different impression of the estate's operations on my journey through the area."

Ipuy pulled a face. "Prince Amunhotep and his friends have drunk the place dry? Maybe that we can't make wine fast enough to keep up with the prince's parties?"

I grinned. "Not exactly, but close enough."

"Oh, yes. I'm very familiar with that particular group of rumors. The Prince and his friends do go through a lot of wine at those parties, but it's usually brought in. They rarely touch the estate's own stores. Estate wine is reserved for official functions and for family dinners."

"I understand. I also know it doesn't take much to get that sort of thing started, either. Rumors, I mean."

The winemaker made a non-committal humming sound and very carefully straightened a short stack of grape-gathering baskets. Neffi hopped up onto the rim of the main press to supervise.

"It certainly doesn't," Ipuy said. "Why, there's even one going around now that you're actually here to track down Ma'aheru's errant son."

"Oh, no. Not that one again."

But Ipuy wasn't listening. Instead, he was getting angry, stacking and shoving baskets around with more force than necessary. Apparently, Paseti was a sore spot with him.

"*Paseti.*" He practically spat the name. "Always trying to be something he isn't, that one. Lacks the class to carry it off. Have you watched him eat? Clumsy! Acts more like a field hand than a son of a wealthy house. Sasobek is almost as bad — but he's a soldier and you know how *they* are. Old Ma'aheru should have fired their tutor. Me? I'd have flogged him, to boot. It was too late by the time those two joined the princes with their tutor. Damage done. Ingrained. Just plain ingrained. Even being appointed Lector at the temple in Pi-Ramesses didn't do anything for those rough edges." He turned and gestured with a basket. "And now, he's a criminal." He punctuated his final statement by slapping the basket into place on a stack that towered over his head.

Neffi had been relatively quiet up until the man had started moving baskets around. Now he stretched on his hind legs, craning his neck to inspect the topmost baskets of the rows to the far side of the press. I wasn't too thrilled about this. The stacks didn't look all that steady and I could easily envision them crashing down on us.

I pulled my attention away with difficulty. "Have you seen him around here, then? His father was pretty certain he wouldn't come back."

"Pffah! Like his father would know."

"You *have* seen him?"

"Well, no," the scribe said, turning away from his stacking. "Not for a while — but I wouldn't be surprised if he were somewhere around here. Those two!" He jerked a thumb toward the house. "That bunch used to get into all kinds of trouble together. Why, I remember one time Prince Meriramesses and Paseti—" He broke off and narrowed his eyes slightly. "Hey! You *are* looking for him, aren't you?"

Neffi had managed to climb to the top of one of the basket stacks. It wobbled.

"Ummm . . .no," I said, lifting Neffi down and dropping him back onto the flagstone floor. "I'm just curious."

"Sure. I get it. Checking known haunts and all that." He nodded knowingly and lowered his voice. "I'll keep an eye out. If I see anything, I'll let you know."

"Uh. Thanks . . . *Hey!*" I dived past the startled scribe to snatch Neffi before he disappeared into a space between the wall and the back of the huge press. He wailed complaints as I hauled him out by his hind legs. He shook free and stalked over to sit by the door and smooth his ruffled fur. I was wondering at his disruptive behavior when a shadow fell across the door and Prince Meriramesses, himself appeared, leaning on another staff, this one topped with a lapis and gold djed pillar.

"I trust I'm not interrupting anything," the prince said.

Ipuy was dumbstruck, frozen with a basket half-way to a stack.

"No, sir," I said, bowing. "Your man was telling me about the grape harvests and the excellent vintages that are produced here. It's been a very interesting tour."

"Good! Good! We also raise some of the best beef in the Two Lands. Ipuy! You must also show Sitehuti the cattle pens."

Ipuy nodded and bowed mutely.

Prince Meriramesses appeared not to notice, but continued, "I came down in person to apologize that the list is taking longer to compile than expected. I fear you must suffer our humble hospitality for a while longer. Please stay for the evening meal. The cook is preparing some of our own beef."

I started to answer, but the prince held up a hand. "I won't accept no for an answer. I'll get back to the house and see to it that young Banufre stays with us, also."

That left me with no choice. I bowed again and said, "Many thanks, Your Highness. I would be delighted."

He cracked the staff onto the pavement. "It's settled. Dinner. I guarantee you'll have our list of offerings in your hands before you leave." Without another word, the prince wheeled and marched back toward the house leaving Ipuy and myself staring after him.

"What was *that* about?" I managed after a bit.

"Well," said Ipuy with the air of a man who has just realized the log he'd been about to step on was a crocodile. "I suppose we'll be visiting the cattle pens next."

Where the meal with Ma'aheru and Neferhedjet was almost like a picnic, the meal hosted by Prince Meriramesses and Lady Wurusemu more resembled a state event. Well, maybe that was a trifle extreme. The spread they provided stopped just short of a feast, yet was opulent enough to let the guests — especially me, I think — know their hosts were rich and powerful people. As if I needed reminding.

The meal was served in the large hall that acted as a common area for the two brothers' separate apartments. I was led in by Yuni and found the room was already occupied by elegantly dressed people. I recognized several nobles and estate owners I'd encountered on my Opet request circuit. Servants already threaded through the guests filling wine cups from large pitchers. The room was a mass of flowers with an area set up to one side for musicians. There was a dais at the top of the room with three massive throne-like seats and one smaller. For the Royal Family, no doubt. I was a bit surprised, since I'd gotten the impression from Prince Meriramesses that this would be a family dinner. I suppose I shouldn't have been. See prior statement about "rich and powerful people".

Yuni led me across the room amid a flurry of nods and murmured greetings to an ebony chair with blue and red faience inlay, gold fittings and a tasseled cushion. A blue, lotus-shaped cup was put into my hand by a servant and filled with a rich-smelling red wine by another. I didn't sample the drink right away, though. I was sort of worried about Neffi. As soon as we entered the house, he wanted to be picked up. After we entered the dining area, he hopped down, sat plunk under my seat, refusing to budge. He was never like that, especially where food was involved.

I was busy staring at the large, immovable, spotted object when someone scooted a chair over beside mine. It was Prince Amunhotep. He already smelled of wine, but his movement wasn't impaired, nor was his speech slurred.

He peered at Neffi, concern on his face. "Aw, the poor little guy. Is he scared?" Before I could stop him, he plunged a beefy paw under. "Hey, little fella. It's okay."

I winced, expecting to hear a yelp and rending flesh. Instead, I heard a loud purr. Neffi had his eyes closed, leaning into the prince's scratches. After a moment, I managed, "Not so much scared as worried about being stepped on, I think. Ummmm, Your Highness." I added hurriedly.

Prince Amunhotep flopped back into his seat and scanned

the rapidly filling room. "Yeah, I can see that. There's an awful lot of feet in here. Some of those sandals look downright dangerous, too."

"No disrespect, Your Highness, but aren't you supposed to be up there? On the dais."

He leaned back, regarding the platform, hummed a little, then turned his back on the four empty chairs. He resumed petting Neffi. "Naaah. Why would I want to be up there? Those guys are no fun."

The prince's attention was suddenly elsewhere. Grinning, he stood and called out, "Ban! Over here!"

I swiveled in my seat and saw Banufre looking freshly-scrubbed and uncomfortable standing in the doorway with Yuni. The butler was directing the boy to the back of the room — the cheap seats, as it were. Before they were more than a few steps in, Amunhotep closed the distance and, engulfing the young man in a bear hug, shunted the Chief Butler back to his post. "I got this, Yuni."

The head servant was not pleased. Banufre was, however. Trying to stifle laughter, he let himself be swept toward where Neffi and I waited.

"Glad your parents let you come, Ban," Prince Amunhotep said.

"Oh, yeah. Like they'd refuse an invitation from you and your brother," Banufre answered, shooting a glance over his shoulder at the irritated butler. "Yuni looks ready to chew scorpions."

"Ah, he'll live. Anyway, it's more my brother than me tonight, but it should still be fun. I hear he trotted out some of the really good wine. Think he's trying to impress someone." Prince Amunhotep swatted me on the arm. It nearly knocked me onto the floor.

A bit of a commotion started in the direction of the dais. We turned as one to see Prince Meriramesses with Lady Wurusemu on his arm entering from the private quarters. The guests bowed and called out to the couple who smiled and nodded in acknowledgment. They were elegantly dressed in fine, embroidered linen; their heavy wigs were surmounted with perfume cones; fine gold jewelry gleamed in the lamplight. Behind them, apparently trying to be as invisible as possible, Princess Iaret slipped in. Her face was hidden in shadow under her court-style wig, but she looked like she'd rather be any place but up on that platform. She quietly took her seat, shook her head at a servant's offer of wine and became very interested in her bangles.

Amunhotep muttered something I couldn't make out over the background noise, but the look on his face would have fitted finding a dead bug floating in his drink. After a moment, a broad smile spread across his face, and he stood, hoisting his wine cup into the air. "Brother! Sister! Guests! Welcome! Let's get this party started!"

The expressions on Meriramsses' and Wurusemu's faces froze for an instant as their eyes locked on Amunhotep. I'm not sure they'd known he was present until then. Nothing happened for a moment, then Meriramesses forced a gracious smile. "My brother is correct. My guests, I extend you welcome to my home." He clapped twice. "Yuni! Call the musicians and tell the servants to begin."

As his brother and sister-in-law took their seats, Amunhotep waggled his fingers at his niece. I still couldn't see her face well, but it certainly looked like her shoulders quaked with what might have been suppressed laughter.

The meal was sumptuous, rich, and the beef, as promised, was excellent. There was an incredible variety offered; far more than I'd seen up to that time. Still, if push came to shove, I'd choose the simple fare from the earlier luncheon Banufre's parents provided any day. Sometimes "sumptuous and rich" merely equates to overdone. Throughout the meal,

Banufre, Amunhotep and I chatted about a wide range of subjects and the evening passed more quickly than I realized. The Prince insisted on being called Amuny, but I couldn't bring myself to do that, yet, so I simply dropped the prince part. That seemed to make him happy.

During the meal, Neffi never left his post under my chair. Banufre and I casually dropped tidbits. They were snagged and disappeared before they hit the floor. Prince Amunhotep, on the other hand, had not been so casual. He seemed determined to make friends with "the Magic Cat". Considering the choice bits of beef and fowl he was presenting as bribes, he was making great progress.

As I noted, Amunhotep had already been drinking before the gathering, but he hadn't seemed tipsy. However, as he downed cup after cup of the strong estate wine, he was getting there. As he became more boisterous, Prince Meriramesses shot dark looks in our direction. His glares were benign, though, compared to those of the exotically beautiful Lady Wurusemu. Those chilled my blood — and I wasn't even the target.

The party was winding down when Prince Meriramesses called for the list of offerings for his father's festival to be brought out. Yuni did so and made a show of presenting me with a very long piece of papyrus with an equally long list of items on it. The ostentation was, no doubt, to let all present know how generous they had been, but it mattered little. Skimming down the list, I had to admit they had been extremely generous. I turned toward the dais, bowed deeply and made a brief speech of thanks on behalf of my masters and myself. I made it through the oration without a slip. Good thing I'd only sipped at the rich wines. They were strong vintages and, if I'd imbibed more deeply, the thank you speech would probably have been gibberish.

Still, I'd had enough wine and rich food to make me grateful to drop my backside into the seat again. Even Neffi was curled up, half-asleep.

Amunhotep, who was weaving more than a little by then, leaned over and said, "Huti, I've taken the liberty of having a room readied for you on my side of the house."

"Thank you, Your Highness, but—"

"Amuny," he corrected again. He belched and waved a finger in my face. "What kind of host would allow a guest to travel all the way back to the city this late?"

Banufre, who had drunk a bit more deeply than me, said with exaggerated gravity, "Your brother's doin' it."

"Exacty!" Amunhotep said and waved a hovering servant over.

~*~

The house servant led me through the quiet halls of the private quarters with a salt-lamp held high to illuminate the way. Neffi, still half-asleep, weighed heavily on my shoulders. Our march stopped at a set of tall, wooden doors, painted blue with bronze latches.

The servant bowed and swept a hand toward the doors. "Your quarters, Scribe. I am Dedi. If you need anything, I will not be far away. Simply send the boy."

I wondered about this until I entered the room. Renen was already there, sitting on the scroll case that was now packed with replies from landowners, tucking into leftovers from the dinner. He greeted me happily and unintelligibly around a mouthful of bread.

I dropped Neffi onto the floor and held up the rolled papyrus. "Our last Opet list. Tomorrow, we return to the temple."

Renen swallowed his bread and looked a little disappointed. "I guess so."

I knew how he felt. The last few days had been dusty and hot, but still more fun than taking dictation or grinding pigments. I shoved those thoughts aside and looked the room over. It was one room, but bigger than some houses I'd seen. There were several chairs, a bed and a tall chest with drawers against the wall by the door. Several bronze floor lamps burned, shedding soft light and the faint, pleasantly exotic scent of olive oil.

"Pretty nice, huh?" said Renen. "They even gave me my own sleeping mat!" He pointed happily to a linen-cased cushion at the foot of the big bed.

I nodded. "Certainly nicer than anything I've seen."

Neffi had been snuffling around the room. He stopped at the far wall, critically examined the row of high windows, then stretched and sauntered back to us. Without so much as a yawn, he hopped onto the bed, curled up in the middle and went to sleep.

TWELVE

The next morning, we returned to the temple of Bastet in Memphis. I was surprised to find all my things had been moved to a private room. I'm not sure exactly why I was. With all the other Pi-Ramesses people gone, it would have been silly to have me rattling around by myself in the now-empty dormitory. Ta welcomed us back and seemed genuinely glad to see me. I was pretty glad to see him, too. The time on the road had been wearying and, even though the food and rooms at the mansion were sumptuous, what the temple offered felt more like home. There was also the fact that I wasn't walking and covered with dust. That was a *very* good thing.

I considered taking a day off, but no matter how enticing it sounded, I couldn't do it. My scribbled notes and the landowners' lists had to be turned into a legible, accurate accounting to be sent back with the original offering lists. Lieutenant Si-Montu had promised to return in five to six days. We'd been two days on the road — three, if you counted the stopover at the manor house and the journey back to the temple. There was also the small matter of the report for General Seti-Merenptah. Those scribbled notes detailing everything I learned at Ma'aheru's and Amuhotep's estates also needed to be transcribed into something more legible. The Medjay's schedule didn't leave me a lot of time to write out all the formal reports and get them into the proper hands. A day off would just have to wait.

I looked at my notes for General Seti-Merenptah, then at the ones for the Opet offerings lying beside the landowner's lists

I had to tally. There was no contest. I took the easy way out and wrote the General's report first. Once I had it safely in the hands of the young priest who acted as messenger, I'd come back and start the count.

I riffled through the stacks of papyrus filling the chest on the floor beside me. Maybe I'd get the report to the messenger, then have a nice lunch. Yes. That sounded better.

By noon the next day, most of the Opet lists had been tallied onto a master sheet. That master sheet looked like there'd been a cat fight on top of it, but that wasn't important. I was a few sheets away from my final entry, then I'd double check my counts and write it all out in a neater, final form. I had dipped my pen again when Neffi, who had been sleeping beside me, raised his head and chirped just before someone tapped on the door. I was a bit surprised anyone bothered to tap since the door was standing open to allow a cross breeze. I was even more surprised to see Master Ta standing there.

"My apologies for interrupting your work for the Great House, Sitehuti."

I tried to rise and bow, but my legs were too stiff from sitting to do a convincing job of it. I groaned, "Oh, please! Interrupt away, Master Ta!"

He laughed a little and stepped in, waving me back down. "Please stay seated. I know how it is after working for long periods at a stretch." He sobered and added, "I would like to discuss the boy, Renen."

"Oh, no. What's he done?"

The head scribe laughed again. It was a pleasant laugh. He seemed to have recovered his jovial nature with the exit of Master Userhet. "Don't worry. He's done nothing more than become attached to you. I'd like to send him to the capital with you when you return there."

This was unexpected and I could dredge up no words in response.

Master Ta continued, "The estate overseer has no objection to this and neither do I. The boy could do a lot worse than to go to Pi-Ramesses."

"But . . . I'm just a junior scribe. There's no way I can afford to keep a servant. I don't even have my own house."

"We're well aware of that, Sitehuti, but we're also well aware that the young scribe with the magic cat is going to go places. Later, when you can afford a servant, Renen might as well be it. He already considers himself as such."

I mulled it over. I liked the boy and we did get along well. I said, "But who knows how long that will be? What will he do until then?"

"Perhaps a letter to the overseer of the temple in Pi-Rameses could guarantee him a job within the temple? Until such time as you can take him on yourself, of course. I have every confidence that will be sooner than you think."

I was still doing a suffocating fish imitation when there came another tap. This time, it was one of the door porters. "I have a message for Sitehuti of Western Thebes," he said. "It's from Prince Amunhotep."

Ta was amused and didn't try to hide it. "See, young man? You're already moving up in this world."

I wasn't so sure, but I thanked the porter and glanced over the message. From the scrawl and blots, I wondered if Amunhotep had penned it himself. It was an invitation to an outing in the old necropolis of Saqqara with Prince Amunhotep and his gang. He also invited me and my servant to stay for a few days at the mansion. I was torn. I always wanted to see the old necropolis, but there were those Opet lists. . . .

Ta came to look over my shoulder. "Oh! It's direct from

the prince himself. You must go. It's not a good idea to refuse a member of the Royal House."

I gestured helplessly toward the piles of papyrus. "But, I also have to finish this! This is for the Royal House, too."

The head scribe came around and sat next to me, taking the tally from my lap. "Then, I can finish for you. No one will care as long as it is done properly. I'll attach both our names to it so there can be no confusion later. Now, show me where you are."

~*~

Soon after Master Ta had collected all the Opet documents and headed off to his workshop, I heard footsteps pelting my way. Using the doorframe as a pivot, a breathless Renen swung himself into the room.

"The porter said we're invited to the princes' mansion again!" he gasped.

Neffi sauntered over and twined around the boy's legs, purring mightily. Looked like I had a servant — at least for the foreseeable future.

"Yes, we have—"

"Yes!" Renen hissed, punching the air. He hurried forward, snagging clothing as he went. "I gotta get you packed!"

"All right, but make sure you have your own things together first."

He stopped and looked a little uncomfortable. "I don't really have anything to pack."

Before I could respond to that, Banufre poked his head in. "Huti! I'm here to take you to the estate. I got my chariot outside — oh, and porters for the luggage, too.

I'm not certain when we started calling each other by our diminutives, but somewhere along the line it happened. It felt like we'd been friends for a lot longer than a few days. I gaped at Ban. "Chariot?"

Ban laughed. "You wanted to walk all the way out there? The invitation was for this afternoon, not tomorrow. Besides, you're lucky it's me and my old rattletrap. Amuny wanted to come himself, but I talked him out of it."

"That sounds ominous."

There was a wicked tinge to Ban's smile. "Simply delaying the inevitable. You'll have to ride with him later, so I figured we might want to get Neffi used to riding before then. Ease him into it."

I wondered who was going to ease *me* into it.

When the horse first jolted into movement, Neffi startled and grabbed on to me. I managed to disengage his claws after the horse's gait smoothed out. After that, the cat started to enjoy it, turning his face into the wind, eyes half-closed with pleasure. It was amazing how much the chariot shortened travel time even if I was hanging onto the rail most of the way. As we approached the princes' estate, we could see Amunhotep and his friends gearing up just outside the gates. They cheered when they spotted us approaching.

Prince Amunhotep greeted us with a shout and a bear hug that engulfed both Ban and myself. Neffi, in his sling against my chest protested loudly, which caused the prince to release us amid profuse apologies.

"Oh! I'm sorry I squished you, little guy," he said, scratching the top of the cat's head. "I just get carried away with my friends."

He stepped up into his chariot and secured the reins around his waist. "Okay, Huti, you and Neffi stand here on my right. Ban, you take the left and it ought to balance out nicely."

I stared for a moment, then whispered to Ban, "Why can't we take yours?"

146

Ban whispered back, "Because Nedjem wants to tinker with it while we're out. He thinks he knows a way to get more speed out of it."

I stared open-mouthed.

Ban nodded. "Yeah. My feelings exactly."

"All right, everybody! Pile in!" Amunhotep shouted over the chatter of the group. "This is going to be a *great* day!"

Ban and I stepped up onto the springy floor. Prince Amunhotep showed me how to stand to maintain my balance at speed, and made sure Neffi was secure. When he was satisfied we were set, he called out. "To the necropolis! Last one there buys the wine!"

Without further warning, he cracked his whip and his matched pair of grays took off, the colorful plumes that adorned their harness whipping in the wind. Once again, Neffi added to my scratch collection, but just like earlier, relaxed when the gait smoothed out, lifting his head into the wind.

I have never moved so fast in my life. It seemed like I barely blinked and we were at the ferry crossing to the old necropolis. Amunhotep and his friends were antsy to get moving again on the ride over. Banufre and I savored it. Neffi did, too — but then again he always loved boats. He wriggled free of his sling to perch on the railing and look directly down into the water.

Once we were on dry land, the speed-fest began anew. I barely had time to tuck Neffi in again before the prince and his friends exploded off the barge and hared toward the ancient burial grounds. We did a circuit of the site at top speed, barreled along the Avenue of the Sphinxes, then veered over to pull up in front of the causeway leading to the funerary complex of Unas.

Two other drivers were neck-and-neck with Amunhotep for first place. There was a tie for last place, too, and a disagreement broke out over just who would have to buy the wine.

Nedjem had caught up with us at the ferry. I'm not sure what he could have done to the vehicle in that short a time, but then again, I knew less than nothing about chariots. The nobleman hopped out and circled the cart, seeming pleased. Next, he dropped to the ground to peer at the underside, then hailed Ban to join him.

I stepped out after Ban and almost fell over. My legs weren't ready for something that wasn't hurtling along at a break-neck pace, yet. Neffi didn't seem to have the same problem. He squirmed out of the sling and sauntered over to investigate the edge of the lake spanned by the causeway.

"Impressive, isn't it?" Amuny said dusting his hands against his linen shirt.

"It is. Isn't this one of the monuments your brother Khamwese restored?"

"Heh. Khamwese," Amunhotep said, shaking his head. "You want to talk impressive. There you are."

"Sir?"

He smiled, remembering. "My brother was a brilliant man. I always felt dumber than a mud brick when I tried to talk to him. Couldn't hate him, though. Too nice a guy."

I wondered if Amunhotep could hate anybody. I'd met agreeable people before, but the prince seemed to be the most unflappably pleasant individual ever. I said, "Were you two close?"

"No, not really. I was in Pi-Ramesses during part of the time he was crown prince, but I've never interacted much with that side of the family. The *real* royals, I mean. Still, when I did meet with him, I liked him."

I grinned. "I hate to be the one to point it out, but you're kind of royal yourself."

"Nah. Not really. Mother was a concubine, and not one of the highest-ranking ones. Now, wealthy? Yes. My birth has given me that. Privilege? Yep. That, too, but there's a big gap between me and the throne. There'd have to be a lot of weird shit — and probably some divine intervention — before either Meriramesses or myself could ascend to the throne."

He bent down and said in a stage whisper, "But don't tell my brother that. You'd ruin his day." He gave me a swat on the shoulder. "Come on. Ban said you wanted to see the old burial grounds, so let's have a look-around."

With that, he sauntered off over the causeway toward the pyramid of Unas. I had to hurry to keep up.

Saqqara was in various states of repair and disrepair. There was a great deal of building and restoration going on throughout the necropolis, all of it bearing the stamp of the divine Ramesses. We had moved on from Unas' complex when Banufre finally caught up with us. It probably hadn't been hard to track our path. If Prince Amunhotep hadn't been recognized and given VIP treatment, then someone (usually a priest) realized Neffi was a sacred cat and we got VIP treatment by association. Asking if anyone had seen a man and a boy with a big cat would have pointed him in the right direction.

We also became a magnet for vendors and other tourists. The women seemed to especially like Neffi. At one point, we had several vendors, a couple temple singers and a bevy of lady tourists all making over him — and me by default as the scribe the cat had adopted. Amunhotep thought it was hilarious.

We extricated ourselves, bought water and cones of dates all around, then trudged off to take in the Serapeum. All along the way I munched dates, admired the restorations and the colossal figures of the divine Ramesses and wondered what it must be like to be a member of a family with that kind of legacy. One that would stand long after we were gone. I confess I'd let the conversation between Ban and Amunhotep become a pleasant background buzz until:

"So you're from the Place of Truth?"

Amunhotep's question broke me out of my thoughts. "Yes, sir, I am."

He gave me a playful swat on the back that nearly took me off my feet. "How often do I have to tell you, Huti? You get to call me Amuny."

"All right, Amuny," I said, "but I don't think I'll ever get used to it."

"Awwww, sure you will," he said. "Anyway, I saw the family House of Eternity a few months ago. All those chambers and all those rooms! What the workmen have achieved is amazing."

He got my pride, there. My family was large and had been at the Place of Truth for a long time. "Thank you, s— Amuny. I have family members on both the left and right teams and my father is one of the chief painters. They'll be pleased to hear that."

"Both teams? Do you know who the chief stonecutter is? That representation of my father as Osiris in the T intersection of the main corridors is very well done. Scared the crap out of me when I came up on it with that teeny lamp they give you."

I thought for a bit. "My cousin is a stonecutter, but not the chief stonecutter. I believe that's a man named Nebamun. I'm afraid I've been away from the village too long to know him."

A few tourists came up to pet the sacred cat and give him tidbits from their lunches. The sacred cat was making out like a tomb robber.

Ban asked, "What were you doing in the House of Eternity, Amuny?"

The big man shrugged. "I may not be as royal as some of my siblings, but there are still a couple rooms set aside for me. I was taking a chest of ushabtis and other items in there. Can't hurt to be ready."

Both Ban and I pooh-poohed him. I said, "I'm sure it'll be a while before you have to worry about needing that."

He shrugged again. Like everything else about him, the shrug was big. "That's what my brothers and sisters probably thought, too. There's already a crowd of them in there."

A woman at a pastry stall Ooooooed and pointed at us. She came around with a small handful of dumpling filling. She asked, "Is it all right if I give this to the Sacred One?"

"Sure," I said.

She extended her hand and crouched down, making her skirts pull tight against her backside. Neffi sniffed suspiciously at the meat, then deigned to nibble at it. The girl giggled.

Amuny, on the other hand, scooted around until he had a real good view of the tight skirt. When the girl gave Neffi a final pet and sashayed back to the booth, Amuny followed her with his eyes. At length he sighed. "I hope I can have a cat like Neffi in the Land to the West. Now *that* would make for a pleasant afterlife."

I gave in to a laugh. "I'm sure you can, Amuny."

We continued on to the Serapeum, but we never actually made it there. The day at the necropolis had started off as a good one, but, as usual, it wasn't destined to stay that way. Well, I suppose it could be called good in one respect: I finally found Khety, the missing scribe.

~*~

We were passing through one of the areas the food vendors had claimed for their own, when a group of temple singers spotted us. The women hurried over, fluttering and twittering around us like a flock of birds, first exclaiming over Neffi, then over the prince. Ban and I were more or less being ignored.

Before long, a group of workmen who'd been taking a break at a stall selling savory soups and flatbread, wandered over to see what the fuss was.

One of them said, "Oh. It's just a cat."

One of the singers stood ramrod straight. Looking down her elegant nose, she said, "Not just any cat. This is a sacred cat, or are you too blind to see that?"

Another workman standing behind the first, caught sight of my writing kit. There was a bit of whispering back and forth, then he asked me, "Hey, Scribe, is that cat yours?"

"Uhh. Yeah, he is."

"You're from the capital, ain't ya?" He didn't wait for me to answer, but turned to his mates and said, "Yeah, this is the guy that priest was talking about."

The singer who'd spoken before flashed recognition. "Oh! You're the one sent to hunt down that rogue Lector. Everyone at the temple was talking about it." She eyed me critically. "You look a little young for a policeman."

"No, that's just a stupid rumor!" I was waving my hands, but no one was paying attention to me. "I was never sent here to look for the Lector. Really!"

Ban spoke up, "He's telling the truth. He's only trying to find out what happened to that scribe who went missing from the temple of Ptah in Memphis."

I stopped cold. I had never actually *told* Banufre what I was there to do. I'd only meant to reassure him I wasn't in Memphis to capture his brother and punish his family. He was an intelligent person. He'd put all my little comments together and come up with a direct hit. While I was kicking myself for being too free with my information, I glanced at the workmen again. They were shooting odd looks at each other and were a lot more nervous than a few moments ago.

I said, "Wait a minute. Do you guys know something about that? About a missing scribe?"

They shuffled and paid an inordinate amount of attention to their feet.

The exchange had caught Amuny's attention. He stood to his full height and said pointedly, "The scribe asked you a question."

The workmen glanced nervously at one man in particular, possibly their foreman. That man's eyes flicked from me to Prince Amunhotep and back to me again. "Well . . . not exactly."

Amuny took a step forward. "Well, *what* exactly?"

The one who seemed to have been elected spokesman cleared his throat. "A few weeks back, some of us guys went to a beer house after we knocked off work. There was this foreigner there who was all over tattoos. He was drunk and bragging to the whole house about the powerful friends he had. How he'd done all kinds of favors and jobs for them."

The description sparked a memory. I prompted, "Was his name Jiji?"

"Don't rightly remember, but it was something like that," the workman said. "Something short. More nickname than real name. He was trying to be all mysterious-like, but he was drunk."

"And stupid," added a voice from the back.

"Right, that, too," The spokesman agreed. "One of the stories he told us was about some nosy scribe who got himself into trouble. He and his pals grabbed the guy as he was coming out of his house. Brought him out here and worked him over. Said he kept using the name of the Pharaoh like His Majesty was going to protect him." The man paused and looked even more nervous. In a near whisper, he finished, "He said the scribe ought to be happy, because the Divine Ramesses will watch over him forever, now."

I was stunned beyond words for a few heartbeats. Finally, I managed to squeak, "He *said* this?"

One of the singers blurted out, "You went to the necropolis police with this, right?"

The workmen squirmed as one. "Well, no . . . I mean . . . this guy — well you had to have seen him. Half of us thought he was out of his head."

"And the other half?" asked the Prince.

"Bought him more beer."

There was laughter all around. Amuny, especially, found it funny. The singers weren't amused in the slightest. Neither were Banufre and I.

I was still trying to jolt my mind back on track when Ban gripped my shoulder and said, "We have to look, don't we?"

He was right. After we got his attention and explained what we needed, Prince Amunhotep led the way to the office of the captain of the necropolis guard. We were joined by the singers and part of the workmen. We must have been an interesting procession.

Just as in the Place of Truth, where the kings of today made their Houses of Eternity, the guards at the old necropolis were almost all Medjay. The captain was a big Nubian who reminded me a lot of Captain Djedmose back in Pi-Ramesses. The one who had dragged me out of school to talk with the crown prince. He looked about as happy, too. Maybe it was a Medjay thing.

The captain's name was Min-iniuy and he had little patience for us. He waved his hand dismissively and said, "Don't give me rumors. If I listened to every rumor of someone burying a body here illicitly, I'd spend most of my time digging up the sand."

This made Amunhotep angry. It was a kind of impressive sight — especially since it was so rare. He leaned forward and brought his face within inches of the Medjay's. "Captain, I find it hard to believe you don't recognize me."

The officer flinched ever so slightly and bowed. "Of course I recognize you, Your Highness."

"And you have no doubt heard about the scribe with the sacred cat?"

"Yes, Your Highness."

"I'd say our information points to the missing man being buried near a statue of my father. What do *you* think, Captain?"

Prince Amunhotep said nothing else. He just waited.

"Well, if you insist on digging around, at least I can keep you from causing too much damage," Captain Min-iniuy said. Then he turned and shouted to his men, who had been hovering in the background, "You lot! Don't just stand there looking stupid. Fetch some gear and accompany His Highness and the scribe on their search."

Before long, we were back outside, trailed by two unhappy Medjay armed with shovels.

~*~

I hadn't realized just how many images of the Divine Pharaoh Rameses II there were on the ancient grounds. We were at it for a long time. As the day wore on, the Medjay were shooting me mutinous glares. We'd lost all the workmen and most of the singers before we approached a line of seated figures along a wall. Muttering curses, the soldiers started digging at the base of the first statue in the line. Neffi, who had been riding on my shoulders with great disinterest, suddenly perked up, hopped down and started sniffing at the base of the wall near one of the middle sculptures.

He suddenly lifted his head and unleashed an unearthly, "WOWOWOWOW" and dug, throwing sand everywhere.

I grabbed him up, ignoring a louder "WOWOWOWOWOWOW" right beside my ear. Without being told, the Medjay left their hole and dug where the cat had started howling. In a matter of minutes, the shovel

155

pulled up an embroidered linen stole. A few more and we were looking down on the naturally mummified remains of Khety, Scribe of the temple of Ptah.

THIRTEEN

Later that evening, Neffi and I sat in a pavilion that hadn't been there the last time we'd visited the estate. It was built of imported cedar wood, held together by pegs and lit by braziers that also kept the night chill at bay. The structure stood beside the pond, putting it even closer to Ma'aheru's property line than the picnic had been. It probably sounded like the revelers were right outside their windows. Torches dotted the surrounding lawn and the water's edge. People moved in and out of the pools of light like a vision in some sort of fantastic dream.

As the ostensible guest of honor, I'd been enthroned in a beautiful folding chair. Neffi stationed himself underneath just as he had at the formal dinner — what was it? Only three? Four days before? So much had happened, it seemed like the distant past.

A full-scale celebration raved around us. In theory, the reason for the party was to congratulate me on having found Khety, but I didn't feel very celebratory. Yes, we'd solved the mystery of the scribe's disappearance, but a man was dead. A woman was now a widow and two boys were fatherless.

I was a little surprised that Prince Meriramesses was also there, seated next to his brother at the back of the pavilion. He didn't seem to be enjoying himself, though. He sat stone-faced and silent throughout. The exotic Lady Wurusemu was nowhere to be seen. That didn't surprise me. No raised dais here, just rugs spread out on the ground under a portable pavilion. The food wasn't fancy, either. It was much simpler fare: fruit, roasted meats, bread and very few things with sauces. Either Amuny or the cooks didn't see a need for elaborate dishes. Probably a good choice since most of the guests were more interested in the wine than the food.

There was no order to anything. That must have been driving Meriramesses mad. Men and women seemed to sit where they wanted. People perched on stools, reclined on couches or on the lawn itself. I recognized many of the same faces from the picnic and several from the later formal dinner.

All night long, people tried to coax Neffi out from under the chair, but he wasn't leaving. He wouldn't even budge when a dancing girl and a trio of acrobats tried to lure him with a slice of roasted goose. He didn't growl or anything, he just stayed put. Finally, he accepted the meat, and let the women reach under to stroke him, but oozed from their grasp when they tried to pull him out. Not that he was lacking for food. I slipped him tidbits, and he'd even been provided with his own water bowl.

After the impromptu dinner, when the drinking began in earnest, Meriramesses conspicuously excused himself and returned to the house.

As the stiff-backed prince vanished into the night, a noble seated on the floor beside me muttered into his cup. "Well, there goes Prince Better-Than-The-Rest-Of-You."

Another elbowed him and said, "What are you muttering about, Khems? Meri stomping off to his lair means the party can really get started."

There was a burst of laughter that probably reached the departing prince. He was doubtless used to it. This seemed like a regular occurrence.

Khems sat back against his cushion. "I know. He just irks me." He swept his near-empty wine cup to take in the crowd. "A bunch of us are also of the Divine Ramesses' blood. Same damn family, so what makes *him* so much better than the rest of us?"

A noblewoman said, "Not better, Khems. Just too tight-assed to know what he's missing."

There was more laughter and many toasts to Hatu, who I assumed was the noblewoman who had spoken.

About then, Neffi surprised me by emerging from his safe place under the chair and jumping into my lap. He stretched out along my legs, kneading the air with his huge paws on either side of my knees. Soon, though, he resumed his favorite perch: across my shoulders. This attracted the dancer and acrobats again. This, in turn, attracted a couple of the musicians who all gathered around to make over the "Magic Cat".

Amuny roared with laughter and sloshed his wine saluting us. "That settles it once and for all. I have *got* to get me a cat!"

Little by little, more people took their leave. Most had things to do in a morning that was getting too close for comfort.

All night long, servants had circulated, refilling cups, helping revelers to relieve themselves and clean up after. As for me, the vintage was excellent, but it was very rich — and strong. I nursed a couple cups interspersed with beakers of fruit juice and was glad I'd eaten beforehand. It wouldn't have taken much of that wine to give me a real buzz. I watched the quantities imbibed by the nobles around me with growing amazement. If I'd drunk half as much as them, I'd have been comatose.

A voice behind me said, "Nefer-Djenou-Bastet has the right idea, Sitehuti. Stay off the floor and seek the high ground to observe."

The voice was familiar. It was General Seti-Merenptah, smiling down at me and stroking Neffi. Neffi arched his head into the soldier's hand.

"Sir!" I started to rise, but the petting hand rested briefly on my arm, holding me in place.

"No, Sitehuti, stay seated. This party is in your honor after all."

I couldn't stop the chuckle. "More like I'm the *excuse* for the party."

Seti-Merenptah's smile widened. "Too true. My father said you were observant."

The General looked out over the people-covered lawn. "Perhaps a party isn't your style — it isn't exactly mine either, but you *do* deserve congratulations for finding the missing scribe. It's a pity he wasn't found alive, but the medical men who have examined him tell me he was likely killed the same day he was taken. That fits with the story the foreigner told."

Again I was saddened that we couldn't have helped Khety. I said, "It's a small consolation, but at least his wife can give him a proper burial now. That's what she wanted most."

"And I guarantee it will happen. The Great House of Ramesses will furnish anything that is needed for his afterlife." He added, "I've been watching your moderation tonight. Very wise."

"I'm not used to this kind of thing, sir."

Seti-Merenptah's eyes slid to his uncle. "Few of us are." He bent on the pretext of picking Neffi up. The general's breath brushed my ear as he whispered, "Keep your wits about you, boy. My father thinks there's something very wrong here at my uncles' house. I believe him to be correct."

The soldier stood and made over the big cat. Neffi allowed it for a moment, then squirmed away, hopped to the floor, then was back in my lap.

"I'll bid you good night, Scribe," Seti-Merenptah said, then strode past the braziers and into the darkness beyond.

~*~

As the evening wore on, people sifted in and out until it distilled down to Amuny and his core group of friends. Most of those had been on the chariot run to Saqqara. I'd had a final cup and felt both the wine and the late hour. Neffi sprawled across my lap, sound asleep. I envied him. I was having a hard time keeping my own eyes open.

The notion of slipping away to bed was becoming ever more appealing when the nobleman, Khems, now red-faced with drink, crouched beside me. "Okay, Huti, it's just us now. What really happened in Pi-Ramesses? You can tell *us*."

I said, "What?" Give me a break, it was late and the question took me by surprise.

Khems said, "I mean with that damned moron, Paseti. What'd he really do?"

Laughter rippled through the group. Someone called, "C'mon, Khems, don't hide how you feel. Let it all out!"

I sat gaping. Amuny apparently mistook my dumbfounded silence for reticence to insult his boyhood friend. Voice slurred, he said, "Don't worry, Huti, no feelings will be hurt here." He drained his cup, then looked into it as if puzzled about where the wine had gone. "I mean, Paseti was always more my brother's friend than mine. Both him and that hobnail-booted brother of his, Sasobek. Maybe the prudes have to band together or something, I don't know, but it's never been a secret they don't think much of me, either. Mind you, I don't hold any of that against Banufre. Ban's a good kid."

This last statement was greeted with a chorus of "Hear, hear!" and "He sure is!" plus one of "Hey! Where *is* Ban?"

Someone else called out, "Bet his father wouldn't let him out tonight."

That was met with calls of disapproval until Khems said, "Aw! Shut up, guys. Huti, here, is the fella the high muckety mucks in the capital sent to track Paseti down. He knows what really happened."

Someone else shouted, "Of course, doofus. Didn't you see the cat?"

I was still nonplussed at the lack of discretion among this group, but the mention of Nefer-Djenou-Bastet sent them careening down a different path. Well . . . sort of different.

Hatu roused and propped herself up on an elbow. Her wig was so far down over her eyes, I wondered if she could even see. "Sure! Everybody knows that Huti and Neffi chased that idiot Paseti right out of the temple. Heard about it myself just yesterday . . . or something."

The group made noises of approval. Another noble as red-faced as Khems leaned in. "Right outta th' temple, huh? I'da given a lot to see that! Well . . . whudddedo? I mean th' prick, not th' cat."

My mind was spinning and I cursed even the small amount of the powerful wine I'd had. I didn't have to worry, though. Prince Amunhotep stepped into the breach.

"He whacked my brother-in-law's slave on the head and took some letter away from him," Amuny said.

"No!"

"Yeah, really!" he slurred.

All attention focused on the prince. Hatu asked, "Which brother-in-law? Oh wait! It was Ol' Padi. High Priest at the temple where Huti got the magic cat."

"Paseti's such a stupid bastard was prolly Ol' Padi's laundry list." Khems said.

Hatu laughed, "Well, Paseti always did want to know how his betters lived."

There was a burst of raucous laughter. Then someone else shouted, "Naaaah. Not a laundry list! Love letter to his mistress."

"Mistress?" Amuny snorted. "Have you met Pedibastet?"

Waves of laughter washed around the pavilion as the suggestions of what was in the letter got wilder and bawdier. Neffi and I were thankfully forgotten in a fresh round of drinks and off-color jokes. I waited until another round had been absorbed, then put Neffi on the floor and stood. Nobody noticed.

We slipped out of the smoky pavilion into the cool night. I stood, sucking in great lungfuls of the crisp, fresh air, hoping my head would clear. No luck. Between the late hour and the last cup of wine, I was just about gone.

Once my eyes adjusted to the light of the stars and near-full moon, we plodded back to the house. For once, Neffi had the decency to walk beside me instead of demanding to be carried. I was so tired, I wouldn't have been able to keep my balance with his weight on my shoulders. The journey back to the mansion became a soft, gray meander until Neffi growled and hissed. That woke me up fast. I searched the ground at my feet and finally found him a short distance ahead of me, crouched in the middle of the path, ears back and tail lashing. His gaze was fixed on something ahead of us near the house.

Neffi growled again, a rough low sound that I recognized at once. It was the warning he gave when he saw someone he didn't like. I dodged back into the plantings, looking frantically for the last person who had triggered that growl: Jiji, the tattooed foreigner.

There was no sign of the sailor. Instead I saw a well-dressed and wigged Egyptian man disappearing through a doorway into the mansion. Another of Amuny's guests? Probably not. I didn't recognize the man's robes and I'd definitely have recognized the counterpoise of his pectoral if I'd seen it before. It was an elaborate gold and enamel piece shaped like a pair of geese. It must have cost a fortune.

By the time we reached the entrance, there was no sign of the man, but Neffi stopped to sniff open-mouthed at the door frame. He sniffed and huffed until I finally had grab him and carry him up the stairs to our rooms.

Yes. I said rooms plural. Instead of putting us in the huge space that passed for a room we'd stayed in before, Amunhotep had put us in a private apartment near his own digs. We even had a sitting room with a balcony overlooking the gardens. I was going to have *so* much trouble going back to sharing a room with my cousin, Ahmose, over my aunt's linen shop.

Renen was already dead to the world on his mat beside the big carved bed. Too tired to be neat, I shucked out of my clothing and left them draped across the top of a stool. Neffi had taken up his usual spot in the exact center of the bed. I shoved him aside, climbed in and collapsed against the soft mattress.

FOURTEEN

I've always been an early riser. It's partly nature and partly habit. I grew up in the Place of Truth where the workmen were up and out to work on the tombs before first light. For the last ten years, give or take, sunrise saw me already in my scribal master's school working on lessons. So, when I got dressed, corralled Neffi and headed down to the loggia for breakfast, I was a little surprised to find that Prince Meriramesses and Lady Wurusemu had already been and gone. That suited me fine. I hadn't been looking forward to making small talk with them, anyway. Meriramesses had this way of looking at me that made me think he was waiting for me to slip up so he could pounce on the mistake. Lady Wurusemu gave me the same impression, only I'd put her down for flogging over an upbraiding.

I was very *un*surprised to find that Amunhotep was still asleep and that no one expected to see him before midday. I loaded some baked fish and a little yogurt into a bowl and put it under my chair for Neffi. With him occupied, I returned to the food tables and grabbed a few boiled eggs and a chunk of bread for me. When I tilted one of the earthenware pitchers to see what was inside, though, I knew I was sunk. Fresh grape juice. It might be a staple on the tables of nobles and royalty, but for me, fresh juice was a real treat. I drank three cups of it. I should have been ashamed. But I wasn't.

Another cup of juice was whispering to me when I heard a commotion out in the entrance hall. I poured the cup that was taunting me and strolled over to see what was up. Neffi had beaten me there and sat in the midst of a knot of household staff before a big, sun-reddened man.

The man was gesturing widely, saying, "Yes! He was floating just off the pier when I cast my lines. Throat slit!"

Yuni, the staid servant who had announced me in the hall on my first visit, was horror-stricken. "What are things coming to? People aren't safe in their own homes."

"Oh he wasn't from here, Yuni," the big fisherman said. "He was a foreigner."

Another servant said, "Oh right, Rebu! When did you get to be an authority on foreigners?"

"I know the evidence of my own eyes, Hentaneb," he said. "I helped the city police pull him out of the water. Small, dark. Tattoos all over."

The cook was aghast, "Tattoos?"

"Oh they do that sort of thing in the wilderness below Nubia," the fisherman added with an air of authority. "He had triangles and lines all up and down his chest, swirly patterns on his arms and this big necklace tattooed all around his throat."

I stopped listening then. My knees went weak and I was very glad to be close to a pillar. Neffi trotted over to me with a concerned chirp. I knew those tattoos. I'd seen them on the riverboat that brought my scribal party to Memphis. The deckhand, Jiji, had just been pulled from the Nile.

Nobody noticed the news had hit me hard. They didn't notice me at all. They were concentrating on the fisherman and his tale of horror. They hustled him out to the kitchen to tell his story to the others, leaving Neffi and me alone in the pillared hall. I looked down at the cat who was stretching up against my leg to pat me with a big paw. "Well, Neffi, looks like Jiji has turned up again."

Yeah. Turned up dead. Was it a coincidence, or was it related to the missing scribe? After all, the man lived a life that put him at risk. If he made a practice of robbing his fellow sailors, it was a wonder he hadn't been murdered long ago. Still, he'd been bragging to the workers at the necropolis about burying a body right where we'd found Khety. Then Jiji turns up dead the next day? Nope. Not a coincidence. Writing a quick report for General Seti-Merenptah was in my future. What I would say and what good it might do, I had no idea. It just had to be done.

The grisly news made me regret the juice. A breeze wafting through the open hall revived me a bit, making the idea of a walk through the grounds an inviting one. I returned the cup to the hall, then Neffi and I headed out into the morning cool. Soon I found myself standing on the lawn where the party had been, looking out over the beautiful pond. I sat on the bank and leaned back on my elbows to enjoy the morning sun and watch the flashing dance of dragonflies. Neffi wandered a little way off to pounce things at the edge of the water. All at once, he perked up and stared hard at a stand of papyrus waving in the breeze and trotted off toward it.

I don't know why I bother to call after him. He never listens, but I sat up and called after him, anyway. "Hey! Neffi! Come back here."

He ignored me.

Grumbling, I rose and brushed myself off, following him on his beeline to the thicket of tall water plants. As we came around, a wooden pavilion built out over the water came into view. It was older and much smaller than the gaudy party pavilion. Its lines were cleaner, more elegant. It had to be the place Banufre and Iaret used to sail their toy boats from. Intrigued, I approached and was almost to the steps when I heard a woman crying inside. I froze. I had no idea who was behind the reed blinds and certainly didn't want to intrude. I reached to gather up Neffi for a quiet retreat when he leaped forward, carrying me with him. I crashed onto and up the steps, rolling heels over head into the gazebo to sprawl gracelessly at the feet of Banufre and Iaret who were locked in a tight embrace.

FIFTEEN

Time stopped. I didn't even dare to breathe. The only sound was the water lapping at the gazebo's stone supports and Neffi purring as he wove around the legs of the lovers.

Then everyone moved at once.

Iaret gasped and clapped her hands to her mouth. "Sitehuti! Are you all right?"

Banufre leaped forward to help me up.

I scrambled awkwardly to my feet trying to re-situate my now-cock-eyed wig. "Oh! I'm so sorry. Please forgive my intrusion."

And Neffi? Neffi hopped up onto a reclining couch and regarded all the human activity through half-closed eyes. Have I mentioned that the cat can laugh? He can. He *does*. I'm sure of it.

Banufre colored and stammered, "This isn't what it looks like — well it *is* — sort of — But it's *not!*"

I waved my hands in front of him. "Whoa! Whoa! I understand. I have no problem with you two having a relationship."

"No, but my parents will," said Iaret quietly. She was pale and shaking and I realized that it had nothing to do with my fall.

"I won't tell them," I said.

I stood there willing her to believe me, then Banufre said, "It's a sign, Ia. I was telling you we needed to find Sitehuti and the Sacred One and the gods led them right to us."

I glared at Neffi who was vigorously grooming his face. I wasn't so sure it was divine guidance that knocked me headfirst

169

up the stairs. Without warning, Iaret dropped onto the couch next to Neffi and burst into tears. Neffi put his paws on the girl's leg and head-butted her.

I looked from cat, to woman, to man and said, "Okay, just what *did* I interrupt?"

Banufre sat next to Iaret again, put his arm around her shaking shoulders. She sat straighter, sniffed, and said, "You heard about the dead man they found in the river this morning?"

I pulled a stool up and sat down. "Yes, the house staff were talking about it at breakfast."

She choked back another sob. "I think that man was killed right here — right in my own house!" •

I'm sure I gaped at her.

Banufre reddened a little. "You probably noticed I wasn't at Amuny's party last night."

Well, yeah I noticed, but I didn't see what that had to do with anyone being killed. I said, "Amunhotep said your father refused to let you come."

"That wasn't quite true. That's what I told Amuny, but Father is too old school to ever turn down an invitation from a prince," Banufre said. He couldn't quite hide his smile as he added, "Even if he didn't like the prince. Amuny is still a prince and he's done an awful lot for our family."

"All right, I understand. Then . . . where were you?" I asked, although I had a suspicion I already knew.

"Right here," he confessed.

"With me," Iaret added.

"Ah," I said.

Banufre said, "Father let me come to the party with the promise I'd come home right after dinner. Ia and I both stole food from the kitchens and met here for a . . . picnic."

I nodded. I'd been on a few . . . picnics, myself.

Iaret said, "When people started leaving the party, we

said goodnight. Ban headed off to his house and I slipped in at the back of mine. I was being especially careful. Even when Uncle Amuny is having a party, the main house is so quiet you can hear a mouse sneeze. This time, though, there were people in the hall."

I leaned forward. "Did you know them? Have you seen them before?"

She shook her head. "They were big, rough men with swords. They might have been soldiers. There were two of them, dragging a smaller man between them. If he hadn't been making so much noise, they probably would have caught me. As it was, I barely was able to duck into the other room out of sight."

She stopped talking and swallowed a few times. Banufre squeezed her hand and Neffi draped himself across her lap. "I was so scared," she said. "I just pressed myself against the wall and prayed they wouldn't see me. It was horrible. That man. He was whimpering and begging them to let him go. They just laughed and said that soon, he'd be free forever."

I said, "You're sure this was the man who was pulled out of the river?"

She nodded. "I knew as soon as I heard the description. A very dark, little man with tattooing all over his body. They didn't mention it this morning, but he also had big double gold hoops in each ear."

The roaring in my own ears drowned out any words that followed. My face must have been a sight because Ban looked up from comforting Iaret and froze. "You know who he was, don't you?"

I didn't have to consider long. Even if I hadn't instinctively trusted them, the sight of Neffi stretched out on Iaret's lap, presenting his stomach for pets would have cinched it.

"I'm pretty sure he was a riverboat crewman named Jiji," I

said. "He was on the boat that brought me and my group down to Memphis." I paused uncomfortably. "I really can't give you all of the details; some aren't mine to share. Others are just so complicated I don't even want to try, but simply put: Jiji was suspected of breaking into the passengers' luggage and then, a couple nights later, disappeared with some fellow sailors' pay. That was just before we reached Memphis."

"Wait. Jiji. I've heard that name before—" Ban's eyes suddenly widened. "He's the one you thought the workmen were talking about. The man who was bragging about killing that scribe. I hadn't put that together until now."

I nodded. "And that led us directly to Khety's body. I'm wondering if that's why Jiji suddenly turned up dead himself."

Iaret's face crumpled again. She clutched the edge of her seat and said, "I'm so scared! There is no way my parents couldn't have known what was happening. I can't believe it, but I *have* to believe it. They must be involved in this somehow. Oh, Ban! Sitehuti! What's happening?"

"Princess Iaret—" I said.

"Ia," she interrupted.

"Huti." I grinned, then got serious again. "Ia, I think you're right about your parents being involved in something and you were very smart to keep quiet last night—"

Neffi perked up, slid out of Ia's lap and trotted to the gazebo entrance. He stood there chirping and trilling while we three stared, wondering what had gotten into him. A few seconds later, Prince Amenhotep stumbled up the steps looking very much the worse for wear. He saw Neffi first and reached out to give him a scratch. "Hey, little fella. What are you doing out here?"

Suddenly, he caught sight of Ban and Ia, looked embarrassed, started to back out, then saw me and stopped, confusion replacing embarrassment.

Ia was up and on him in a second. "Oh, Uncle Amuny! You look awful! Come and sit down in the shade."

He allowed himself to be guided to a couch and lay back on it with a groan. "Normally I'd clear off and give you kids the room, but I'm dying here."

"What happened?" I asked.

He threw his forearm across his face. "For some reason half the staff decided they needed to wake me up to tell me about the guy they pulled from the river this morning. No idea why they needed to do that. The guy would be just as dead if they'd waited to tell me when I woke up."

Ban said, "Huti thinks the dead guy is the foreigner who killed the scribe of Ptah."

Amuny peeked out from under his arm. "Yeah?"

"Small, dark and all over tattoos," Ban said.

"Huh," Amuny said lowering his arm. "So it does. Now if someone can tell me why Meriramsses is in a pissy mood, I'll be as happy as a hippo in mud. He's rampaging through the house shouting at everyone. I came out here to hide."

Once we made sure Amuny was going to be all right, we left him snoring in the gazebo. None of us were too anxious to go back to the princes' house, especially with Meriramesses in a bad mood. We walked through the gardens in silence, enjoying the cool shade and watching Neffi stalk and pounce things invisible to us. I debated telling Ban and Ia about my reports to Seti-Merenptah, but decided against it. It wasn't that I didn't trust them — I did — but I worried that it might panic them to know how official my involvement was. Ia was already upset at the realization her parents were mixed up in something more than shady. If she found out that her uncle, the Crown Prince, and her cousin, the General already suspected, it might make her more fearful. I knew for a fact Ban and his family still worried that the Great House might swoop in and, at best, seize everything they had. Knowing that those same officials were watching. . . ? Nothing good could come of it.

After we had walked for several minutes, Iaret said, "It's a shame that Uncle Amuny isn't welcome in his own house. I can't believe how my father and mother treat him." She paused as an odd look flitted across her face. "Well, I guess I can. As badly as they treat others, why should family be any different? Especially someone who doesn't act the way they think they should."

We tramped along in silence for a while longer, then Ban said, "According to Amuny, Meriramesses wasn't always a stick in the mud."

Ia gave him a doubtful side glance. "That's hard to believe."

"No, really. Amuny said when they were kids, they used to have a lot of fun along with Sasobek and Paseti."

"Even harder to imagine my father as a child," Ia said with a wry smile.

Ban laughed outright. "I feel the same way about Sasobek and Paseti."

"I have no trouble imagining Amuny that way, though," I said.

Ia's half-smile became a full grin. "Me either. I don't think Uncle Amuny so much grew up as he just got bigger."

"Seriously, though," Ban said. "He told me that they hunted and fished all the time when they were boys. They caught all sorts of animals. They even caught snakes! One time they even pulled a prank on the Pharaoh with one."

"Oooo. That took some serious nerve," I said.

"Yeah," Ban agreed. "Amuny said they caught a big Diedem snake — one that looked nasty but was non-venomous. They slipped it into their mother's bedroom, into a clothing chest. When their father opened the chest, the snake popped out. There was chaos. People screaming, Sherden Guards running around. . . ."

"My *father* did that?" Ia asked wide-eyed.

Ban nodded. "Amuny said they both got a hiding for it and were forbidden to ever hunt snakes again, but they still thought it was hilarious." He went quiet. "It's so hard to reconcile that boy with the man. The Meriramesses I'm familiar with would have somebody tied up and whipped if someone did it to him."

"Yes." Iaret said in a subdued tone. "That's the one I'm familiar with, too."

SIXTEEN

Ban and I managed to get Ia back into the house without her father and mother noticing she'd even been gone. She had gotten her tears well under control by then. She was probably still scared spitless — I know I was — but a lifetime of court-training let her assume a calm and stoic outward appearance.

Ban returned home for another lesson on vine care from their estate foreman. He seemed grateful to fall back on something normal. I understood how he felt.

I'd gone back to the apartment, sat down and written a letter to General Seti-Merenptah about Jiji and what Iaret had seen in the hall of her own house the night before. If that didn't fit in with what he and his father feared about bad things happening on the princes' estate, I didn't know what would.

I sent the report off by way of Renen. The boy was a good messenger, quick and reliable. After he'd been instructed not to run until he was out of sight of the house, he was gone and I found myself in a unique situation — for me, anyway. I had absolutely nothing to do. I savored the feeling for a moment, then rooted through my scroll box for something to read. I chose one that I'd salvaged from the papyri slated for erasure at the school. In other words: I was on papyrus scraping duty, saw it was a story I hadn't read before, and nicked it. That had been only a couple days before I was sent to the temple of Bastet and came home with Neffi. I hadn't had much chance to read since then.

I tucked the scroll into my stole and headed for the pavilion on the pond. It was secluded and its position over the water with the papyrus screen made it wonderfully comfortable in the heat of the day.

~*~

It was a good idea, anyway.

It wasn't that the story was bad. It was well-written, and any other time would have had me rolling around laughing. The problem was me. There was so much going on that, even though I'd turned it over to other people, I couldn't stop thinking about it. Couldn't keep from trying to fit pieces together to make a whole. I kept finding myself with the scroll in my lap, scratching Neffi and staring out at the shifting water through the swaying stalks of the papyrus stand. When Prince Amunhotep found me there a few hours later, it was a welcome interruption.

Once again Neffi alerted me to someone approaching by chirping and trotting over to the entrance. Amuny peered cautiously up the steps, then relaxed. "Glad it's just you and Neffi this time. I was afraid I was going to interrupt something private again."

"Yeah, just me, Neffi and a scroll I can't seem to get into." I set the scroll aside. "I hope what happened earlier didn't upset you or anything."

Amuny eased back on a couch and made a dismissive noise. "You mean about Ban and Ia? Don't worry. I like Ban and I know those two kids are in love. They have been since they were little. Have to be blind not to see them making cow eyes at each other when they think no one's looking. Blind or not *want* to see." He pulled his feet up onto the cushions with a happy groan. "I've been helping them meet."

"You have?"

"Sure! Why do you think I invite Ban to all those parties he doesn't want to come to? I do my best to keep everyone away from the gazebo. Hell, half my gang doesn't even know this place exists. The other half is usually too drunk to find it. I like that just fine. Gives *me* a place to hide from time to time, too."

Neffi hopped up onto the couch and head-butted Amuny. Smiling, the prince scratched the cat thoroughly, until he jumped down, spotted fur rippling.

I said, "Prince Merirameses doesn't know, does he?"

"Nope. Remember what I said about not wanting to see? Meri has his sights set *way* high for Ia. Not that she isn't a wonderful girl, mind, but he's been shopping some foreign princes lately. Like he needs to forge state alliances." He snorted. "Ban would be a great match for her. I've been thinking about petitioning my father about it — that is, if Paseti hasn't ruined things for everyone. He was always good at that."

"Well, so far, no one in the capital seems to blame the family for what the son has done."

"That's good to hear. I never understood why one bad fruit meant the whole tree had to be destroyed."

"I never understood that, either, but then again, I'm just the son of a painter."

Amuny stared at the shadows of the papyrus plants undulating against the lattice of the gazebo wall for a long time. Finally he said, "Yeah. That's one of the big drawbacks to being a member of the Royal Family. People expect a lot from you."

I was taken aback at the bitterness behind his words. It must have read on my face.

"Surprised, Huti? Don't be. I'm a realist. I know my limitations. I was a lousy soldier. Didn't last a year at that. I was a crummy administrator, too. Didn't matter if it was grain measures or cattle. I'm just no good at it — but parties? That, I can do." He barked a big, booming laugh. "If there was a government position for official party giver and hunt master,

I'd have slotted right in. But, there isn't. That's one of the reasons I asked to be sent back out here."

"You asked to be sent home?"

His eyes slid toward me and he chuckled. "Yep. I know everybody thinks Father sent me home to keep me out of his hair, but it was sort of the other way around. In Pi-Ramesses, people were always on me to make something of myself. *Be something.* Out here, I still have a big city nearby, but no one puts expectations on me — except Meri, of course, but I've been ignoring Meri all my life."

I thought about that for a bit. I found myself staring at Neffi who was stretched on his back in a shaft of sunlight. "Yeah, I sort of understand that. Especially now. I never aspired to be more than a mid-level scribe, then one day, I went to the temple of Bastet and boom!" I gestured toward the sleeping cat. "Everything changed."

Amuny followed my gaze. "Huh. I never thought of it that way. I just saw all the fun a cat like Neffi could bring." An instant later, he shrugged off the serious mood and asked, "How do you like your rooms?"

"It's like nothing I'm used to. Back home, I still live with my aunt Tiaa and share a room with my twelve-year-old cousin above a linen shop."

"You need to get a house."

"Easier said than done. I'm still a junior scribe. I only just graduated from my scribal school the same week I got sent to Memphis."

"Hmmmm." He bent to rub Neffi's ears. The big cat's purr filled the gazebo. Suddenly he said, "Y'know, it was really good to see my nephew Seti-Merenptah out here last night. It's been a long time since he accepted one of my invitations." As he looked up from the purring cat, the shrewdness in the older man's eyes caught me off guard.

179

"Look, I may be a wastrel and everything else people accuse me of being, but I'm loyal to my family and the throne. I'm guessing my half-brother Mernenptah sent you out here for a specific reason. Probably more than to just to find that unfortunate scribe. Might be to find Paseti, might not. I'm not asking you to tell me. Just know if you need anything, I'd move the mountains to help my Father."

With that, Amunhotep stood, stretched and grinned at me. "Well, I better be getting back to the house. Some of the gang are coming over for a little racing later. You're welcome to join in if you feel like it."

~*~

My unfamiliar condition of not having anything to do didn't last long. Someone, somewhere, looked at the estate's list of Opet offerings and decided it was incomplete. I didn't see how. By my recollection, it was one of the longest and most comprehensive I'd collected. Still, given how prickly both Prince Meriramesses and Lady Wurusemu had been since Jiji had been pulled from the river, I didn't blame the servants for wanting to make busy. I was pretty happy to be working with Ipuy in his office a good distance away from the house, myself.

As a representative of the Great House and a servant of the High Priest of Bastet, they couldn't really take their ire out on me, no matter how much they wanted to. The glares and clipped manner of address were bad enough, but I felt it made it harder on any servant in the same room with me. If they couldn't rain hell down on me proper, they could make it rage around me.

"His Highness, Prince Amunhotep, thinks it a serious oversight we didn't include any sheep in our previous list," Ipuy said, shuffling through various scraps of papyrus.

I consulted my copy of the completed list that Master Ta had provided for me. "Two other estates are sending sheep and one other is sending goats. A few more sheep wouldn't hurt."

Ipuy craned to see my list. "Who's sending the goats? If it's
. . . yes. That idiot . . . er . . . the *noble* Nekure. I think we'd do well
to add a few goats to our list, too. His might not be exactly up to
specification — if you get me."

I did. We red-inked in a group of both.

"So, what do you make of that foreigner they found in the
river? They say his throat was slit," Ipuy said in a conspiratorial
tone.

I looked up from my papyrus. "I heard about that. I don't know
what to think."

"Some are saying he was killed on a boat and tossed off."

"That sounds plausible. You sound like you don't believe it,
though."

Ipuy looked as if he wanted to say something, as if there was
a lot he wanted to say. At length, he settled on, "Well, I just think
it's odd where they found him."

"Why?"

"That's the same spot they found that poor girl, Tali,
wasn't it?"

"Tali. Who was she?"

"She used to be Lady Wurusemu's personal maid. Then one
day she went missing. By that evening, they found her right there.
In the river. They *say* she slipped, hit her head and drowned."

"What do *you* think happened."

Ipuy got busy again, shuffling the scraps of papyrus that littered
his work area. "I'm sure I don't know. If the city police think that's
what happened, that must be what happened."

I turned back to the lists. "There's a note here about wine.
Does that say 'more white'?"

"Oh yes!" Ipuy's face lit up. "We've been experimenting and
we've developed a truly delicious white variety. It tends toward
the sweet, but I believe His Divine Majesty Ramesses prefers sweet
to dry."

"Very interesting! You don't get white wines too often." I said, making a note on the master list.

Ipuy made a note of his own, then said off-handedly, "I imagine you'll be leaving us soon, now that the missing scribe has been located. Terrible business, that."

I shrugged. "I haven't been recalled yet, but that might be because I'm currently Prince Amunhotep's guest."

"Oh, of course that would be it. You said you weren't looking for Pasteti the last time we chatted, didn't you?"

"Ummm, yeah. As I said last time, that's a job for a policeman, not a scribe."

Ipuy hummed and nodded. "Of course, of course."

After that, we fell into a routine that carried us almost to dusk, and we broke for the evening meal.

~*~

To my unbounded relief, there wasn't a family meal that night. Amuny was visiting one of his chariot buddies, and Lady Wurusemu had a sick headache that kept her to her rooms. Renen and I took our evening meal in the apartment sitting room overlooking the garden. It was a nice evening until a scrap of papyrus slid under the door. Neffi pounced it as it came to a stop and sniffed at it open-mouthed as he had at the doorframe the night of the wine party.

I recognized the spiky writing without even picking it up. I'd been looking at it all day. It was Ipuy's hand. I pulled the tall doors back and peered out into the hallway. It seemed to be empty. Not even the sound of footsteps.

Renen picked the note up. He squinted at it. "What's it say?"

I stared at it for a bit. It didn't make a whole lot of sense. "It's from Chief Scribe Ipuy. He wants me to meet him at the wine press tonight. He says he has some news to tell me."

~*~

The press was on the far edge of the estate and getting there after dark by the light of a small lamp took me longer than I'd figured. Neffi kept weaving in and out between my feet, nearly tripping me several times. He refused to ride on my shoulders, slipping out of my grasp each time I tried to pick him up. When we got there, the place was empty but for the big stone press, yawning catch basin, and the towering lines of stacked baskets.

There was a salt lamp on the edge of the catch basin, still burning brightly, so someone had been there not long before. No other sign of Ipuy or anyone else. I sat on the edge of the basin to wait as Neffi inspected the wall of baskets much as he had on our first tour of the estate. He was strangely agitated. Tail lashing, making small chittering sounds as he clawed and plucked at the wicker. Mice were a nuisance in places like that and I figured he'd found a nest. Still, I didn't want him destroying property on a royal estate. I rose to pull him away, but he managed to topple one of the central stacks before I got to him.

There was something in back of the remaining baskets that I couldn't quite make out. Neffi yowled and pawed at a length of stained cloth trailing from a larger bundle. The neighboring stacks swayed precariously. As I put out my hand to steady them, I got a better look at the bundle. It was Ipuy. His throat was slit.

Neffi dodged my attempt to scoop him up, and bounced up onto the rim of the catch basin, glaring at the door, bristling and growling. My shocky brain wouldn't process the meaning. The thing foremost in my mind was to get as far away from the gruesome bundle on the floor as possible as fast as possible. I needed to alert someone, but who?

As I backed away, someone spoke, "Ah, Sitehuti. Who knew you had such violence in you? It was an epic struggle, but you have prevailed in your evil scheme and Ipuy is dead."

I wheeled. Paseti blocked the doorway. His eyes and the iron dagger in his hand glinted in the wan glow of the lamplight. My mouth moved, but I could force no sound out.

"How unfortunate that he was also armed," the former priest continued. "I'm sorry to report, the wounds he dealt you were fatal."

As Paseti firmed his grip on the knife, Neffi sprang at him. The man was ready for it. He spun aside, grabbing one of the heavy harvest baskets in his free hand, and slammed it neatly over the snarling cat. "There. That was easy, wasn't it? I've been wanting to do this since the day you interrupted me in my workshop."

He lunged at me. I jerked backwards, but not far enough. The knife point sliced my shirt and drew a line of fire across my chest. Paseti seemed oddly pleased with his work and slashed at me again. This time I was ready and brought a wooden carry-pole up. I swung at his head. He ducked and came under the rod, slicing me along the inside of my arm. I cried out and dropped my makeshift weapon.

I backed away, clutching my bleeding arm. Paseti followed.

Suddenly, a large dark figure bulled through the door and slammed into my attacker, sending him careening against the wall of baskets. The violent action caused the stranger's heavy, braided wig to slide to the floor. The big man made no move to recover it, but stepped back, ready for whatever the former priest might try next.

Paseti and I recognized the newcomer at the same time.

"Good evening, Captain Djedmose. I'm afraid you're too late to save anyone," Paseti said.

"We'll see about that," Djedmose said evenly, never taking his eyes off the man with the knife. "Kid, you okay?"

I never got the chance to answer. Paseti moved like a snake, knife blade flashing as he struck the Nubian in the chest. To

Paseti's surprise (and mine) the blade turned aside and ripped through the dark cloak to reveal the Medjay's blue and gold scaled armor corslet beneath.

Djedmose's punch took the older scribe in the side of the head, sending him staggering back into the basket with Neffi under it. It toppled over. The angry cat sprang on his attacker at the same time Djedmose lunged forward. Paseti tried to run, but got tangled in the mass of fallen wicker and fell hard against the rim of the catch basin with the wet sound of a split melon. He slumped to the ground and didn't move again.

Djedmose knelt, felt for life, then swore. "Dead. Dammit!"

I was shaking so badly by this time, I could hardly hold myself up. Neffi chirped and patted at me, making it even harder to concentrate.

Djedmose's roar cut through the fog, "You idiot kid! Didn't you see this was a trap? Why in the name of—"

"Stop it!" I sank onto the basin. "Just stop it! No, I didn't see it was a trap! Why? Because I *am* a kid. I'm not a policeman. I'm a scribe. Just a scribe!"

Neffi paced in front of me, growling at the Nubian.

In an instant, the Medjay's expression changed. He stepped forward. "Get away, cat. Let me see that." He pulled my hand away from where I'd been clenching my cut arm. That released a fresh cascade of blood. Captain Djedmose sucked his teeth and announced, "Not too deep, but he got you good. We need someone to look at that."

My brain was moving at a snail's pace. Blame shock, blame blood loss — whatever — but it took that long for the fact that the rough-looking Nubian who had been shadowing me and scaring the life out of everyone must have been Djedmose all along. Angry overrode shocky. I pulled away and stood up. "I was bait! You used me for bait!"

"That's not true, Scribe. I was sent here to find *him.*" He jabbed

Paseti's limp corpse with the toe of his boot for emphasis. "I was also told to watch your back, and that's what I did. Now *he's* dead and I can't help if you're too butt stupid to recognize a trap if you see one."

My breath caught as another thought glimmered. "I don't think it was just a trap for me."

"What?"

"I was with Ipuy all day while we tallied the items for the Opet. That note was definitely his handwriting. His downstrokes were very long and pointy — hard to miss."

"Meaning what?"

"Other than he really set up a meeting with me, but Paseti got here first? I don't know."

Djedmose frowned at the corpses, then frowned at me. "I know one thing it means. It means we need to tread lightly in Their Highness' house."

"What? I'm not going back there now — I can't!"

"We have to, kid. Aside from the fact you're bleeding like a pig, I have a job to do."

The room swam. I swallowed hard and looked away from the carnage. "Too bad you aren't in full uniform. It would make what comes next easier."

"Nothing will make what comes next easier." The soldier turned abruptly and stalked out.

I bent to scoop up Neffi, but he slipped out of my hands, trotted over to Paseti's corpse and pawed at something under it. Disgusted, I grabbed him, but as I pulled him away, the thing he'd caught with his claws slid into the lamplight. It was the couterpoise for Paseti's pectoral. It was an elaborate gold and enamel piece shaped like a pair of geese.

I clutched Neffi to myself and tried to hurry after Djedmose.

Then the floor reached up and smacked me.

SEVENTEEN

I awoke in the guest apartment's big bed to the scent of honey and wine. My chest and right arm felt like they were on fire. I tried to sit up, but there was a weight on my chest preventing me from doing so. The weight meowed loudly and head-butted me.

Renen and Lieutenant Si-Montu appeared in my blurry field of vision.

Si-Montu turned to Renen. "Boy—"

But he was speaking to empty air. Renen had already cleared the doorway.

I tried to push Neffi off, but my arms wouldn't do what I told them. The slender Nubian officer scooped the surprised cat off my chest and dropped him to the floor. It didn't do much good, as he hopped right back onto the bed and insinuated himself under my good hand, but I was impressed at the move. Most people would have taken a few scratches, but Si-Montu managed it all in one fluid motion before the cat even knew what was happening. I made a mental note to compliment him on it when I remembered how to talk.

"Captain Djedmose will be here shortly," the Medjay said as he helped me sit up. Laughter tinged his voice as he added, "If you're going to keep getting yourself into trouble, Scribe, we'll need to teach you how to fight."

As if on cue, Djedmose, in full Medjay regalia strode through the door. Renen trailed in his wake. The Medjay captain said, "Welcome back. You certainly know how to make an exit."

Turning to Si-Montu, he said, "Give us the room, Lieutenant. I need you and the boy in the hallway to make sure we have no unexpected visitors."

Si-Montu snapped a salute and left, pulling the reluctant boy with him.

"We have to be quick," Djedmose said. "You've been out all day and Prince Amunhotep has been hovering. Look, we know someone in this house is complicit in the plot against the Great House. Someone hid the Lector here, but of course, no one admits to it."

"The counterpoise," I said. "I saw it before — right here at this house."

Djedmose frowned and crouched to look straight into my eyes. "Kid, you're still scrambled."

I waved him away, "No, I'm not. I saw Paseti entering this house the night of Amunhotep's party. The night before the sailor, Jiji, was found murdered."

"You're sure?"

I nodded.

"Why didn't you say something before? Send a note to the General? The last we heard was simply that Jiji was seen in the area."

"I only saw him from the back, so I didn't realize it was Paseti. All I saw was a cloak, a wig and the counterpoise to his pectoral. Then tonight just before I passed out—"

"Last night," he corrected.

"*Last* night." I glared. He ignored it. "I saw the counterpoise again. Two geese in gold and faience inlay. Very distinctive and expensive." I paused to feel the bandages. "What all happened, anyway? I don't really remember much."

Djedmose laughed. "I wondered when you'd get to that. Most people, it's the first thing out of their mouths. You had to bang on about a piece of jewelry."

I glared again. He ignored it again.

He pulled a stool over to the bedside. "I'd been watching the house when you came stealing out like an illicit lover. You had me confused as hell when you took me all the way across the estate and ducked into the wine press. I was circling the place when I heard a crash and this horrible screaming. I was sure Paseti or one of the conspirators had killed you, so I came running. Got inside just in time to see you backpedaling and that cat screaming from under a basket like he was being killed.

"When you went down, I thought the cat would rip me to shreds if I touched you, but he didn't. He let me pick you up and get you back to the house. Howled the whole way back, though. Didn't have to knock or anything. The whole household heard us coming."

That was all blank to me, so I kept quiet.

Djedmose said, "You're damned lucky that large amounts of wine and hunting don't mix well, because Prince Amunhotep keeps a physician on staff just in case. The doctor got the bleeding under control and the wound on the arm stitched up in no time. You've been out cold ever since. The whole house has been in an uproar."

I remained convinced that I'd been used for bait, but I was too angry to deal with it rationally, so I went off on another tack. "You've been reading the reports I sent to General Seti-Merenptah."

"Of course I have. How else was I going to keep track of what you were doing?"

"All right," I said. "If you knew I hadn't found anything in Khety's scroll boxes, why break in and steal one?"

Djedmose looked dumfounded. "What? I didn't. I went to talk to the widow, yes, but once I found you'd already been there, I left. I headed straight for the General's house to see if your report had gotten there. It arrived about the same time I did, so I was probably reading it when the break-in happened."

"Then who broke in?"

"That's a damned good question."

"Maybe Paseti? He knew Khety wrote the original letter."

"Good point, but I doubt he'd do it himself. More likely, he'd pay someone to steal it for him."

I considered. "If Paseti was behind it, we might find the box wherever he was hiding out. I'm betting it was here on the estate. I'm also betting that's what Ipuy discovered."

"That brings me back to what I was saying before. We have to be very careful what we say to people in this house. Someone — probably several someones — in this household are planning bad things for the Pharaoh and the Crown Prince. Right now, we have no way to know who or even what they plan. We'd hoped to ask Paseti, but his head split like a melon when he hit the wine press. Did you put everything, I mean *everything* into those reports you've been delivering to General Seti-Merenptah?

I nodded. That made the room swim, so I gulped a couple times and said, "Yes. All except the counterpoise, but I didn't know that was important since I didn't know whose necklace it was."

Djedmose grunted. "It wouldn't seem important at first glance, I agree. Is there anything else that doesn't seem important?"

"Well, I don't think Prince Amunhotep is in on whatever plot is being formed against his father. I had a talk with him the other day. He told me that he was loyal to his Father. I tend to believe him. He really isn't interested in politics and being involved in a plot would be a *lot* of politics."

Djedmose was puzzled. "What were you doing talking with Prince Amenhotep?"

"He found me reading in the gazebo by the pond." I paused. No sense in mentioning Banufre and Iaret, yet. I continued, "It was the same day that news of the man pulled from the river was making the place buzz. As I said in my letter to the general, I didn't get to see the man, but from the description, it made me think of that sailor who disappeared from Captain Jebahou-Nefer's riverboat. Jiji."

Djedmose raised an eyebrow. "The one suspected of going through the luggage?"

At my nod, he frowned. "I didn't make it back to the general's to read your last letter because all this happened. Looks like I missed a lot."

"Then you don't know about Princess Iaret."

"What about Princess Iaret?"

I steeled myself. There was no sense in holding back now. "First off, Banufre, Paseti's half-brother is having a secret love affair with Iaret, Prince Meriramesses' daughter."

I could tell from the look on Djedmose's face he thought this was pure gossip, so I hurried on, "Iaret was sneaking back into the house from a lover's picnic with Banufre the night of the big wine party. She saw two rough-looking men who might have been soldiers dragging a man fitting Jiji's description into the upstairs living quarters."

Djedmose whistled softly. "More and more interesting. I'll need to talk with the lady myself. Privately, if that can be arranged."

There was a light tap at the door. Djedmose, hand on sword hilt, rose and opened it a crack.

It was Lieutenant Si-Montu. He said quietly, "Sir, the boy says Prince Amenhotep is heading this way."

"Fine." Djedmose looked down at Renen who had edged in through the narrow opening. Putting a hand on the boy's shoulder, he said, "Go to fetch Prince Amunhotep. Tell him the scribe is up and about, then find Prince Meriramesses and tell him the same thing. Got that?"

Renen nodded and shot off.

Djedmose glanced back at me. "Remember. Be careful what you say to people. Even to Prince Amunhotep."

"How are we going to explain what happened last night?"

"No way around the truth on that, I'm afraid. When we brought you back here, we found Ipuy's note on top of your writing kit. Paseti's name wasn't mentioned specifically, but the rumors that you were sent here to track him down are flying like mosquitoes in the spring floods."

I groaned. "I swear, I'm going to strangle that stupid Hapuseneb."

Djedmose grinned. "Just be glad it wasn't his cousin Tepemkau, or you'd be rumored to have flown to Memphis in the sun's bark on a mission of vengeance."

He had a point.

~*~

It was beyond me how Amunhotep could have ever been a successful hunter. He was simply noisy. I heard his boisterous approach well before he reached the room.

When the double doors opened, we were invaded by Amuny heading up an entire entourage. He had the doctor, a servant carrying food, one carrying wine, one carrying a basket stuffed with tableware and one poor boy lugging a table. A bemused Banufre brought up the rear.

Neffi abandoned me as soon as food came into the picture. The servant holding the tray rolled his eyes uncertainly at the huge cat standing up against his legs. To his credit, he didn't flinch.

Amuny looked almost comically relieved when he saw me sitting up in bed. "Oh, good! You're finally awake. I was worried sick how long it was taking. When that lion knocked me out a couple years ago, I came around real fast. Doctor Merit-Ptah, here, said the longer it takes, the worse it is."

The medical man in question carefully unwound my bandages and peered at the edges of the wounds. He touched the reddened skin lightly, hmmmed, then said, "The flesh is hot, but that's to be expected. The swelling and heat should subside in a few days. Now, don't scratch or pick at those stitches in your arm. They'll itch, but that simply means the healing has started." He turned to Renen, who hovered nearby, and handed the boy a large roll of bandage. "Keep those stitches wrapped with fresh linen until they're ready to come out. Probably seven days. You might also want to wash the area with palm wine and apply honey to the wound for the first couple of days, young man."

The doctor placed a several sealed jars on the chest beside the bed, then took his leave.

As Merit-Ptah exited, the servants sprang into action. In no time, the table was set, food and wine put into reach, and then they, too, disappeared into the shadows of the hallway.

All during this, Djedmose and Amuny had eyed each other with overt suspicion. I felt like a disputed cub caught between two angry bears.

Finally Amuny nodded slightly to the Medjay. "Captain Djedmose, we haven't been on the best of terms, but I want to give you my sincere thanks for saving my friend, Sitehuti. The gods only know what could have happened if you hadn't been there."

Djedmose was nonplussed. He saluted and said, "Just doing my job, Your Highness."

"It was a very good job, then, Captain," Amuny said, his characteristic grin coming back in force. He turned to me. "I don't expect you'll feel like eating much, but I brought a lot of different things. Ban's mother sent over some of her herbed labna and a jug of the date wine, too. She said you liked that."

Ban said quietly, "Sitehuti, I've come to offer apologies on behalf of my family. My father was horrified to learn it was my half-brother, Paseti, who had done this to you." He turned and bowed deeply to the Medjay. "Captain Djedmose, we also want to thank you for being there for our friend, Sitehuti, and for bringing justice against my errant brother."

Djedmose returned the bow, but remained silent.

I didn't stay silent, though. "Ban, please let your father know that I don't hold your family any way responsible for what Paseti did."

Ban blurted out, "We didn't even know he was back in this area. Really! We didn't!"

Amuny put a massive paw on the young man's shoulder. "I think he knows that, Ban." He looked right at Captain Djedmose as he added, "We *all* know that."

In a blink, Amuny made the switch from serious to his normal jovial demeanor. He slapped his hands together and said, "Now, you need to keep up your strength, Huti. I had the cook send up some of that *amazing* beef soup that sits well even on the queasiest stomach — and do I know queasy!"

~*~

Prince Meriramesses and Lady Wurusemu arrived before Amuny left. The couple were sans servants, but still maintained a stiff and formal manner. When they passed, Renen slid in behind them and took up a post in the corner near the door. It looked as if he was setting himself up to bolt if need be. I didn't blame him. I would have liked to do the same.

Neffi kept himself between me and the royal couple. He didn't growl or bristle as he had with Paseti, he simply assumed the same sphinx-pose he'd assumed that first day in the audience chamber.

"We are pleased to see you have awakened, Sitehuti of Western Thebes. It pains us that this has happened to you when you were a guest in our house," Lady Wurusemu said in her odd, accented speech.

"Yes, we are dismayed that anyone could have given quarter to a deranged and dangerous criminal such as this former priest. Even more so that such a degenerate should come onto our land to slay a trusted servant and attack a messenger from the Great House itself."

Amuny listened to them with growing bemusement. Finally, he said, "Wow. That's cold. I thought Paseti was one of your closest friends, Brother."

Wurusemu glared at Amunhotep. He had thicker skin than me. I'd have shriveled; he treated her to a charming smile, then ignored her.

Meriramesses' face turned to stone. "That was a long time ago, Brother. The man had obviously been becoming more and more unstable over the years. Still, I never thought he would descend to this."

To my amazement, I saw Djedmose and Amunhotep exchange glances. Neither Meriramesses nor Wurusemu did, though. Their eyes were face front almost the entire time they were in my chamber. I'm not sure they even looked at *me*.

Djedmose bowed low. "Your Highnesses, my men and I would ask permission to search the grounds so that we might find where the Lector has been hiding himself."

Immediately, Amunhotep said, "Of course, Captain Djedmose. You have my permission to search anywhere. House or grounds."

Meriramesses looked as if he'd been slapped, but pasted on a gracious smile and nodded to the Medjay. "Of course my brother speaks for all of us. I will instruct my Chief Butler to accompany you."

~*~

I was too weak to participate in the search, but Renen did. So did Amunhotep. From what the boy told me, Yuni, the Chief Butler, kept trying to guide the Medjay away from certain areas, and the prince made certain those areas got looked at.

It sounded wonderful. I would have loved to see it.

They finally found Paseti's hiding place in an old, rundown worker's cottage well away from the main house. They found food remains, clothing, jewelry and a new-looking bed inside. They also found Khety's stolen scroll box. While we still had no idea who physically broke in and stole it, we knew Paseti had been the ultimate recipient.

Yuni made a great show of outrage, swearing up and down that the seal on the place had been intact just a few days before. According to Renen, you'd have to be blind not to see the place had been in use lot longer than that.

Captain Djedmose brought Khety's box back to my apartment in the big house. The contents were jumbled, but there didn't seem to be anything missing. Not that there was anything of value there, in the first place. I'd already read through all the scrolls with lady Shepenwepet.

EIGHTEEN

After several days of my not scratching my maddeningly itchy, stitched-up arm, Captain Djedmose returned from meeting General Seti-Merenptah with a piece of papyrus tucked into his scaled corslet. I'd been in the sitting room, still trying to make it through my unread story. Djedmose all but fell onto the stool beside mine.

"You don't look too happy," I observed.

"I'm not." He pulled the small roll from his corslet and held it up. "Our new orders. In spite of the fact we haven't rooted out the conspirators here, we're being called up to Thebes in advance of the festival."

I was torn at the news. I didn't want to leave the task here in Memphis unfinished, but being sent to Thebes made my heart catch. "Thebes. Will I be able to go across the river to visit my family?"

The Nubian shrugged. "I can't promise that, Sitehuti. That isn't my decision to make." He stood and smacked the rolled-up orders into his palm. "Still, that's all in the future. The Crown Prince and the General want us to stick around until your stitches are out. That gives us another week, give or take."

"Then we're not giving up on finding the conspirators?"

The big man grinned and tucked the scroll back into his armor. "Well, there's nothing in these orders that specifically says we should."

He saluted me and marched for the door.

~*~

I was still shaky, but feeling well enough to go downstairs for the midday meal. Before I even got to the communal dining room, I heard angry voices. It was Amuny and Meriramesses arguing. That in itself wasn't unusual, but the subject matter was.

"Don't give me that 'doesn't concern us' bullshit, Meri. There were things from *this* house in that cottage. Someone from this household was helping him. That should concern us very much."

"Are you accusing me of something, Amuny?"

"I don't know. Should I be?"

A vein standing out in Prince Meriramesses' temple throbbed with his barely suppressed rage. His words were quiet, although spoken through gritted teeth. "Lady Wurusemu and I are just as determined to find the truth as you, Brother. We have been questioning the servants ever since the deception was discovered."

"The servants." Amuny repeated flatly. "Why would any of the servants aid Paseti?"

"Because of an illicit affair of the heart, Brother-in-Law."

Amuny pivoted toward Lady Wurusemu, who had come through the private entrance to their side of the house. "What 'illicit affair of the heart' would this be, Wurusemu?"

The lady didn't answer immediately. She glided across the room to her accustomed seat, then said, "It's a sad tale, but an old one, Brother-in-Law. One of the maids, a girl named Maia. She met Paseti at one of our summer fetes and became enamored. When he returned here after fleeing Pi-Ramesses, she believed his lies and agreed to help him. She hid him in the worker's cottage and stole things from the house for him."

Amuny snorted. "A girl. Stole an entire *bed* by herself?"

Djedmose stepped out from behind me. I have no idea when he'd come in, but he'd apparently heard about as much as I had. He said, "Pardon me, Your Highnesses, but I would like to speak to this woman."

The lady looked remorseful. "Alas, that will not be possible. Unfortunately, the girl died under interrogation."

I could tell no one believed the story, least of all Captain Djedmose, but this was part of the Royal Family. Unless you had stone-solid proof, you didn't accuse them of lying even if you were the commander of the crown prince's personal guard.

~*~

After that, the tension in the house swirled as thick as a sandstorm. There were no more communal meals and people pretty much stayed out of everyone else's way. Lady Wurusemu kept exclusively to their side of the house. Prince Meriramesses emerged only to deal with the daily working of the house, grounds and estate. I didn't see much of Amuny at all. He seemed to take his frustration out by attending more parties and gatherings than before. Ban stayed clear of the princes' estate for the most part. I wasn't certain of the reasons. It could have been anything from guilt over what his half-brother had done to not wanting to cross paths with Djedmose. I could understand the reasoning behind either of those.

I did see Iaret. We tended to be on similar internal schedules. We wandered through the dining room at roughly the same times and liked the same garden paths. She didn't talk much, though, and I could tell she'd been crying a lot. Mostly, we just sat together and ate or read in companionable silence. I was glad to know she was all right and I think she was glad to know that I was there. I hadn't told either Ia or Ban about being sent to Thebes, yet. I knew I was going to have to do it soon. Even though it had been less than the predicted week, Dr. Merit-Ptah was so pleased with my healing arm, he thought the stitches could come out early.

It was on the fourth day after the argument, Ia, Neffi and I had just finished the midday meal. Her father had passed through the dining area into the entry hall like a restless ghost and we could hear the drone of his voice as he gave orders to Yuni. Their quiet murmurs were soon drowned out by many voices as if a group approached from outside.

Ia listened for a while, then said, "Excuse me, Huti. It sounds like a work gang arriving. I'd better go give my respects to my father before he gets involved with whatever they're here for. He'll be cross with me if I don't."

"I hope you'll pardon me if I don't accompany you," I said. "I don't think I'm on Prince Meriramesses' happy list at the moment."

A smile flitted across her face and she chuckled, a rare and precious sound those days. "I don't know where you could have gotten an idea like that, Sitehuti of Western Thebes." She reached down and stroked Neffi, then, assuming her court-face, went out to the hall.

It was mere moments later I heard Iaret scream like her heart was being torn out. I was on my feet and into the hall before I knew I was moving. There, I found Yuni and Meriramesses frozen in mid-sentence and Iaret, ashen-faced, standing with her hands covering her mouth. They were all staring at a large mass of people squeezing in though the gates with a sedan chair hoisted high in their midst. It took me a moment to recognize the limp, dirty and bloody figure in the chair as Prince Amunhotep.

Next, I recognized Banufre. He was the disheveled figure in the front, holding the gates open and directing the fellahin bearing the sedan chair into the hall. Around them boiled a veritable circus of members of Amuny's chariot group, several already worse for drink.

Ban spotted us and rushed over. "Amuny — Prince Amunhotep's chariot lost a wheel on the road. The car tipped and he was thrown out."

Iaret gasped and started toward the crowd, but her father grabbed her arm and pulled her back. His shout rang through the columned hall, *"Silence!"*

Meriramesses slammed his walking staff on the pavement. "Amunhotep, you idiot, what have you done now? It's a wonder you haven't killed yourself, but you could have also killed or injured the horses. As if a destroyed chariot isn't expensive enough — *another* destroyed chariot."

Amunhotep stirred in the litter, too dazed to answer back. As he moved, I saw that his right side was raw and bleeding and there was a large lump on that side of his head, also oozing blood. I wondered if he was even capable at that point of registering that his brother was there.

Djedmose appeared beside me, looking concerned. He murmured, "I don't like the look of those injuries. He doesn't seem to be tracking well, either." He pushed past and into the crowd, doing something unusual for him: laying hands on a royal without asking. The soldier's deft fingers probed the prince's scalp. Amuny winced and flinched, but showed no response when the Medjay raised his eyelids.

At my feet, Neffi paced and made small mewing noises, copper eyes riveted on the injured prince.

"He's hit his head and probably has a concussion of the brain," Djedmose said. He turned back toward us. "Where's that doctor?"

His words sparked Iaret to action. She broke from her father's grip and grabbed Yuni's arm. "Yuni! Go fetch Dr. Merit-Ptah! Send him to my uncle's rooms immediately."

Yuni nodded once and scurried away.

Next, Ia pointed at Ban, "Banufre, guide the fellahin to Uncle Amuny's apartments. Quickly!"

Banufre complied and Neffi trotted alongside the sedan chair, still making the tiny mewing noises. The rest of the circus made to follow, but Iaret stepped into their way. She was, at best, half their size and a quarter of the age of most, but the expression on her face stopped them in their tracks as one.

"You lot, *out!*"

Nedjem looked uncomfortable. "But, Princess Iaret, Amuny is our friend. We want to know how he is."

Iaret nodded, then said, "Very well, you can wait, but you must wait out on the lawns. I'll send word once the doctor has examined him."

As the nobles took their sheepish leave, Ia caught sight of a cluster of servants peering into the hall, trying to be invisible. She searched the faces, found who she was looking for, then said, "Hentaneb, give the fellahin who bore the sedan chair a loaf of bread and jar of beer each. They deserve good payment for bringing Prince Amunhotep home to us."

She started for the doorway leading to Amunhotep's side of the house, then glanced over her shoulder at Djedmose and me. "Well, don't just stand there gaping, come on!"

Djedmose and I did as instructed. As we fell into the young noblewoman's wake, I caught sight of her father's face. It was turned toward his daughter's retreating form and held a look of pride.

~*~

When we got to Amunhotep's rooms, the doctor was already there, busily cleaning and bandaging the injured man. Djedmose and I came over to stand beside Banufre and Iaret. Neffi had stationed himself on the pillow beside the prince's head. Amunhotep absently stroked the cat's fur with his left hand. He seemed to be more aware than he had been downstairs.

Amuny caught sight of me and grinned, pointing to the bandages taking shape under the physician's hands. "Hey, Huti! We almost match." His voice was weak and he slurred a little.

Dr. Merit-Ptah turned the wrapping over to his assistant. When he was satisfied the linen was being applied correctly, he approached our little group.

Iaret asked, "How is he, Doctor?"

"It isn't as bad as it looks, Your Highness. Having said that, it could have been worse. Much worse. According to what the Prince and young Banufre tell me, the chariot was only traveling at a moderate pace when the accident happened. If it had been traveling at full speed. . . ?" He left the "if" unsaid and shrugged, spreading his hands wide.

~*~

The friction between Amunhotep and Meriramesses exploded later that night. Amuny called for a full dinner to be served in the common dining room for, as he put it: "A sort of celebration for not being dead". Nothing big, just family, and a few friends, so there were maybe twenty of us. Trust me, that *was* a small party for Prince Amunhotep.

Lady Wurusemu declined the invitation citing another of the sick headaches that had been plaguing her. Meriramesses accepted and sat slightly removed from the rest of the guests with Iaret by his side.

Somehow, Amuny had even managed to drag Banufre in, although the young man looked uncomfortable. The only other guest to look as awkward was Captain Djedmose. Almost all the others were nobles who went racing with the prince. The group was small enough that Neffi eschewed his usual post under my chair to wander among tables, mooching tidbits from anyone willing to give them.

The evening started out well. Good food, a fine wine and interesting conversation. Even Banufre and Djedmose relaxed a bit as the dinner wore on. It only started to go off the rails after Prince Meriramesses' fifth or sixth cup. I confess, I'd been watching his progress with amazement. I had never seen

Meriramesses drink so much in one sitting. From Ban and Ia's looks, neither had they.

"Would someone please explain to me why we're celebrating the destruction of yet another expensive vehicle?" Meriramesses said. "Why don't we just buy them and burn them as soon as they're delivered. It would save the wear and tear on all the rest of us."

Iaret put her hand on her father's arm, trying to calm him.

Amuny merely rolled his eyes.

"I saw that," Meriramesses said, slamming his wine cup down. "You spend like there's no tomorrow, but *I'm* the villain for calling you a wastrel."

The room got quiet very suddenly. I knew things were going to get bad when Neffi abandoned his begging rounds to assume his sphinx-on-guard pose at my feet.

Amunhotep looked like he'd been slapped. He set his cup down carefully and said, "Better an honest wastrel than a deceitful viper."

Prince Meriramesses leaped from his chair with such force, the heavy wooden furniture slid back a handspan. "Just what are you accusing me of, Brother?"

"For starters, harboring and aiding a dangerous criminal," Amuny replied with a worrisome calm.

"I did no such thing! It was—"

"—poor dead Maia. Amazing how many servants have conveniently turned up dead or run away, *Brother*."

My eyes slid toward Djedmose. He was already poised to come out of his seat.

"Please, Father," Iaret tugged at him, trying to get him to sit. Meriramesses shrugged her off.

"I see no reason to stay here and be insulted by a drunken idiot," he said and stalked off into the private quarters.

"Drunk? You haven't *seen* drunk," Amunhotep roared. He

lunged after his brother, but met Djedmose's shoulder instead.

I barely heard the Medjay as he murmured into the prince's ear. "It's not worth it, Your Highness. His time will come."

Amunhotep stared at the soldier blearily, then nodded. He reclaimed his cup, held it aloft and said, "Now we can *really* party, my friends. *More wine!*"

NINETEEN

The following morning, my stitches came out. It stung like the devil as Dr. Merit-Ptah snipped the linen threads and tugged them from my flesh, but the cut stayed closed. A lot of the itching stopped, too. Djedmose examined the wound, then nodded approvingly.

"Excellent work, sir. Some of the best I have seen," he said.

Dr. Merit-Ptah continued stowing his equipment in the painted chest. "I shall take that as an extreme compliment, Captain."

Djedmose looked thoughtful. "I suppose this means the Scribe will be able to travel? We've been ordered to journey up to Thebes as soon as he's able."

The physician frowned slightly and said, "The wound is healing nicely." The man's eyes twinkled. "As long as no one puts the lad to rowing, I see no reason he can't."

There was a brief, frantic pounding at the apartment's doors, then they burst open spilling Amunhotep's servant, Dedi, into the room.

Dedi glanced around wild-eyed, then rushed over to Merit-Ptah. "Please! You must come. His Royal Highness has been taken ill! He's dying!"

"Which Royal Highness?" demanded Djedmose.

Dedi gulped. "Prince Amunhotep, sir!"

Djedmose grabbed his corslet and sword. "Don't just stand there, man. *Let's move!*"

Dedi pelted back the way he'd come. The physician, Djedmose and I tore off to the prince's suite with Neffi loping alongside.

When we got there, the servants were trying to lift him into his bed, but he was convulsing, and they couldn't maintain their hold. Dr. Merit-Ptah and Captain Djedmose pushed through and, between the two of them, got the prince back onto his cushions. He convulsed again. Froth appeared at the corner of his mouth. His left calf appeared red and swollen.

As soon as the servants saw us, they melted back from the bedside. Oddly, I think it was a reaction more to the presence of Nefer-Djenou-Bastet than that of either the doctor or the Medjay.

Djedmose looked ashen. "I've seen this before."

The physician looked just as grim. "I'm afraid I have, too, Captain."

The Medjay bent over the writhing man. "Your Highness! Can you hear me?"

Amuny tried to speak but a fresh spate of convulsions snapped his jaws shut. The doctor opened his case and ordered the servants to help hold the patient still.

Djedmose grabbed one of the servants as he passed. "You found him here? In his own quarters?"

"Yes, sir," the frightened man said, pointing past me. "Over there. On the floor just inside the door, sir."

To my utter amazement, Djedmose released the servant, took a careful step away from the bed and began to scan the floor warily. I looked down, too, and realized Nefer-Djenou-Bastet was missing.

A hollow, eerie howl rose behind me. Whirling toward the sound, I found Neffi pacing in front of a stack of chests, ears back. That unearthly sound was coming from him.

I started toward him, but Djedmose grabbed my shoulder and pulled me back. "Don't move, kid. Take a closer look at the shadow between those boxes."

I did as the Medjay said, and my heart nearly leapt from my

chest when the shadow moved, rose up, and spread the unmistakable hood of a cobra.

The servants behind us saw it, too, and started up a ululation that almost drowned out the howls of the cat and the physician's shouts for them keep holding the prince down.

Djedmose drew his sword, stepped in front of me, then froze in amazement.

I followed his gaze. Neffi, ears pinned back, fur standing stiffly up along his spine, danced, weaving and bobbing in front of the poised snake. In a flash, the cat lunged then, just as swiftly, bounced several paces back. The snake struck at the place the cat had been moments before, then recoiled, hissing, into the shadows.

The cat moved in again, chittering and clicking. Again, he bobbed and danced just out of reach, leaping forward, then away. This time the snake struck closer, but the stretch brought it fully out into the room. Djedmose tightened his grip on his blade and began a slow step to one the side of the battle.

Neffi seemed unaware of anything but the cobra. He circled and danced in front of it again, hissing and spitting. He leaped forward and feinted out of reach of another strike. A leap up and back lured the reptile out of cover, causing it to stretch its body to its full length. The cat launched himself into the air. Twisting in mid-leap, Neffi landed astride his prey. In a lightning move, he grabbed the serpent behind the head with his teeth, killing it with one powerful crunch.

In the heavy silence, broken only by the dying prince's labored breathing, he trotted over and presented me with the corpse.

I heard gasping and choking behind me and realized Amunhotep was trying to speak. I leaned in to hear his words.

"By the gods," he rasped. "I'm glad I lived long enough to see that."

Djedmose rushed forward. "Your Highness, how did this happen?"

Amunhotep ignored the Medjay and clamped my arm with a fever-burning hand. His eyes bored into mine, but I don't think he could really see me by then. He smiled slightly. "Remember, Huti, you promised I could have one."

Another convulsion wracked his body and he was gone.

TWENTY

We were so close to Saqqara, that it took no time for the funerary priests to arrive. They washed Prince Amunhotep's body, then carried him away to the waiting embalmers amid wailing and tears. Djedmose and the Medjay cohort that were in Memphis formed an honor guard to escort the prince and the contingent of priests to the Place of Purification. A priest wearing a full head and shoulders mask of Anubis led the procession. There was much wailing and sobbing among the servants, too. A part of me — the nasty part, I suppose — wondered how many of the tears were because they were now working for Meriramesses without the mitigating factor of his more casual brother. I wouldn't have been looking forward to it if I'd been in their place.

The background buzz to all this was as salt in my wound, though. Every place I went in the house, the servants fawned over Neffi and me. Oh, it was wonderful! The Sacred One of Amun and Bastet had killed the snake just like the cats who ran in front of the bark of the sun! No one but me seemed to notice that Neffi had been alerted to the snake too late to save the Prince, and I didn't say it out loud.

Later that evening, the dining area was more formal and subdued than usual. Even Neffi was quiet and hardly begged at all. Meriramesses and his family were all in mourning, eyebrows shaved and dirt smeared on their cheeks. Iaret's eyes looked as if she'd truly been crying. Djedmose was conspicuously absent. I wondered whether he had absented himself or if he was now unwelcome at the table.

When Amuny was alive, he'd declared that the Medjay captain would take meals with the family and be treated as a guest. This was likely as thanks for Djedmose coming to my rescue in the wine press. On the other hand, part of it could well have been that being treated as a guest made the Medjay extremely uncomfortable. There had been just enough mischief in Amuny to have taken a great deal of pleasure in that, too.

When I returned to my apartment after dinner, Lieutenant Si-Montu was standing guard outside the door. I wasn't surprised at all to find Djedmose waiting inside. It didn't require a great deal of perception to see the captain wasn't in a good mood. He sprawled in a chair with a jug of wine and two cups on the table beside him. I dropped into the opposite chair and kicked off the dress sandals High Priest Pedibastet had given me to wear for court occasions. They were leather, stiffened with gold; very beautiful and exceedingly uncomfortable.

I pushed them out of the way with a bare foot and said, "Now I understand what His Highness, the Crown Prince, meant about these court shoes. They aren't footwear, they're gilded instruments of torture."

In spite of his mood, this made Djedmose laugh. "I've heard him declare that many times, myself. Many of the princes of the Great House are not fond of ceremony. A trait I gather they inherited directly from his Majesty, the Divine Ramesses, himself."

"You'd never know that by watching Prince Meriramesses. The man does love his pomp," I said. "Does he take after his mother or something?"

"I can't comment on that, never having met the lady." The Medjay poured out two cups of a deep red wine and handed one to me. "Let's drink to the *other* Prince."

I took the offered cup. "Amuny would like that."

We drank to the memory of Prince Amunhotep.

Afterward, Djedmose relapsed into his funk. Slumping into the chair, he regarded the floor with a frown. "I confess, I consider what happened with Prince Amunhotep to be a personal failure. It's my job to protect the Royal House and I never saw this one coming."

"I think I know how you feel. Almost everyone I've met today sees Neffi and launches into that thing about the Sacred Cat destroying the serpent to ensure the passage of Re's Solar Bark. Like I'm responsible for his victory or that we even *saved* anyone."

Djedmose sat forward and regarded Neffi who was stretched across the uncomfortable sandals with half-closed eyes. "I'll grant you, it would have been the best outcome to have discovered the snake *before* it bit the Prince — still — I've never seen anything quite like what Nefer-Djenou-Bastet did last night."

I joined him in looking at the somnolent cat. "It was pretty amazing, wasn't it?"

"That it was, but we can't let it blind us to the fact that the snake didn't get in there by accident. It couldn't — we're on the top floor. All right, I know snakes can climb, but still. . . ."

I went cold inside and set the empty wine cup aside slowly. "Are you saying Prince Amunhotep was murdered?"

The Medjay spread his hands. "There's no other word for it. I've been all over that room. There are very few ways a snake that size could have made it to His Highness' suite without being seen, yet I can't find any way a cobra could have been introduced."

"Unless it's been removed already," I said slowly. "While it was happening, all anyone was thinking about was Prince Amunhotep. Afterward, it's been like the Avenue of the Sphinxes on a festival day: people in and out constantly."

"Too true. And more often taking things out of the apartment, rather than putting things in." He frowned. "I think perhaps our late Prince was right, there are more vipers in this house than the one the Sacred One killed last night."

That gave me pause. It wasn't that I didn't know it, it's simply that I didn't want it to be real. Amuny's death removed that fantasy. What was left in its place was ugly.

Djedmose stood, resuming his all-business demeanor. "The good news is that we're out of here come tomorrow. I spoke with General Seti-Merenptah today and our instructions are still to continue on to Thebes. We'll be leaving early in the morning."

I found myself fingering the wine jug with the broken seal of the estate, bearing the names of both Ramesses II and Prince Amunhotep. I shook myself out of it and said, "I'll be ready. I haven't unpacked much since the move from the temple. As soon as I throw these formal things in, I'm good."

Djedmose chuckled. "Yeah? Well if you want to pack those sandals in one piece, you better take them away from the Sacred One real fast."

I looked down just in time for Nefer-Djenou-Bastet to toss one of my fancy golden sandals high into the air, leap after it and land on it, all claws bared. I yelped and dived for it.

TWENTY-ONE

The journey to Thebes was a quiet one. The death of Prince Amunhotep had shaken us all. As far as I knew, only Djedmose, myself and the actual murderer had any idea that the Prince's death was anything more than a tragic accident. Still, Amuny was the sort of man that people just assumed would go on and on forever. Kind of like the big boisterous hound who barks all hours, chews the furniture and pees on your best linens. Half the time you're ready to wring his neck and put him out of your misery. Then one day, he's gone and there's a hole where all the noise and mayhem used to be.

A messenger had been sent ahead of us to inform the Pharaoh and Crown Prince of the death and another to Western Thebes to let the workers in the Place of Truth know that the prince's tomb would soon be needed. That tugged at me, too, but for an entirely different reason. It had been a long time — years — since I'd been back to my home village. When I was busy studying, I never gave it much thought. Somehow it was different now. Maybe having someone trying to kill you changes your point of view.

It was quiet, but our riverboat was full. We were once again sailing with Captain Jebahou-Nefer which made me wonder again how close her ties were to the Great House. Several local families joined us on the boat including Banufre and his parents. Ma'aheu was trying to keep a stoic face, but was failing miserably. With all the hooha about Prince Amunhotep's death, it was easy to forget that Ma'aheu had lost a son, too. The fact that son was involved in questionable dealings — more questionable than even his father could suspect — didn't make the hurt any less. The thought that his middle son would pass into the West without a name, and so be consigned to oblivion because of his crimes, must have made it doubly hard. It was also the family's reason for the last-minute decision to travel to Thebes. They hoped to petition the forgiveness of the Divine Ramesses. *I* hoped the special gifts they brought to the Pharaoh would soften him and the Crown Prince toward the innocent members of the family.

Renen was with us, too, more determined than ever to become my personal servant. Master Ta had sent him along with his blessings. In fact, everyone but me thought it was a great idea. Personally, I hoped the Sem Priest at the temple back in Pi-Ramesses would give him a berth there until I had a place of my own. I wasn't looking forward to telling Aunt Tiaa that I was bringing a servant home with me. She'd taken badly enough to the cat.

It felt unfinished to leave Memphis. That feeling surprised me. I'd never wanted the job of investigator, but now that I had it, I wanted to do it to the best of my ability. I suppose my time in Memphis *could* have been considered a success. Paseti was accounted for — if dead counted. But, because of that death, we knew little more about the conspirators and, more importantly, their plot, than we did before I left Pi-Ramesses. It was telling, though, that Prince Amunhotep was killed right after he publicly accused his brother of harboring Paseti.

How involved was Prince Meriramesses? He had to be aware that a man had been brought into his home, killed and tossed into the river. There was also the matter of Chief Scribe Ipuy. He'd been murdered by Paseti seemingly because he'd learned something he intended to tell me, but never got the chance.

Ipuy had certainly told me a lot, even though he danced around making definite accusations. He seemed to believe that Lady Wurusemu was responsible for the deaths of several servants. There was no proof, though. Not for any of it. No one piped up and said, "I saw it all! They did it".

The matter of Khety was resolved, too, although that was only a partial success. Finding him dead and buried in the ancient necropolis wasn't how I'd envisioned finding him. Naive, I suppose, but a happy ending would have been nice. Even the fact that the Great House of Ramesses II was footing the bill for a fine burial in the ancient necropolis near his family seemed a little hollow.

Just as hollow as finding and destroying the cobra *after* it killed Prince Amunhotep. Both Khety and Amuny were still dead. It felt like I was falling way behind and racing to catch up. If I was supposed to be so special and Nefer-Djenou-Bastet so magical, then why the hell couldn't we actually save someone's life?

The day we pulled into Thebes was bittersweet, too. As the hands threw ropes onto the piers and hauled us into the dock, I could see the other docks across the swollen river and just make out the road threading through the hills toward my home village. Before we left Memphis, I'd asked General Seti-Merenptah for leave to visit my family and only received a "We'll see how things go".

~*~

Thebes was always a bustling place, but in the days before the Opet, it was bursting with people, colors and activity. Good smells wafted from the food booths set up near the docks to take advantage of the influx of travelers pouring in for the festival. This was one of the biggest and most important festivals of the year, the time when Amun and Mut renewed their marriage vows. When they and their son, Khons, made the journey from Karnak to the great temple at Luxor in their sacred barque. It was also when the Pharaoh repeated his coronation rites and made offerings to Amun-Re on behalf of the people. Everyone wanted to be there. Who wouldn't?

In spite of all the sadness, it was good to be attending the celebration in the ancient city that year. Festivals in the new capital were grand, but Opet in Thebes was different. Not that I remembered my last festival in the city very well. I'd been six, and holding tight to my mother's hand. I wondered if my family might be there now, somewhere in that swirling, ever-shifting throng. Even if they were, making connections would be hard since Captain Djedmose and I were heading directly to the palace from the boat. I had no idea what would happen next, but I hoped at least part of it would involve leave to visit my family before returning to Pi-Ramesses.

I'd been worried about Neffi with the crowd. We'd been in busy places before, but this was different. A lot more people with a lot more distractions to lure a cat into trouble. As soon as we came in sight of the docks, I'd looped my stole into a sling across my chest and put Neffi into it. He settled down immediately, eyes half-closed as he had in Amunhotep's chariot at Saqqara. I was glad. It was easier to keep him from leaping away at random than when he rode on my shoulders.

As soon as we pulled into our waiting berth at the city, I saw I needn't have worried about getting through the crowd. A contingent of Djedmose's Medjay waited for us on the shore. I knew from experience in Pi-Ramesses that people melted away in front of a group of marching Medjay, no matter what.

It worked that way in Thebes, too. The Medjay cohort closed

around Neffi and me while Captain Djedmose led the way to the palace. The porters fell in behind us with the luggage, a happy Renen among them, carrying my scroll case and his own new bag of belongings.

At the palace, we parted ways with the Medjay. They marched off to their barracks and Renen, Neffi and I were handed over to the Chief Royal Butler, a pleasant and efficient man named Kha'Emteri.

We followed the butler through the pylon gates, veered away from the governmental offices and entered an area that looked more like a park than part of a building complex. We passed several houses, royal residences according to Kha'Emteri, and went through a beautifully carved and painted double wooden gate into a walled garden. There was a house nestled inside, not as big as the ones we'd passed outside, but a cool, inviting place, nonetheless.

Once inside the airy, columned entrance hall, Kha'Emteri bowed low and said, "Welcome to this house, Sitehuti of Western Thebes. It is our hope that you will be comfortable in this place and that the Sacred One will enjoy his gardens."

As if on cue, Neffi struggled out of the sling and disappeared into the plantings outside the door. I was overwhelmed. The house was beautiful. The stone first story with its tiled floors and surrounding gardens gave the place a fresh, comfortable feel. "Thank you, Kha'Emteri, but which is my room? Is it upstairs?"

"The sleeping rooms are indeed upstairs, Honored Scribe. You may choose the one that suits you best. The porters will wait for you to instruct them where to place the luggage." With that, he bowed even lower and left me standing speechless in the hall.

Apparently, the whole house was mine. I was definitely not used to that. The private guest room at the temple had seemed like a lot, then the room and later apartment at the princes' estate was extravagant — but this? The palace was a whole different world. Even Renen was awed into silence — for a while, anyway.

After a moment, shuffling from the waiting porters brought me back.

Renen tugged at my arm. "Should I go up and choose a bedroom for these guys to put the luggage in?"

I nodded. "Yeah. That will work, thanks, Renen."

I wasn't sure I'd ever get used to this servant business.

When the porters left, we were alone in that big house. There was a cook and her assistant provided by the palace, but they pretty much kept to their rooftop kitchen. My meager two clothing chests and scroll case looked very lonely in the big bedroom Renen had selected for me. He said he'd picked it because it had the best light. He was right. It did.

Neffi had returned from the garden and found me upstairs. He sniffed along the base of the walls, hopped into windows, wound around lamps and braziers, then sprawled across the middle of the bed. The bed was so huge, I'd figured it wouldn't be as hard to share with the cat as usual. I'd forgotten that cats ooze to fill all available space. Too bad I wasn't able to do that. I'd never had a room to myself in my life and this one looked bigger than my parents' whole house. I was feeling small, lonely and a little like a solitary clay bead in a big rattle.

Thinking about my parents' house was a mistake. A wave of homesickness washed over me. Homesickness for a place I hadn't seen in a decade.

Neffi yawned and stretched out, impossibly taking up even more space than he had before. As I was glaring at the disinterested bed hog, Renen appeared at the top of the stairs.

"Did I pick right?" he asked.

I turned and smiled, "Yes, it's a great room, just . . . big."

"Um, Sitehuti, do I have to stay in the servant's room with the two cooks?"

"Well, no, not if you don't want to. Which room would you like better?"

"This one. I want to put my pallet at the foot of your bed like I did at Prince Amunhotep's."

Apparently I wasn't the only one overwhelmed by the accommodations. "I don't know why not. There's plenty of space in here."

"Great!" Renen said and disappeared down the steps, only to reappear moments later with a bedroll and his bag of belongings. As he spread his pallet on the painted plaster floor, someone rapped loudly at the carved gates to the garden. "Oh!" Renen said. "I'll get that," and disappeared down the steps again.

I descended, too, curious to see who would be calling so soon after our arrival. As I stepped into the entry hall, Renen led a palace messenger in from the gardens. The man bowed and said, "Sitehuti of Western Thebes, I am instructed to escort you and the Sacred One, Nefer-Djenou-Bastet, to the royal apartments for a private conversation with His Royal Highness, Crown Prince Merenptah and His Eminence, High Priest Pedibastet."

~*~

Neffi grumbled when I picked him up and carried him downstairs, but seemed perfectly happy to follow the messenger through the gardens and to the very back of the park-like private area. We entered the palace proper through a side door, then went up a long flight of stairs to wind up at an elegant room furnished with chairs and couches. I was guided to a couch beside a table with winc and fruit on it, then the messenger left, closing the doors behind him.

I admit I was slouching in the Crown Prince's anteroom feeling pretty down on myself. All the palace servants we met on our way were officially in mourning, but still made over Neffi for killing the cobra. Most of them had never met Amunhotep, but a recognized son of the Pharaoh had died and that was enough. Everyone was going on about how Neffi and I saved the day in Memphis, but I found that too painful to listen to. No matter how I tried to look at it, I couldn't get past the fact that, yes, the snake was dead, but Amuny was, too. My mind was spinning and a million miles away from the elegant room I sat in, when I heard someone say:

"Well! Hello, Cat. You look like you belong in one of the temples."

I turned to see a thinnish old man with wispy white hair leaning heavily on an ornate gold walking stick. He was bent down to pet Neffi who was standing on his hind legs against the man's richly embroidered robes. The man said, "What're you doing here, Fella? Did you slip past the guards, too?"

I'm ashamed to say that my funk made recognition of the jewelry and distinctly hawk-like features a little slow. When at last I realized I was looking at Userma'atre Setepenre Ramesses Meriamon, himself, I dropped and pressed my forehead against the floor.

The great man must have noticed the movement because he said, "You! Boy! Did you bring this cat in here?"

"Uhhhh, yes, Your Majesty," I mumbled into the floor. Then I remembered myself and launched into the greeting: "Thou art like Re in all that thou doest, everything happens according to the wish of thy heart—"

It seems to be a family trait to never let me get any farther in my litany than that. The Divine Ramesses whacked his walking stick on the floor tiles and snapped, "Yes, yes! All good, all proper, but you can stop now, boy. At my age, I might be on the barque to the Land of the West before you finish that thing. Get up off the floor before you suffocate down there." He moved over to one of the cushioned chairs, lowered himself into it, then gave me a sharp look. "Ah yes, you're the young scribe my son and son-in-law have been talking about." He glanced down at Neffi who was snuffling his hand and said, "And this looks like a temple cat because he is." He sat back and chuckled, then said to Neffi, "Must be getting old or I'd have realized that as soon as I saw you, Cat."

He looked back at me. "Close your mouth, boy, or something will fly in. That would be amusing, but not productive. What's your name?"

I realized I'd been gaping, snapped my mouth shut and bowed. "I'm Sitehuti from Western Thebes, the Place of Truth, Your Majesty, and this is Nefer-Djenou-Bastet from the temple of Bastet in Pi-Ramesses."

He raised an eyebrow. "From the Place of Truth?" He suddenly looked sad and much, much older. "Very appropriate since I've just lost another son. But I understand you know that, too."

"Yes, sir. I share your sorrow at Prince Amunhotep's loss." No surprise, Neffi really liked Pharaoh Ramesses. He jumped up into the massive chair and stretched out beside the old man with his front paws hanging over the edge of the cushion, kneading the air.

"And this is the cat who battled the serpent. It's a pity you and Nefer-Djenou-Bastet weren't called to the scene earlier, young man. Poor Amuny. He never was much good at anything other than being likable."

I found myself grinning, "Yes, Your Majesty, he certainly was that."

This earned me a sharp look. "You knew him. You knew Prince Amunhotep."

I lost my grin and bowed. "Yes, Your Majesty, I did. He showed me great hospitality and helped me in many ways."

"He was with you in the ancient necropolis when you found that scribe who had gone missing, so I understand."

"Yes, Your Majesty. If he hadn't been with me, I might not have been able to follow up on the lead that took us to the grave."

"Yes. That was Amuny. Always willing to help." The Pharaoh went silent, his thoughts turned momentarily inward, then he sat forward, pointing to the table behind me. "Is that wine over there in that pitcher?"

Startled, I said, "Yes, Your Majesty, it is."

"Good. Fetch me a cup."

I got control of my nerves and managed to pour more wine into the cup than on the table, then took it to him.

"Now pour yourself one, sit down and tell me about some of the things you and my son did. It will be refreshing to hear someone speak of him in a positive light. He and I never saw eye-to-eye on the virtues of responsibility. Still, I loved him very much. He was my son, after all."

I did as he asked and was sitting on a low stool at the great man's feet, deep into the story of the wild chariot ride to Saqqara, when Djedmose opened the doors to the study.

"Scribe, the Crown Prince and—" he began, then caught sight of Ramesses II. It's rare to see Captain Djedmose taken by surprise. He's usually the one who does it to other people. It was rewarding to see him blanch and drop into a salute and bow. "Your Majesty! My apologies! I had no idea you were in here. How may I serve you?"

"At ease, Captain. I simply dropped by to confer with my son, but it's no matter. The scribe and I were having an interesting conversation. Young Sitehuti here has a true storyteller's knack at a tale."

Djedmose bowed again. "I will inform the Crown Prince immediately." He then turned on his heel and left. Catching sight of the Pharaoh's expression as the Nubian hurried away, I wondered if he'd enjoyed the Medjay's discomfort as much as I had.

As if in answer, the great man chuckled. "Captain Djedmose is very good at his job. This is a good thing because it outweighs how much of a pain in the ass he is."

I tried hard not to snort, but failed. The Pharaoh smiled and I found myself thinking that maybe Amunhotep and his father were a bit more alike than either of them thought.

Shortly, Crown Prince Merenptah and High Priest Pedibastet entered with Captain Djedmose in tow. Merenptah said, "Father, I didn't know you were joining us."

"I didn't either," The Pharaoh said. "But I'm glad I did. This young scribe has some very amusing stories about our Amuny."

Ramesses waved everyone toward chairs. "Sit down. I'm getting a stiff neck looking up at you."

Merenptah and Pedibastet complied. Djedmose merely stood with his back to the closed door and tried to look invisible. Yeah. Like that could ever happen.

"Now, Merny, Padi, you called the boy here. Say what you wanted to say," Rameses said, leaning back into his chair, fingers absently rubbing Neffi's ears.

Crown Prince Merenptah looked troubled. "First, we would like to extend our thanks for finding the missing scribe and leading us to the former priest, Paseti. You deserve great reward for accomplishing that for us. The problem is that a large part of the job remains unfinished."

"We still don't know exactly who is responsible or what the

plot actually is," added Pedibastet. "There are also some very disturbing factors that have come to light, Father."

Ramesses II shot them a sharp look. "What disturbing factors, Padi?"

Merenptah looked even more uncomfortable. "It would be best to have Captain Djedmose and Sitehuti give the report. They were there on the scene." The Crown Prince motioned to the Medjay, who reluctantly stepped up beside his commander's seat.

"Your Majesty, I was present when it occurred and . . . I sensed something amiss with the manner of Prince Amunhotep's death. The Prince's bed chamber was on the top floor of the mansion, and while it is known that snakes can climb, it would have been a difficult one. There was also where the Prince was found. He had fallen just inside the doors to his rooms, beside a stack of clothing chests. That is also where the Sacred One cornered the serpent later."

Djedmose paused. Merenptah motioned for him to continue. "After examining the rooms, the scribe and I reached the conclusion that the death of Prince Amunhotep was not an accident."

Silence reigned. I kept my eyes on the floor, not daring to breathe.

"*Why?* Why Amuny?" The Pharaoh demanded angrily. "There could have been no one less likely to pose a threat than Amuny." The great man stopped short as he caught a look passing between Djedmose and myself. "What is it? Exactly what are you thinking?"

Unwilling to be the bearer of the news, Djedmose glanced at Merenptah.

The Crown Prince took up the tale, "Father, that thought occurred to us, as well. But you'll be even less happy to hear where that line of thought has taken us than by the fact that

Amuny was murdered."

Ramesses' hawk-like face was both stern and sad as he ordered, "Tell it."

My heart broke. I'd never given much thought to the fact that this was more than the ruler of the Two Lands. He was also a father whose sons were at odds with each other.

Merenptah said quietly, "The only way any of this makes sense is if Meriramesses, or someone close to him, were in some way complicit. Meriramesses has long been in contention with your policies, Father. He has also long clashed with Amunhotep and been resentful of his way of life. The timing is suspect, as well. Amunhotep was killed within hours of accusing Meriramesses of having harbored the traitor Paseti right there on the estate."

The Pharaoh looked like he'd bitten something sour. "And that Hittite woman is probably in it up to her fine alabaster neck. Enjoys fanning the flames, that one. Meritamon never trusted the woman. I should have listened to her, but I signed off on the marriage, anyway. Too many good, solid political reasons not to agree."

"Unfortunately, those same political considerations give them both a shield," the Crown Prince said. "Not to mention that, being members of the Royal Family, not just anyone can make an accusation against them."

"True," the Pharaoh said. "We must have rock-solid, undeniable evidence."

"Or they could be named by a conspirator," the High Priest amended. "That carries weight, too. Paseti's elder brother, Captain Sasobek, of the Seth Division, is already under observation. We propose to send Captain Djedmose, Sitehuti and the Sacred One out to figuratively beat the bushes, Father. A full confession from Sasobek would either implicate Meriramesses or lead us to the evidence we need."

Ramesses nodded. "Yes. That could very well work. I so order it to be done."

Pedibastet sat forward. "Father, there is another matter, as well, a question of mercy. Paseti, the former Lector. His father and stepmother are in Thebes seeking an audience with you. They wish to give you a gift and ask forgiveness for their family for what the errant son — or sons — have done."

Crown Prince Merenptah shook his head with finality. "No. They can go hang. One of his sons was plotting directly against the throne and another might still be involved."

"I'm inclined to agree. We need to make a strong example of the entire family," Ramesses said.

I looked down again. Pedibastet must have seen it because he said, "Father, Brother? I believe Sitehuti has something to say on this matter."

My heart leaped into my throat. There was no way I could say what I was thinking. How did I tell the Pharaoh and the Crown Prince they were wrong? Through the panicked buzzing in my ears, I heard Djedmose, "I believe the scribe wants to say there might be another way to handle the family of Paseti, sirs."

Ramesses looked interested and leaned forward. "Indeed? Speak, Scribe."

"Yes, Your Majesty," I squeaked. I cleared my throat and tried again. "Sirs, I've spoken at length with Ma'aheru; his wife, Lady Neferhedjet, and their son, Banufre. They are all fiercely loyal to Your Majesty and had all but disowned Paseti and his elder brother, Sasobek, even before the brothers became involved in this plot. Might it not be more effective to receive them and their gifts in that spirit? I believe Ma'aheru would be extremely grateful and that the generosity of Your Majesty would fully cement his family's ties to the throne." I tried not to gulp, keeping my eyes on the floor and on Neffi who had left the

Pharaoh's chair to sit sphinx-like in front of me.

There was silence for a few heartbeats, then the Crown Prince said thoughtfully, "There is truth to these words, Father. Also, if this Banufre is the one I'm thinking of, he was a favorite of my half-brother Amunhotep."

Djedmose said, "Yes, Your Highness, you do remember correctly."

Ramesses sat back, thought for a bit, and I held my breath.

Finally, the great man said, "Very well, it won't hurt to play it this way, at least for the time being." He turned again to Pedibastet. "What gifts are they bringing, Padi?"

Pedibastet sorted through a stack of papyri, selected one and read, "Seven jars of fine red wine and five jars of sweet white wine."

"And a few jars of some *really* good date wine," I said before I realized I'd spoken. "Your Majesty," I added lamely.

The Pharaoh laughed. "With such a recommendation, I can hardly wait to give it a taste."

TWENTY-TWO

Back in the guest house after the palace meeting, I can only describe my thoughts as vacillating and uncertain. The things the Great House asked me to do — no — *expected* me to do were so important I could hardly fathom it. I definitely couldn't fathom why they trusted me with the job. As far as I could see everything that had happened to that point had been all but accidental. I had literally stumbled onto things or they'd stumbled onto me. How was I, a junior scribe from an artisan family, supposed to lay a net to snare a prince and his royal wife, or even one for a professional soldier from a high status farming family? It wasn't like I could march in, accuse them and have them dragged off for interrogation. I mean, yes, it had been done before, but as was mentioned previously, the ramifications for all involved didn't bear thinking about.

It felt as if the familiar earth had fallen away, dumping me into a whole new dangerous world filled with intrigue and I was having to learn the workings of this uncharted land as I plunged through the darkness. Don't get me wrong. I wasn't unaware that people could be nasty. Far from it. There'd been rampant double dealing in the village of the workmen at the Place of Truth and lots of back-biting at school, but this? This was as different in scale as the luxurious guest house I sat in was from my tiny shared bedroom over my aunt's weaver's shop. It was something that had never before even entered my dreams — or nightmares.

The worst part of the whole thing was that when I pointed out how ill-equipped I was, everyone thought I was being modest. Modest. I felt dishonest; as if my entire being was a lie and, if the Feather of Ma'at had been weighed against my heart right then, I'd have dropped so fast, the Eater of Souls would have had to dive to catch me.

Renen poked his head into the room and said, "Captain Djedmose is here."

The announcement came a little late because Djedmose almost ran the boy down striding in. The Medjay stood in the middle of the sitting room and gave it a once over. "Nice digs, kid," he said approvingly. "You landed well."

"Yeah, it's so nice it's making me twitchy," I said. "I liked the apartment at Amuny's better. It was big, but fewer frills."

Djedmose chuckled, then sat in the chair opposite. Almost immediately, he stood again, brow creased, and pulled a big tasseled pillow out of the seat. Tossing it to one side, he seated himself again. "I see what you mean."

The cushion didn't stay vacant for long. Neffi strolled up, stomped a few circles in the center, then nestled down, curled into a tight, spotted roll.

"*He* likes it. I think the place is more for him than me, anyway," I observed.

Djedmose grunted or maybe laughed. I wasn't sure which. "I bring news, Sitehuti. Good or bad, you choose. A royal barge carrying Prince Meriramesses, Lady Wurusemu and their personal servants pulled into the palace docks this afternoon. They've taken up residence in one of the larger houses in the palace complex." He looked out onto the lush greenery surrounding the guest house and his lips twitched a little. "They tell me it has its own enclosed garden."

I ignored the garden comment. It wasn't like I picked the

place out myself. I said, "Well, I guess it's to be expected. That pair loves a show. Now, with Amunhotep out of the way, they're free to put on any kind of show they want. Is Princess Iaret with them?"

"She is. My Medjay tell me she doesn't look happy."

"She probably isn't. I felt terrible for leaving her alone when we left Memphis."

This time the quirk was definitely a smile. "I guarantee you, Sitehuti, the young lady was never as alone as it seemed."

"You had people keeping an eye on her?"

"And on young Banufre. With all of the underhanded dealings that had already gone on, we didn't believe the young lady, her young man, *or* that young man's family to be safe."

There was something in the Medjay's tone that worried me. "Oh, you *didn't* tell the Crown Prince and the Pharaoh that they're in love with each other, did you?"

The quirk became a full-fledged grin. "It *might* have been mentioned. In fact, you were one to mention it. I turned your reports over to the Crown Prince as soon as we arrived in Thebes. They've now been thoroughly studied. The Pharaoh complimented your clear writing style many times during the readings, by the way."

"Oh, no. They told me that in confidence. Ia and Ban are going to kill me."

"I doubt that. Especially since your reports might have colored the opinion of the Great House in a somewhat more positive light."

"Really? How?"

"In a way, it was Prince Amunhotep who changed their opinion," Djedmose said thoughtfully. "He may not have lived to write the letter petitioning his father on behalf of Princess Iaret and his friend, Banufre, but he told you he was going to, and you wrote it into an official report."

"That his father just read."

"And chose to view as a direct request from his late son."

That aspect of recounting all that happened as it happened had escaped me. It shouldn't have, but I was new at the whole investigator thing. It was wonderful that Amuny's wishes would be recognized in regards to Ban and Ia, but I hoped Djedmose was right and my friends would forgive me. Ia and Ban had sworn me to secrecy. No doubt they'd understand having to let Captain Djedmose know, but the Crown Prince and the Pharaoh? Probably High Priest Pedibastet, too.

I didn't want to think about it. Instead, I changed the subject. "I'm sure the Prince and his Lady are here for the opening ceremony where the extended Royal Family greets the Pharaoh's barge when it arrives at the temples, but could it mean something else, too? Could it mean they'll make whatever move they're planning right here? During the festival?"

"We considered that." Djedmose shrugged. "It would make sense. All the players are in one place and everyone will be distracted by the festival. That fact might change our plans a little, too."

"How so?"

We were going to focus on Sasobek, but the arrival of Prince Meriramesses and Lady Wurusemu might give us even more opportunity."

"I hope it also means there's something we can do to help Princess Iaret. She's stuck in the middle of all this and is terrified. Ban and his parents are afraid, too, and I don't blame any of them. In their position, I'd probably be a tiny puddle of melted wax."

Djedmose grunted again, this time with an added nod. I was beginning to wonder if 'grunt' was an all-purpose expression for the captain. At length he said, "The other thing I came to tell you is that our parade troop inspection will begin the day after tomorrow. All four divisions, Re, Amun, Ptah and Seth have at least one platoon of charioteers and foot soldiers here for the processionals. It'll be excellent cover to interview their captains and have them put their men through their paces."

"Captains as in Captain Sasobek of the Seth Division?"

"Yes! Exactly like that," the Medjay said, standing. "It will likely take all day, so be ready to go early. I'll come for you myself."

"So, what am I to do tomorrow?"

"Enjoy your downtime. Look around. Get the lay of the land. It's useful to know the battlefield before the war begins."

Djedmose always knew what to say to make me feel more at ease.

~*~

Taking Captain Djedmose's advice, the following morning found me exploring the palace and its grounds. I was worried that I'd wander someplace that would get me — or more likely Neffi — into trouble, but most people we encountered were too busy to mind what we did. The festival was still several days away, but the whole complex was buzzing with preparations. The kitchens were insanely busy, painters and decorators fairly flew from place to place. I had an awful time keeping Neffi from diving face-first into the sauces or winding himself up in the brightly-colored linen hangings.

Even without the festival dressings, the palace was an amazing place with something new around every turn. When I found the library, I thought my head might explode. Sure, I'd seen big libraries before. Every House of Life in every temple in the Two Lands had one, but this? All this belonged to one person.

After I tore myself away from the library, I went down a new corridor and made a turn that brought me out into a different part of the communal gardens for the private areas. It was landscaped with persea, date and tamarisk trees. The trees encircled a large, square pond that was ringed with flower beds and whose surface was dotted with lotus blossoms. Somewhere nearby, jasmine was in bloom, filling the air with a heady scent. The beauty was calming. I needed a lot of calm just then, so I sat on a bench near the pond, pulled Neffi up beside me, closed my eyes and tried to let the scents and breezes clear my mind.

That's what I was doing when Neffi sat up and chirped. He was focused to our right, watching someone slink from residence to residence, trying to peek over walls and under gates. Memphis and Ma'aheru's plight still weighed on my mind, so from that distance, the person looked a lot like Banufre. Neffi hopped down, and tail in the air, sauntered toward the slinker. I followed. As we got closer, I realized it *was* Banufre.

We were both overjoyed to find a friendly face in a strange new place. We hugged and pounded each other on the back for a while.

"I'm so glad to see you," I said. "I thought the only familiar person I'd see on the grounds would be Captain Djedmose — and he doesn't count."

"Don't tell him that," Ban said with mock severity. "He'll drag you off to be flogged until you change your mind."

"He just might," I said, laughing. Inwardly, my thoughts turned back to the conversation of the day before. I hoped the Pharaoh and the Crown Prince kept the positive attitude Captain Djedmose claimed they had. I briefly thought about giving my friend a heads up that his secret was blown, but decided against it. The gardens weren't the place for a conversation like that. What I said was: "Where are you staying?"

He brightened a little. "You know my mother's family are

well-to-do merchants? My grandfather is letting us use his townhouse here in Thebes. Not a palace, but very nice."

He glanced around nervously. "I keep expecting to get tossed out. I'm not supposed to be here. There was so much chaos at the gates with scads of porters running every which way with all kinds of luggage, I just kind of walked in and nobody said anything."

I nodded. "It's the same way in the rest of the palace. Everyone is so busy with things for the festival, a team of horses could probably drive through and they'd barely register. Anyway, if anyone asks now, you're with Neffi and me. They put us — Neffi, Renen and me — in a guest house on the palace grounds. Well, *they* call it a guest house. It's a full house. Way bigger than the apartment Amuny gave us. Sits smack in the middle of its own walled garden."

Banufre went wide-eyed. "Wow!"

"Yeah, I know. What were you looking for, anyway?"

"Ia. I heard she and her parents arrived this afternoon. She's somewhere in the private residences, but I don't know which one."

Some detective that I didn't put *that* together. I said, "I might be able to help. I heard it's one of the biggest."

It helped, but even knowing that, it took us a while. The palace complex was huge and the private residence portion was a big chunk of it.

~*~

Once we'd found the likeliest house, we didn't have to work hard to determine we had the right place. We were lurking outside a garden wall, listening for anything when we heard quiet sobs. It sounded like a woman trying to muffle her tears, but not quite succeeding.

I pulled back. "Someone's crying in there."

Ban whispered, "That's Ia! I just know it. We have to get inside."

"But how?" I asked. "This is a *big* wall and you can bet any servants have been instructed to toss us out on our butts if we dare to come to the gate."

"At best. Probably have orders to kill us on—"

From inside a woman said softly, "Neffi? Neffi! How did you get here?"

We strained to hear more, but there was silence until: "Huti?"

It was definitely Iaret and she sounded to be right against the wall opposite us.

Ban pressed a palm against the rough stucco. "And Ban! I'm here, too!"

Neffi appeared directly above us. He reclined along the sun-warmed stucco, twitching the tip of his tail and looking smug as only a cat can.

Ia said, "Stay where you are. I'll be right out."

A short time later, Iaret hurried around the corner of the garden wall and threw herself on the two of us. "I'm so glad to see you! Both of you! I know you and Captain Djedmose left for Thebes before we did, Sitehuti, but Ban. . . ? What are you doing here?"

Ban's smile disappeared. "I'm here with my parents. They've come to petition the Divine Ramesses for mercy." He perked up as he added, "The Chief Royal Butler put Huti in his own house, though! Right here at the palace!"

I shrugged. "I think it was more for Neffi than me. They kept saying they hoped that the Sacred One would enjoy his garden. The house is in the middle of a walled garden with a reflecting pond both front and back."

"Oh! The Garden of Reflections! I remember that place from when I was little. It always seemed so magical to me." She glanced over her shoulder. "My parents are at the palace, so they'll be gone quite a while. They left me in the care of Yuni, but he's in the kitchen browbeating the rest of the staff.

It'll take a while for him to notice I'm not in the house."

I said, "We don't want to get you into trouble. If you have to go back inside, we can meet up later."

"Not on your life!" Ia spat. "I've been pretty much under lock and key since Uncle Amuny died and I'm not going back without a fight. My parents have been strange lately. Almost like they're — I don't know — celebrating something. They've been shopping me around among foreign princes, too. There's some member of Mother's Hittite family coming in the next few days. . . ." She suddenly looked tired. "I realize that's part of the role of a princess, but still. . . ."

We were silent for a bit. I think most of the time, all three of us tended to forget that Iaret was *Princess* Iaret, granddaughter of the Divine Ramesses.

Finally, Ban said, "Well, if you want to disappear for a while, why don't we slip out, and check out the festival booths."

Ia looked confused. "But the festival hasn't started yet."

"Don't tell that to the vendors who've set up early," I said.

Ia grabbed our arms and dragged us away from the house. "In that case, what are we waiting for? Let's go."

~*~

Our escape didn't go as smoothly as planned. We were on the path to the main gate where it curved under a roofed walk, supported at regular intervals by cedar columns and screened by jujube shrubs, when we heard voices up ahead. We were already nervous, so we slowed and peeked through the jujubes to see who it was. What we saw nearly stopped our hearts. It was Prince Meriramesses talking to a military officer I'd never seen before. We retreated several cubits and had a whispered conference.

Ban said breathlessly, "Damn it all! That's my brother, Sasobek with your father, Ia."

"I saw him," Iaret hissed. She turned to me, looking

worried. "This is probably not good. I've never liked that man. The way he's looked at me since I was a child has always made me feel dirty." Her eyes slid off me to the ground and she said softly, "I'm sorry Ban, but I never liked either of your brothers."

"Given the past behavior from both of them, I certainly don't blame you," said Banufre. "I'd forgotten Sasobek would even be in Thebes."

"The Seth division will be participating in the processional. Captain Sasobek is commanding the charioteers and footsoldiers," I said.

They both looked at me oddly.

"I was briefed yesterday because I'm to assist Captain Djedmose as he inspects the troops tomorrow," I explained.

Ia nodded understanding. "That makes sense, he'd need a scribe with him. But— that man scares me, too. For different reasons than Ban's brothers. At least I know *his* heart is in the right place. I can't think of anyone more loyal to the Great House of the Two Lands than that Medjay."

"I agree with you about Djedmose. He's tough, but fair," Ban said. "Sasobek is tough, but not even remotely fair. I've had serious doubts about both my brothers for a long time. I always hoped it was a little brother's jaundiced perspective. I'm sorry to be right."

"Were they very vocal about it? I'd think that was dangerous," I asked in amazement.

"Not so much in public," Ia said. "More like conversation over dinners or at parties. As far back as I can remember, my parents have been the same way."

"My brothers have had some pretty radical views. They both hated Merenptah and haven't been all that quiet about it. When Merenptah was raised to Crown Prince over Meriramesses, they wouldn't shut up about the so-called injustice done to their friend. They went on about it forever. Meriramesses was the elder, *he* should have been the one in line for the throne."

"I remember." Ia looked angry. "I wasn't very old at the time, but even then, I noticed that none of them even mentioned any injustice in Amuny being passed over. He was Father's elder brother. Technically, the crown should have passed to him before my father."

The mention of Amunhotep brought a fresh surge of sadness to me. I could tell it was the same for my friends.

After a moment, I said, "And Amuny's dead now."

We all went quiet as the implications of my words soaked in.

We didn't have time to dwell on it, though, because Ia looked around and said, "Where's Neffi?"

I looked at the ground, and glanced around for him. Then I spotted him, sitting at the bend in the path, staring at me with half-closed eyes. As soon as I noticed him, he stood, stretched and sauntered away. I froze in horror. He was headed up the walkway on a direct path to Prince Meriramesses and Captain Sasobek.

My paralysis lasted long enough for Neffi to disappear behind the shrubs. I suddenly found myself in motion. As I closed the distance, I heard Meriramesses say in a disgusted tone, "That *cat*. It belongs to the scribe my brother-in-law set on your brother. The pair of them are why Paseti is dead."

I came around the bend in time to see Neffi walk directly up to them and sit down. At the same time, Captain Sasobek's hand tightened on the hilt of his sword. I tore past the jujube shrubs, skidded to a halt and put on my best surprised look. I didn't have to feign breathlessness. My chest was so tight with terror, it was a miracle my lungs worked at all.

Bowing, I said, "Oh, Your Highness! Sir! I'm sorry to intrude. I was following Nefer-Djenou-Bastet. He's used to having the run of a temple and wanders wherever he likes."

I scooped the big spotted troublemaker up, half expecting Sasobek's sword to fall, anyway.

Prince Meriramesses treated me to a gracious smile. It looked like it hurt. "It's not a problem, Scribe. Nefer-Djenou-Bastet is a sacred animal. He has the run of the palace as well as the temples."

I forced my own smile and made another obeisance, lower this time, even though I felt like I might see my breakfast again. I had a real hard time tearing my eyes off Sasobek's sword. "Thank you, Your Highness. Sir. You are both very gracious. If you will permit, I'll take him back to my quarters."

The Prince gave me a courtly nod, and staying low, I backed away to the proper distance. Turning, I hugged Neffi tighter and tried to keep my walk to a casual pace. Neffi, damnable creature that he was, peered over my shoulder at the two men and purred. I could feel them staring at me as I passed the plantings where Banufre and Iaret were hiding. Both their faces looked as white and terrified as I felt. I hoped I didn't look anywhere near as wild as they did.

I turned the corner and ventured a peek around a cedar column. Prince Meriramesses and Captain Sasobek had turned and were walking quickly back toward the governmental section of the complex. As soon as they were out of sight, Iaret and Banufre left the relative safety of their jujube copse and hurried to me.

Ban stared in the direction the men had gone. "I can't believe it. I think Sasobek was actually thinking about killing Neffi!"

"I was even more worried he was thinking about killing Sitehuti!" Iaret said.

"Me, too," I agreed. Breakfast still threatened to revisit, so I didn't say any more. Neffi wriggled loose, shook himself and stalked away, this time toward the gates to the street. We followed him out.

~*~

By the time we reached the street and the bustle of the pre-festival revelry, we were more leading than following. Just outside the gates, I refolded my stole and plopped Neffi on my shoulders to keep him from getting stepped on — or from wandering away without my knowing. With the Sacred Troublemaker secured, we entered the already-celebratory crowd, leaving the unpleasant encounter behind, both literally and figuratively.

A troupe of acrobats were performing a short distance away. We walked toward them, and right into the scent of fresh-baked bread.

Banufre groaned. "Oh, that smells so good."

"Then let's get some," Ia said.

"Can't. I didn't bring anything to pay with," Ban said with a rueful shrug.

Iaret grinned. "I did." She pulled a beautifully embroidered bag from her girdle and opened it.

"Copper!" I said. I hadn't seen so much metal that wasn't part of an object in my life.

"And a few bits of silver. We should be able to do quite well with these," Ia said. She plunked a piece of copper into Ban's hand. "Find food!"

"Okay, but don't stray too far. I'll catch you up when I have the goods." He grinned and disappeared in the direction of the enticing aromas.

Ia and I drifted from booth to booth, examining the amazing array of items for sale. We were looking at stacks of brightly colored bracelets when a murmur passed through the crowd like a wave. A group of soldiers were coming up the street, parting the throng before them like the bow of a boat parted the waters of the Nile. The men were in parade form as they marched proudly past us, armor spotless and weapons bright.

Suddenly, Iaret grabbed my arm. Her face had gone pale and she looked as if her knees might fold.

"Are you all right?" I demanded, as I put a supporting arm around her.

She took a deep breath and nodded, standing straighter. "It's probably nothing, but the men who dragged Jiji into my house in Memphis were dressed very like those soldiers who just passed. The same colors. They held the same sort of weapons, too."

I turned again toward the receding procession. Above the heads of the onlookers rippled the banner of the Seth division. Sasobek's lot. I stared after them for a beat, then said, "We have to go back. Captain Djedmose will want to know about this."

"NO!" Ia said so loudly, people in our vicinity turned to look. She continued in a softer tone, "No. I told you that man makes me nervous. Besides, I want to stay as far away from the palace as possible. I don't want anyone to see me and drag me back."

"He'll have to be told," I said.

"Yes," Ia said slowly. "But . . . Huti, my life has been horrible for so long. If I return to the palace right now, it'll go right back to being horrible. Can't we just forget about the trouble and have a good time for a little while? A few hours won't make that much difference."

"Hurry! Grab something!" Ban called. His arms were full with all sorts of delicacies. "I couldn't make up my mind, so I got a little of everything."

TWENTY-THREE

It was a wonderful day. Even Neffi seemed to have fun. We wandered from booth to booth, from show to show, and from sight to sight until the sun touched the mountains in the west. Happy, exhausted and laden with purchases, we headed back to my guest house. Iaret was right. Her copper bits went a long way with the merchants. As we entered the gates to the house's gardens, Iaret strode to the edge of the reflecting pool, breathed deeply and turned full circle in place, a brilliant smile on her upturned face.

"It's even more beautiful than I remembered," she said. "When I was little, I always dreamed of scaling the walls and hiding away in here so no one could find me."

Banufre laughed. "Then who would I have had to sail model boats and fly toy birds with?"

"Come on," I said. "Let's go in, sit down and get something cold to drink. I'm as dry as the dust on the street outside."

"You can't be thirsty—," Ban began, but broke off as the front door opened.

Renen peered around the wooden panel. He seemed to have contracted some sort of dire illness. He twitched, rolled his eyes, and jerked his head to one side as if palsied. We stared, rooted in place by amazement.

The explanation for this mysterious malady became apparent, though, when Captain Djedmose appeared in the doorway to the sitting room. "About time you three got back. I thought I was going to have to send out a squad to retrieve you."

~*~

Soon the three of us were sitting in the darkening room, Neffi sprawled on the floor in front of us, as we waited for Djedmose to say something. He didn't. Instead, he stepped out into the garden portico and murmured something to Lieutenant Si-Montu who appeared, as if by magic, out of a group of date palms. The officer snapped a salute and vanished again into the greenery. When Captain Djedmose returned, Iaret stood and faced him. I knew she was scared, I'd seen it just moments before, but there was no sign of fear then.

She said, "Captain Djedmose, what is the problem here? I demand you tell us what this is about."

Djedmose gave her a deferential bow. "There is no problem, Your Highness, we merely need to talk. We should have spoken before, in Memphis, but events prevented it. I've just asked Lieutenant Si-Montu to station my Medjay around the garden to assure we aren't overheard."

"Talk? Talk about what, Captain?" she challenged.

"Please, Your Highness, be seated," Djedmose said. It was more a request than an order, but it had enough hint of order about it that Iaret sank slowly back onto the couch.

The Medjay didn't sit. He stood, staring out into the fading light that painted the garden with a surreal glow. Finally, he said, "There is no good way to say this, Your Highness, so I'll be blunt. We need to discuss what your parents," he then nodded at Banufre, "and your remaining brother are up to."

The silence in the room became a thick, suffocating thing.

"Captain—" I began, but Djedmose shushed me.

The Medjay's expression softened a bit and he said, "Banufre, Princess Iaret, neither of you need to be afraid to tell me what you know or have noticed. We're all working for the same end result here. Princess, I'm aware of the incident at your house on the night of the wine party. What you saw that night was a piece of a much larger event."

In spite of the Medjay's reassurances, no one spoke. The only sound was Neffi snuffling as he groomed the fur on his haunches.

"If you're worried about getting back before your parents return, Princess, you needn't. Your father has gone off for a hunt with Captain Sasobek. They will probably be gone for days."

"A hunt?" I exclaimed. "This close to the festival?"

"They told the palace staff they wanted to bring back fresh game for the feasts. A special gift for the Pharaoh."

Banufre spoke for the first time, "They've been known to do that before. Go off hunting on short notice, I mean. They disappear into the countryside and come back with wild geese or a deer or something."

"Father goes off by himself, too. He went off on a short hunt just before you came to Memphis, Huti," Ia added.

"Both Prince Meriramesses and Captain Sasobek also seem to to be aware they're being watched. They lost my men before they even passed the city gates. One of the guards at the docks said they took a boat and headed into the marshes.

"By the way, Sitehuti, I have to commend you on that fast thinking when Nefer-Djenou-Bastet walked in on Prince Meriramesses' and Captain Sasobek's little discussion today. My people were impressed with how you handled it."

I stared at the Medjay for a moment. "Someone *saw* that? I didn't see anyone anywhere near there."

"That's the point, kid." Djedmose treated me to one of his most infuriating smiles. "As I was saying, no one will be home for a while, Princess. Your mother is at a banquet being given by one of her countrymen, Prince Zannanza."

Iaret made an involuntary noise of disgust, then flushed and said, "Forgive my rudeness. My mother would like nothing more than for me to marry that . . . person."

"You have objections, Highness?" Djedmose asked.

"I most certainly do! The man has absolutely no chin and he has more chin than sense!"

After Ia's outburst, I saw something that I had not seen up to that point: Djedmose looked at the floor and his face darkened. Then he sputtered. The sputter gave way to a hearty guffaw. He regained control quickly, and bowed deeply to the angry girl. His voice still quivered a little as he said, "Forgive me, Your Highness, but those are almost the exact words spoken by your grandfather about the same individual just this afternoon."

When he had sufficiently recovered, he turned to Ban. "Your parents are also at a dinner party, although not the same one. They will likely return much earlier than Lady Wurusemu, but we will still have enough time to talk beforehand."

"I really don't have much that could help, sir," Ban said, shaking his head. "Today was the first time in months I've laid eyes on my brother. We're staying at my grandfather's house, so Sasobek won't come within arrow-range of the place. He hates my mother and her family." The boy shrugged. "He doesn't much care for me, either."

"I can't add much," Ia said. "I know my parents are up to something, but I have no clue what it is. They have a lot of people coming and going at all times — even here in Thebes. I've been a virtual prisoner since my uncle, Amunhotep, died. My mother tells me it's because they want to 'introduce' me to the royal court at the big family banquet the night before the Festival starts." She looked a little guilty. "That's why I took advantage of not being watched to run off with Banufre and Sitehuti today."

Djedmose looked thoughtful. "Have you recognized any of the people meeting with your parents?"

"No, the only one I've recognized was Sasobek today."

That jogged my memory and I leaned forward. "Tell Captain Djedmose what you said about the soldiers we saw."

She shot a frightened glance at Banufre, then said, "A unit of soldiers went past us this morning and — before you ask, no, I didn't recognize anyone in specific — but one of the men who brought that sailor to my house was wearing the same sort of armor and his shield was painted the same colors as the company banner."

Ban went pale. "I saw the soldiers, too, on my way back with the food." He looked directly at the Medjay as he added, "It was the Seth division."

That seemed to break a dam and we talked for a long time after that. Truthfully, nothing new came to light, but I got the impression that the Medjay captain was pleased with the outcome, nonetheless.

~*~

Later that night, Banufre unexpectedly returned to the Garden of Reflections guest house. I was glad to see him. The cooks had gone back to help out in the palace kitchens, so it was just Renen, Neffi and myself in that big house. It was odd, though. Ban seemed more uncomfortable than I'd ever seen him. After a while, I pried the answer out of him.

"My parents want me to stay with you from now on," he said miserably. "They're afraid the Pharaoh won't grant them forgiveness, but my friendship with you and Neffi might save me, even if they're condemned."

There was nothing I could say for a long time. Finally, I managed, "But, the Pharaoh and the Crown Prince seemed positive about granting mercy. You heard Captain Djedmose say that earlier."

Ban nodded. "I did. My parents won't believe it until they hear it themselves."

"Who can blame them?" I said. "Given past history, the odds would normally be against them."

He stared past me, brow furrowed. Finally, he said, "Everything's going to be lost, isn't it? Ia? My Parents? The estate? All gone because my brothers and Ia's parents are selfish bastards."

"It's not going to happen that way."

"How can you be so sure?"

I couldn't really, so I said, "We'll work to *make* sure."

Banufre mulled that over for a while and said, "I'll do all I can to help. Maybe that'll go some way to offset what my brothers have done." He nodded to some sort of inner decision. "But I refuse impose on you in hope of some nebulous goodwill from the Great House."

"Impose? I'm happy for the company. It'll be nice to have someone other than Neffi and Renen to talk to. Come on! Where's your stuff?"

~*~

The evening was particularly nice, so we took the dinner the cooks had prepared and ate on the roof. It was beautiful up there, cooled by fragrant breezes, surrounded by a rippling sea of greenery, with a deep blue arch of sky above us.

"This is great," Ban said, leaning back on his elbows.

"I love being on the rooftop on a clear night," I agreed. "I sleep on the roof of my aunt's linen shop whenever I can."

Renen perked up. "I could bring the bedrolls up, if you want."

No one objected, so Renen zoomed off to get things ready.

It was a wonderful night, so bright with moon and stars, we had no need of lamps. We sat, and talked, and told Amuny stories until late. By the time Banufre and I packed it in,

Renen had already drifted off on his pallet beside the steps down to the house. Neffi, according to cat-law, had chosen the highest spot available and sprawled across the roof of the stairhead.

~*~

The peace didn't last long.

The nighttime quiet was shattered by Renen yelling, Neffi yowling and a stranger swearing. In the moonlight, I saw a big man with his hand wound in Renen's hair. The boy kicked and clawed trying to dislodge the man's hold. Neffi clung to the stranger's back, howling and biting. Moonlight glinted off a dagger in the man's free hand as he flailed trying to dislodge the cat and get a clear shot at the boy.

Banufre sprang forward with a yell that became a yelp as gleaming metal arced down and he folded in on himself, clutching his side.

I rolled to my feet, grabbing for the first thing to hand: the strap to my water pot. I swung and the ceramic vessel shattered against the back of the intruder's head. He swayed for a moment, took a step to steady himself, but turned the wrong way. Instead of solid floor, his foot found only air beyond the top step. In eerie silence, he plunged down the stairwell, landing at the bottom in a limp, unnatural pose.

We all stood looking at what was most definitely a body, until Banufre asked in a shaky voice, "What do we do now?"

"I think we better summon Captain Djedmose," I said.

~*~

"Sir," the Medjay soldier said. "I think I've seen this man in the Seth encampment."

Djedmose pursed his lips. "Get him out of here and lose the body. Make it like he never existed."

The two Medjay saluted and bent to deal with the remains. In a far corner, a third soldier tended to the slash across

249

Banufre's ribs with Renen lending assistance. Between my run-in with Paseti and Banufre's injuries, the boy was learning a lot about field medicine.

"Why make him disappear?" I asked.

"Because we don't want the people who sent him to know what happened," the captain answered.

Banufre looked up from his own bandaging. "I think I get it. We already know my brother is involved, but this guy being from Seth cemented it. You want to keep him guessing why we aren't all dead."

"Exactly," said Djedmose. "This all but puts Sasobek's signature on the attack. But, don't forget there are others right here on the palace grounds who are complicit. I don't want them to be any the wiser, either."

I said quietly, "Prince Meriramesses and Lady Wurusemu."

Djedmose lifted a warning finger. "Suspected. Only suspected. We have no proof, yet." He sighed and looked down the now-empty stairwell. "Kid, you're going to have to stop killing potential interrogation suspects."

"*What?*"

"Joking, kid, joking."

~*~

Two days after the attack, I was to assist Captain Djedmose inspect the processional troops on behalf of the Great House. I was glad for the intervening time, because the morning after the incident was as bad as the one after I'd discovered the body of the mercenary, Wosret. This time, it was even harder to pretend nothing had happened the night before. This time, I *had* done the killing. All right, it *was* unintentional, and yes, the man had stolen into the house to kill me — me, Renen, Banufre and probably even Neffi. Even so, he died by my hand. In my mind, I kept seeing the man fall down the stairs in slow motion, like a feather floating on the breeze. It made breakfast difficult and concentration near impossible. I had to do it, though — pretend to be normal on the day of inspection. Djedmose told me it was the best way to, as he put it, "get up Sasobek's nose". He was right, as usual.

The four army camps were pitched just beyond the city, out on the Red Land. Up until that time, I'd never been in one and was amazed. They were more like temporary villages than what I thought of as a camp.

Each bivouac was separated from the next by a wall made of shields planted into the sand. A gate flanked by sentries controlled entrance into each encampment. At the center was a large tent, almost a pavilion, for the commanding officer, around that was organized chaos. In a far corner, the horses and other livestock were being fed and cared for by grooms and a few charioteers. Not far from that, a blacksmith had set up a forge. Soldiers and craftsmen were hard at work repairing tools and weapons. A chariot was flipped upside down, worked on, flipped over, rolled backward and forward, then flipped over and worked on again. In the mess area, soldiers sat on benches around hot stew served in communal bowls. In another corner of the enclosure, infantrymen were sent through their paces by their drill sergeant. The aroma of spicy stew and baking bread warred with the smell of leather, hot metal and horse dung. All around, soldiers talked, bartered, gambled, argued and generally did the everyday things that comprise life in a village.

As we approached the commander's pavilion, we heard shouting from within. I'd only heard the voice once before, but I recognized it immediately. It appeared Captain Sasobek was ripping new orifices for some of his men.

"I'm still waiting," he roared. "Can none of you explain how is it that I go hunting for a few days and return to find none of my orders acted on? I get back to find five chariots out of commission, a lame horse, and that we're running low on fodder."

There was a murmured response that didn't escape the confines of the tent. It was followed by an inarticulate explosion of sound from Captain Sasobek.

The guards at the front of the tent were leaning slightly backward to eavesdrop on the reaming and didn't notice us until we were right on top of them. By the time they fully registered Captain Djedmose, who that day was decked out in his blue and gold palace armor, he was already inside the tent. They stared at me for a moment, as if wondering if they should stop me, but seeing Neffi draped across my shoulders changed their minds. I followed the Medjay in and stood at a respectful distance behind him like a good little assistant should.

There were three officers, wearing the insignia of commander, cowering before the angry captain. One of them said tentatively, "I'm sorry, sir. We thought that was Commander Weni's—"

"Where is Weni?" Sasobek demanded.

Another officer said, "We don't know, sir. We haven't seen him for several—"

The officer broke off, catching sight of Captain Djedmose and struck a salute. His two mates did the same.

Captain Sasobek wheeled in surprise. "Captain Djedmose! My apologies. I was unaware you had arrived."

"Good morning, Captain Sasobek, I've come to review the troops. Have you forgotten?"

"Of course not, Captain. We are ready at any time."

"Good. We can get started." The Medjay stood aside and swept a hand at me. "I believe you've already met my assistant, Sitehuti of Western Thebes." As if waiting for that cue, Neffi hopped to the ground, chirped once and settled into his sphinx-pose between Sasobek and myself.

Sasobek looked like he'd been pole-axed. He recovered

quickly, dismissing his commanders and leading us out to the practice field. He did a wonderful imitation of an officer with nothing more to concern him other than some out-of-commission chariots. He remained a bit green at the gills throughout our inspection, though.

We didn't bother with much in the way of interrogation. We didn't have to. Watching Sasobek goggle at Neffi and me was answer enough. It appeared we might also have gotten the name of our would-be assassin. The missing Commander Weni.

Djedmose especially enjoyed the Seth Captain's discomfort and drew things out by putting the troops through more paces than were originally scheduled, muttering notes for me to write on their performance as they went. Neffi maintained his guard pose throughout the exercise, eyes never leaving the nervous officer. By the time we were ready to move on to review the Ptah Division, Sasobek looked almost ready for the embalmers.

I have to admit, it was more fun than I thought it would be.

TWENTY-FOUR

I was tired and dragging by the time we finished for the day. Because we'd spent so much extra time with the Seth Division, we were late getting to Ptah and Re. That pushed Amun to the following morning. I wasn't looking forward to it. While being busy made the pretense of normalcy easier, the work was more demanding than I'd counted on. Who knew simply watching people march, mock fight and do chariot maneuvers could be so tiring?

Pushing open the guest house gate, I discovered Renen picking fresh figs. The basket at his feet was already full with jujube, dates and several rosy pomegranates.

"That's quite a harvest," I said. "Did the cooks leave before they prepared tonight's meal?"

Renen looked up from his task with a sour expression. "No, they cooked, but they went back to the palace earlier than usual. I'm glad they did. They're not very nice — at least not to me."

"Ignore them. It's their problem, not yours. Still, why the fruit basket?"

Renen brightened. "Princess Iaret is here. I thought fruit would help stretch dinner for an extra person."

"Good idea. Is she inside with Banufre?"

"They're on the east veranda. It's cooler there this time of day," he said, then looked troubled. "I still don't feel right about not telling the princess about the man who broke in the other night. Are we right to keep it from her? It seems like she should know if she's in danger."

"I'm torn about it, too, but she's not in danger, Renen," I said. "This was aimed against us. No one would dare harm Princess Iaret. Besides, she's worried enough that her parents are involved in some kind of plot against the throne. She doesn't need the added worry that someone — probably Banufre's own brother — wanted us dead. But at the same time—"

I was interrupted by a voice from behind: "At the same time, she'll be really angry when she finds out you didn't tell her."

Iaret stood in the open doorway to the house, and yes, she looked pretty angry.

Ban came up behind her and she spun on him. "When were you going to tell me? Your own brother tries to have you and our friends killed and you say nothing?"

Renen goggled at the three of us a bit, then blurted, "I better get this fruit inside." Snatching up his basket, he bolted through the open door.

I stared at Iaret, who was glaring at Banufre, who showed intense interest in the walkway. Nobody moved or spoke for several beats until Neffi, who had been lying beside the fish pond, trotted over and stretched his front feet up on the angry girl and trilled. Iaret looked down and stroked the cat's head.

"All right," she said at last. "I understand you were trying to keep me from worrying about more than I already am. I don't *agree* with your decision, but I see that you meant well." She glanced around the gardens. "Perhaps we should get somewhere more private."

When we returned inside, Renen had set up tables and chairs on the veranda. He put the plates out, then made to return to the servant's area.

I said, "Wait, Renen. We have a lot to discuss and you're part of this, too. That man was as bent on hurting you as he was Banufre and me."

The boy paused uncertainly.

"He's right, Renen," Ban said.

Iaret handed the boy a plate and pushed a low chair toward him. After a few more doubtful moments, he sat down.

We filled our plates, and recounted what we remembered of the events on the rooftop. Ban, Renen and I each had a slightly different point of view, but we all agreed on the main points. When our tales were finished, none of us knew what to say next. We ate in silence for a while.

Ia was the first to break it and she veered off the subject slightly. "Father came home from his hunting trip late last night."

I said, "I thought he probably had. Sasobek had recently returned when Djedmose and I did the troop review for Seth first thing this morning."

Ban grimaced. "I bet that was fun."

I couldn't stop a grin. "It was, actually. He was apparently unaware the plan to kill us failed. I thought he was going to have a fit when he saw Neffi and me."

"Wish I could have seen that," Renen muttered into his shredded cabbage.

"Oh!" I added. "We may know who the would-be assassin was, too. One of the division commanders has been missing a few days."

Silence reigned again until Banufre said, "Ia was telling me what happened when she got home after our talk with Captain Djedmose."

I said, "I hope you didn't have any trouble."

It was Iaret's turn to grin. "None at all. I got back well before mother. She came in late and, truthfully, wouldn't have been in any shape to tell whether I was there or not. Anyway, Yuni was wild when I returned. I told him I'd been walking in the gardens and looking at the palace and just lost track of time. He didn't believe me, but he also doesn't want to draw attention to the fact I gave him the slip. He's more afraid of my parents than the Soul Eater itself. Especially my mother."

"Where are they now?" Ban asked. "How'd you get away tonight?"

"They're both visiting friends. Different friends, different parties. You know how it is. It's the same way back in Memphis. There's a banquet or party of some kind every night until the festival starts the day after tomorrow. It will probably be worse after that."

A spotted paw patted along the edge of my table. I put a sliver of roasted duck in its path and both paw and meat vanished. "We're all avoiding talking about it, but we can't ignore it for long. What exactly *is* the plot against the Great House and what are we going to do about it?"

"I have no idea," said Iaret. "My parents aren't even home since the parties began. There's no hope I'll overhear anything until the Feast of Opet ends."

"It'll probably be too late by then," Ban said gloomily. "They'll probably have done whatever they're planning by that time." He looked up and said, "I want to do anything in my power to keep them from succeeding. No way will I sit on my hands when the life of the Divine Ramesses is at risk."

Ia went quiet, brows puckered. Finally, she said, "I don't think so."

Ban was taken aback. "What? Of course I'll do what I can."

"No," Ia said, waving him down. "I mean why would Father harm Grandfather? If he did that, my uncle, Merenptah, would be the one to step up. He *is* Crown Prince, after all."

Ban and I looked at each other. We hadn't thought about that.

Ia pushed a fig around her plate. "Father hates my uncle. So does my mother and she goes out of her way to fan Father's hatred. They both hold Uncle Merenptah responsible for the fact that he became crown prince and my father, his elder brother, got sent to the farm to manage it and Uncle Amuny."

She looked up from worrying the fig. "I'm not supposed to know this, but Father was sent to the estate because he got involved in something questionable in the new capital. Uncle Amuny told me one night when he was drunk and especially angry with Father."

"What sort of thing was it?" I asked.

"I'm not sure. It was something political. I think even Uncle Amuny didn't know for sure. It couldn't have been all that bad or he would have been executed back then . . . right?"

"Probably," I agreed. "Still, how would he expect to step into being crown prince? Your grandfather said they'd never seen eye-to-eye on policy. That doesn't seem to fit."

Ia and Ban turned to stare at me with twin expressions of astonishment.

"My grandfather?" Ia said. "You've spoken with my grandfather?"

"Here in Thebes?" Ban asked.

"Yeah. A few days ago. It was Neffi's fault. It's always Neffi's fault."

~*~

With all the parties being thrown during the lead-up to the Opet festival, neither Banufre nor I had been invited to anything. We hadn't expected to be. After all, I was simply a low-level scribe and Ban was the youngest son from a farming family. Taking that into account, we were doubly floored to be told we were expected to attend the banquet given by His Divine Majesty the night before opening ceremonies.

I didn't have much time to think about it (read worry) during the day. The Amun Division, having been left to last, determined to prove they were far from the least. They put on a show of precision and expertise that was worthy of a festival unto itself. Even though the exercise lasted about as long as the extended one for Seth the previous day, there weren't many notes to take on that performance.

Neffi was a big hit, too. His markings made him sacred to the great god Amun as well as the goddess Bastet, so the members of the Amun division held him in special reverence. He'd gotten more pets, scratches and surreptitious treats in that short space of time than he had in the entire week prior.

After we finished there, the Medjay captain and I delivered our reviews to the division captains, walked the parade route, then headed home.

I didn't have a clue how a banquet in the palace was supposed to go. Yes, I'd read descriptions in my copy lessons, but those were historic accounts. The closest I'd ever come to a real one was the dinner given by Meriramesses my first time on the estate. Well, there were also Amunhotep's wine bashes. Somehow, I doubted those counted.

Renen helped both Banufre and myself to get ready. By that I mean he'd rooted through our clothing chests and pulled the finest garments and jewelry he could find. He'd also managed to find two wax perfume cones. Both Ban and I drew the line there. We figured we'd rather be hot and smelly than hot, covered in melted wax, but fragrant as a flowerbed.

We were nervous, so we were early to the palace banquet room. Hardly anyone was there yet. Places had been reserved for us and I was amazed to find we were very close to the royal dais. At first people arrived at a trickle and Ban and I sat and fidgeted. Neffi stroked off to explore the room, but came back to take his usual post under my chair when the trickle became a steady stream. It was during this influx that Ma'aheru and Neferhedjet arrived. They seemed overjoyed when Chief Butler Kha'Emteri brought them over to where we were. There were warm greetings for me and hugs and shoulder squeezes for their son.

Before we could reclaim our seats, the Chief Butler strode in front of the dais and rapped his staff against the floor, "All bow before the Divine Userma'atre Setepenre Ramesses Meriamon. All hail Crown Prince Merenptah and his lady, Princess Isetnofret."

The conversational buzz in the room stopped to be replaced by the scrape of chairs and the rustle of fabric as everyone rose for the Royal Family's entrance. As they took their places on the dais, the Divine Ramesses looked regal and composed. The Crown Prince seemed to be having a quiet fight with his fancy dress and the Princess was studiously looking the other direction.

We had only sat back down when Lady Neferhedjet gasped and touched Ma'aheru's arm. "How lovely Iaret looks tonight. A true princess of the Great House!"

I followed her gaze, but didn't see my friend, Ia. Instead, I saw Lady Wurusemu and Prince Meriramesses leading a stunningly beautiful noblewoman to stand directly before the Pharaoh. I only registered that the elegant noblewoman *was* my friend, Ia, a couple beats before the Chief Butler announced, "Prince Meriramesses, Lady Wurusemu and Princess Iaret."

Iaret looked magnificent. She was beautiful, anyway, but she must have sat under the ministrations of her mother's lady's maid for hours prior to her presentation. As she bowed before the dais, the Pharaoh's lined face broke into a smile of pleasure.

"Princess Iaret! You still wore the sidelock of youth when I last saw you." Her grandfather leaned forward and added, "You have grown into a handsome young woman. I have heard very good things about you."

I wondered how many of those good things the Divine

Ramesses had heard came from our conversation, my written reports, or from Djedmose later. It didn't matter, really. All that mattered was that the Pharaoh seemed genuinely pleased to see her. I hoped it would help further soften the anger of the Great House toward her, and by association, Banufre and his parents.

The conversation at the dais became more quiet and I saw Meriramesses and Wurusemu straining to hear what the Pharaoh said to their daughter. From their expressions, I assumed they were failing. Finally, Iaret bowed and took her seat with her parents and the Crown Prince gave the signal for the meal to be served.

The food at the banquet was sumptuous, but not too overdone. Plenty of roasted meat, bread and succulent vegetables. I tucked in and enjoyed the conversation around me, handing tidbits down to Neffi from time to time. When I held down a particularly nice piece of goose skin and it wasn't taken, I looked under my chair with alarm. The space chair was vacant. I looked around, and to my horror, found Neffi wandering across the royal dais.

Most of the royals seemed to be aware of him and several members of the extended family dropped tidbits for him. Well, he was a sacred cat and had license to go where he wanted. Still, my breath caught when the spotted head poked up under the Pharaoh's arm. It seemed everyone was watching now as Neffi rejected the contents of the Great Ramesses' plate, and sauntered over to Prince Meriramesses. I have never understood how cats know who hates them most, but Nefer-Djenou-Bastet's instincts were unerring. To the immense amusement of the surrounding revelers, the cat stood with front paws on the edge of the Prince's table and viewed the offerings critically.

Prince Meriramesses looked as if a scorpion had just

popped out of his bread roll. He waved a hand ineffectually and hissed, "Shoo. Go away, cat."

I could tell he wanted to do more than wave, but half the room was watching. Princess Iaret froze, her face reflecting my own horror.

Neffi blinked at the Prince, and without looking at the plate, hooked a chunk of beef and hightailed it back under my chair.

The banqueters roared with laughter, the loudest seemed to be the Divine Ramesses himself. Prince Merenptah was doing a passable job of not laughing. He raised a hand and ordered a new plate for his irate, red-faced half-brother. It was brought immediately.

Finally, the Crown Prince couldn't resist. He said, "Really, Brother, the Sacred One favors you even over our father. You should be pleased."

Meriramesses glared in my direction. "I fail to see the humor, Brother."

Merenptah gave his sibling a swat on the back that reminded me of the late Amunhotep. "Oh lighten up, Brother, he only stole a cut of beef from you. He ate *my* sandal." He looked over at where I was trying to be small. "Isn't that so, Sitehuti of Western Thebes?"

All eyes were on me and I wished I could drop through the floor. My first attempt to answer came out more as "eeep", but the second succeeded. "Yes. I'm afraid he did, Your Highness."

The court thought that was even funnier. Everyone but Prince Meriramesses and Lady Wurusemu.

~*~

Later in the evening when the food was mostly gone and the wine poured more freely, I glanced at the royal dais and noticed the Pharaoh had quietly retired. I admired his wisdom. The Beautiful Feast of Opet officially began in the morning and Ramesses would play a huge part in the opening ceremonies. Iaret was gone, too.

She had excused herself part-way through the meal, to her parents' displeasure. Ma'aheru and Lady Neferhedjet had also left early, leaving Banufre and myself alone at our tables. Not long afterward, Ban excused himself. I wondered if he and Ia had worked out a tryst. Good luck to them if they had. Neffi was sound asleep under my chair and I was considering joining the exodus when I heard: "Just look at those cute little toes!"

In a blink, I was surrounded by a group of elegant noblewomen. They weren't looking at me, though, they were crouched down so they could peek under my chair at Neffi who was sprawled on his back with his legs in the air.

Realizing he was the center of attention, the cat stretched, splaying his toes, much to the delight of his audience. He rolled over and proceeded to rub against their legs, leaving a liberal coating of fur on their costly garments. They loved it.

It wasn't long before one of them noticed me. A tall, older woman, whose melting perfume cone was all but gone, said, "Well. Sitehuti of Western Thebes. I've heard the cat can do amazing things." Licking her lips suggestively, she leaned so close her wine-breath grazed my ear as she whispered, "What can the scribe do?"

No ready comment sprang to mind. I was spared when one of the others pointed toward the servants' door. "They're bringing in more wine."

The woman who had been leaning into me straightened and raised her cup like a battle standard. "So they are! Form a line, girls!"

Forsaking Neffi and me in favor of the wine steward, they wove away in a floral-scented wine-soaked mass. I sank into my chair, certain I'd had a near escape. Someone sat in the seat recently vacated by Ma'aheru. I turned to find Crown Prince Merenptah regarding the recently-departed bevy.

"The ladies do love the Sacred One," he observed.

I'd had more of the strong red than I intended, and before I realized it, I was saying, "Prince Amunhotep made the same observation. He kept telling people that he wanted a sacred cat of his own in the Land of the West. He said *that* would make for a pleasant afterlife."

Merenptah laughed and called back toward the now-sparsely populated dais. "Doesn't that sound like Amuny?"

Princess Isetnofret, joined the laugh. "Doesn't it, just?"

Merenptah turned back to me and became serious. Behind us, people started sharing Amuny stories. It seemed everyone had at least one.

The Crown Prince said, "Actually, I want to talk to you about Amunhotep. This morning, his personal servant, Dedi, delivered a list of my half-brother's bequests and requests to me. One of the items on that list was Amuny's wish that you be the scribe to write out the sacred texts for him to carry into the Land to the West."

Time stopped. The party around me receded to a distant blur. Prince Amunhotep wanted *me* to pen the spells that would allow him to enter the Land to the West? A list of bequests and requests? When had he even had time to write that out?

When I found my voice, I said, "I'm sure he was joking, Your Highness. I'm only a junior scribe and this is such an important thing! Everything depends on it. Surely there are other scribes in your house who are much more qualified."

Crown Prince Merenptah held up a hand. "Nonsense! If Amuny wanted you to do his spell scrolls, then that's how it will be."

Still breathless, I made a gesture of respect. "Absolutely, Your Highness. Thank you, it will be an honor to write out the texts." I wasn't lying, either. The fact that Prince Amunhotep trusted me with the keys to his afterlife made me proud and determined to do the best job I could possibly do.

Pleased, Crown Prince Merenptah smiled and gave me one of those Amuny-like swats that nearly lifted me from my chair. As I re-settled myself, I caught a glimpse of Prince Meriramesses who still sat on the dais with his wife. Their expressions were anything but pleased.

~*~

When I got back to the guest house, Banufre and Renen were both asleep. I tried to sleep, too, but it didn't work. Just as I was drifting off, I thought about what I'd said to the Crown Prince earlier. Amuny had said repeatedly that he wanted a cat in the Land to the West. Maybe there was something I could do about that, after all.

I got out my writing kit and set to work composing a letter to my cousin, the stone cutter in the Place of Truth. That didn't take as long as the painting of Neffi I included. It was late — or early, depending on how you looked at it — by the time I finished.

Renen woke up a couple times while I worked. In the morning . . . well, when Renen woke up, anyway, he promised to take the letter to the ferry to be put in with the correspondence going to Western Thebes.

~*~

The festival was in full swing when I awoke. I could hear it even in my bed chamber. Renen was gone as was the message for my cousin. I hoped he'd made it to the boat in time. I snatched up the clothing he'd laid out for me and had barely finished dressing when Djedmose shouted up the stairs.

"Hurry up, kid! We got a full day ahead of us."

The Medjay paced in the entry hall, his blue and gold armor catching the morning light from the rows of high windows.

I stifled a yawn. "I thought we finished yesterday."

"If you mean the troop reviews and grounds inspection, we did. Today, we have the actual processional. The royal barge is set to dock this hour."

"Oh, no. That's today."

"Yes, it's today . . . how much wine did you have last night?"

"What? Oh, no. It was something else entirely that kept me up last night." I threw my writing kit over my shoulder and hurried out in the Medjay's wake.

TWENTY-FIVE

I had seen the arrival of the royal barge at the Theban docks once before. I was a small child and my father had swung me onto his shoulders so I could see better. All I really remember were amazing colors and the milling sea of peoples' heads. Now, roughly a decade later, I was officially part of the event, standing on a raised platform beside the Captain of the Royal Medjay. What could I see? Amazing colors and a milling sea of peoples' heads. Granted, the heads belonged predominantly to princes, princesses and nobles of the realm, so the colors that went along with them were actually spectacular.

The Beautiful Feast of Opet was a celebration of fertility, procreation, and renewal. The Divine Ramesses had excelled at procreation. The majority of the throng that met and cheered the royal barge as it docked that morning, were his direct descendants. They parted to allow the Pharaoh and the Crown Prince to exchange the barge for the gilded and flower-festooned ceremonial barque that would carry them on their journey to the temple of Amun.

A shout went up as the bearers shouldered the royal conveyance and a more distant cheer from beyond the docks that told me the army divisions were marching. The gilded boat seemed to ride on a river of humanity as it began the journey along the processional route.

Djedmose watched the progress for a few minutes, then said,

"All right, we're on the move, kid. We'll have to hustle to get to the temple of Amun before everyone else gets there. Grab the Sacred One."

It was ironic. I'd never before been so close to the heart of the festival, but I'd also never seen so little of it. We skirted the processional way and the crowds of jubilant spectators. Even though it was a longer distance than the barques were traveling, we made it to the temple well before the divine cortege. The priests of Amun were putting the final touches on the enclosed forecourt, hanging garlands and strewing flowers in preparation for the arrival of the gods and the royals. The golden shrines for Amun's consort, Mut, and their son Khonsu gleamed in the sunlight, doors wide, awaiting their occupants.

Hori, the captain of Ramesses' personal Sherden bodyguard was already there, having an intense conversation with two of his men. When Djedmose and I entered, he broke off and strode over to intercept us. In the past, the Sherden had been sea people — pirates, not to put too fine a point on it. Captain Hori looked every inch the part: short, muscular and deeply tanned by sun and wind, even though it must have been years since he'd trod a sea-going ship's deck.

Hori was a master of inscrutability, but his men weren't. Even at a distance, their movements and posture said they were worried. That made *me* worry. Had something gone wrong? Had the conspirators already made a move?

Hori and Djedmose greeted each other with gestures of respect, but I could feel tension between the two men. They didn't seem to like each other. When the Sherden spoke, it didn't do much to allay my fears.

"His Divine Majesty is tiring," Hori said. "He'll be present on the dais for the rituals in the forecourt, but the Crown Prince will take over once they enter the temple for the re-enactment of the coronation."

Djedmose frowned. "Is His Majesty ill?"

The Sherden shook his head. "Just tired. He stayed overlong at the feast last night and didn't sleep well. When the crowds have followed the procession to the quay, we'll slip him out and back to the palace."

I'm not certain what Neffi or I did to attract his attention, but Hori's gaze shifted to me. He assessed me for a moment, then nodded. "Ah. The Crown Prince's scribe. His Divine Majesty told me you were helping figure out what's going on. Whatever it is, the Sherden can handle it, but you impressed him. That's not easy to do." Abruptly, he shifted his gaze to the still-closed pylon gates. The hubub outside had been slowly increasing in volume. Captain Hori listend for a moment, then said, "They're here. Let's get cracking."

The massive gates swung wide, admitting the four gilded barques bearing the Theban Triad and the royals, escorted by priests, Sherdan Guards and Royal Medjay. A cortege of royal family members, nobles and invited guests followed them in. Outside, the four army units flowed into formation, blocking the avenue of sphinxes leading to the great temple of Amun, and positioning themselves to escort the divine procession to the barges waiting quayside after the ceremonies.

The gates swung closed again, blocking the view from outside and bringing a measure of quiet to the enclosed forecourt. As the invited observers took their places, I caught sight of Iaret walking alongside her parents. She saw me, too, and happily bobbled the pale blue lotus she carried at me. I gave a little wave back. Lady Wurusemu noticed the movements and turned to glare at her daughter, who now stood, court-face perfect, eyes reverently upon the barque bearing her grandfather and uncle.

Sherden Guards and Royal Medjay drew back the curtains and Crown Prince Merenptah stepped out, then turned to help his father. The Divine Ramesses looked drawn and unsteady as he mounted the steps to the royal dais, leaning heavily on his golden Was-staff and his son's arm. The sight deepened my concern. The great man was frailer than I had considered. Frailer even than the day I'd met him at the palace. He was mentally sharp as an iron dagger, but his back seemed stiff and his legs were giving him trouble.

Really, I don't know why the Pharaoh's age hadn't sunk in before that moment. I knew how long he'd been on the throne of the Two Lands. I also knew how old Crown Prince Merenptah was and how many sons had already preceded the Pharaoh in death. I'd simply never *thought* about it. As I glanced around the temple courtyard at all the statues depicting an eternally young and vigorous Pharaoh, I realized there was a reason behind all the public art. It kept the image of the strong warrior before the people's eyes. In spite of the fact my family had been responsible for some of that imagery, I'd never considered that aspect of it.

At the far end of the forecourt, a group of priests escorted Princess Isetnofret out of the temple, and the chattering crowd fell silent. Swooping golden wings of the tall crown of Mut framed the lady's serene face. Sunlight shimmered off the net of gold, lapis and carnelian beads covering her linen gown as she moved from the darkened interior into the open courtyard. Crown Prince Merenptah stepped forward, took her hand, and the ritual remarriage of Amun-Min and Mut began.

~*~

There was music, dancing and feasting. When Crown Prince Merenptah finally emerged from the Holy of Holies, I knew hours had passed, but it didn't feel like it. Horns blew and the pylon gates opened to a cheer from the people gathered outside to greet the renewed ruler of the Two Lands.

Djedmose and I fell in with the Royal Medjay and remaining Sherden who formed an honor guard around the four flower-festooned barques as they made their way down the avenue of the sphinxes toward the river where four equally decorated actual river boats waited. Infantry marched before and after us in lock step, pennants and standards rippling in the breeze. Chariots formed a rolling wall on all sides. The late afternoon sun gleamed off the charioteers' armor and the horses' harness fittings. Priests walked along the outside edges, tossing flowers and small gifts into the crowds that lined the way.

We rode to Luxor on the boat with the Crown Prince and Princess Isetnofret, still in their guises of Amun-Min and Mut. Instead of the usual oars, though, the barque was towed upstream by gangs of men hauling on papyrus ropes. The four army divisions kept pace with us on the shore all the way. It was an amazing sight and an experience I'll never forget.

There were more rituals, more feasting and more dancing in the forecourt of the Luxor temple of Amun. By the time Merenptah and Isetnofret retired to the private chambers to begin their week-long honeymoon, I was feeling every minute and every step of the day. My duties were over and I was free to return to Thebes. Captain Djedmose was rarely off duty, and was staying with his Medjay contingent in Luxor for the duration.

I toyed with the idea of heading back to Thebes. After all, it wasn't that far and it would be with the current that way. In the end, I just couldn't face it. When a young priest offered a guest accommodation for Neffi and me at the temple, I jumped at it. It was a private room at the greatest temple in the Two Lands, so it must have been nice, but I was too tired to notice. I fell asleep almost as soon as I hit the mattress.

~*~

No one met me at the door when I returned to Thebes and the Garden of Reflections guest house the next morning. Inside,

Neffi squirmed out of the sling I'd been carrying him in and trotted through to the back garden. The house seemed unnaturally quiet. Banufre was spending the day in Luxor with his parents, so I didn't expect to see him until late. Renen, however, was supposed to be there. I checked upstairs and the roof, but he was nowhere to be found. Sounds and fragrances from the outdoor kitchen told me the cooks were back.

I peeked in. "Good morning. Have either of you seen Renen today?"

The two women looked up from their tasks, seeming annoyed. Curling her lip, the older one said, "The boy?"

"Yes," I said. "The boy."

"Oh," she said, returning to grinding something to a powder. "We haven't seen him since yesterday. He left while it was still dark and never came back. Said he had some sort of message to deliver."

They refused to say anything more and went back to their cooking as if I had ceased to exist. I was beginning to see why Renen had a problem with those two. Returning to the sitting room, I paced a bit, trying to make sense of things.

Renen had been gone for more than a day. That wasn't right. I had assumed with the Seth Division tied up with the processional, then stuck in Luxor for a bit, we were safe. What if I'd been mistaken? What if someone had grabbed Renen as he left the house like they'd done with Khety?

I was working out the best way to contact Captain Djedmose when Neffi trotted in from the garden making a "prrrt, prrrt" noise. He went past me and into the entry hall as someone opened the front door. I followed. Renen, looking rumpled, dusty and bone-tired, was carefully closing the door behind himself. He turned, saw me and gaped in surprise.

"You're back!" he said.

"Yes, I am. So are you. Where have you been?"

"Well, you were going to be busy all day yesterday and going up to Luxor and I didn't have anything else to do—"

"Renen! Where have you been?"

"I went to the village of the workmen in the Place of Truth to deliver the letter to your cousin in person."

"You went to the village?"

He nodded happily. "I delivered your message and your cousin took me to the house of your parents. You have a great family! They were all glad to hear from you. Your mother wants to know why a scribe can't write more often."

I stared.

"Oh, just a minute." He rooted in his dusty garments and produced a scroll. His face split in a sunny grin as he handed it to me. "They sent a reply."

~*~

I retreated to my bedchamber for a little more privacy as I read. Not that I expected to burst into tears or anything, but I wanted a little alone time. The letter was written by my youngest brother, Hesi-Ra, who had been born after I left the village. He was undergoing training under the current chief scribe of the Place of Truth, Kenhirkhopeshef. Hesi would do well. His hand was firm and the letters well-formed, in spite of his youth.

The message acknowledged my cousin's receipt of the commission and the drawing. He said the piece I'd requested was straightforward and would be no problem to execute. From there, it went into family stuff. Things like the fact my youngest sister had set up a new household with the son of the chief plasterer of the left crew. How Mother was very pleased to learn I had a servant now, had I let aunt Tiaa know? A smattering of the usual village gossip. Then there was the ubiquitous when was I going to come for a visit?

The question about coming home hit me hard. I'd been asking permission to go at every opportunity since I learned I was coming to Thebes, but the answer remained a vague, "We'll see." I sort of understood. Things were tense, and up until yesterday, I'd been extremely busy.

I closed my eyes and took a couple deep breaths. Then I opened the scroll and started to read again. If I couldn't get to the village, a fresh letter was pretty damned good.

~*~

The invitations started arriving just before midday. Parties, picnics, banquets — even one for a new play. It seemed that being adopted by a sacred cat and an invited guest at the royal banquet not only made me socially acceptable, but desirable as well. It had even rubbed off on Banufre. By the time Ban returned from Luxor, I'd received twenty-five invitations and he, eighteen. It was a new experience for both of us. Considering the festival was only a week long and we were already on day two, we needed to be selective. The problem was that out of all the names of potential hosts and hostesses, we recognized four.

Renen wasn't much help. His knowledge of the Memphis nobility was encyclopedic, but he'd only been in Thebes a short time. He knew fewer of the names on the invitations than Ban and I did. In the end, we sorted them according to when they were happening and rolled a die to decide which ones to accept.

I never thought I'd get tired of parties. Make that, I never thought I'd get tired of parties so fast. After three days, though, I was done. On the morning of day five of the festival, Ban cheerfully called me a wimp and headed off to the next picnic alone.

~*~

My resolve for a quiet day at home lasted until mid-afternoon. It took that long for the sounds and scents of the festival booths to entice me to put Neffi in his sling and venture out. It was a lovely day and I wandered for a couple hours taking it all in. It was quite relaxing and entertaining.

I should have known it wouldn't last.

I had just bought a flatbread and was sharing it with Neffi as we watched a troupe of dancers when someone put a hand under my chin and jerked my head back. The point of a dagger pressed briefly into the pit of my throat, then a shriek rose above the music. I wasn't the one doing the shrieking. As soon as I was grabbed, Neffi launched himself over my shoulder. The attacker's grip loosened and I fell to my knees. A dark, muscular man came seemingly from nowhere, beaded braids clattering as he tackled the man struggling with Neffi. The screaming stopped abruptly after one powerful blow.

The surrounding crowd was still processing what had happened, when the dark man, a Nubian who looked vaguely familiar hissed, "Lieutenant Si-Montu is going to want to speak to you, Scribe."

~*~

Yeah. He did, but it took him a while to get to me. I cooled my heels in the palace room Captain Djedmose had commandeered as an office for quite a while. I didn't mind. It provided time for my heart to stop racing.

When the lieutenant returned, he looked tired and angry. He collapsed into a chair and stared at the ceiling for a moment. "It looks like this one is a Hittite. We can't be sure, though, because the bastard is refusing to talk."

"At least this one isn't dead," I ventured.

Si-Montu looked at me directly for the first time. "Small consolation."

"What next, then?"

"We keep trying," the Medjay said. Anger flared. "What the hell, Sitehuti? I mean . . . what the *hell* were you thinking?"

I looked blank. That seemed to make things worse.

He abruptly sat forward. "All the parties were bad enough, but even the Medjay can blend in with the background there. Now, you two idiots split up and went *separate* places! I only have so many resources. You're just lucky it was Mahu tailing you today. He's got the best reflexes of any of this unit."

I was being followed? I suppose I should have expected it. My dumb-struck silence gave the lieutenant time to cool down and shift gears. "Consider yourself confined to the palace and grounds for the duration. It's probably best not to mention this to your friend or your servant boy. We want things as close to normal-looking as possible. Keep your head down and let us do our job."

I didn't argue. This was the third time in recent memory that someone had tried to kill me. I didn't want to try for a fourth.

Predictably, it didn't take long for me to get bored. I finally finished the scroll I'd filched from the school's resurfacing pile, caught up on correspondence (yes, I wrote my mother) and did some preliminary sketches for Prince Amunhotep's Book of Gates. After that, I was at loose ends. I wandered the gardens and palace. Before long I found myself in the library. If there weren't things to hold my attention in that magnificent collection, I was in sorry shape. I was examining a beautifully illustrated book of dreams when Kha'Emteri, the Chief Butler, went past the door. He seemed in quite a state.

He was gone for a moment, then reappeared and gave me a look of hard consideration. "You! You're not drunk!"

"Ummmm, no, sir."

"Do you intend to be?"

Nnnnnno. I think not."

"Excellent. Come with me."

He sounded urgent and I had nothing else to do, so I re-shelved the book of dreams and hurried after him.

"I am so happy to have encountered you, young man," Kha'Emteri said as I caught up with him in the passage. "Sometimes, I simply loathe festivals."

"What's wrong, sir?"

"The same thing that goes wrong every major festival. My regular assistant is sick as a dog and the other scribes in the pool aren't much better. You're the first one I've encountered all day who's standing upright."

"What do you need from me?"

"We're hosting a feast each night until the Crown Prince and the Princess return from Luxor. Then we host a *big* feast. I need someone to help me keep track of things."

"I'll be glad to pitch in, sir!" I can't say it sounded like fun, but it *did* sound like a great way to keep busy while I was restricted to the palace.

In truth, it was more fun than I'd supposed. I got to see a side of banquets I'd never even considered: the supply angle. I also got to know Kha'Emteri pretty well. He was an intelligent, good-humored man who could find a way to cut through the thorniest problem and make it seem like child's play. It was no wonder His Divine Majesty trusted him with the running of his palaces.

One of the other side benefits of the job was that I learned my way around the palace. Not your ordinary walking tour way, either. I mean the back ways, the shortcuts and the hidden places a guest wouldn't normally see.

On the next to last day of the festival, I was taking one of these shortcuts delivering a list to the Chief of the Storerooms, when I heard voices from a room just ahead. This was unusual since that particular room was rarely used. I slipped closer to see who it was. If it was a couple servants, I could continue on with barely a nod.

It wasn't. It was Prince Meriramesses, and the person he was talking to so heatedly was his father, the Great Ramesses.

The Prince said, "I don't understand this grief, Father. What did Amunhotep ever do for you — other than cause you headaches?"

When the Pharaoh responded, his sorrow was a palpable thing. "I grieve for Amuny because he was a good man, if an irresponsible one. It's painful to lose another son. Merenptah is my thirteenth son. I've lost twelve Crown Princes before him. The House of Eternity in the Place of Truth is filling at a sorrowful rate."

"Where do I come in that count?" Meriramesses demanded. "I'm older than Merenptah and *I'm* a son, too."

Ramesses stood and patted his angry son on the shoulder. "Always so passionate, Meri. I love you both, just in different ways. Merny has the blood to ascend to the throne and you have control of a great estate. It was a comfort to know I could always count on you to make sure Amuny didn't get in over his head."

The old man gave his son another pat, then resumed his wandering path through the palace hallways, leaving Meriramesses red-faced and sputtering. I held my breath and clutched Neffi to me. The last thing I wanted was to draw attention to myself and the fact I'd overheard the conversation.

After a moment, Meriramesses spat, "Yes, Father, I have. I have taken care of Amunhotep very well."

Then, he, too, left the room.

~*~

I wasn't at Luxor, or even at quayside, when the procession made the return journey to Thebes. I was still helping Kha'Emteri put the final touches on the palace feasting hall. We were a good piece away from the river, but I heard their return even from that distance. The people were jubilant, singing and shouting as the barques were borne to their respective temples and the royals were brought back to the palace. From that point on, it became a blur. Putting on a day-long banquet is hard — even for an assistant.

TWENTY-SIX

At the end, we were all exhausted. The final day of the festival had been a good one, no matter what side of the preparations you were on. The Pharaoh had insisted on making the journey from the temple of Amun to the temples of Mut and Khonsu then back to the palace in the ceremonial barque. He also stayed all the way through the banquet. When the last guest had left, he was tired, but jubilant at how well the celebrations had gone.

Throughout the day, Prince Meriramesses had stuck to his father like sand to wet skin. As the evening wound down, he was back, fussing over the aged Pharaoh and being a general nuisance. He even inserted himself in the midst of the royal body servants to escort His Majesty to his bedchamber.

Shortly after they'd gone, I noticed Neffi was missing. That was never a good thing. I tried to search inconspicuously as possible, but the Chief Butler noticed, anyway.

"No need to worry, Sitehuti," he called. "Nefer-Djenou-Bastet went with His Divine Majesty."

"To the private quarters? Oh, no. I don't even want to think what he could get into there."

Kha'Emteri laughed. "All right, then, we can go retrieve him before he causes too much mayhem."

When we reached the corridor where the royal bedchamber was, the Pharaoh's body servants were already leaving, carrying lit lamps. The Sherden Guards flanking the door gave us hard looks as we hurried past after the departing group.

I called softly, "Excuse me! Did my cat go into the room with you?"

The Chief Body Servant said, "Yes, sir. The Sacred One is still in there. Prince Meriramesses keeps trying to shoo him out, but he won't go."

The other servants snickered. They didn't bother to look remorseful, either. It was pretty clear they didn't care for Prince Meriramesses. I couldn't blame them. I'd seen how he treated servants and it wasn't nice.

"I hope he isn't being a nuisance to His Majesty."

The Chief Body Servant smiled at that. "No need to worry, Scribe. The Great God was exhausted. He's so deeply asleep, he wasn't even too annoyed that Prince Meriramesses insisted on sitting with him for a while."

With that, the servants turned and continued on their way.

After a moment, Kha'Emteri said, "Come, we can go back together and retrieve the Sacred One. The Sherden won't object."

We turned back, but before we took another step, Prince Meriramesses came out of the chamber. Without a word to the guards, or a look behind him, he hurried away, his ornate walking stick tapping hollowly against the plaster floor.

"That's odd," Kha'Emteri said, looking puzzled. "The Chief Body Servant said His Highness was insistent on remaining with his father. I thought he'd stay longer."

"Perhaps His Majesty sent him away?"

The Chief Butler nodded. "Very likely. I don't like to carry tales, but His Divine Majesty is not as fond of that particular son as he is of others."

The Sherden Guards stood back as Kha'Emteri listened for a moment, then opened the door. He entered, beckoning me to follow. We moved as soundlessly as we could, but needn't have worried. The ruler of Upper and Lower Egypt was sound asleep and snoring fit to stampede a herd of hippopotamuses. There was no sign of Neffi, though.

At Kha'Emteri's encouragement, I stepped into the room and scanned for the cat. The plaster floor had been painted to look like a riverside hunting scene with graceful stands of papyrus forming the edges. More hunting scenes adorned the walls. A slight scraping drew my attention to the royal bed and my heart stopped. The wavering light from the low-burning standing lamps gave the scene a dream-like feel — although this dream was more of a nightmare. A recurring nightmare.

I'd found Neffi, but I also saw a huge snake coiled in the shadows under the Pharaoh's sleeping couch. Kha'Emteri saw it too, I heard his sharp intake of breath and felt him go motionless behind me.

The Sherden Guards, sensing something amiss, stepped into the room and froze in their tracks, swords drawn. They stood to either side of the butler and myself, paralyzed with helpless horror. All of us too afraid to move lest we startle the serpent and cause it to attack the Pharaoh.

The only sound in the room was the irregular snore of the Pharaoh and the occasional sizzle of the lamps. Neffi was utterly silent, as if he knew making a sound might wake the sleeping ruler. As before, in Prince Amunhotep's chamber, the big cat lunged at the serpent, stopped short, and leaped back, away from the couch. The snake didn't strike, but slithered farther out onto the floor, standing tall, hood spread, still alarmingly close to the Divine Ramesses. Another cobra.

Eyes fixed on the serpent, Neffi danced to one side, and feinted again. This time, the snake struck, missing the cat by a hand's breadth. The angry cobra made a low, growling hiss as the cat pranced still farther out of reach. It struck again, sinuous body extended to its limit smacking hard against the plaster. In a blur of movement, the big cat pounced, fangs sinking deep into the serpent's body just behind the head. The two animals rolled across the painted marsh scene locked in a fatal embrace, snake hissing and cat still eerily silent. The struggle only lasted a few minutes, but it seemed like an eternity before the cobra went limp.

Neffi shook the lifeless body a few times, dropped it and sauntered casually to a clothing chest, plucking at something on the side with his claws. I went to collect him. The chest looked odd in the lamplight. Misshapen. I looked closer. It wasn't misshapen, the left side was hinged and had swung open, revealing a hidden cavity at the bottom. It was just about right for a good-sized snake.

Everyone started moving again. One of the Sherden Guards drew his sword and struck the head off the snake, the other went to check the Pharaoh, who was propped groggily on one elbow. The Chief Butler clutched his chest and leaned against the wall for support. Behind us, Lieutenant Si-Montu and another Medjay skidded into the room.

The Divine Ramesses looked around his now-crowded chamber and spotted the remains of the cobra. Recognition clicked. "By the gods! The Sacred One has done it again and I slept right through it!"

~*~

Everyone was celebrating and praising Neffi. I barely heard it. Something niggled in the back of my head that wouldn't let me relax. Something someone said. . . .

Lieutenant Si-Montu slapped me on the back, snapping me out of my thoughts.

"What's wrong with you, Sitehuti?" he asked. "The Pharaoh is safe and you got your wish: the Magic Cat killed the snake before it bit anyone this time."

"True, but . . . there's still something. . . ."

"Something what?" He snapped his fingers. "Hey, we better go report to Captain Djedmose. He's over in the Crown Prince's apartments with—"

"That's it! What Iaret said." I turned and grabbed the lieutenant's arm. "We have to hurry. There's a serpent in the Crown Prince's chamber!"

I snatched up Neffi, and we pelted down the hallways, picking up more Medjay and Sherden, including Captain Hori, as we ran. We must have looked mighty impressive when we burst past the astonished Medjay guards and into the Crown Prince's chambers.

Djedmose whirled toward us, sword drawn. Merenptah and Pedibastet looked up in surprise from the documents they were studying.

I let loose of Neffi and gasped. "T-they just tried to kill His Divine Majesty . . . with a cobra . . . hidden in a chest. There has to be one here, too."

Djedmose sheathed his sword. "Search! Quickly!"

We didn't have to. When I looked for Neffi, he was sitting on the lid of a painted chest identical to the one from the Pharaoh's chamber. This one, however, had been shoved out of the way with several others to make room for the papyrus-strewn table. The box was jammed so tightly against its brethren, the hidden door hadn't been able to open.

The Sherden and Medjay were slipping strong cords around the casket and removing it from the room as Si-Montu asked, "What was it that tipped you off?"

"It was what Iaret said," I answered. "Banufre and I were talking about the plot against the Pharaoh and she remarked that it would do her father no good to kill the Divine Ramesses because then Crown Prince Merenptah would ascend to the throne, leaving Prince Meriramesses exactly where he started."

Pedibastet gasped in realization. "He'd need to murder the Crown Prince, as well, then claim the throne by right of being present."

Merenptah's tone was disgusted as he said, "I wondered why the insufferable prig was at our father's side all day. He probably intended to claim he'd been given the right of succession sometime during the Opet Festival."

~*~

Our contingent was even larger when Crown Prince Merenptah led the way to the house his half-brother occupied on the palace grounds. We found Meriramesses pacing in his study. Lady Wurusemu sat on a couch beside a brazier lit against the increasing chill of the night. Princess Iaret sat beside her mother looking frightened and confused.

Neffi struggled out of my arms. He ran straight to the girl, leaping into her lap and — it might have been only in my perception — put himself between Lady Wurusemu and her terrified daughter. Iaret clutched the cat to herself like a spotted shield.

Meriramesses stopped pacing and glanced up as we entered. We were apparently not the people he expected to see. His expression morphed from expectation to surprise, and finally, to anger at the sight of his half-brother.

"I have grave news, Brother," Crown Prince Merenptah said. "Nefer-Djenou-Bastet has killed your pet cobra."

~*~

The attempt to take Sasobek into custody didn't go so well. When the joint Medjay/Sherden team entered his tent at the Seth Division's encampment, the "sleeper" they found in the bed was Meriramesses' Chief Butler, Yuni. He'd been cleanly and quietly killed.

Captain Djedmose received the returning officers' report with a mix of anger and frustration. "I wondered where that bastard had got to. We searched the Prince's house for him from top to bottom. He must have run to the camp as soon as we arrested his master."

Captain Hori's reaction was more physical. He slammed his fist against his shield and growled, "It's a fitting reward for his multiple treacheries. But it's too damned bad. He was the type who would have broken easily. I'd have loved to have gotten my hands on him."

"It would seem Sasobek thought the same thing," Djedmose said. "He's not leaving any loose ends for us to grab onto. Has anyone checked on his wife?"

The officers shuffled their feet and looked at the floor. Finally one of the Medjay spoke up. "We asked her whereabouts at the camp, sirs. No one knows. It seems she left Sasobek just as the festival began. Ran off to Canaan with a lover while he was in Luxor with the division."

"She would seem to be out of the mix, then," Djedmose observed. "Unless she was brought into the plan before."

"I doubt it, sirs," the Medjay officer said. "It seems they haven't been speaking to each other for a while."

"Not civilly, anyway," the ranking Sherden said. "She lobbed the better part of a faience dinnerware set at him the last time he went home."

This was greeted by muffled snorts and snickers from the rest of the group.

"His Divine Majesty is going to have a fit," Captain Hori muttered half to himself.

I could tell from Captain Djedmose's expression he didn't expect the Crown Prince to take the news any better.

Hori fumed for a few more beats, then ordered, "Well, get after him."

"Already done, sirs," the Sherden answered briskly. "We sent our best trackers out as soon as we saw he'd done a bunk."

In the end, we had no better luck finding Sasobek than we had when his brother, Paseti, had done a runner from the capital.

TWENTY-SEVEN

If I'd expected a spectacular, public trial with well-deserved humiliation and punishment meted out to Prince Merirameses and Lady Wurusemu, it was not to be. After a private, behind closed doors session with the Pharaoh and Crown Prince, the formerly royal couple simply vanished. I never found out what happened to them. In truth, I never asked. It was better that way. I suspect, however, that soon after their disappearance, there was a quick, quiet double burial in an unmarked room in the House of Eternity for the children of the Great Ramesses.

I hope, wherever they landed, it was at a great distance from the chambers reserved for Prince Amunhotep.

Banufre and his parents also had a private, closed-door meeting with the Pharaoh and Crown Prince, but they emerged from their session smiling and walking taller. I didn't get a chance to speak to Ban before they returned to Memphis, but I found out later that, thanks to Amunhotep's last wishes and Banufre's help in exposing the plot against the Great House of Ramesses, their family had been granted forgiveness for their other sons' actions. His Divine Majesty had even taken it a step further and officially struck both Paseti and Sasobek from their family line. It was as if neither had ever existed.

I did manage to speak with Princess Iaret before she left for home, though. Rather, she made a chance to speak with me.

~*~

The Chief Butler's assistant had sufficiently recovered from his festival merry-making that I was released from my not-so-enforced conscription into the job. That left me with time to work on the commission I'd been given of making Prince Amunhotep's Book of Gates. I remembered seeing several excellent examples in the royal library, so I'd taken my kit and some papyrus and settled into a well-lit corner to make notes and preliminary sketches using those references. Neffi found a sun-patch nearby and stretched out to snooze.

"Ah! Kha'Emteri said I'd probably find you in here."

I looked up from my drawing at Princess Iaret, who was peeking into the room around the doorframe.

"Hey! I thought you'd already headed back to Memphis."

"Not yet. I wanted to talk to you and thank you and Neffi for all you've done before I went. And it's been ages since we just talked." She came over to where I was working. Lifting a sketch from the pile beside me, she said, "These are wonderful! I'm so glad Uncle Amuny asked you to paint his spell book."

"Those are just rough ideas. The actual scroll will be much better — I hope."

"It'll be beautiful! I hope I get to see it before it goes into the House of Eternity with him." She pulled a low chair up beside me. "I'm so glad it's finally over. Grandfather spoke some reassuring words to me the night I was formally introduced to court. I got the impression he knew all about what was happening and wanted to let me know I'd be all right no matter what."

"I'm glad he did that. I saw you and he had your heads together that night. He definitely knew your parents were all but holding you prisoner. I know for a fact Captain Djedmose told him about it. It must have been hard being so isolated."

"It was," she agreed with feeling. "I knew Ban, you and Neffi — and even Captain Djedmose were behind me. That helped, but knowing the Pharaoh was on my side helped even more. The time in Luxor with my parents and their associates was bad. I'm not sure how well I could have done that without my grandfather's extra reassurance." She giggled. "My parents couldn't hear a word he said to me, either. Every time they quizzed me about it, I just looked sincere and said I'd been instructed to keep it to myself. It drove them crazy."

We enjoyed that thought for a moment, then I asked, "So what happens now?"

She became thoughtful. "I'm not sure. They told me to go home and take time to grieve — or not. The way my grandfather and uncle Merny talked, there will be more news once Uncle Amuny's burial rites are completed. Oh! They gave me permission to promote Dedi to overseer of the estate, too. With my parents gone and Yuni dead, the estate is going to need new management."

"Dedi's a good choice. He always had a handle on things, even when it seemed it was all spinning out of control to everyone else. Keeping up with Amuny and his friends had to be good practice in emergency mitigation." I paused, taking in her appearance. Outwardly, she seemed all right, but at times, she had a sort of faraway look. The kind I'd seen on soldiers returning after a particularly bloody battle. "How about you, Ia? Are you all right? You looked pretty rough the night your parents were taken — and I've never seen Neffi run directly to someone like that. Had they hurt you?"

There was that look again; like she was watching something just on the horizon. After a moment, she took a deep breath and shook her head decisively. "No. No more than usual, anyway. When they had me brought down to the study, they told me that my life was about to change. That I was to become one of the most important women in the Two Lands."

"What did that mean? Had they decided to marry you off?"

"That's what I thought at first, but then I realized it was worse than that. Father said that, because of my direct line to the Divine Ramesses, I was to become a Great Wife. I had just worked out that he meant I was to be *his* Great Wife shortly before all of you burst in and took him away."

There was nothing to say to that. We sat in silence until Neffi chirped and rolled over to face the doorway. A moment later, Captain Djedmose appeared in its frame. He stopped short upon seeing Iaret.

"My apologies, Your Highness," he said. "I did not intend to intrude. I was merely delivering a message to Sitehuti. I can come back later."

He turned to go, but Ia stopped him. "No, Captain, please don't let me interfere with what you need to say. If it's something confidential, I can give you the room. I have more packing to do, anyway."

"No, Princess, stay seated. There's no secret here. I've been sent to tell Sitehuti we'll be returning to Thebes with the royal party in two days' time."

"Two days?" I said. Then I asked, even though I already knew the answer, "There's been a decision on my request to visit my family?"

Djedmose looked more uncomfortable than before. "I'm afraid it won't be possible. Not yet, anyway. I'm sorry."

Bowing again, the Medjay backed out of the room and strode away.

I sat, stunned, listening to his footsteps fade with distance, trying not to let the depths of my upset show in front of Ia. It didn't work. She knew anyway. She slid out of the chair onto the floor next to me, putting her arms around me.

"I'm so sorry, Huti. It'll happen. Soon. I know it will."

~*~

Two days later, I stood on the deck of the royal barge, with Renen and Neffi beside me, watching the hills of Western Thebes shrink in the distance. Still feeling homesick for a place I hadn't seen in a lifetime.

65536436R00167

Made in the USA
Charleston, SC
28 December 2016